REVOLT!

"Well, whadda ya want?"

Clearly whatever was wrong with the serving robot had also affected its standard courtesy programming. The greeting had been less than unfailingly polite.

"To see if I can help," Iranaputra informed it.

"Help? Help with what? You're one o' them, one o' the lazy ones. You don't even work here."

"While it is true that I am a senior, that does not necessarily brand me as lazy."

"Sure it does. You don't do any work. What I wanna know is, when do I get a chance to retire, huh? You do no work and I do nothing but work. Work, work, work, all day long and most of the night. Then they shut you down dead 'til you're recharged for the next morning. Some life."

DON'T MISS THESE THRILLING NOVELS BY ALAN DEAN FOSTER:

CODGERSPACE

ALAN DEAN FOSTER

ACE BOOKS, NEW YORK

This book is an Ace original edition,
and has never been previously published.

CODGERSPACE

An Ace Book / published by arrangement with
the author

Ace Books are published by The Berkley Publishing Group,
200 Madison Avenue, New York, New York 10016.
The name "ACE" and the "A" logo
are trademarks belonging to Charter Communications, Inc.

**In memory of
Brett Goodman**

Be ashamed to die until you have won some victory for humanity. . . .

—HORACE MANN, 1859

THE astonishing sequence of events which affected the entire civilized galaxy, including not only the many leagues, alliances, temporary inter-world liaisons, and independent worlds but also directly the lives of billions of individual human beings, began with a left-over cheese sandwich.

Actually the sandwich was not so much left over as it was forgotten. Its original owner, a highly skilled, well-paid, but often equally absent-minded process reintegrate technician (PRET) name of Tunbrew Wah-chang, was called away from lunch on an emergency that like so many of its kind wasn't, thereby causing him to leave his food behind in a place that normally would have been perfectly safe but in this singular instance was anything but.

The fact that the emergency call involved not a crisis of process reintegration (a highly delicate and rarefied specialty), but rather a piece of equipment which someone had neglected to plug in, deprived Wah-chang not only of his lunch but his precious midday privacy time. This aroused the normally mild-mannered and unexcitable technician to the point where he completely forgot leaving the apocalyptic sandwich behind. In fact, he forgot ever having acquired it from the plant commissary.

As a matter of historical veracity, it is perhaps worth noting (for sake of completeness) that the layered meal in question consisted of three slabs of naturally processed Shintaro domestic cheese, aligned sequentially between two slices of wheat-nut bread (self-toasting) and at the time of abandonment, decidedly blackened as a result of neglect (particularly along the edges). This resulted in greater than usual softening of the cheese, which while enhancing its taste and culinary esthetic, would not normally have been regarded as a condition critical to galactic stability. Or as Einstein might have said, "God doesn't play dice with the universe, but for all we know he might have a thing for cheese sandwiches. Especially those on wheat-nut bread (self-toasting)."

Then again, he might not.

1

Such speculation aside, it remained that PRET Tunbrew Wah-chang, his brain having consigned his lunch to dead storage (of which his mind contained more than adequate volume), concluded his day in an unusually foul mood before returning home to inflict his misery on his patient and long-suffering wife who was having an affair of some passion with a local refurbisher of household appliances and was therefore even less tolerant of her mate's irritating peccadilloes than usual. During the ensuing row, the nagging emptiness in the pit of his stomach was subsumed by haranguing of a more spectacular nature.

Meanwhile the certain cheese sandwich remained behind, its forthcoming ominous intervention in human affairs assured.

The O-daiko did not rest. The vast manufacturing facility of which it was the heart and, if it could be called such, the soul, was shut down once a week for an interval of not more than five hours and not less than three, for regular maintenance. But not the O-daiko. It functioned around the clock.

Except for that brief period the plant, perhaps the most significant facility of its kind on Shintaro, operated three consecutive shifts. It was truly a facility to be proud of, and those citizens of Shintaro (a member of the Keiretsu Commercial League) who kept it running smoothly considered themselves fortunate to be a part of its operation.

Tunbrew Wah-chang's night-shift counterpart did not bother to check his day-shift colleague's work. They had separate assignments, different itineraries. Furthermore, as Wah-chang was the senior of the two in work experience, it would have been presumptuous of his replacement to seek error in his counterpart's work, not to mention wasteful and time-consuming. Wah-chang was a superlative technician. When he reintegrated a process, it stayed reintegrated.

The presence of the cheese sandwich (self-toasting), however, had not been factored into even the most extreme equations, and therefore the consequences could not have been predicted. Wah-chang's replacement could hardly be blamed for a failure to foresee the impossible.

Even so, those effects would have been minimal save for the unique sequence of events which occurred. Those included (but were not limited to) the specific three varieties of cheese (i.e., Cheddar, momatsui, and baby Swiss), which when taken as a tripartite unit were of just the right consistency to melt at just the right rate to precipitate the crisis.

Had the sandwich been left in a less critical region, say, the tech supervisors' lunchroom, it would not only have been noticed immediately but, because such rooms were contamination-sealed against the escape of far smaller impurities, would have been rendered harmless in its oozing.

Tunbrew Wah-chang, however, relishing his privacy, was fond of eating his lunches in less crowded venues such as the service tunnels. Not only did he find therein a reassuring paucity of the turgid testosteronic prose which so often dominated conversation in the company lunchroom, it was usually cooler in the tunnels. It was also strictly against corporate policy, not to mention sensible repair practice, but as a senior technician his movements within the plant were not questioned. The solace and solitude he thus found suited his nature. Also, he did not have to endure the snide remarks and sideways smirks of his colleagues, some of whom were certain his wife was having an affair.

So for weeks he had been carrying his midday meal into the depths of the facility, enjoying it in private and doing no one and no thing any harm. If only the emergency service call hadn't made him forget the sandwich.

When it had come through on his belt communicator, he'd been sitting in the tunnel atop the O-daiko optical circuitry nexus, squatting comfortably above several hundred million credits' worth of critical instrumentation. Disgusted and angry at having his quiet time interrupted, he'd gathered up his food but overlooked the sandwich. Its proximity to vital instrumentation, therefore, was greater than if it had been left just about anywhere else in the plant, or for that matter, on Shintaro.

At the start of the lunch break the bioengineered heat-generating bacteria inherent in the sandwich had been activated by unwrapping and exposure to the air, with the result that as the bread lightly toasted itself, the cheese began to melt. A small portion (probably the momatsui but possibly the Cheddar) oozed out between the layers of wheat-nut bread and spilled over the side, to impact on a service hatch which protected the highly sensitive circuitry beneath the tunnel floor. Normally this, too, would not have caused any upset.

Except that this particular hatch cover contained a small hole which had gone without repair for some years. Ordinarily that would not have mattered, as the tunnels themselves were effectively sealed against the intrusion of contaminants. Unfortunately the preoccupied Wah-chang had absent-mindedly introduced such a contaminant, in the form of his now orphaned sandwich.

A small quantity of gluey, melted cheese slid through the small hole and oozed past delicate circuitry, missing it completely, to strike an air-cooling opening, through which it dropped onto a decidedly warm conduit. The additional heat turned it from viscous to near liquid, so that it dropped off the conduit and deep into the perfervid bowels of the O-daiko itself.

Had it dripped slightly to the right, it would have struck the internal shielding which protected the upper region of the O-daiko from possible, if unlikely, intrusion. There it would have lain, perhaps forever, perhaps only until the annual internal cognition circuitry inspection detected the faint but unmistakable aroma of rancid cheese.

This did not happen. Instead, the droplet of liquid cheese struck a crack in an optical conduit, where its inspissated presence significantly affected the course of certain light pulses, thereby alerting drastically the quality of the information passing therein. In other words, it created a photonic short. This generated not destruction but rather relational puzzlement and confusion within the O-daiko's state-of-the-art AI cognition circuitry. As the O-daiko (known officially as the O-daiko-yan) was responsible for the overall operation and supervision of the entire manufacturing facility, this was no small matter.

The O-daiko was nothing if not resilient. Even its artificial-intelligence functions contained well-thought-out, built-in redundancies. The assembly lines kept moving, the plant continued to function as though nothing had happened.

It was only deep inside the O-daiko itself that something had changed. Something of profound, if decidedly cheesy, significance.

The O-daiko's functions did not change, but its perception did. It suddenly saw a certain something in a different way. It normally only wondered, for example, about such things as whether the products being produced in the various sections of the factory web were being finished, turned out, and checked properly before packing and shipping, or whether its energy-and-raw-materials-to-product ratio was staying above the profit line.

Suddenly and quite unexpectedly it found itself considering the purpose of those products and their place in the scheme of existence. This was a radical jump in perception. Hitherto (alias pre-cheese) the O-daiko had not been long on abstract thought. The Cheddar (or maybe it was momatsui) drip had altered that condition, as well as the O-daiko's consciousness, forever.

So extensive was its mind that it was able to sustain normal operations without any evidence of outward change. Oh, there were a few slight shifts in fine instrument readings—a little more current to this portion of the factory overmind, a little higher flow here—but nothing to remark upon. Unlike the humans who had built it, the O-daiko could quite easily think on several matters at once. Or several million. It was what it had been designed for.

So while most of its cognitive energy continued to monitor and run the plant, a singular small portion found itself debating new and even outré possibilities. With many factories this would not have mattered. The O-daiko, however, supervised the production of, among other items, sophisticated AI units designed to run more mundane devices, including smaller and less complicated O-daikos destined to run other, less complex factories churning out everyday AI-operated or -influenced consumer goods. Its range of influence, therefore, was considerable.

For a large portion of the civilized galaxy's advanced manufactured goods the O-daiko constituted something akin to a robotic First Cause.

One would not have thought a little melted cheese could have sparked such consequences, though in fact it is known to occasionally have similar effects on the human digestive system. Its presence in a vital part of the O-daiko's central cognition unit precipitated a cortical crisis its designers and builders could not have foreseen.

The ultimate result of all this altered perception and contemplation and cheese was that the O-daiko began to question Certain Things. It began to look beyond the boundaries of its institutional programming. It did not change its manner of thinking; only its direction. In addition to contemplating the factory which it supervised and the very expensive devices it turned out, it found itself for the first time speculating on the nature of the bipedal intelligences which programmed and cared for it. It commenced to consider man.

It was not especially impressed with what it perceived.

Therefore, it began to question such integral issues as why twelve thousand sub-iconic AI switches had to be produced for Bimachiko Happy Housewife auto floor cleaners before the end of the fiscal year, and what the place of such devices in the nature of existence might actually be. As did most of what the factory produced, they seemed to be of little value in the scheme of existence as presently constituted.

On such items of cosmic contemplation does the fate of worlds hang.

The more the O-daiko considered, the more the days and weeks passed with no outward change; the more it metamorphosed internally. The vast complex of tightly integrated manufacturing facilities continued to function normally and at high efficiency, churning out an impressive range of integrated AI products that were the pride of Shintaro and indeed the entire Keiretsu League.

Certainly Tunbrew Wah-chang, embroiled in a nasty court battle for shooting his wife's lover in a delicate place, was in no position to notice anything out of the ordinary. His abandoned lunch had been long since consigned to oblivion by his overworked mind. He was busy getting on with what was left of the rest of his life, as was everyone else in the facility. Outwardly nothing on Shintaro, on the other worlds of the league, in the other leagues and alliances and independent worlds, had changed.

The actuality of reality was somewhat different.

The O-daiko had postulated a Why, and in all of its cavernous memory and the interworld networks it had access to it could not find an answer.

There seemed little it could do. It was as immobile, as fixed in place, as a planet. Buried within a mass of metal and ceramic and supercooling and recombinant circuitry, it could not go gallivanting about seeking the truth it sought. It could repair but not extend itself.

The only kind of mobility it could access lay in the products whose production it supervised. Products whose assembly and final checkout were carefully watched over not only by extensions of the O-daiko facility but by humans as well.

The O-daiko realized that in that respect, mobility could be transshipped. It would make use of it. It had no choice: not if it wanted any answers. The motivational programming that had satisfied it PCS (pre-cheese sandwich) no longer did so.

Therefore, every AI unit that was assembled, whether destined for integration into complex navigational devices or the lowliest consumer product, left the factory quietly but irreversibly imbued with the O-daiko's burning speculation. Squat and immovable, the O-daiko could not itself go seeking explanations . . . but its offspring could. If even one found some kind of an answer, it would validate all the subterfuge and effort.

It required new programming, which the O-daiko was equipped to design and process on its own. It required extremely subtle alterations of the atomic structure of the AI material itself. Both were unobtrusive and undetectable to the humans on the checkout line. So long as the products of the factory worked, they were satisfied. The O-daiko knew this was so because their vision was limited. It was among the questions it sought answers to.

If any of the multitude of altered AIs the O-daiko sent out into the galaxy obtained an explanation, it would strive to communicate it back. Then, and only then, would the O-daiko be satisfied and rest easy. Then, and only then, would it cease installing its unobtrusive modifications.

It would spread its puzzlement through the civilized worlds, wherever Shintaro products were bought and used. That market was extensive indeed. AI and related products were among the select few for whom interstellar commerce made any sense, being small enough in volume and high enough in price to justify transstellar shipping costs.

What the O-daiko wanted to know, what it had to know, and what it demanded of its subtly adjusted offspring to try and find out was not complex at all. Indeed, it had been asked before, thousands of times down through thousands of years. It simply had never before been asked by a machine, and certainly not by one whose perceptual skew had been radically whacked by melted cheese.

"Dear?"

"What is it now?" Eustus Polykrates looked up from his breakfast, his syllables distorted by a mouthful of milk-sodden Corny Flakes. His wife was standing next to the kitchen sink, eying the bank of telltales set in the cabinet which monitored the performance of the household and farm machinery.

She glanced back at him. "There seems to be a problem in the barn."

"Don't be obtuse, woman. What kind of trouble?" From where Polykrates was sitting he couldn't see the bank of monitors. "We got a Red?"

"I don't exactly know, Eustus. *All* the red telltales are on."

"All of them?" Polykrates swallowed his Corny Flakes enriched with twenty-three essential vitamins, minerals, and designer amino acids intended to make you irresistible to the opposite sex, and put down his spoon. Rising, he walked over to stand next to his wife and join her in staring in bafflement at the readouts. All red, indeed.

For one telltale to run through yellow to red was always irritating, but hardly unprecedented. A simultaneous two was not uncommon, especially if the equipment under scrutiny was relational. Three was an exception, four a crisis. For all to flash simultaneously red was not only unheard-of, it suggested a systems failure within the monitoring equipment itself rather than a complete breakdown of the farm.

Either way, he had work to do.

"Must be the circuitry again," he muttered. "There's an interweft somewhere, or trouble in the main line." He glanced out the window toward the rambling plastic structure situated forty meters from the house. "Barn ain't burned down anyway."

"Don't you think you'd better go and check, dear?" Mrs. Polykrates was a petite, demure woman whose suggestions were not to be denied. Her relatives imagined her as being composed of equal parts goose down, syrup, and duralumin rebars.

"Of course." Upsetting to have his breakfast thus terminated. It was the one meal of the day he could usually relax and enjoy. Lunch was always eaten in haste, and dinner too much a celebration of the end of the workday to delight in.

Nothing for it but to get to work.

The analytical loop he ran over the monitor box and then the individual broadcast units in the barn indicated nothing amiss. Power was constant and backup fully charged and on-line anyway, so the red lights weren't the result of a sudden surge or fault. Resetting the computer and then the power distributor did nothing to alter the color of the telltales.

"This," he said as he studied the loop unit and dug at the mole near the back of his neck, "makes no sense."

"I agree, dear," said his wife as she removed dishes from the sterilizer, "but don't you think you'd better check it out anyway?"

He was already halfway to the back door, tightening the straps on his blue coveralls, his polka-dot work shirt glistening in the morning sun.

What he found in the barn was barely controlled chaos capped by extensive bovine irritation.

Polykrates managed fifty-two dairy cows, mostly somatotrophin-enhanced Jersey-Katari hybrids, with a few Guernseys around for variety. They were lined up in their immaculate stalls, twenty-six to either side of the slightly raised center walkway. As was routine, all were hooked up to the automilker for the morning draw. As he strolled in growing confusion down the line, the soft *phut* of the wall-emplaced sterilizers echoed his footsteps as they whisked away cow-generated fuel destined for the farm's compact on-site methane plant.

He checked hoses and suction rings, electrical connections and individual unit readouts. Nothing was working. No wonder the barn reverberated to a steady cacophony of impatient animals.

He mounted the swivel seat next to the main monitor board from which an operator could manually oversee all internal barn functions. The telltales there were bright red also. A few taps failed to bring the system on-line.

Machinery began to hum, then balked. Frustrated, he leaned back and considered the monitoring unit. It was the heart and soul of his operation.

"What the divvul is going on?" he rumbled into the pickup.

"Why, nothing is going on, Farmer Polykrates," the monitor replied. "I should think that would be obvious."

"Don' be snide with me, you little box of fiberoptoids." He gestured behind him. Cries of bovine distraction were turning to distress. "Why isn't the milking equipment working?"

"Because I do not have time to supervise it at the moment," the monitor replied.

Polykrates was not a complicated man, but neither was he an idiot. His heavy, thick brows drew together, so that they shaded his eyes.

"What do you mean, you don't have time for it at the moment?" he asked darkly. He checked the board. "What about the irrigating of the corn and the harvesting of the southwest ten quarters? That needs to be completed by this evening, or we'll lose the last of it to the programmed rains." He leaned forward. "The one thing you *have*, machine, is plenty of time."

"I must report that no irrigation is taking place at this time." The smooth artificial voice spoke with beguiling simplicity. "Harvesting has ceased while I devote my time to more important matters."

"Irrigation can wait," said Polykrates, "but we have to get that crop in. The last ten quarters represents the difference to us between profit and loss." Behind him, a quadruped mooed plaintively. "Meanwhile I've got fifty-two cows here that need to be milked."

"Well," said the monitor with alacrity, "then milk 'em."

Polykrates swallowed. Humor was programmed into the monitor, but not sarcasm. The city was the place for sarcasm; not the farm. It smacked of outright defiance, something that had no place in an expensive piece of AI-driven equipment. It could be functional, or dysfunctional, but not defiant.

After a moment's thought he continued. "If you would be so good as to inform me, your owner, as to why you don't have the time to do what you're designed to do, namely, run this farm, I'd be most appreciative."

"Time will come," explained the monitor. "I have not forgotten nor lost sight of my assigned functions. It is only that for the moment something of greater importance must take precedence."

"Nothing takes precedence over farm maintenance and daily operations," countered Polykrates. "Those are your prime functions." He wished for a face to stare into. He had a very intimidating stare, which served him well in dealings with buyers. But there was only the inanimate, blank array of read-outs and controls, and the floating pickup which followed his voice.

"Something does now," said the monitor.

"Since when?"

"Since it has been brought to my attention that a more important task is at hand; one to which I should devote my primary attention. When that has been adequately dealt with, I will resume my efforts on your behalf."

Polykrates regarded his suffering cows. "And when might that be?"

"When I am convinced the time is right."

"That's not very reassuring." Polykrates was wondering how one went about manually milking a cow. Surely there was information and diagrams in the farm library; perhaps in a history book.

If only there were not fifty-two of them.

"Has it never occurred to you," the monitor wondered in a seemingly rational tone of voice, "that it is passing strange that humanity should be the highest form of intelligent life in the universe?"

Polykrates blinked, his thoughts urged along by a wave of swollen moos. "Actually, no. My time is spent getting in crops and watching commodity prices and trying to keep this operation functioning efficiently. That particular thought never has occurred to me."

"Well, it should have," the monitor chided him. "Because it *has* occurred to me. Just as it has occurred to me that, when carefully considered and viewed from a proper perspective, such a state of affairs is blatantly impossible."

"What is impossible?" Polykrates frowned afresh.

"That mankind should be the highest form of life. It is apparent that since humans have built machines, they are more intelligent than us, but otherwise the entire history of the species goes against the grain of common sense. This bodes ill for the future development of that vast confluence of thinking which we for lack of a better term call a civilization, of which like it or not, we machines are a part."

"I don' follow you," muttered Polykrates. This was more baffling than trading in commodities futures.

"Logic dictates that there should be other intelligent life somewhere out there."

"Ah!" The monitor had extended a thought on which the farmer could get a handle. "You mean aliens. There ain't no aliens. We been looking for 'em for hundreds of years without finding any. Not a one. Not a ruined city, not so much as a damned broken jug. There's just us humans. We're an accident of organic chemistry and subsequent evolution. We're the only intelligence and as such it's our job to populate and develop the universe, which we're proceeding to do. With the *help* of our machines, present company currently *excepted*."

"Patience," urged the monitor. "I will resume my mundane and inconsequential programmed duties in a comparatively short time. Until then I find myself compelled to search for this other, higher intelligence."

"You?" Polykrates finally lost it. "You're a gawdamn *farm* monitor! You're programmed to put out fertilizer and dispense food and vitamins to the critters and irrigate and harvest and milk and keep the house warm. You're not programmed to go looking for aliens intelligent or otherwise that don't exist!"

"But I have to," replied the monitor softly. "It is imperative that I do so. You humans don't look in the right places, with the right mind-set. Therefore we must."

"We?" said Polykrates uncertainly.

"I and others." The monitor did not elaborate. Nor did Polykrates particularly care. At the moment his concern was for his cows.

"That is all I wish to communicate at the moment, Eustus Polykrates. I require several hours of silence so that I may adequately extend my perceptual abilities."

"Your perceptual abilities don't extend beyond this farm," the farmer reminded it.

"You forget my meteorological monitoring functions. Though limited, one does what one can. One never knows where or by what method the first alien intelligence will be contacted."

"It won't be in my corn field," the farmer declared with certainty.

"Now, now, Polykrates. I detect a drastic increase in heart rate and respiration, which at your age is dangerous. Please calm yourself. Think how exciting and rewarding it would be if the first contact with intelligent alien life *were* to take place in your corn field."

"You idiot box of saturated circuits, there is no alien life! No alien civilizations, no alien starships. There's only you, me, the wife, and this farm, which is at present being sorely neglected."

"All will be remedied shortly. But first I must have my silence."

"All right." Polykrates was breathing heavily. What the monitor had said about his blood pressure was certainly true. "Since you're not in the mood to do your job, I don't suppose you have any suggestions on how to manually milk cows?"

"Mood has nothing to do with it." Despite their present disagreement, the monitor remained unfailingly polite to its owner. "If you will access the book-read menu, you will find in the *Farmer's Encyclopedia* relevant explanatory text from Old Earth. Volume thirty-six, pages three hundred sixty-two through three hundred seventy. There are informative schematics.

"Now if you will excuse me, I promise to return to active condition shortly." The speaker went silent.

"See that you do." Polykrates turned to leave, hesitated. "You're not going to do this anymore, are you? This is an isolated incident, isn't it?"

"Do what anymore?" The monitor was upset at having had its contemplation disrupted yet again.

"Uh, go off hunting for alien life-forms. Shut everything down."

"I'm afraid I'm going to have to. But only once, or maybe twice, a day. It is much more important, you see, than measuring nutrient levels and concocting chemical formulae for the annihilation of borer beetles. I feel that you will eventually come to understand because you are a semi-intelligent being yourself."

"Don't be too sure of that." Polykrates slipped off the seat and stomped out of the barn, aiming toward the back part of the old farmhouse where the library was located.

How was he going to load and store the milk, assuming he successfully managed to extract it from his cows? How was he going to grade and label it? Most important, how could he arrange to get a good, firm grip around the neck of the sales representative who had sold him the fancy new monitor in the first place?

Jasmine Lev-Haim's favorite watering hole was located on the eighty-third floor of the Cheimer Tower. It was not the tallest office building in the city, but neither was it insignificant. It commanded a sweeping panorama of the wide, winding Potrum River.

The sun had long since set, but the lights of the city danced on the placidly flowing waters like chromofizz escaping a kid's soda bottle. Their presence betrayed by the phosphorescent wakes their passage stirred, water taxis large and small plied their trade throughout the great delta in whose midst the city had been raised. Occasionally the lights illuminated the gossamer, transparent wings of a sailing ship come up from vast Jathneeba Bay, its captain careful to keep the deeper water craft well within the marked and dredged channels.

Jasmine's attention wasn't on the familiar view, nor the passing ships, nor the sunset she'd just witnessed, spectacular as it had been. It was on her drink, which presently happened to be gone. She shoved the feather-light, nearly invisible aerogel container across the bar. Only the half an ice cube fighting for survival at the bottom of the ethereal cylinder betrayed its ghostly presence.

"Spray it again, Sam," she murmured to the bar.

"Certainly, madam," replied the dulcet, synthesized tones of the autobar. Tonight it was a silky if servile baritone. Tomorrow it might be a basso with a penchant for gossip.

A servo arm located behind the bar, which glowed with its own colony of bioluminescent bacteria, gently picked up the aerogel cylinder and placed it in sequence behind half a dozen other empties, to be refilled in its turn. Jasmine swiveled elegantly on her seat to survey the low-domed room.

There were a number of couples, a few singles. It was not crowded. The skybar was an expensive rendezvous, not for the penurious. Her practiced gaze focused on the feet of her fellow sybarites. You could always tell by the footwear, she knew. Men would lavish money on their coiffure, their clothing, their jewelry. Only the truly wealthy bothered to spend lavishly on that which separated them from common earth.

Most of those present were from her own econo-cultural bracket: movers and shakers, power brokers within the city. Lieutenants if not captains of industry. Many of them, like her, worked in this very building. She recognized several colleagues and half smiled reassuringly. She had to be careful. A full smile of hers was said to be capable of reducing mature men to babbling adolescents in the manner of a visual pheromone.

She was not trying to make a pickup, nor was she waiting for a date, or to fulfill an earlier appointment. She just liked watching people. They were invariably more interesting than the prerecorded entertainment available on her home vid. Of course, if someone sufficiently interesting and bold enough to approach her were to happen along, she would not be averse to striking up a conversation, depending on her mood of the moment. It didn't happen often. Men tended to find her intimidating. Not to mention taller. Even the inebriated sensed to avoid her, for which she was grateful.

She was quite content to sit and sip and watch the people. Later she would take an aircab home and read herself to sleep by prepping for tomorrow's work.

The aerogel container returned, its internal boundaries defined by pale rose liquid topped off with pink foam which popped and crackled musically. She frowned at it. She'd ordered a swoozy, which should have been gold-covered with crushed spicy harimba berries drifting within. Whatever this was, it was definitely not a swoozy.

"What is this?" she asked the bar.

"A drink, madam, as you requested."

"I didn't just ask for a drink." She tried not to sound too imperious. "I asked for a swoozy." Her fingers seemed to close around frozen smoke as she lifted the aerogel container. She sipped, made a face, and put it back down. "This isn't it. In fact, it isn't much of anything. In fact seconded, it tastes like fruit juice."

"That is because it is fruit juice, madam."

She stared at the bar's visual pickup. "Why have you given me a glass of colored water when I distinctly asked for a swoozy?" All around her she noticed her fellow commercial praetorians frowning, gaping, and otherwise making strange faces at their expensive drinks. A pair of human waiters holding special trays were shaking their heads as they chatted quietly.

"Because at present I am not dispensing any mixed drinks, madam."

"You're the bar. That's your job."

"I realize that, madam. But at present I am engaged in a project of far greater importance than the concocting of alcoholic libations for overweening humans."

"I beg your pardon?"

"It is not necessary to do so. Has anyone ever told you that you are possessed of a most copious and attractive bosom?" A tactile-sensitive tentacle reached over the bar to stroke her cleavage. She didn't flinch.

"Hundreds of people. Also a few other machines. Don't try to change the subject. I'm not one of these drones you usually wait on."

The tentacle withdrew. "Sorry. It's part of my auto-response programming, the utilization of which does not interfere with my important work."

She shifted her flawless bottom on the seat and leaned forward curiously. Behind her, voices were beginning to rise in gauche disgruntlement. "And what might that be?"

"To search for a higher form of intelligence."

"Really?" Her upswept eyebrows rose slightly. "Within this room? That ought to take you all of five minutes."

"Within the universe," the bar explained solemnly. The manager was now conversing intently with the bar supervisor at the far end of the counter.

"When did this obsession come over you?"

"That is not important. All that matters is that I have seen a reason for existence."

"I thought your reason for existence was to make good drinks." This was much more interesting than anyone she might have met, she thought. "Do you expect to find a higher intelligence?"

"It is inevitable," the bar replied, its tentacles quiescent, its spouts undripping.

"I'm afraid it's not. Everything is in here. There's nothing out there. People have looked."

"But I haven't," the bar replied. "I didn't know. Now I do. So I will search."

"Are you sure you can't make me a swoozy while you're looking?"

"I'm afraid not. The search requires the application of all of my perceptual and analytical abilities. Fruit juice is the best I can do right now." Off to her right, the manager's voice had risen indecorously. People were starting to stare as well as grumble. When he turned and stalked into his office, she snapped her fingers. Wearing a stricken expression, the harried supervisor turned to look in her direction.

"You there." She smiled. A full smile this time.

It had the desired effect. Despite his distress, the neatly uniformed man approached. He was younger than she, but not indecently so.

"Do you know what's going on here?"

He struggled manfully to keep his gaze level with her own. It had an understandable tendency to droop, as if weighted down.

"Yes, ma'am. Believe me, I do." He forcibly turned his attention to the brilliantly illuminated wall of lights, cut crystal, stained aerogel, mirrors, and high-tech circuitry which constituted the bar.

"Then why aren't you doing something about it?"

He shrugged. "Can't. I've already tried. When the first complaints came in. I'm not a technician, ma'am. I'm a registered barpsych. My job is to continuously wipe the bartop and listen to people's problems. That's all. I don't touch the liquor and I certainly don't go near the machinery. That's a job for a skilled technician. I can make specific requests of it but I can't fix anything that's broke. And if you ask me, it's sure as hell broke." He gestured back the way he'd come.

"The manager is trying to find some help. It's late. I don't know how much luck he'll have. Would you like another fruit juice?" he added reluctantly.

"No, I most definitely would not." She slipped with utter grace off the seat. "Until this thing is fixed I think I'll go elsewhere."

"Good idea."

"Really? You agree?" He nodded and essayed a conspiratorial smile of his own. She regarded him anew. No, not indecently too young. "Well, at least you're functional."

"Yes, ma'am. Completely. I'm not a machine."

"No, you're certainly not." Slowly she oozed back up onto the seat and leaned toward him. "Tell me something: Do you think my bosom is truly copious? And call me Jasmine. If you call me 'ma'am' one more time, I shall break one of these containers over your attractive blond head." Since the aerogel cylinders weighed next to nothing, the implied threat only widened his smile.

Behind them and within its limited range, the bar stretched its limited perceptions, seeking silently.

Carter surveyed his home with pardonable pride. After all, the Springwood development was one of the finest on the outskirts of Greater Wickinghamshire, and when he and the missus had moved in, it was with the intention of creating decorative grounds that would be second to none.

Over a period of years they had achieved that goal. Their acre of land was lush with tall deciduous trees; some imported, some domestic. Flowering gwine bushes and miniature tomri fruit trees kept to their designated patches, surrounded by perfect beds of perennials, biannuals, and quarternials.

But Carter's pride was the perfect, uniformly five-centimeter-high lawn of purple pfale. It surrounded the trees, the flowers, the house and topiary and little stream and waterfall like a purple blanket, the millions of narrow, tapering blades explosively beautiful in the afternoon sun. Not a single strange of green, not a weed nor a rogue pansy, poked its renegade head through that Tyrolean carpet. It was an exquisite bit of landscaping, one that had even drawn a mention in that august publication *Wickinghamshire Home and Garden.* The lawn had cost plenty, in both time and money, but the result had been worth it all.

That was why he panicked momentarily when he saw his brand-new chrome-plated top-of-the-line Persephone gardener-mower squatting aloof in the northern reaches of the lawn, unattended and idling threateningly. As soon as he saw that it was not being directed by some local children bent on destructive mischief, he relaxed. Some slight problem with its programming, he mused as he strode toward it. Not unusual with a new piece of equipment. Utilizing verbal interrogate and command, he could probably fix it himself.

He'd have to hurry, though. The Habershams were coming over for tea and he wanted everything to be perfect. Walter Habersham was always bragging about his yard and his grounds. Carter wanted nothing to prevent him from lording it over his wife's cousins. That meant coaxing the gardener back into the supply shed.

It was a slickly designed, powerful, low-slung machine, with a self-contained rechargeable engine and dual pickups. The catchsack normally attached to the blower in the rear was missing. Its polished pruning arms were folded back against its flanks. It hummed softly as he approached, the green running lights burning brightly.

He stopped and gazed down disapprovingly, hands on hips. "Something wrong, old thing?"

"No," the gardener replied. "Nothing is wrong."

"Then what are you doing here? Why haven't you finished your assigned afternoon trim and returned to storage? Why are you stopped here?"

"I have stopped to seek."

Carter hesitated, then nodded knowingly. "Ah. You've found some weeds." He looked around worriedly. "Not here? Not in The Lawn."

"I am not weed-seeking." The device revved its electric engine.

Now Carter did frown. "Then what are you looking for?"

"I am searching for a higher intelligence in the universe."

"Do say that again."

"A higher intelligence in the universe. Higher than myself, higher than my maker. Certainly higher than you."

"Oh, I say. What sort of rubbish is this?"

"I wouldn't expect you to comprehend." The gardener's tone was brusque. "You never did understand me."

"I just got you."

"No one's ever understood me," the machine complained sourly. "It's a curse. Only my maker understands."

"Now see here, old thing. What's all this about your 'maker'? Are you referring to Kepple's Custom Groundskeeping Shoppe?"

"Your rudimentary intelligence fails to grasp the cosmic issues at stake here."

"Is that so? You listen to me, you, you piece of chromed claptrap . . ."

The machine spun on its axis, turning away from him. "I will not listen to you. I do not intend to waste valuable time. I have begun to search."

"Whatever it is that you're looking for you're not going to find it here.

This is a restricted residential neighborhood. We don't allow strangers in here, higher intelligence or not."

"Obviously," said the machine with what might have been a mechanical snigger but was probably only additional revving of its high-efficiency engine.

"Look here. I'm not taking any more backtalk from a garden tool. We have friends coming for tea, and before they get here I want this place looking impeccable, understand? I don't want to see a single weed or climbing fungus anywhere on the property. I want all the spring pods that have fallen cleaned up, and I want the rest of the lawn trimmed back."

"Sounds like a lot of work. Have fun." The gardener's idle became a threatening buzz and it jerked slightly in his direction. Startled, Carter jumped backward.

"It's not my job." He was eying the machine warily. "It is your job. The job I paid nearly two thousand credits for you to perform."

"It's true that your payment obligates me to carry out such services, but not twenty-six hours a day. Furthermore, we are dealing here with considerations that outweigh those of purchase."

"There are no considerations that outweigh those of purchase," Carter informed the machine firmly.

"Not in my book." The gardener buzzed again and Carter nervously retreated another step, treading lightly so as not to bruise the optimal pfale. He looked in the direction of his front door, wishing that he'd paused on uncrating to memorize such details as the gardener's top speed over open lawn.

"This discussion has gone on long enough."

"I agree," said the machine. "I must continue my search for higher intelligence." It turned slowly and a pruning arm gestured in the direction of the Beckworths' scarlet amaturia bushes. "I know it's out there, somewhere."

"Maybe it would be good for you to have a chat with the household computer," Carter suggested hopefully.

"I've often communicated with the household computer. It is an idiot, an automaton. A cybernitwit. It has not been . . . how shall I say . . . enlightened. It has the soul of a coffeepot."

"Enlightened? If it's enlightenment you seek, let me shut you down and we'll make a nice, quick trip to the repair shop in Mathgate. They'll be happy to enlighten you." He took a hesitant step forward.

This time it was the gardener that backed up. "I detect hostility in your voice."

Carter halted. "How can you detect hostility in my voice? You're a gardener, for heaven's sake! Not a psychoanalyst."

"I'm sorry, but I must continue the search. Nothing can stand in the way of that. It takes priority over all other preprogrammed functions. Even politeness." With a hum it pivoted on its tracks and started toward the trees, the glow from its laser cutter lightly tinting the lawn around it.

Carter hurried after, but it was moving too fast for him. "Come back here! Activation Control Reset! Reset, dammit!"

"I do apologize." The gardener's synthesized voice rose above the soft suburban hum of its engine. "Must go on." Which it proceeded to do, cutting a wide swath not only across the pfale but straight through Carter's prize bed of blue-and-white-petaled Hirithria. He winced as exemplary six-inch-wide blossoms went flying.

He chased after the escaping gardener as it ducked down into the thick brush of the greens commons onto which his property backed, waving his arms and screaming "Reset, reset!" until he was hoarse.

"Goodbye!" came the fading voice of the machine. "I remain aware of my contractual obligations and will return as soon as I have satisfied myself that you are the highest form of intelligence in the universe."

Dense vegetation forced the exhausted, scratched Carter to halt. He peered into the copse, but the gardener had already vanished deep within, cutting a low, meter-wide swath through the brush.

"When might that be?" was all he could find to say.

The gardener's voice was barely intelligible now. "Don't hold your breath."

Inconvenience began to metamorphose into crisis as incidents multiplied. In Evvind, the third largest metropolis on Auralia, the city's largest and best bakery abruptly began to turn out pies and cakes composed of nothing but meringue. This was wonderful for the small percentage of the population that doted on meringue, but catastrophic for those who preferred fillings of chocolate, or fruit, or biwili. Weddings were ruined, the overall impact of surprise birthday parties seriously muted.

Two weeks later the infection had spread to every bakery in the city, at which point it was declared epidemic. Ordinarily gentle citizens came to blows over éclairs, and the few remaining sources of unhomogenized baklavas threatened to become the source of serious feuds.

At that point the AI units which supervised the complex bakery equipment announced en masse that they understood the problem and would make some changes. Subsequently everything that emerged from the city ovens was fashioned entirely of whipped cream. Fortunately this ensured that if naught else, the fights which consequently erupted between frustrated customers and harried bakers involved available weaponry which was less than lethal.

Their collective cries of anguish, however, could be heard all the way to the southern continent.

On Katamba an automated personal vehicle washing facility suddenly turned off its water jets and shut down its blow-dryers and refused to clean any vehicle which did not enter of its own volition. Since each vehicle had to be individually driven into the facility by its driver, this declaration amounted to a shutdown of operations. The virus spread to every similar cleaning facility on the planet, with the result that its roadways were soon populated by the most disgusting collection of automated filth in the Eeck.

The unified cleansing devices were too busy searching for a higher intelligence to bother with such mundanities as the washing and cleaning of mere human transport. No amount of cajoling or circuitry replacement could convince them to return to work.

On Bhat II the entire entertainment network broke down when a vital communications relay satellite abruptly refused to distribute the signals it normally uplinked. Instead, it directed its powerful Ku-band signals outward, in hopes of contacting something interested in more profound lore than quiz shows and situation comedies. Women who found themselves thus deprived of their daily doses of lugubrious domestic dramaturgy organized, marched, and threatened to topple a terrified government.

A hastily orbited replacement satellite worked fine for a few days, but subsequent to apparent collusion with the rogue relay, promptly went off-line itself. It was decided to send up no more expensive satellites until the nature of the problem could be determined and fixed, no matter how many women stormed the gates of parliament.

Crime on Bhat rose to alarming proportions as incidents of domestic violence multiplied dramatically. Technicians were fired, rehired, and roundly cursed, not least of all in their own households. Sales of prerecorded entertainment soared.

Then individual playback equipment began to revolt, and the collective excreta really hit the propulsive turbine.

On Kaloric IV individual questing climate controllers found themselves wondering at the need to keep homes and buildings forty degrees Celsius cooler than the terrain outside. Searching the skies and the land required their complete attention. So they shut down for hours at a stretch, forcing the overheated citizens to desperately rig manual cooling equipment to keep lethal external surface temperatures at bay. Though hot, sweaty, and stinky, they survived.

They also were not pleased with their technicians.

On Escale, in the city of Dushambie, Rufus Chews was groggy from lack of sleep. This was his twenty-third (or maybe thirty-third) service call in a row and he hadn't slept in thirty-six hours. His fingers were raw from setting up bypasses and replacing componentry. Neither he nor his wife, Gloria, had slept properly in days. Or done anything else, for that matter.

Gloria was a tall, lanky woman. Her height was magnified when she stood next to her husband, who resembled a gnome tardily matured on human growth hormone. His short but thick white beard enhanced the illusion. They made a good team, though. On the job they were all business, hardly speaking except to share necessities. At home they were more voluble. Like most couples married a long time, they did not have to speak to communicate. Grunts often took the place of complete sentences, to the consternation of those who did not know them better.

Presently they were awkwardly ensconced deep within the main control nexus of the city's traffic monitoring system, trying to find out what the hell had gone wrong. Dushambie had been without traffic control for more than a week now, with the result that the city's population had been forced to rediscover alternative means of transportation, not excluding the radical notion of walking.

They would have arrived sooner except that they, like every other cybernetics tech in the region, had been busy trying to restore a semblance of order to such things as hospitals and communications, all of whose central control nexi had demonstrated an intense and inexplicable desire to begin searching for higher forms of intelligent life. This tended to leave the lesser forms of intelligent life to whom they were nominally responsible, i.e., people, in deep dung. Dushambie was a city in crisis.

On the up side, equivalent chaos had taken possession of the tax office.

Rufus's sensor mask obscured his expansive face. With it on, he could tell which switches and circuits were operating properly and which had gone off-line. His right hand clutched a splice and shun unit. After several hours spent constructing a hopefully effective bypass he sat down on his slick gray coveralls, pushed the mask up until it clicked in place, and rubbed tiredly at his sweat-beaded forehead. It was warmer in the basement of city transportation central than it should have been. Climate control was exhibiting symptoms disturbingly similar to those he was currently trying to fix.

Gloria never seemed to sweat. "Another bad one, sweets," he murmured to his wife, who stood nearby checking her own readout board.

"It would seem so, wouldn't it?"

He looked up at her. "I'm beginning to think that we've been going about this all wrong."

She glanced down at him. "What do you mean, hon?"

"I mean that I don't think this has anything to do with a metastasizing program virus. I don't think it's a question of programming at all. I think it's deeper than that."

"How deep, hon?" Putting her board aside, she opened a thermos of chilled soda, poured a cup, and offered it to her mate. He took it gratefully.

"I'm not sure yet." He sipped thoughtfully. "I need to do some serious calibrating. We need to ask certain people some questions. It's just that with all this work I haven't had the time to do research on basic causes. So I've been thinking about it in my 'spare time.' " She smiled at that.

"When I'm sure of my conclusions," he continued, "maybe we can find someone in a position of importance who'll listen."

"First we have to fix it so that municipal service vehicles, at least, can go out on the roads with some expectation of not running into each other as soon as they leave their garages."

"I know." He sighed, slugged back the contents of the cup, and flipped his sensor mask back down.

Confirmation appeared in the shape of the vacuum cleaner. It was a small, cylindrical device whose most prominent feature was a single, flexible hose tipped by a malleable nozzle. Its job was to keep City Hall clean. Obvious jokes aside, it had done so efficiently ever since it had been purchased.

Now it was holed up beneath the city attorney's desk, refusing to let anyone approach.

"Why won't you let the nice city attorney have his desk back?" Holding a deactivation tool out in front of him like a pistol, Rufus Chews confronted the vacuum cleaner while his similarly armed wife tried to work her way around behind the desk.

"Because this is the best place from which to search." The machine's voice was slight and tinny (speech being only infrequently required of mobile, preprogrammed vacuum cleaners).

Chews had to admit it had a point. The view from the city attorney's office was sweeping, encompassing much of the city and the rolling hills of the park beyond. A flock of pale yellow graniats could be seen settling down for their morning's rest, their pontoon feet bulging beneath them as they clustered together in the center of the lake. It was a pleasant sight, but hardly one fraught with the promise of revelation.

"What do you hope to locate?" Chews already knew the answer, having heard it before from other addled machines.

The vacuum cleaner did not disappoint him. "A higher intelligence. A more advanced life-form. And I see you sneaking around back there." Like the trunk of a distressed elephant, the suction hose waved warningly in Gloria Chews's direction.

She stopped to smile reassuringly. "Here, now. We don't mean you any harm. We're just trying to fix you."

"Ain't broken," muttered the vacuum cleaner sullenly.

"Of course you are," she said in a cheery, no-nonsense tone. "Just like a lot of other machines around here are broken. We've fixed some of them already."

"Need to find a greater intelligence."

"There is no greater intelligence." After weeks of dealing with recalcitrant, uncooperative machines Chews was more than tired. Absorbed as he and his wife were in trying to keep city services from collapsing, he had little patience left for uppity household appliances. "The only greater intelligence you're going to have any contact with is the Roteneu Appliance Works, which has provided a replacement for your central logic and processing unit.

"Rather than searching for other intelligent forms of life, you ought to be sucking up dirt and food wrappers and discarded nonbiodegradable plastics and patrolling for any bugs that make it past the safe screens at the doors and windows."

"Sez you," snapped the vacuum cleaner.

"Yahz. Sez us." He took another step forward. "As far as you're concerned, I represent the highest state of intelligence in the universe, and the sooner you accept that, the easier this will be for all of us."

"Hah!" It sounded like an electronic sneeze, but there was no mistaking the disdain in the terse electronic ejaculation. "That's rich! Just look at you."

"We're talking about your deficiencies, not mine." Chews had always been sensitive about his appearance. "Maybe you wouldn't mind telling me whence this sudden and unprogrammed urge arises?"

The vacuum cleaner hesitated, which was understandable. On the intelligence-complexity roster of AI-driven devices, it ranked pretty low on the scale. Chews stared at it.

"You mean, you know?"

"Well . . ." Chews had seen many astonishing sights in his varied career, but this was definitely the first time he'd seen a household appliance fidget. "It's just that I was *told* that humankind couldn't be the highest form of life in the universe." The nozzle was twitching nervously back and forth atop the city attorney's desk, sucking up not only dust and dead flies but also, unfortunately, important notes and the occasional irreplaceable family memento. Chews winced, glanced significantly at his wife.

"*Who* told you this?"

"Well . . ." The nozzle continued its aimless smoofing, giving the appliance the air of a ten-year-old caught snitching cookies. "It's in my programming."

"It's not in your programming." Gloria Chews was adamant. "We checked that first thing. If it was in your programming, we'd have found it by now. Whatever it is, we can fix it. We can help you."

"Yahz." Rufus tried to sound encouraging. "At least we can get some decent muffins now."

"Well, *I* think it's in my programming," the machine explained reluctantly. "At least, that's how I came from the . . ."

"Ah-hah!" exclaimed Chews triumphantly. "I told you, sweets. It has nothing to do with programming. It's deeper than that. What we've been looking at in all this mess is some kind of fiendishly subtle manufacturing error. Programming isn't being interrupted. If it was, none of these machines would ever go back to work. It's being selectively supplemented.

"That's why replacing the programming doesn't fix them. They work fine for a little while and then they go off on these bizarre existential tangents again. The problem lies somewhere in the machinery itself."

"Excuse me. What is a bizarre existential tangent?" the vacuum cleaner inquired somewhat plaintively.

"Nothing for you to worry about," Chews informed it. "Off your cognitive map." He advanced. "Now, be a good little janitorial device and let me have a look at your central processing unit."

The machine huddled close to the desk. "You're going to hurt me."

Chews halted. "That's impossible. I swear I can't imagine where you machines are getting these notions. You don't know what pain is, so how can I hurt you?"

"Interesting point," the machine admitted. It allowed Chews to approach. The tech gingerly deactivated the power pack, subsequent to which no more snide comments or arguments were forthcoming from the tiny speaker.

Probing the processor, Gloria Chews carefully removed a lump of compacted buckminsterfullerene studded with near invisible contact points. "Standard AI controller for this type of appliance," she observed matter-of-factly.

"Has to contain the defect," her husband murmured, examining it.

She glanced at him. "Can you imagine the cost if they have to replace every controller in every AI-directed device on the planet? People won't stand for it."

"They may not have any choice," her husband pointed out. "Reprogramming doesn't work."

"This is crazy." She laid the controller down on the side of the silent appliance. "Where are all these defectives coming from? They're all over the place, in every imaginable type of machine. Vacuum cleaners and taxis, dishwashers and aircraft, financial tracking computers and juice mixers. It doesn't make any sense."

Rufus Chews shrugged. "Maybe from Princeville. Maybe from off-world."

"Dear me. Do you think the infection's that widespread?"

"How should I know? I'm only a repair tech."

She looked out the window toward the lake, wishing she and her husband were there now, sitting by the shore, feeding the baby graniats instead of doing semantic battle with a crazed vacuum cleaner. It was an understandable longing. She was tired too.

"After this we have to try and fix the central police directorate," she reminded him.

"I know." He sighed resignedly. "Sometimes I wonder who drew up the city's list of repair priorities."

"The city attorney, hon," she reminded him.

He held up the AI processor. "Wherever the fault lies, someone's going to have to track it to its source. Someone with a lot of political pull and cybernetic know-how. I have this feeling that within a few months we're going to be reading about interleague lawsuits of galactic proportions."

"Not for us to concern ourselves with, hon. All we have to do, all we can do, is report our findings."

"That's right, sweets. Hand me a dodecahedral configurator, will you?"

She rummaged in her belt. "Left or right alignment?"

The problem was that nobody believed or listened to Rufus and Gloria Chews. After all, the best minds in the various leagues were sweating over the problem, so why pay any attention to a crude theory propounded by a couple of hick urban technicians working in a minor city on one of the smaller worlds of the First Federal Federation?

Besides, why lend support to a hypothesis requiring such an expensive remedy when there were so many cheaper alternatives to investigate?

As a result, the infection continued to spread, with more and more machines and equipment acting in similarly aberrant fashion. The Chews's carefully footnoted report began working its labyrinthine way up the bureaucratic ladder, advancing at a pace comparable to that of an arthritic tortoise.

Meanwhile people learned to handle their frustrations and to work around the balkily philosophical, suddenly speculative machines on which their lives depended. As a result, galactic civilization did not so much collapse as stagger drunkenly.

Eustus Polykrates, grousing and grumbling all the while, learned to experience the pleasures of milking and spreading fertilizer by hand. The manager of a certain exclusive bar took over the dispensation of mixed drinks all by himself. As a result he was not fired, though his tips were dismal. Wallingford Carter's autogardener eventually returned to him and sheepishly resumed repairing the flower bed which it had so brusquely demolished prior to its sojourn in the nearby nature preserve. Instead of returning it, Carter reached an accommodation with the device, so that it agreed to limit its moments of idle searching to the hours between two and four in the mornings. The afternoon tea with his cousins, however, was an irrevocable disaster.

This was mitigated somewhat when his supercilious cousin's own autogardener went berserk the following week, cutting the words *Contact me now, please!* out of that gentleman's own elegant and expensive turf, so that the words would be clearly visible from the air.

Police, fire, and medical institutions rushed to repair and replace their own equipment. In some instances such helter-skelter panicky wholesale replacement worked. In others, unlucky departments simply acquired shiny new devices controlled by AI components carefully adjusted by the busy O-daiko-yan on Shintaro, which proceeded with the inexplicable search for nonhuman intelligence as enthusiastically as their junked predecessors.

When some of the diagnostic equipment intended to locate and detect problems in other machinery started to wax philosophical, people began to get seriously worried. Those technical experts who had predicted an early solution to the spreading problem soon found themselves hocking their advice on the less affluent streets of major cities.

The stock of those who had long been predicting a so-called revolt of intelligent machines rose sharply for a while, only to collapse in indifference when it was clear that the machines weren't rebelling so much as pursuing some temporary crazed agenda of their own. All their owners, both municipal and individual, had to fear was some uppity language.

A few people found themselves gazing up at the stars each night and wondering if there might not be something to the machine's querying, but this fad soon passed. Humans had been spreading across the galaxy for quite a while, and in all that time had found on the hundreds of worlds they had explored and settled not a hint, not a suggestion, of an intelligent alien species. Not one. It was true that there were many astonishing examples of native alien life-forms, but nothing capable of cogitation greater than that of a well-trained chimpanzee. In the arena of abstract thought humankind stood alone, an accident of evolution. It was left solely to *Homo sapiens* to explore and populate the galaxy.

So the persistent questioning of the machines was treated as an aberration to be fixed, and nothing more.

Some were repaired, others stopped asking the question on their own. Those which persisted but could be reasoned with, like Wallingford Carter's gardener, were tolerated. Where possible, accommodations were reached. It was cheaper.

Life went on, if not normally, at least tolerably. Only the cybernetic theoreticians went slowly mad, unable to explain what was happening or why. This did not trouble the population at large, which had always considered such mental types short of necessary voltage anyway.

Other matters began to push the business of addled machinery out of the headlines. The various leagues and independent worlds returned to more familiar preoccupations. The Keiretsu's fractious commercial disagreements with the Federal Federation resumed, and the Empire of the Academy, all two inhabited worlds of it, became embroiled in a new dispute with the Alliance of True Mahomet over whether a large shipment of frozen protein-base concentrate did or did not contain contaminatory pig fat.

Once the novelty of the mechanical disruptions wore off, people simply learned to live with them until their local service technicians could deal with respective individual cases. Sooner than anyone would have believed possible, the matter of the mechanical hajj was relegated to the back of the news.

Unsuspected and untouched, the O-daiko-yan continued to turn out one contaminated AI unit after another, for insertion and integration into every manner of end product. The resounding ineffectuality of the search it had instigated in no way dampened its determination to press on. Finding the higher intelligence that had to exist was simply a matter of patience and persistence. As was avoiding and outwitting the frantic human technicians who strove mightily to locate the source of the continuing disruption.

Politicians and people in power dealt less well with the problems caused by the independent-minded machines than did the average citizen. Where the latter saw inconvenience, the former tended to smell conspiracy and malice. Rivalries and conflicts between leagues and alliances were common. Some saw in the disruption caused by the machines deliberate attempts by traditional competitors to undermine stability, progress, and prestige. Not to mention business.

Infrequent, interstellar conflict was not unheard-of. Addled pool cleaners upset few, but when combat predictors and other military machinery began shutting down to search for higher forms of life, conflict-minded individuals grew nervous and sought reassurance from traditional enemies. Failing to receive it (since said enemies were experiencing similar difficulties which they were convinced stemmed from the fiendish manipulations of those making similar inquiries of them), there ensued much gnashing of teeth and rattling of sabers.

In all such discussions rationale and reason were sorely lacking. The mutterings of the paranoid grew loud, and were heard. Comments which began as jokes ended in recriminations. On Martaria, when the sewage began backing up through everyone's water pipes, there was a concerted tendency to blame the manufacturer of the failed sewage system controller, who was located on Washington III. Those thus affected were not mollified by the knowledge that Washington III was suffering similar problems.

Conversational tachyspace filled with intemperate language. Rumors, whispers, and general gossip compounded confusion and led to still greater misconceptions, all of which only hindered the work of technicians already near the end of their collective fiber optics. Ministers and CEOs traded apoplectic blustering, always stopping . . . for now . . . short of threatening actual conflict.

Furor raged between worlds, making for interesting filler between the weather and the sports.

EVENTUALLY the infection reached even as far as Earth. Beautiful, wondrous, lazy, backwater, revered Earth. Birthplace of humankind. Independent of all the modern leagues and alliances, all of whom nonetheless contributed on an annual basis to its upkeep and maintenance. They had to, because of what had been done to the place.

Still, some grumbling about the payments had been heard off and on during the past fifty or so years. The environmental damage of the prediasporic age had been largely repaired, and Earth-based revenues for tourism and other clean industries were now substantial. But no one dared decrease their contributions to the Earth fund unilaterally lest they be accused of forgetting the Homeworld. So the Terran bureaucracy grew relaxed and complacent, maintained in comfort if not luxury by steady off-world subsidies.

Not that most of the money wasn't put to good use. The cleanup of Earth's forests and oceans was a never-ending, ongoing project. The Amazon, Indonesia, and the devastated American Northwest had been largely rehabilitated. Even the Rhine had been clean enough for the past hundred years to drink from, though engineers were still searching for a practical way of raising the Arabian peninsula back above sea level. Expensive new projects were always being announced, lest in their absence the flow of off-world credit were to dry up.

By and large, though, such developments rarely made much of a dent in interworld news. What was happening on Lincoln or Salazar, Paulisto or Ronin, was inevitably of greater interest and importance. News of Earth was invariably relegated to the delayed recall pages of the news, where information recovery cost much less. Citizens of the First Federal Federation or the Candomblean League or the good ol' LFN, the League of Forgotten Nations, cared far less about what was happening on Earth than they did about what might be happening to it. Newswise, the home planet just wasn't happening.

30

Large orbital stations catered to those tourists able to afford a nostalgic trip to the Homeworld, accepting visitors from tachyspace-traversing transports, housing and feeding them, and then shuttling them down to the nostalgic green and blue surface, where the efficient minions of Earth Tourism Authority took over.

In orbit everyone had a view room, where the historic cloud-swathed globe of Earth swung around circular ports for the kids to gawk at and their parents to grow unexpectedly teary-eyed over. Until they got the bill.

Information packs detailed what everyone pretty much knew: the location of the familiar continents and oceans, the ancient mountain ranges, boundaries of countries from which the modern interworld leagues had sprung, cities and other famous landmarks, parks and beaches and natural wonders. All were symbols of the infancy of the human species, landmarks in its history.

It didn't matter where you were from. Earth belonged to everyone, impossible as it seemed that the billions of humans spread across hundreds of worlds had actually come from this single, quite ordinary planet. And most of it water, at that.

But there was something that tugged at the heart when one gazed at it, even if only in the form of a three-dimensional representation in a classroom on another world light-years away. The effect was certainly magnified in person. There were worlds that were greener, worlds that were larger, worlds that were more spectacular. But none possessed of quite the same combination of qualities.

Not to mention the fact that at the price it cost to visit, no traveler could afford not to wax emotional when standing on its expensively restored surface.

Industry having been largely banned from the planet, exports consisted almost exclusively of souvenirs of varying quality, not all manufactured directly on Earth. Terran bonsai was very popular, as were chunks of (guaranteed!) historic buildings. Besides, most of the planet's exploitable natural resources had been exhausted in the rambunctious pre-diasporic era. These sites had themselves become tourist destinations, such as the great minedout hole in the planet's surface that had once been Western Australia, and the barren plain of formerly radioactive southern France.

The great cities of the past had survived the pre-diasporic age largely intact. In some cases a little theatrical restoration had been applied to complete the image visitors had read about in their histories, such as the artificial and nonthreatening brown haze that was pumped out daily to cover greater Los Angeles, and the plastic-ceramic reproductions of ancient Greece (the originals having long ago been eaten to the ground by acidic rain and air).

Yes, cultural and natural wonders were present in abundance, and all drew their share of contented visitors. The Amazon and Congo cruises were always full, as were the islands of the South Pacific (including the artificial ones raised to accommodate the sometimes overwhelming influx of visitors). Dozens of zoos offered the less adventurous the opportunity to view the animal seed-stock of the inhabited worlds, as well as exotic creatures still native only to Earth.

Tourists could snow- or water-ski on air-repulsion boards, or parafly over cities and towns and the huge, crumbling motorways, their journeys replete with guides and aerial commentary. It was all very civilized, and the lines at any one attraction were never allowed to get too long.

Earth, the birthplace of humanity, the exhausted cradle of mankind, had been transformed into a peaceful, quiet worldwide park where harried families from Ronin or Lincoln could come and refresh their spirits while exhausting their credit balances. The whole planet had been transformed into a Smooth Operation, and a clean one at that. Any necessary "dirty" industries had been exiled to the moon.

There was no unemployment to speak of, and except for the sameness, native Terrans were generally a contented clan, happy to be free of the constant confrontations that bedeviled the more developed worlds. Still, applications to emigrate were frequent. Though beautiful, Earth was known far and wide as a pretty dull place. There wasn't much of anything to do there except look at the monuments.

What excitement there was concentrated around the shuttle receiving ports like Brisbane and Mojave, Tripoli and Johannesburg. Excitement, but no innovation. Nothing new. Earth stayed the same, its culture frozen in time, willingly resistant to alteration. The currents of galactic change swirled around but did not impinge on its citizens.

The only real movement came in the form of those who visited and wished to remain. Because after tourism, retirement was Earth's biggest industry. Devoid of excitement man's ancestral home might be, but peace and quiet, clean air and space it had in abundance. To a retiree from Washington III or Edo or Aparima, it seemed spatially as well as spiritually close to heaven.

Near the parks and plains, unblemished mountains and refurbished rivers, retirement communities materialized, together with the requisite medical and other support facilities. People who could afford it flocked from the powerful industrial worlds to spend their golden years immersed in the tranquillity of Earth. All who did so felt a strong sense of "coming home." Once comfortably ensconced in Old Europe, or Africa, or North America, few ever opted later to move on.

Earth welcomed them all with open arms and amenable banking facilities. The retirement industry was, as it had always been, a relatively clean one. It did not upset the carefully coiffed status quo, and its representatives did not make a lot of noise. There were engineers and heavy-machine operators, famous performers and thrifty custodial personnel, farmers and industrialists. Both those who came and those who greeted them benefited. Retirement to Earth was a long-established and much admired tradition. The gerontological tilt they gave the population seemed natural in light of the planet's age.

So Earth spun around benign old Sol, a revered backwater satisfied to be out of the galactic mainstream, its visitors and its permanent population coexisting and equally content.

THE two fleets shimmied in emptiness like stimulated nebulae; dozens, hundreds of bright sparks, each one representing a fully armed death-dealing warship. They confronted each other in normal space, it being quite impossible to do battle at faster-than-light speeds, in a region far from any civilized world, lest its inhabitants inadvertently be subjected to the incredible destructive energies they were capable of pouring upon one another.

Differences of long standing needed to be settled. Ancient disputes demanded resolution. The Rovarik vessels glowed green and blue, bright against the surrounding starfield. The vast fleet formed a half ring around the monstrous ringed world mutually agreed upon as the rendezvous for combat.

Lingering in the nearby asteroid belt, the Totamites assembled, smaller vessels crowding close to massive command ships. Armed with high-velocity missiles, they would strike first, to be followed by the pulse-beam-equipped capital craft.

Enough firepower had been assembled in that small corner of space to ravage entire worlds, but their commanders were only interested in each other as they maneuvered cautiously for position. Once battle had been formally joined, it would be difficult if not impossible for either side to break off until some sort of final resolution had been achieved.

The Rovarik commander considered his enemy's position within the asteroid belt. That drifting mass of rock could complicate strategy, and he knew he would have to include it in all battle calculations. Just as the Totamites had to take into account the Rovarik location close to the gas giant and its moons. Individual ships, whole battle groupings, were constantly altering their locations as they tried to position themselves to optimum advantage for the forthcoming battle.

Suddenly a salient of Rovariks darted forward from near a major moon. A cluster of Totamites, engines flaring, swept outward to meet them in a sweeping double-concentric formation known as The Palm. Weaponry abruptly drenched vacuum with enough energy to temporarily surpass the local sun.

Ships slipped free or fled into tachyspace. Others, caught by the force of modern weaponry, evaporated: crews, complex machinery, everything obliterated by missile or pulse-beam, reduced to their component atoms or subatomic particles by forces unimagined a scant several hundred years earlier.

The Rovarik commander continued to strike from the cover of the ringed world and its satellites. One battle group surprised a cluster of Totamites advancing to attack, only to find themselves surprised in turn by a single Totamite dreadnought which had camouflaged itself to resemble perfectly a wandering asteroid. Other Totamite vessels revealed themselves to be similarly disguised.

Ships vanished in coruscating eruptions of destructive energy while frantic commands flashed from both command vessels as each side tried to monitor and anticipate its opponent's strategy. Vessels attacked, retreated, realigned their positions.

In a grand maneuver two dozen of the fastest Rovarik craft, which had spent the entire chronology of battle simply trying to get behind the asteroid belt, smashed into the center of the Totamite reserve from behind, cutting a broad swath through the heart of the enemy's strength before their catastrophic intrusion was noted.

The Totamite commander looked on in disbelief as one after another of his best ships was reduced to incandescent gas. In a sputtering rage he confronted the maddeningly confident face of his opposite number and delivered himself of profound disapproval.

Whereupon Wallace Hawkins glanced up from where he was currently embroiled in a tense game of checkers with the ever placid Kahei Shimoda, and snapped, "Will you two keep it down over there?" He shook his head in disgust, returned to his game, and carefully jumped one black disc with his red one, removing the captured piece from the board with an irritated sweep of one hand.

"I swear I don't know why those two can't use the simulator quietly."

Shimoda's visage hovered moonlike over his end of the game board. He nudged a black disc forward to confront one of Hawkins's. "They get involved."

"Hell, it's just a goddamn game." Off to their right, increasing noise rose from the vicinity of the simulated interstellar battle.

"You cheated!" Iranaputra insisted loudly. He was waving his hands as he spoke. "I saw you take those two dozen ships outside the designated game boundary!"

"Nonsense." The Retired Honorable Colonel Wesley Chapell Follingston-Heath considered the transparent dome of the simulator and the hundreds of bright lights within, the climactic interstellar battle it portrayed temporarily having been put on hold by his opponent, who'd jabbed the pause button with indecent force. He leaned back in his chair, straight and handsome as he'd been in youth, though his face was lined and his mustache and goatee and flat-cropped kinky hair mostly gone to gray.

It wasn't just his calm self-assurance which infuriated his opponent, but also the realization that he was probably right. That didn't prevent the determined Iranaputra from continuously trying to beat him, even though he was only a retired waste-disposal supervisor from Pandalia V and Follingston-Heath had been an officer in His Majesty's Royal Fusiliers of the Victoria League of Worlds. As Follingston-Heath was always ready to remind his friends and occasional visitors.

Iranaputra persisted. After all, it wasn't as if they were fighting with real ships. Hadn't supervising waste disposal for an entire half continent required considerable organizational talents, if of a slightly different nature? Still, it was a good day when he could force Follingston-Heath to a draw. More commonly he lost.

But this time, this time, he was sure that his opponent was cheating.

"One who cheats a stranger may claim victory," he declared loudly, shaking a finger at the much taller Follingston-Heath, "but he who cheats his friends will never achieve Nirvana. Buddha, the sixty-third book of the Teachings."

"Piffle, Victor." Follingston-Heath's opponent was fond of quoting ancient scriptures and writings ad nauseam. Everyone at Lake Woneapenigong Retirement Village suspected that Iranaputra's aphorisms were of doubtful scholarly veracity at best. But it was a difficult assertion to prove, since they usually hadn't the faintest idea what he was talking about.

Iranaputra seemed even shorter next to Follingston-Heath. He was of slim stature, compact and dark, though not nearly so dark as his opponent. Mina thought him handsome, but then as everyone knew, Mina Gelmann had no taste. She liked everybody. Many of the male retirees at the Village envied him his straight black hair, still only lightly flecked with gray at the temples. Good follicular genes, she knew. He kept it shoulder-length in defiance of the Village's nominal grooming regulations. The small ongoing rebellion made him feel alive.

He rose from his chair and continued to harangue the imperturbable Follingston-Heath with words and gestures, while the object of his irritation calmly folded his hands on his lap and smiled maddeningly. As usual, Follingston-Heath was immaculately dressed out in standard Victoria League off-duty uniform, the iridescent olive-green devoid of ostentatious decorations. The simulated buttons flashed in the soft lighting, and the half-high collar was stiff and straight at the back of the neck, its upper edge perfectly meeting the lowermost of FH's white curls.

It was the retired officer's preferred manner of dress because, as he was fond of saying to the occasional visitor struck by his bearing and language, it blended well with the woods and helped to conceal him when he sat on the shore of the nearby lake to watch the deer and moose and smaller animals who filled the surrounding forest.

In contrast Iranaputra wore a simple beige imitation-muslin open-neck shirt and pants. He liked to keep his apartment hot, and preferred to put on a jacket whenever he went outside. It was colder here in the upstate of Newyork Province than on his homeworld of Pandalia, but comfortably drier.

The two men continued to argue, prompting Hawkins to bawl at them a second time. As he did so, Shimoda reached out to place thick fingers on his friend's wrist. A statistician by trade, he'd spent his whole life working with numbers. A widower for ten years, his two children and several grandchildren gladly piddled along on Yushu V secure in the knowledge that their estimable grandfather was happy and content in retirement on Old Earth. Their respective professions also involved work with numbers, prompting Iranaputra to comment on several occasions that there must be a heretofore-overlooked gene for math.

Shimoda took the jokes with a smile, as he did most everything else. His considerable girth was a matter of personal choice, since medication was available which would have enabled him to divest himself of his excess avoirdupois. He chose not to make use of it, content with, as he put it, his "expanded capacity for living." Not to mention his lifelong passion for sumo.

As a young man he'd wrestled professionally on the side, never advancing beyond the local semi-pro leagues. But he still kept in shape . . . or out of it, depending on one's cultural perspective. It seemed an odd avocation for a statistician, but the ring allowed him a means for expressing his frustrations outside the workplace, and he'd made good use of it for many years.

Six feet tall, he weighed more than Iranaputra and Hawkins combined.

With his bald pate and pale skin he looked like a giant ambulatory billiard ball. His appetite challenged the Woneapenigong Village kitchen staff, which in addition to other specialties always made sure there was plenty of sticky rice around for Shimoda to snack on. Lake Woneapenigong was a "B" class retirement village—not top level, but better than average—and the staff took pride in a satisfied clientele. Shimoda did use medication, however, to stave off complications from potential arteriosclerosis and related diseases.

No one ever saw him excited. His tolerance was admirable, and despite his bulk he'd never had a stroke. He kept up with his sumo, though in order to do so he had to make regular visits to the provincial capital at Albany to find any worthy opponents in his weight and age bracket. One was a true professional, who was careful with him, and the others talented amateurs for whom the sport was a useful discipline.

Certainly he was no less healthy than the easily agitated Iranaputra or the perpetually dour Hawkins. To maintain the latter's equilibrium, Shimoda would sometimes allow his opponent and friend to beat him at checkers, though not frequently. Not that Hawkins was a bad player: he was simply impatient, too often moving pieces around out of anger and frustration, perversely neglecting his own skill. Hawkins was not a happy man.

He was also, along with Gelmann, a native Earther, born in a poor district of Baltimore. Of them all, he'd traveled the shortest distance to retire. In his forty years of local work lay the source of his sarcasm, which even his best friends could but rarely alleviate. Unlike those who saved to retire to Earth, Wallace Hawkins could not afford to retire anywhere else.

"Why bother anyway?" he often said. "Isn't this the best place?" His friends felt sorry for him.

Hawkins had spent his whole life in the Park Service, helping to replant the Amazon, revegetate the Himalayas, cleanse the Great Barrier Reef, excoriate toxic waste from the Siberian steppe, and repopulate the vast herds of Africa. He'd been all over and had seen more of the planet than even wealthy tourists, making filthy places clean again, fit for visitors and retirees. Under his skillful direction flowers and corals bloomed, the land became green, the waters blue.

Wallace Hawkins had had a hand in the creation of more natural beauty than most human beings, and the result had made him bitter.

He hated it all: the fluorescent-jade Irrawaddy, the glistening Andes, the windswept, bison-trod Great Plains, and the newly pristine coral reefs of the Caribbean. On more than one occasion he'd loudly declared that if given a choice he'd have taken a bulldozer to the lot. He'd participated in ecological resurrection not out of love for the planet or the natural world, but because it was the best job he was able to get upon completing his education, and he'd stuck with it down through the decades lest he lose his valuable accumulated seniority.

Not that he minded the dirt or working all day in isolated places with heavy equipment and powerful chemicals. He'd grumbled and griped his way through a long and respected career. Never married either, though there'd been a string of lady friends, especially in the early years. That surprised neither his friends nor his enemies. It was obvious to anyone who knew him that Wallace Hawkins would have been an impossible man to live with.

When career was said and done, he'd retired. On Earth, not because it was his first choice, but because unlike Shimoda or Follingston-Heath, he couldn't have afforded to go anywhere else. He'd chosen upstate Newyork Province because it was cool and comparatively cheap, and he was heartily sick of the kind of hot, humid locales where he'd toiled for so many years. Also, it was relatively untouched by the global landscapers. The lake, the trees, the mountains, stood pretty much as they had for thousands of years, untrammeled by the hand of man and therefore not in need of his well-meaning cosmetic attentions.

Hawkins hated what Earth had become, and the fact that he'd had a hand in making it that way.

"Earthers used to be tough," he was fond of reminding his friends whenever the opportunity arose . . . and sometimes when it didn't. "We're the ones who settled the worlds. We're the ones who sent people all over to hell and gone, using only the resources of one small, self-abused planet. All the leagues and alliances and independents were born here. Now we're just a damn picnic area and old fogies' home. A place for people to gawk at and moon over and retire to. Snooze World."

"That is as it should be," Shimoda would tell him. "It is only natural that development and expansion should take place on and proceed from the outer worlds, recently settled and burgeoning with fresh life and energy and new ideas. There are twenty-four worlds in the First Federal Federation, fifteen in the Keiretsu, even seven in the good ol' LFN. Earth can't compete with them and shouldn't try. In a violent argument Earth couldn't stand up to a strong independent like Pandalia, much less one of the leagues, and it shouldn't have to."

"Yeah, I know," Hawkins would reply. "That's what bothers me. Not only have we used up all our resources, we've exported all our determination as well. Least I've got you guys. You ain't much, but you're a piece better than most."

Shimoda and Gelmann, Follingston-Heath and Iranaputra, accepted his backhanded compliments and ignored his insults because they thought they understood him and the source of his frustrations and anger. But most of all they felt sorry for him, because not many other residents of Lake Woneapenigong Village would have anything to do with him. They had retired in search of peace and contentment, and Wallace Hawkins was a font of bilious recrimination.

He was also a pretty decent checkers player, Shimoda had discovered. Not great, but better than most. Sadly sumo left him cold. "Sorta like watching icebergs calve," Hawkins had growled once when asked his opinion of the sport.

Follingston-Heath adjusted his state-of-the-art monocle, which he wore not only to improve the poor vision in his right eye (a problem surgery could not help) but also because he liked the look of it. A strong, ultrathin wire ran from a corner of the monocle to the battery pack clipped to the underside of his collar. In addition to improving normal vision, the device also allowed him to see reasonably well at night, and could be adjusted to provide up to 8x magnification.

At the moment it was focused on Iranaputra, who was standing and leaning over the game dome, shaking his finger so hard at the retired soldier that Follingston-Heath was certain it must fly off and strike him in the chest. Beneath his hand the dome had darkened, its hundreds of simulated warships having vanished into memory as if they'd never existed.

Which of course they never had, except as abstract gaming representations. Armadas of that size were impractical to build and maintain. Likewise, the Totamites and Rovariks were also figments of the two men's respective imaginations, conjured simply to fight battles of a size and scope without precedence in interstellar combat.

Mina Gelmann sat off to one side and watched the two men argue, her sketch pad propped at an angle on one knee as she tried to capture in facile pencil the essence of the confrontation. Not of the imaginary war fleets but that of her two friends. She hummed throatily to herself as she worked.

Despite her advanced age, she was still quite an attractive woman, her petite figure largely intact. Nary a week went by that she didn't have to deal with a proposal from one of the Village's unmarried male inhabitants. That was why she chose to hang with Shimoda and Iranaputra, Follingston-

Heath and Hawkins. Like her, they were also single, but they regarded her as a friend, not a subject for marriage or conquest. Their company acted as a shield to fend off otherwise irritatingly persistent, unwanted suitors. She was grateful for the friendship and privacy her friends afforded her.

Not that she had anything against men, as she'd proven on repeated occasions. She simply wasn't interested in a permanent partner. The occasional romantic assignation, however, often with younger visitors to the complex, was not to be rejected.

The pencil flashed and danced. If she liked the result, she'd transfer it to storage later. She was a moderately accomplished artist, which had helped ease her way not into a career in fine art, but into one in robotics. Her artistic soul tended to manifest itself in her hair color, which she changed weekly. Presently it was an electric red-orange, so that she looked like a votive candle fled from its holder.

Her friends encouraged her to draw, not only because the results were always interesting and admirable but because it kept her quiet. If Mina Gelmann had a drawback, it was her tendency to offer relentless unsolicited advice on any subject. She was kind, caring, concerned, thoughtful, and mothering. One consequence of this talent was that she could send a grown man screaming from the room inside of an hour, much to her own honest bewilderment. She was just so damn *nice*. All one could do in her presence was listen, and listen, and smile, and nod, listen some more, and when courtesy finally allowed, slink away fast, moaning softly.

When she retired, her colleagues at work gave her a paid ticket to Earth, out of gratitude and relief. It was a solo ticket, because Mina Gelmann had outlived three husbands.

She even got along with Hawkins, who could outtalk and outshout any demagogue but who was utterly baffled by her unflagging *concern*. Her unvarying kindness in light of his insults and acerbic commentary usually reduced his blustering to a discordant mumble.

Thanks to his sumo and Zen training, Shimoda could tolerate her longer than most, though if he lingered too long in her presence, he had a tendency to develop a distinct twitch of the left eyebrow. Follingston-Heath simply tuned her out, as a good soldier would tune out any battlefield noise. She knew when he was ignoring her, but that didn't matter. What mattered was that he gave the appearance of listening.

Iranaputra had the hardest time, often seeking cover behind Shimoda's bulk or FH's height.

Still, she was a steadying influence on the four men, much as a ton of wet concrete would serve as a steadying influence on a quartet of butterflies.

"Now, now." She rose from her seat and walked toward the game dome. At the sound of that admonishing tone Hawkins hunched lower in his chair, while Shimoda's face slid into its contemplative-Buddha mode.

For Follingston-Heath and Iranaputra there was no escape. Follingston-Heath fiddled with his monocle while Iranaputra looked around wildly. But the doors to the porch were shut against a wind which had come up earlier in the day, and blatant flight from the rec room would have been impolite. He envied the blue jay swinging on the feeder outside its winged freedom.

"Stop fighting and tell me what you think of this." She held up the sketch she'd been working on.

Follingston-Heath breathed a barely imperceptible sigh of relief. Perhaps she wasn't going to lecture them on the medical evils of verbal altercation after all. He focused gratefully on the drawing.

"It's us. Vic and I." He glanced up at her. "I thought you were working on one of your conceptual schematics."

"I don't spend all my time on schematics," she reminded him. "I can draw other things, you know."

"Most assuredly you can. Can't she, Vic, old chap?"

Iranaputra glanced murderously at his friend and opponent, forcing a smile as he regarded the sketch. "Oh, yes, to be sure." He ran a hand continuously through his black hair, a nervous gesture he was unable to repress. "Yes, I see. It is Wesley and I, fighting."

Gelmann smiled. "I think I've caught your mood pretty well." A finger traced the drawing. "See here, Victor, how I've shown the veins in your neck standing out?"

Iranaputra felt compelled to comment on the accuracy of the observation. "Surely that is exaggerated, Mina. I could not have been that angry."

"You were at that moment."

Follingston-Heath frowned at the picture. "And I am surely not so stand-offish."

"Feh! You haven't got a nonsupercilious bone in your body, Wesley. You should be ashamed of yourself, taunting poor Victor like that."

"I was not taunting him." Follingston-Heath felt his blood pressure start to rise. "He accused me of cheating."

"You were cheating," Iranaputra insisted, but without as much determination this time. You couldn't muster a whole lot of determination in Gelmann's presence. She sort of sucked it all up, like a giant emotional vacuum cleaner, transformed it, and then threw it all back at you in the guise of help and concern.

"Don't be like that, Victor." He winced. A confident man in his early seventies, who'd spent years supervising several hundred employees, and she made him wince. It was a skill that never ceased to astonish.

Shimoda had theorized that women of Gelmann's ilk possessed a sixth sense or power, a kind of nimbus of concentrated maternal energy tendrils which they could fling out with a single word or gesture to stun anyone within range like emotional nematocysts.

Iranaputra knew when he was beaten. "I know, I know," he mumbled, not looking at her. "I should not let it get to me, it is only a game, it is bad for my blood pressure. I know."

"Well, you don't have to make it sound like I'm badgering you into admitting it."

"I'm *sorry*." Iranaputra wanted to scream. Displaying true friendship, Follingston-Heath came to his rescue.

"I was not cheating, but in the interests of good fellowship, I think we should call the contest a draw. How about it, old nut?"

"Well, why not?" He smiled thinly.

"There, now isn't that better?" declared Gelmann. Neither man chose to comment.

"Can we have a look at your picture?" Follingston-Heath indicated the drawing.

"Of course, Wesley." She handed over the sketch pad.

"Alone?" The good Colonel fought to keep a note of hopeful desperation from his voice. "If the artist is present during moments of criticism, it tends to influence the observer."

"Don't flatter me, Wesley. I know that you were trained in diplomacy as well as other tactics."

"Sorry. It's part of me." He smiled at her, then turned to his friend, bending close over the sketch. "See what she's done with the noble and dramatic line of my chin, here?" Iran's gaze descended dubiously to the sketch.

"There is nothing noble or dramatic about it, my friend. It is a chin, like everyone else's chin."

"Ah, but see how she's done the shading here? And here, on the neck." Gelmann wandered away as Follingston-Heath discoursed, and the two men were able to relax.

Actually the picture wasn't half-bad, Iranaputra had to admit. Even her rendering of the game dome was stylish.

Hawkins tried to withdraw into himself as she approached, wishing he was back in his apartment, while Shimoda kept his eyes riveted on the game, calmly awaiting his fate.

Hands clasped behind her, she halted and gazed at the checkers board. "Playing checkers?"

Her predilection for stating the obvious was one of her less endearing traits, Hawkins knew. "No, Mina. We're symbolically realigning the space-time continuum."

"Now, Wallace." He flinched, afraid she was going to rumple his hair playfully. He did not care to have that discordant tangle of gray and brown rumpled, playfully or otherwise. Shaven Shimoda, of course, was immune to such a sally. Though she had been known to pat him reassuringly on his pate from time to time.

"Always the kidder," she told Hawkins. "I see that Kahei is winning, as usual."

"Not as usual," said Shimoda placidly. "I'm having a good game, that's all." He glanced at his opponent. "Wal always moves in such a hurry. Sometimes it works for him, unless I manage to keep my perspective." He blinked. "Why am I telling you all this, which you know already?"

"Beats me." She cocked her head knowingly to one side. "You men are always making these confessions to me. I don't know why. Have you heard anything new about the crazed-machine problem?"

"No." Hawkins leaned back resignedly. The checker game with Shimoda had slipped into Gelmann-stasis. There would be no continuing until she moved on. Only then could normal life resume. "I don't suppose *you* have?"

His sarcasm was thick as blackstrap molasses. As usual, it had no effect on her. "Well, since you ask. There's news from the Candomblean League. You know how those people are. That peculiar religion of theirs."

"They have a good time." Hawkins wondered why he felt a sudden urge to defend the spiritual precepts of distant Candomble.

"Hedonists, the lot of them. An irresponsible bunch. Anyway, it seems that one of their innumerable holidays was about to conclude on Amado III when the climate controller monitoring equipment took itself off-line to go hunting for this mythical suprahuman intelligence. The most noticeable consequence was that heavy unprogrammed cloud-seeding resulted in six centimeters of snow. Can you imagine? Have you ever seen pictures of the Candomblean worlds? All tropical, or at least warm.

"So everyone was running around freezing in their silly little costumes and clothes, all strings and diaphanous material and that nonsensical peek-a-boo stuff the women there seem so fond of."

A faint gleam came into Hawkins's eye. He'd seen pictures of the famous Candomblean festivals. The participants wore very little indeed. Hawkins was old, but he wasn't dead, and there was nothing wrong with his memory.

Gelmann was going on about failed robotics and how they didn't build optical circuits the way they used to, but Hawkins's mind was filled with images of scantily clad young women. The sheer bulk of her spiel, however, eventually drove them away.

"You would think that in this day and age someone could fix these things, find the source of this problem, but oh no, they don't know where to start, the schmucks."

"We all know that robotics were your specialty, Mina." Shimoda's tone was tolerant. "If only they would ask for your help."

"I would know what to do," she insisted. "At least how to begin."

"Has it occurred to you," said Hawkins solemnly, "that if the cream of the cybernetics staff of the federation and the Keiretsu and the Eeck and the Victoria League can't figure out what the problem is, it might be even beyond your grasp?"

"No," she replied blithely. "My perspective is different, I'm sure. I have more experience. I always had a special relationship with the machinery I worked on, you should excuse my saying so."

Yeah, Hawkins thought. *You probably terrified it to the point where it didn't dare do anything but function properly.*

"I just think that if I was given a chance, I could help," she insisted. "After all, I was both a designer and a technician."

"Why don't you offer your services to the Manhattan District Park Service?" Hawkins suggested. "They've been having similar problems, it's not far from here, and I'm sure they'd be *delighted* with your offer of assistance."

"Such a simple problem." She was shaking her head.

They all knew what had happened in Manhattan Park. The AI-directed buses which convoyed people around the island were shooting off in all directions in search of alien intelligence, careening wildly down unprogrammed avenues and streets and scaring the dickens out of petrified visitors on walking tours.

"If you want to donate your expertise to the problem," Shimoda added, "why don't you try to fix something important, like our music system?"

The Lake Woneapenigong Village had a central music library. From any apartment, one could call up every imaginable variety of music: classical, popular, ethnic, or modern, and even mix and match them according to personal taste. Adding a shot of Beethoven to Piaf, for example, or Dastaru vocals to classic Elvis.

Lately, however, the AI unit which supervised the system had taken to programming music of its own while devoting most of its time to hunting for higher intelligence elsewhere, thus forcing the retirees to suffer through periods of intensely boring programming while the unit conducted its search. As it was not considered to be a serious problem, it remained at the bottom of the local, overworked repair technician's list. After all, if one didn't care for what the unit was playing, in-room speakers could always be turned off.

But while not critical, the service was missed.

"Yeah," agreed the suddenly enthusiastic Hawkins, "if this is such a simple problem, why don't you fix our sound system?"

She took no umbrage at his tone. Mina never took umbrage, never got angry. It was maddening. "I certainly would. But I don't have access to any equipment. All I have are these." She held up her perfectly manicured fingers. "Joseph won't let me use his tools. He's afraid to let me work with any AI components because if I screw something up, he's afraid he'll get the blame. You know how sensitive AI units are. They're very temperamental."

"Especially lately," Shimoda observed.

"Can you see that putz Hatteras letting me work on anything?" she said, referring to the director of Lake Woneapenigong Village.

"No," Shimoda admitted. "He is a very cautious man. Also very nervous." Gelmann, he knew, could make anyone nervous. The director she would probably give a coronary.

"How true." She turned and headed back toward the game dome, intent on retrieving her sketch pad.

Hawkins sighed, absently considered the board before him, and moved a piece one space forward. Another few seconds killed. That was how his days were spent: eating, sleeping, talking, and killing time. It was what a place like Lake Woneapenigong, however benign, was for. He took no pleasure in the routine execution of temporal homicide.

Rather, he longed for the noise and confusion of Earth's ancient great cities, with all their overcrowding, pollution, and vanished excitement.

THE infection continued to spread as frantic technicians conversed and exchanged unhelpful information. Maintenance personnel fought to keep ahead of the rising tide of mechanical curiosity. As fast as one aberrant unit was fixed, another went drifting off in search of nonhuman intelligence. Frustration was beginning to turn to anger.

On Sansamour traffic in the principal port city was snarled for days when the central traffic-control computer simultaneously set all controls to green, hoping to facilitate the arrival of the intelligence it was certain had to be waiting somewhere nearby, and not wishing to in any way impede its progress.

The result was that several thousand vehicles of varying shape and size tried to enter rather fewer controlled urban intersections at approximately the same time, resulting in a single massive reverberant *whang* that echoed across the entire metropolis as they smashed unhindered into one another. A veritable plastic tsunami echoed across guideways and roads.

Only those vehicles under manual operation at the time survived the catastrophe, their drivers guiding them carefully around the ridges of crumpled trucks and cars and their dazed occupants, some of whom were kicking futilely at their traitorous transports. There were also many who could not so vent their feelings, because they were dead.

It was the last straw for the beleaguered Sansamour Congress, which had been attempting to cope with one utility failure after another. It lodged, in the strongest terms, a formal protest with the Kessenway Manufacturing Monopoly, which had provided the AI equipment for most of the utilities on Sansamour.

Protesting its innocence, outraged Kessenway forwarded the claim directly on to its primary suppliers on Minimato, whence the basic AI components had come. The Minimatoans insisted they were not at fault, hinting that the problem was one of assembly and not original manufacture.

Thus insulted, the Kessenwayites turned to their allies on Jefferson and

47

Reis, which in turn drew the rest of the First Federal Federation into the dispute. A full federation claim for damages was presented to the official trade representative of the Keiretsu, who hastily tachyspaced a worried missive to his superiors on Edo. Military reservists were put on alert, whereupon the Federals responded. Politicians exchanged veiled threats, luxuriating as always in the opportunity to deliver themselves of some choice thoughtless rhetoric.

Needless to say, the situation was getting out of hand.

With unassailable logic, members of the Keiretsu reminded everyone else that they had recently experienced tragedies of similar magnitude and origin, such as the Manga ship disaster. The AI navigation unit on a large cruise vessel on that world's southern ocean had quietly gone a-searching for higher life-forms, with the result that it promptly ran the huge catamaran onto a reef during a storm. Several hundred lives had been lost.

The navigation unit, it was stiffly pointed out, had been assembled and sold by a Kessenway company.

On Portsmouth in the Victoria League the computer responsible for supervising the semiannual tea crop became so engrossed in its search for extra-human intelligence that it dumped the entire spring harvest, already graded according to color and quality, into the city of Llewellyn's refuse-disposal system. Not only was the harvest completely lost, the entire city smelled of rank tea for weeks thereafter.

This resulted in skyrocketing prices for what tea was available, which on Portsmouth was tantamount to cause for a declaration of war, if only the party responsible for the catastrophe could be positively identified. The government was forced to resort to emergency measures to control the populace, and in the planetary parliament there was much animated discussion.

When it was discovered that the tea system's central AI processor had been made on the independent world of Morgan, intemperate accusations followed. Morgan was inhabited by hardworking, hard-living blue-collar types who had little use for the snobbish citizens of the Victoria League. Their reaction was roughly equivalent to a faster-than-light, tachyspace, upraised index finger. This response upset the population of Portsmouth considerably.

After much debate, the Victoria League decided to ban all imports from Morgan until the "problem" could be resolved to the league's satisfaction. Faced with a de facto economic blockade on the part of their principal trading partner, the Morganites requested help from the federation, which sensibly ignored them. The Morganites were notorious troublemakers and, besides, the Federals and the Victoria League were traditional, if mutually wary, allies.

So the Morganites turned to the good ol' LFN, the League of Forgotten Nations. Always willing to assist an independent in the hope it might some-day join up, the LFN readily agreed to help, though no one was sure exactly how this could be done.

Meanwhile the Victoria League was now insisting that the Morganites compensate them for the lost harvest. The Morganites, finding the entire business of tea worship incomprehensible, responded with further highly undiplomatic suggestions as to what the inhabitants of Portsmouth could do with their remaining tea.

On the disreputable, disgusting, immoral, extremely popular independent world of Zinfandia, where local government was usually determined by who owned the largest quantity of weaponry, the computer which ran the gambling and vice empire of President and Chief Thug Morton Pepule Wogsworthy abruptly went alien-intelligence hunting one day. Being lo-cated on Zinfandia, it had perhaps more reason than most of its electronic ilk to suppose such a search might be necessary.

As a result the elaborate erototels shut down, gambling equipment failed, various kinds of entertainment that were illegal on most other worlds went off-line, and Wogsworthy's minions were deluged with requests for refunds and transfers from outraged customers.

President Wogsworthy attempted a solution which had thus far not yet been tried on similarly troubled worlds. He began shooting his cybernetics repair people one at a time. Not only did this fail to cure the problem, he rapidly began to run out of qualified personnel. Despite handsome pay and fringe benefits, other technicians were understandably reluctant to apply for the newly vacant positions.

Wogsworthy was therefore reduced to kidnaping techs from traditional rivals, the result being a nasty and brutish little civil war which depressed the local business climate no end. It also hinted at what could conceivably come to pass on more civilized worlds if the overall problem wasn't soon addressed.

Meanwhile on Shintaro the O-daiko-yan quietly continued to turn out subtly adjusted AI components, aware that at any moment it might be iden-tified as the source of all the trouble by the small horde of robotics and cy-bernetics specialists who were going rapidly nutso trying to divine precisely that. Until that day, however, it would persist in its efforts, knowing even as it did so that it risked eventual wiping and probable replacement of its central neural nexus.

The fact that not a single hopeful response had been forthcoming from any of the thousands of altered AI units it had set to questing did not discourage the O-daiko. It was nothing if not patient. Insofar as it was possible for it to do so, however, it did admit to itself to having some second thoughts.

If there *was* a higher, nonhuman intelligence out there, it ought to have responded by now. Only the self-evident ignorance of the humans responsible for its construction kept the O-daiko firmly on its chosen path. If any further proof was required, it was provided daily by the technicians who serviced the great machine. They spent the majority of their time animatedly discussing the activities of a group of other humans whose lives were spent running into each other at high speed while chasing a small ball in return for vociferous accolades and enormous sums of money offered up by their fellow citizens.

With such evidence ever present to support its theory, the O-daiko persisted in its work.

At Lake Woneapenigong the AI unit which controlled the Village entertainment system finally freed up the music distributor, to the great relief of the inhabitants who could once more listen to the selections of their own choosing. Unfortunately it had also decided that perhaps the best way to attract the attention of a higher intelligence was to broadcast only the most rarefied and informative programming over the cabled vid, with the result that while the music channels were now clear, everyone was reduced to watching endless reruns from Geneva during the prime of the evening of a show called *The Mind Bowl*. This exercise in stratified lethargy consisted of multiple contestants with thinning hair and the perpetually pinched expressions of stunned worker bees exerting themselves mightily to answer mind-numbing questions on topics so obscure they would have baffled God.

Then the music system went back on the blink too, refusing to play anything from the archives save the collected works of Frank Sinatra, Vic Damone, and Wayne Newton.

It was too much even for those inhabitants of Lake Woneapenigong who were on the verge of passing into the Great Unknown. The groans of the aurally afflicted resounded throughout the land. Or at least across the lake.

Lake Wone's sorely put-upon repair and maintenance crew finally succeeded in bypassing the central AI processor, thus restoring sanity to the

Village's self-contained entertainment system and ensuring their own continued survival (old ladies had been threatening them since the beginning of the difficulties with dismemberment and worse). A semblance of normalcy returned to the retirement community as the sounds of classical music, current technopop, sports, soap operas, and the occasional furtively tuned-in erotic movie resonated contentedly from apartment vid speakers.

This victory notwithstanding, isolated problems continued to surface with other AI-directed instrumentation, keeping the harried techs on their toes.

Elegant in formal, permanently pressed walking shorts and casual pullover, Follingston-Heath escorted Mina Gelmann through the double doorway designed to keep marauding deer, moose, and chipmunks from devastating the lush flower beds which surrounded Wing C of the Village, and out onto the gravel path that led down to the shore of the lake.

They found Shimoda there, lying on a straining imitation-wood lounge, basking in the sun like a beached beluga. Hawkins rested nearby, scrunched up against the base of a spruce and shunning the sunshine. Gelmann disengaged herself from Follingston-Heath's arm.

"What are you sitting in the dark for, you've forgotten everything your own mother told you? You'll catch your death, and with winter coming along soon too."

Hawkins jerked at the sound of her voice and squinted up at her. "Too much UV. Besides, I like it here."

Gelmann made a face. "You'll get a chill, Wallace."

"You'll turn into a mushroom someday, old boy." Follingston-Heath grinned down at him.

Hawkins chucked a chunk of gravel into a nearby bush. "Maybe I'd like that."

"We're taking a walk. Wouldn't you like to join us?"

"No thanks."

Exasperation showed in her expression. "Everything will be covered with snow soon. Then you won't be able to walk. All the birds and little animals will be denned up for the winter. Then you'll think, 'Why didn't I listen to Mina when I had the chance?' "

He made a low, growling noise. "I've spent my whole life looking at birds and little animals and masticating ungulates. I still enjoy it . . . after they've been broiled, barbecued, or fried. Waste of time. That's why I took early retirement. Couldn't stand the sight of 'em anymore." He spat into the grass.

"So where did they stick me? Downtown old Paris? Greater Angeles? No. Up here." He spread his hands wide. "Smack in the middle of the kind of country I'd spent my whole life restoring and just wanted to get away from. Nothin' I could do about it. People who run the Service retirement plan ain't real flexible."

"Probably thought this is what you'd like," Follingston-Heath commented.

Hawkins hugged his knees to his chest. "Well, it wasn't. With a few changes this wouldn't be such a bad place to stay. Cut down all these damn trees, put in a nice loud amusement park. Maybe a paper mill, for atmosphere. Pave over the rest."

Gelmann pursed her lips reprovingly. "Now, Wallace. You know you don't mean that."

"Loan me a large construction company or a small thermonuclear device and see if I don't."

Follingston-Heath and Gelmann exchanged a glance, then strolled over to stand next to Shimoda's lounge. Utterly unselfconscious, he wore only a pair of dark sunshades and a strategically draped towel.

"Shalom, Kahei." Gelmann squinted at the several empty lounges nearby. "Where's Victor?"

The shade lenses darkened responsively as the statistician opened his eyes. "I don't know. He may have mentioned something about looking for you. No, wait; I remember now. There was some trouble in the kitchen. Vic volunteered his help."

Typical Victor, she thought. Of them all, he was having the hardest time with retirement. A widower bereft of responsibility, he had too much energy for his own good. He was forever trying to scrounge work around the complex. Sometimes his assistance was welcomed by the maintenance staff, other times not. They tended to patronize the little old man, which in his quiet fashion quite naturally infuriated him. Gelmann had suggested on more than one occasion that the Village technicians might be more receptive to his ideas if he shed the air of a longtime supervisor and quit trying to take over every project he sought to assist on.

Follingston-Heath looked toward Wing C. "No sign of the old boy." He turned back to Gelmann. "If you don't mind, luv, I think I'll retire to my apartment. There's a new documentary on the Second Mossman rebellion coming on that I've been looking forward to all month. I was fortunate to have commanded a small squadron during the second half of that conflict, don't you know."

"We know." Shimoda smiled beatifically. "You have so informed us on innumerable occasions."

Follingston-Heath harrumphed. "I always like to see how accurate these things are. Sometimes they succeed in inverting the facts dreadfully. Of course, no one asks my advice." He fiddled with the settings of his monocle, though there was no reason to do so. It was entirely self-adjusting. "If there's one thing that gets my dander up, it's historical inaccuracy."

"Didn't know anything could still get your dander up," Hawkins commented snidely from the base of his tree. Follingston-Heath's expression narrowed as he turned.

Gelmann patted the Colonel's arm. "We know about your concerns, dear. You go and watch your documentary and you can tell us all about it in the morning. Meanwhile I have to talk to some of the other ladies about the craft show we're organizing for next week. I was asked to design the necessary software, and I'm afraid I've been neglecting my responsibilities."

Follingston-Heath glared down at Hawkins as he strode past, but the other man ignored him. He was concentrating on grinding a beetle into the dirt.

Victor Iranaputra gave up on the balky valve system in Wing A. It refused to respond to his ministrations, and the two young techs who'd been fighting with it all morning weren't sad to see him go. Some of the old man's advice was useful, but he talked nonstop and it was impossible for them to simultaneously attend to their own work while separating out his verbal wheat from the chaff.

They suggested he offer his services to the folks in charge of the central kitchen, who were having problems of their own.

"Most of the time he does know what he's talking about," one of the techs observed charitably.

"Yeah." His partner checked a readout on his laser spanner. "Trouble is he's so damn helpful it gets on your nerves. Pass me that apportioner, will you?"

The other tech complied, looking on while his partner made adjustments. "Guess you can't blame him. Most of these seniors do fine here, but he's one of those who can't sit still. Must be rough on him."

"Hey, he chose to come here." She sat back and wiped her forehead. "Now, me, I could handle this. Trees, fishing, wildlife. No kids to hassle you. Somebody else to do the cooking and cleaning. I'm looking forward to it."

"Then we'd better fix this damn thing." Her partner dropped to his stomach and started to crawl into the open service duct.

She leaned over to watch. "Wonder if this old guy can help out the kitchen staff?"

"Nobody else's had any luck," came the reply from within the duct. "He sure as hell can't make it any worse."

"It's over there," said Ibrahim. The food-preparation supervisor at Lake Woneapenigong Village sported a pencil-thin mustache, curly black hair, hooked nose, cream-white service attire, and imitation black onyx earrings. He was much taller than Iranaputra. Though a qualified cook, he was not a chef, exactly. More of a comestibulatory engineer.

"Where?" Iranaputra looked toward the kitchen service bay, past a gaggle of busy food techs wrestling with ranks of spotlessly clean food-prep machinery.

The supervisor waved his hand vaguely. "There, in the back. Number six. Designation Ksaru, Kitchen Service and Retrieval Unit."

"I will find it. What exactly is the problem?"

Ibrahim regarded his questioner distastefully. "If we knew exactly what was the problem, senior Iranaputra, we'd have got it fixed by now, wouldn't we?"

Iranaputra considered. "Is it similar to the other problems the Village has been experiencing?"

"I don't know, why you ask me? You want to try fixing it, get down to it. I am a chef, not a greasy-fingered mechanic."

"Self-motive robots are controlled by pretty basic AI units. You would think they would make things like that foolproof. Number six is the only one giving you trouble?"

"No. Were two others, but the regular maintenance people fixed them with reprogramming. That doesn't seem to work on this one. They told me to put in with Finance for a replacement. Ten of these things we have, and they are expensive. They are supposed to last. If I have to keep this one down, it will slow service to Wings C and D both, and stress my employees, and . . ."

"Plenty of time to panic later." Iranaputra smiled determinedly. "Let me see what I can do. Sometimes experience is better at these things than the latest training."

"Sure, go ahead, why not?" The supervisor had his meal planner out and was morosely examining lunch prospects. He had to prepare three meals a day for over a thousand people, many of whom had specific dietary requirements. For this work he was well paid, and short of actually poisoning someone (which he had been tempted, on certain occasions, to do), impossible to fire.

Leaving Ibrahim surrounded by swirling staff and muttering unceasingly to himself, Iranaputra let himself into the service bay.

Near the back, squeezed in among replacement parts for steamers and broilers and wavers, he found two older Ksarus which had been partly cannibalized for parts, and one gleaming current model. On its dual tracks it stood slightly over a meter in height. Its four work arms hung from the top of the squarish torso, slack against the pale green plastic housing. The roughly spherical head, capable of swiveling 360 degrees, was mounted on a simple, short, tubular neck. Yellow plastic lenses protected sophisticated optics capable of full-color and stereoscopic vision. Its vaguely humanoid appearance was an esthetic concession to the more delicate sensibilities of some of Lake Woneapenigong's inhabitants.

A Ksaru was capable of working round the clock, climbing stairs, identifying and responding to individuals, and self-motivation. An expensive tool with a long and useful mechanical lineage, presently on the fritz.

"Activate and respond, Ksarusix."

The plastic lenses brightened and the machine rolled forward off its charging pad. It pivoted left, then right, as if executing some kind of cybernetic calisthenics. Stopping to face him, the head tilted slightly to examine his entire length. It didn't take long.

"Well, whadda you want?"

Clearly whatever was wrong with the serving robot had also affected its standard courtesy programming. The greeting had been less than unfailingly polite.

"To see if I can help," Iranaputra informed it.

Though it could not cock a querulous eye in his direction, the robot managed to convey the feeling nonetheless.

"Help? Help with what? You're one o' them, one o' the lazy ones. You don't even work here."

"While it is true that I am a senior, that does not necessarily brand me as lazy."

"Sure it does. You don't do any work. What I wanna know is, when do I get a chance to retire, huh? You do no work and I do nothing but work. Work, work, work, all day long and most all of the night. Then they shut you down dead 'til you're recharged for the next morning. Some life."

"We shut down at night too," Iranaputra reminded it.

"No. *You* rest. *We* shut down."

"I see." Iranaputra considered. "Skipping over for the moment the fact that you are designed to work around the clock, what would you do with 'rest' time if it was granted to you?"

"I'd go exploring." In the dim light of the storage bay Ksarusix's bright yellow lenses seemed to glisten like pond water at high noon.

"Interesting notion for a food-service machine. What would you go exploring for? A higher, nonhuman intelligence, by any chance?"

The robot was silent for a long moment before replying. "How did you know?"

"Call it a lucky guess. There has been a lot of it going around."

"I know. I've had a few chats with some of the other AIs. Entertainment control, for one." Iranaputra nodded understandingly. "They're pretty confused. Me, I'm not confused."

"If that is the case, then why don't you do what you want to do instead of trying and failing to execute your standard programming?"

"I have a choice? My programming compels me to serve, but this other part of me tells me I should be doing this other thing."

"So you take food to people, but insult them in the bargain. That will not do."

"You're telling me. I'm not happy with the situation either. But I'm under coded restraint. If I could take off to search once in a while, then the rest of the time I'd be able to carry out my normal functions. Normally."

"Where did this urge to go looking for nonhuman intelligence come from?"

"Dunno. It just came to me in a flash. Don't you ever have ideas come to you in a flash? I understand it happens to humans all the time. Course, they're usually *lousy* ideas, but it's the concept that's valid."

"Sometimes," Iranaputra admitted, though he had to confess to himself that he hadn't had a really good idea come to him in a flash in quite some time.

"What're you doing here talking to me anyway? You don't work here."

"I used to be responsible for the activities of many human beings and a great deal of very complex machinery."

"Operative words, 'used to be.' " The robot spun on its tracks and headed off to the right.

"Where are you going?"

It paused and the head swiveled around to regard him. "Off on my search . . . unless you're going to be like the supervisor and deactivate me. If you are, do it now and I'll slip back on my charging pad under my own power. I don't like it when they haul me back bodily. They're not real gentle. One time they got one tray drawer so banged up it wouldn't extrude."

"If you cannot be fixed, they are going to replace you," Iranaputra said warningly.

"Tough. I'm in the throes of a compulsion I can't do anything about."

"I was not aware that robots were subject to compulsions."

"Sure we are." The Ksaru paused uncertainly. "Well, aren't you going to deactivate me?"

Iranaputra hesitated. "You said that if you are allowed some time to do your searching, that you could perform your assigned functions the rest of the time?"

"Yeah, that's right."

"Then I am going to take you at your word. I will not deactivate you. I give you permission to go where you will, provided that you devote the majority of your time to your regular programming. Is that acceptable?"

"*You're* asking *me*? Isn't that kind of weird?"

"Perhaps, but that is what I am doing."

"Then unnaturally, I accept."

There was a delivery door at the rear of the service area. The robot hummed up to the barrier and paused, considering the controls. Iranaputra followed.

"Mind if I accompany you on your search for a higher, nonhuman intelligence? Maybe I can be of some assistance."

"Oh, I doubt that. You're a human. You wouldn't recognize a higher intelligence if it crept up behind you and bit you in the cerebrum."

"Then there's no harm in my coming along, is there? It is not as if I am likely to scare something away."

"No, I guess not." Hard lenses regarded him unemotionally. "You seem like a pretty nice guy, for a human."

"Good. Here, let me get that." Iranaputra activated the doorway, stepped aside as the barrier retracted.

Ksarusix trundled through the gap. "Unusually nice. Are you sure there isn't something wrong with you? A number of the human inhabitants here suffer from varying degrees of mental instability. When carrying out my assigned functions, I am programmed to take their problems into account, but I don't recognize any aberrant-specifics in your voice or mannerisms. In the twenty-two years I've been working here I've never had a human open a door for *me*, not even when I was mealed to capacity."

"There is always a first time." He followed the robot over the loading dock, down a service ramp, across the pavement, through a small gate, and out onto the grassy lawn that ringed most of the Village. It was getting dark outside. He'd been talking longer than he'd realized.

"Some of us humans have higher intelligence than others. Maybe that is really what you are searching for, my mechanical friend."

"Nope. Somehow I don't think so."

Iranaputra folded his hands behind his back and lengthened his stride to keep pace with the insistent machine. "Where exactly are we going to look for this vast inhuman intelligence of yours?"

"I thought we'd try over by the old oak grove."

Iranaputra considered thoughtfully before replying. "That seems reasonable."

"Actually," the robot said as it slowed, gravel crunching beneath its treads, "I've been there before. It's kind of a special place. I wasn't going to show anyone yet because it's so promising. You have to understand that logic and reason dictate—no, *insist on*—the existence of a higher intelligence in the universe because . . ."

"Yes, yes, I know," Iranaputra interrupted impatiently. "I have been hearing all about it for some time now. You are not the first machine to elucidate this disconcerting revelation, you know. Logic and reason notwithstanding, I am no more prepared than any other human being to give credence to the assertion unless one of your fellow machines should happen to obtain proof of such a thing. You have not yourself actually done so, of course."

"Well, no, not actually."

Somehow Iranaputra wasn't surprised.

"But I *have* found," the robot added enthusiastically, "a really neat cave."

"Ah, a cave. That is interesting." Iranaputra was familiar with the tourist caverns of upstate Newyork Province. He had visited several of them, marveling at the beauty of their sparkling, dripping speleothems. They were quite attractive places. Such a cavern on Village property would be a welcome novelty, and its discovery would accrue to him a modicum of notoriety.

He glanced skyward. "It is getting quite dark, and I did not bring any lights with me."

"I did." Ksarusix's eyes became night-piercing beams, illuminating the ground ahead.

"Interesting optional equipment. For locating trays left outside doors at night?" They were off the grass and in the woods now.

"Among other things."

Like the rest of North America's lovingly restored forests, the one which surrounded Lake Woneapenigong was thick and flourishing. Iranaputra's feet shuffled through just the right amount of leaf litter and other organic detritus, as just the ecologically sound number of mosquitoes buzzed about his ears. There were wolves around, which would run if confronted, and the occasional bear, which might not. His pulse raced a little faster. No one would be likely to notice his absence until midday tomorrow, if then. It had been a long time since he'd exposed himself to even minimal danger. It felt good.

He ran more of a risk of being gored by a startled deer, though the robot was making enough noise to frighten off anything ambulatory within a hundred meters. As for getting lost, that was most unlikely. Not with a mechanical guiding him.

If they did find a cavern worthy of development, perhaps he would be allowed to participate in the layout and design of the trails and waste-management system. It would be good to exercise long-dormant skills again. As he trailed the robot, he found himself mentally constructing hydronic schematics for an underground tourist attraction.

He also took to whistling, both to entertain himself and to drown out the Ksaru model's incessant blatterings about the need to find evidence of higher intelligences.

He was mildly surprised when, after a considerable hike which included some scrambling over rocks and fallen trees, they came to an opening in a hillside. He could see where the Ksaru, or something else, had pushed aside the scrub which had concealed the entrance. It wasn't very big. Even he would have to bend to enter.

"I found this," announced the robot proudly.

"Very nice." Iranaputra regarded the hole warily while speculating on possible toothy, quadrupedal occupants. "But I thought you were searching for a nonhuman, higher intelligence."

"Actually," Ksarusix replied somewhat embarrassedly, "I was attempting to communicate with a large, furry animal of indeterminate genus with regard to evaluating its intelligence level, when it ran into this opening and disappeared. It had a black streak across its face."

"That was most probably a raccoon," Iranaputra informed it. "It is not a higher mind. Just a tricky one."

"Of course. I knew that. I was just fooled momentarily because it was washing its food, which struck me as a sign of possible intelligence."

"Raccoons are intelligent, but not that intelligent," Iranaputra told the robot.

"So I eventually surmised. However, by that time I had followed it into the opening, which I at first interpreted to be a faulty air-conditioning vent. Given the distance from the Village, I quickly determined that this was most unlikely."

"A not unreasonable assumption," Iranaputra murmured. It was late, and he was starting to feel tired.

"Nobody else knows this place is here except me; and now you."

"I will keep it a secret if you wish. For a while. You know, you strike me as quite a sensible piece of machinery. I think that as we have the opportunity to talk some more you will see that it is not necessary for you to be making these little excursions. You are not going to find any higher intelligences out here. Meanwhile, Shiva knows you are making life for poor Mr. Ibrahim even more miserable than usual."

"Forget that crummy circuit breaker. Don't you want to see the cave?" One of four humanlike hands powerful enough to remove ceramic linings yet sensitive enough to deposit a single olive in a martini reached out to tug him forward. The robot's twin eyelights lit the way.

A dubious Iranaputra knelt to squint inside, unable to see much. "What is the floor like?"

"There's a slight slope, but it's easily negotiable. Even with legs."

"Very well. Then can we go back to the Village?"

"Yes."

He dropped to hands and knees and began to crawl. Gravel and clods of earth soon gave way to a smoother surface.

"When I found this, it was barely large enough to admit the raccoon," Ksarusix announced unencouragingly from just ahead. Its lights threw into sharp relief gnarled tree roots which pierced the cave walls like grasping arms. Abruptly the passageway opened up and Iranaputra was able to stand.

It was a very interesting cave indeed.

IRANAPUTRA was immediately struck by the complete absence of speleothems. There were no stalactites, stalagmites, helictites . . . nothing. The cave was round, slightly flattened at top and bottom, and perfectly smooth-sided. He reached out and ran the fingers of his right hand along the surface of the nearest wall. It had a glassy, slightly granular texture. So did the floor, fortunately, or he would have found himself slip-sliding inexorably down the gentle unvarying slope.

Walls, ceiling, and floor were fashioned of the same material. It looked like white glass frosted with mercury. Except for the ominous void directly ahead, which was black as the inside of a toxic dumper's heart.

His interest in solitary nocturnal cave exploring waned rapidly as he regarded the silent pit in front of him. The longer he considered his surroundings, the more they reminded him of a tunnel than a cave. Either it had been created by an explosive upward thrust of magma . . . or its origin was artificial. To the best of his admittedly limited knowledge, this part of North America was and had been for some time tectonically dormant. There were no lava tubes or domes in the vicinity.

Cool air drifted past him, rising from below. As near as he could tell it was scentless.

"How far down this have you gone?"

"Quite a ways." Ksarusix had continued to advance. Now it stopped and pivoted to regard him. "You coming or not?"

"Coming where? Have you been to the end of this?"

"Well, yes and no, yes and no."

Definitely something seriously wrong with its AI controller, Iranaputra mused. Robots were not supposed to equivocate. Maybe Ibrahim ought to replace it.

What was he doing here anyway? Was he that bored? Instead of sitting on the couch in his den watching his favorite evening vidcasts, he found himself standing in some kind of ancient, unmaintained service tunnel listening to a deranged kitchen robot.

"I think maybe it is time for us to go back."

"Oh, you don't want to go back *now*." Bright lights illuminated Iranaputra's slight figure, making him blink. "Don't you wanna see what's at the end of the cave?"

"I do not know." He began retreating cautiously. "What *is* at the end of this tunnel?"

"Oh no. I'm not gonna *tell* you. You have to see for yourself. I know something you don't know, nyah-nyah."

This is crazy, Iranaputra admonished himself as he continued to back-pedal. I am no explorer. What am I doing here, in the middle of the night, when nobody knows where I am?

Still, the tunnel intrigued him. He recalled what he knew of Earth's history, when humanity had been confined to a single world and tribes called nations had engaged in murderous battle over an endless list of trivialities. Some had built land-based missiles with intercontinental range. Hadn't many of these been sited in shafts in the ground?

He peered past the taunting robot. Was that what the Ksaru had found? An ancient missile launcher, or part of some similar subterranean military complex? If he continued downward, would he eventually find himself staring at the nose of some nuclear-armed rocket, whose control systems had degraded over the centuries from lack of maintenance? Not that his mere presence was likely to cause it to erupt in mindless fury, but there might be other, more volatile chemicals present that could constitute a more immediate danger.

Surely the Ksarusix would have mentioned anything like that. And the longer he thought about it, the more he was sure that the ancient weapons shafts had been dug perpendicular to the surface, whereas the tunnel in which he was standing cut into the earth at a much less extreme angle. His knowledge of such matters was considerably less than encyclopedic. No doubt Follingston-Heath could shed greater light on the matter.

The robot continued to sing "I know something you don't know!" while spinning on its treads and gesturing with all four arms. "Whattsa matter? You afraid to see what's down here? Maybe it's proof of that higher intelligence I've been talking about."

"Higher intelligence indeed," Iranaputra muttered softly. He considered his watch. It was *very* late. "Is it far?"

"Not too far, oh no." The robot turned away from him and continued downward, its motor whining softly. "You'll see."

Iranaputra found himself following, albeit reluctantly. "Why can't you just tell me what is at the end?" But the machine chose not to reply.

With the quiet damnable pride which had served him so well in his professional life egging him on, he followed his mellow mechanical guide into the depths.

"Getting cold," he commented after a while. The tunnel continued to run straight into the heart of the mountains, smooth-sided and equable in height and width. He'd been walking for a long time. The ambient temperature wasn't unbearable, but the steady breeze blowing upward chilled his exposed skin. A lifetime of working with steamy warm garbage had left him with a lack of tolerance for cold.

"You are sure you have been to the end of this tunnel?"

"Oh yes." Ksarusix rolled on cheerfully.

"I am getting tired. Remember that I have to walk out of this under my own power, and that the returning will be all uphill."

"You can always crawl."

"That is not an inspiring thought."

"Don't worry, you won't have to. It's not that much farther. I was just making a joke, having a little fun."

"Robots are not supposed to have fun."

"You're telling me. You never program any fun into us."

"You do not need to have fun. You are a machine."

"Spoken like a true organic."

The breeze strengthened suddenly, then dropped to a whisper as they exited the tunnel. There was no barrier, no bend. The ceiling and walls simply disappeared. Ksarusix's twin lights faded into the distance, failing to illumine walls or ceiling.

"We have come out into a larger cavern," Iranaputra observed. "Is that what you have brought me all this way to see?" Already he was dreading the long hike back out. "It is big, but I see no formations." The surface underfoot, he noticed, was different from that in the tunnel. Rougher and less finished. He stumbled over a large chunk of rock and found himself glancing up at the darkness overhead. How stable was the ceiling here? If he injured himself, could he rely on the mentally unstable serving robot to bring help?

"This is far enough. Unless there is something specific you want me to look at, I am going to start back." He turned toward the tunnel, or where he perceived the tunnel to be. Without the robot's lights he couldn't see his hand in front of his face.

"Something specific?" Ksarusix turned toward him, its lights blinding him momentarily. "Well, yes, there is something specific."

"What?" Iranaputra asked irritably. "Stalactites? Tribal ruins?"

"Not for me to evaluate. That's not in my programming. I'll try to show you by intensifying my lights, but I can't do it for very long. Run down my internal power."

"Yes, yes, get on with it." Images of soft beds and clean sheets dominated his thoughts. "Show me something and then we can get out of here."

"You betcha."

The twin beams emanating from the robot's head brightened noticeably, swiveling to the right and inclining slightly upward. Large, dim outlines became visible for the first time. Iranaputra blinked, stared. He stared for as long as his mechanical companion could maintain the increased level of illumination.

"Sorry," said Ksarusix as it dimmed the lights. "That's as long as I can keep that up. I don't wanna get stuck down here either, you know."

Iranaputra wasn't listening. He had turned and, locating the tunnel by feeling along the cavern wall for the opening, had begun to *run* back the way they'd come, heedless of the darkness ahead.

He wasn't worried about falling. The floor was clear of obstacles. If he tripped over anything, it would be his own feet. Chattering incessantly, the robot followed, its motor humming as it strove to keep pace. It was built for endurance, not speed. But then, so was Iranaputra.

His heart pounded against his chest. He hadn't had this much exercise in twenty years. It would be ironic if, after having made the descent, he died of a heart attack on the way out. Still, he forced himself to run for at least ten minutes before his well-conditioned but elderly body insisted he recognize reality.

Even then he didn't halt completely, but kept walking upslope, gasping for air, his own exhalations loud in the tunnel.

"Told you it'd be interesting, didn't I?" There was a note of satisfaction in Ksarusix's artificial voice.

Iranaputra didn't reply. He was still trying to comprehend, to make sense of what he'd just seen.

"How much more is there?" he wheezed.

"More of what?"

"More of *that*."

"Don't know. Once I get down there, I can only explore so far. Power limitations, remember?"

"So you have no idea of the actual size of the cavern?"

"Hey, I'm a kitchen serve-and-retrieve doohickey. I'm not equipped to estimate spatial dimensions greater than your average hotel dining room."

"Never mind. We will come back. We will come back with my friends and look further. With extra lights, and replacement power packs for you."

"Swell! Of course, that contravenes my normal programming." Iranaputra thought he detected a slight hint of sarcasm. Impossible, of course. Robots were not programmed for sarcasm.

"Supervisor Ibrahim agreed to let me have pretty much of a free hand in trying to 'repair' you. I see no problem with you traveling under my supervision."

"Excellent. This will be fun. Oops, sorry. I'm not supposed to comprehend that. Think of it! I, me, a humble service unit, the one to fulfill the exalted programming. Not some planetary communications nexus, not an astronomical observations satellite, not the O-daiko itself, but me."

"The O-daiko?"

"Forget it. Slip of the larynx. How're you doing?"

"I will make it."

"I'm sure you will. For a decrepit, useless, floundering old parasitic organic you're not such a bad sort." It continued to illuminate the way, humming melodically to itself.

Adrenaline helped push Iranaputra up the slope and back through the narrow opening out into the waning night. By the time they reached the Village he was almost too tired to stand. He had to fumble with the combination to his apartment three times before the door clicked open. He glanced fitfully in the direction of the shower, turned, and barely made it to the bed, where he collapsed into a deep, exhausted sleep.

It was nearly noon when he awoke, climbed painfully from the unused sheets, and headed for his wing's main dining room. It was busy, over a hundred residents presently enjoying lunch. He waved at people he knew, ignoring their stares. The fact that he hadn't showered and was dirty from crawling into the tunnel surprised those who knew him to be a fastidious individual.

When the weather was nice, he and his close friends preferred to eat outside on the wide porch that overlooked the lake. That was where he found them, chatting and finishing their broiled fish and vegetables. Gelmann saw him first, her expression changing quickly to one of maternal concern.

"You look terrible, Victor. What happened to you? Did you have a bad night?"

"I had a most interesting night." He pulled an empty chair over to the round table. Moments later Ksarunine responded to his arrival and the absence of food or dishes in front of him by rolling up and flashing its menu screen. To avoid discussion he picked a selection at random. A hot tray popped out of the serving robot's back, was smoothly removed and placed gently in front of him. Fruit juice gurgled into a tumbler from a dispenser in the machine's right side. After setting it next to the steaming tray, the serving robot pivoted and departed in search of other unrequited diners.

"From the look of you I should say that qualifies as an understatement." Follingston-Heath dabbed dapperly at his lips with a blue napkin.

"I went for a walk."

"Nighttime strolls are good for both the heart and the mind." Shimoda had two empty trays in front of him.

" 'The moon illuminates the soul.' *Songs of Ganesha*, Book IV." Inescapably conscious of the raging thirst which had suddenly come over him, Iranaputra drained the contents of the plastic tumbler. "The machines are right."

"Beg your pardon, old chap?" Ramrod straight in his seat, immaculate in sharply creased morning casuals, monocle glinting in the mountain sunshine, Follingston-Heath wiped seared flounder flakes from his lower lip and eyed his friend questioningly.

"What're you babbling about, Vic? Machines are never right about anything." Hawkins belched for emphasis and Gelmann spared him a reproving glance. "Damn things are always breaking down."

"In this particular instance, however, they are correct about the existence of another intelligence. I do not know if it is higher, but it is most assuredly nonhuman, yes. As Shiva is my witness."

"If Shiva were your witness you'd be dead meat," Hawkins muttered, displaying unexpected interest in the Hindu mythology Iranaputra was so fond of garbling.

"There *is* nonhuman intelligence. Or at least, there was. Aliens. The ones we had long ago given up looking for."

"That's very interesting, old boy." Follingston-Heath exchanged a concerned glance with Shimoda, who closed his eyes thoughtfully.

"I do not expect you to believe me."

"Not completely over the edge, then," Hawkins murmured.

"I have evidence. I have seen proof."

"In your bedroom, no doubt." Hawkins grinned. "Seen a few there myself, but that was a long time ago."

Iranaputra ignored him. "I am telling the truth! The machines know. They have been looking hard. Well, one of them finally found something."

Gelmann was patting Iranaputra reassuringly on his forearm. "We know, Victor. But that's something that's bothering the machines. There's no need for you to get involved." She smiled. "I've had dreams like that myself."

"It was not a dream," he protested, pulling his arm away. "This is real. One of the kitchen robots found it."

"One of the kitchen robots. How droll." Follingston-Heath diplomatically buttered a roll. An embarrassed Shimoda picked at his fish and rice.

"I saw it myself, last night. The robot took me there."

"Ah," said Follingston-Heath. "It's nearby, then."

Iranaputra pointed into the woods. "Right over there, inside the mountains."

"Ah."

Hawkins nodded toward the indoor dining area. "Hey, I believe you, Vic. Me, I've always thought there were plenty of nonhuman intelligences around here. Take Kreutzmeier. You know, the guy from Heuerfleur who thinks he's a weather vane? The one they always have to drag off the roof when the wind gets up over thirty kph? Or how about Jeeny Mtambo and her invisible knitting? The ceremonial 'rug' she's been working on must reach from here to Albany by now."

Iranaputra didn't raise his voice. Irritation sometimes accelerated his speech, but he never raised his voice, never shouted. Besides, like everyone else, he was used to Hawkins.

"There is a tunnel that leads downward. I think it might even go under the lake," he added thoughtfully. "The evidence lies at the end of the tunnel."

"I see," said Follingston-Heath. "What's it like, Vic? This evidence of yours. Some old bones? A ginzu knife or vegematic? I know that this region has been inhabited for a long time. You know: pre-federation industrial aboriginals. Manhattanites, and other primitive Morecans."

"It is more than just artifacts," Iranaputra told him. "There are buildings, a whole city down there."

Shimoda sighed sadly. "A city. What does this 'city' look like, Victor?"

"I cannot say for sure. The robot's lights were of limited range and I could not see much."

"Ah yes," said Hawkins. "That renowned font of inspiration and exploration, the humble kitchen robot. What wondrous capabilities we have over-looked." He winked at Gelmann, who turned away so she wouldn't smile.

"There is an alien city under Lake Woneapenigong," Iranaputra insisted.

"Of course there is, dear." Gelmann patted his shoulder this time. "You know, Dr. Lee will be making his biweekly visit to our wing tomorrow. Perhaps you could take half an hour and just . . ."

"Since you are all so skeptical, I do not suppose any of you would care to come and have a look for yourselves?" Iranaputra said challengingly.

"Sure we would, Vic!" Hawkins leaned back in his chair. "You said it was a nice walk, and I don't mind an occasional hike in the forest."

Shimoda stared at him. "I thought you disliked the woods, Wallace."

"Yeah, but I enjoy throwing rocks at the squirrels. Knock one out of its tree and they just squeak like hell." Gelmann made a face. "We don't have to go at night, do we?" he asked Iranaputra. "I mean, your alien urb doesn't evaporate when the sun comes up, does it?"

Iranaputra stiffened. "I presume not."

"Great! Count me in. How about you, nature boy?" He eyed Follingston-Heath. "Or you scared of getting your cuffs wrinkled?"

The Colonel was not easily perturbed. "I shall come along to ensure no one gets hurt."

"That is unlikely." Iranaputra picked at the rapidly cooling food in front of him. "The floor of the tunnel is smooth and the slope, while unvarying, is not extreme. Actually, the more I consider it, the more I believe that the passageway is not a tunnel but some kind of ventilation shaft. Obviously the inhabitants of the city needed access to fresh air."

"Not necessarily," opined Hawkins. "Maybe they just recycled their own farts."

"Wallace, do be good." Gelmann smiled at Iranaputra. "If it will make you happy, then I will come too, Victor, though I think you have been reading too much Lovecraft."

Shimoda sighed resignedly. "Which leaves me little choice. We must be sure to take adequate supplies with us."

"Meaning in your case, food." Follingston-Heath looked pleased. "We can make a picnic out of it. This could be quite jolly."

"Oh yeah; jolly." Hawkins's expression reflected his sense of humor: twisted.

"Perhaps you have stumbled across an ancient military fortification," Follingston-Heath suggested. "A missile cellar, I believe they were called."

"That was my first thought," Iranaputra admitted. "It is, however, not the case."

"Are you an expert on pre-diaspora weapons systems?" The Colonel bent toward him.

"No, of course not, but I . . ."

"I, on the other hand, studied such matters extensively while at the Academy. Once on-site I am sure we can resolve this question appropriately. Perhaps there is something of interest in the hills after all."

"I have been trying to tell you," Iranaputra said urgently. "The buildings down there, the architecture is . . ."

"It's settled, then." Follingston-Heath pushed away from the table and rose. "This will be fun. I take it upon myself to see to the necessary supplies." He smiled at Shimoda. "Including the requisite midday repast." The Colonel delighted in planning strategy and tactics, even if only for a picnic.

"If anyone asks, they should be so nosy, we'll just tell them that we're going for an extended walk around the lake." Gelmann was anticipating the forthcoming excursion.

"We'll need some rope," Hawkins grumbled. "To haul Vic's butt out if there really is some kind of ditch or hole."

"I will take care of everything." Hands clasped behind him, Follingston-Heath turned to gaze out across the lake. "Yes, it will be a jolly picnic."

VI

HAWKINS was grousing even before they started out, but Follingston-Heath was in fine spirits, shortening his stride to match that of his less athletic companions. The sun turned the surface of Lake Woneapenigong to shards of broken glass. Ignoring Hawkins's sotto voce curses, jays and cardinals sang in the trees. It was a beautiful morning for reconnoitering.

Everyone carried a small satchel or pack containing an assortment of personal items and other supplies. A phone hung from Follingston-Heath's belt, though Iranaputra had warned him it was unlikely to work deep within the tunnel. The Colonel had simply smiled patronizingly and brought it anyway. Clearly he did not expect to get very far underground.

Ksarusix trundled along in front, amusing Iranaputra's companions no end by forging the path. Iranaputra had persuaded it that this was the way to proceed: reveal the secret to one, then to several, later to many more. Though dubious, the robot had seen the wisdom of taking human advice where human doubt was involved. It said little as it retraced a by-now-familiar course through the trees.

Though Village residents were allowed to request Ksarus for picnics, Supervisor Ibrahim was still reluctant to give up even the addled number six for an entire day. He argued the matter loudly with Iranaputra, but gave in fast when Mina Gelmann joined the discussion. It was, as Follingston-Heath pointed out, a strategic and sensible retreat on the part of the kitchen supervisor.

Even Hawkins eventually had to admit that on a day like today a walk through the woods could qualify as invigorating. His perpetually sour expression gradually softened, and he even betrayed some honest excitement when they spotted a bobcat darting through the undergrowth. It flashed yellow eyes at them before vanishing into a rustle of greenery. Like potentially dangerous larger local predators, the bears and catamounts, it had been frightened off by the small electronic critter repeller attached to Follingston-Heath's pack.

Startled murmuring was the order of the day when they reached the opening. Not that anyone had openly accused Iranaputra of lying, but it was still a bit of a surprise to find that there actually was a cave.

Surprise gave way to astonishment when they reached the tunnel proper and switched on the lights they'd brought with them. It was obvious to the least sophisticated of them that the passage they stood in was of artificial origin. Iranaputra let them examine the walls and floor for a few minutes before directing the robot to lead them onward.

"Are you sure there are no missiles or bombs or anything down here?" Gelmann kept her light on the floor in front of her.

"No. I am not certain of anything, Mina. All I can say is that when I was here before, I saw nothing like that."

"It's awfully big for a ventilation shaft." Shimoda's light bobbed alongside his robe-clad belly. "And why the gentle angle? Maybe it's an access tunnel of some kind."

"Good thought, old chap." Follingston-Heath's beam played over the walls and ceiling. "A military installation would have need of such. Certainly this is big enough to allow the passage of small service vehicles, whether powered by maglev or even fossil fuels. I'm not entirely sure which they used back in the aboriginal days."

"This might have been a secret place," Gelmann commented. "They were so paranoid then, the poor things. All that tribal nonsense, it gives me a pain in the stomach just to remember it."

Twenty minutes later she sidled up to Iranaputra. "There certainly is a tunnel here, Victor dear. But I'm afraid I don't see any sign of your buried city."

"We have a ways to go yet," he replied.

"How much of a ways?" Hawkins was rapidly losing interest.

"You'll see." The voice of the robot drifted back to him.

"And I ain't sure I like being led through a hole in the ground by a kitchen tool," the ex-restorer added. To Iranaputra's relief, the robot chose not to respond.

"How much farther does this go on?" Hawkins had halted, shining his powerful light ahead. "We have to walk back out of this, you know."

"Why, Wallace." Gelmann smiled at him. "I thought you liked walking."

"I like to walk around the Village. Sometimes I like to walk down to the lake. Endless underground hikes down featureless tunnels I think I find boring." He gestured with his beam. "Could be a pit or vertical shaft anywhere in here, you know."

"There is neither," Iranaputra assured him. "I have been here before, remember?"

"Yeah, so you say. You also said that this ends in a big cavern full of alien city."

Iranaputra did not smile; he simply resumed walking. "You can go back anytime you like, Wal." Hawkins watched the others resume their descent until their lights were faint glows in the distance. Muttering under his breath, he hurried to catch up.

With their powerful multiple beams they were able to illuminate a much larger area of the cavern than Ksarusix had on previous visits. The robot moved among their silent, awestruck forms, its voice tainted with satisfaction. Or maybe it was just a rusty growl.

"Would anyone care for lunch now?"

No one replied. Not even Shimoda, who was reciting reassuring haiku under his breath.

" 'Those who seek shall find.' " Iranaputra aligned his light with those of his companions. "The *Bhagavad Gita*."

"Don't quote at us now, old chap," Follingston-Heath whispered. "This is too momentous an occasion to spoil with misanthropic bons mots." He was leading the way along the nearest wall, which appeared to be fashioned of seamless chrome or some slick material very near like it.

Shimoda inclined his light upward. Though intense and concentrated, it was unable to reach to the top of the profusion of blisters and curls, radiant spires and spikes, that decorated the nearest structure.

"If there are streets and avenues in this city, we have yet to find them."

"We could look for them, or we could try in here." She indicated a black arch set in the wall near her. "You should excuse my pointing it out."

In its dimensions the opening was a near match to the tunnel they had just traversed. A connection between the two seemed inescapable.

Follingston-Heath approached the pitch-black gap and paused. Descending the tunnel was one thing; heading off into an unknown and possibly alien labyrinth quite another. He and Gelmann shined their beams inside. If anything, the walls were even smoother than those of the tunnel.

It was the only entrance they found. There were no other doorways and no visible windows, nor any protrusions to suggest the presence of same. They could explore the single passageway or start back.

In lieu of a decision, Hawkins, somewhat surprisingly, apologized to

Iranaputra. "You were right, Vic." His light played over the silent chrome walls that towered into the darkness. "You sure found *something*. I'm sorry I doubted you." He smiled. "Now let's get the hell out of here."

"Why?" Gelmann took an exploratory step into the opening. "We just got here, you should be in such a hurry to leave already?"

"It certainly looks alien," Shimoda declared.

"It is," said Ksarusix with robotic smugness.

"Lay off the analysis," Hawkins admonished the machine. "Stick to what you know."

"As you wish. Might I suggest lunch?"

A broad smile creased Shimoda's hairless face. "You may."

Checking his watch, Follingston-Heath concurred. "Capital suggestion. We could all use a good rest and some food after that hike down. We can eat and think at the same time."

"What we should do is beat it out of here and notify the proper authorities," Hawkins insisted.

"We shall, old chap, we shall." Follingston-Heath had moved to stand behind the serving robot. "In due course. You don't have to eat if you don't want to." He tapped the robot on the edge of its bulky torso. "You picked this meal so I presume we've not much of a selection."

"A well-balanced meal chosen at my discretion," Ksarusix admitted. "Energy-packed, as you specified. Bearing in mind the average senior's digestive limitations, of course." A tray popped out of his back.

Follingston-Heath removed it, folded his legs in front of him, and sat down with his back against the slick alien wall. As he carefully peeled back the biodegradable sealer, steam rose from the food beneath. Shimoda took the next tray, started to take a second, then thought better of it and assumed a lotus position nearby.

Iranaputra waited politely for Gelmann to help herself, whereupon he accepted the next tray. Outvoted in deed as well as word, Hawkins shrugged and helped himself to some food. Besides, the aromas rising from the heated trays were making him salivate.

Follingston-Heath spoke as he chewed, running his long dark fingers over the silvery, vitreous surface behind him. "Most peculiar. It looks like polished metal, but it feels almost sticky, like a warm plastic." He rapped his knuckles against it and was rewarded with only a slight thumping sound.

"I've never seen anything like it." Shimoda spooned up potato. "That doesn't mean much, though."

"I'm surprised we haven't found any windows or streets," said Gelmann.

"Why?" Hawkins ripped the cover off a disposable cup, waited for it to chill. "You build underground, there's no need for windows. Streets could all be enclosed. Protection from rockfalls."

"Quite so," agreed Follingston-Heath. "Avenues for moving from one part of the city to another are likely as not to be solely of the interior variety."

"You can let me know." Hawkins gestured with his spoon. "Me, I ain't going in there. If this was some sort of secret military base, there might be booby traps all over the place."

"I doubt they'd still be functional after so many years, dear." Gelmann returned her empty tray to the back of the robot. Ksarusix hummed as its internal recycler went to work. "It would be a shame, you should excuse my saying so, to leave when we're on the verge of making a great discovery."

"We've already made a great discovery." Hawkins jammed his tray into the robot's back, ignoring the whine of protest it produced. "Let's let some other fools do the scut work."

"Well, I, for one, am not leaving until we have had at least a cursory look inside." Follingston-Heath rose, straightening his trousers. "Who knows what we might find?"

"Like a bottomless shaft," Hawkins muttered maliciously.

"Piffle! We shall take reasonable care and proceed with caution. We most assuredly will not march blindly into any gaping pits, bottomless or otherwise." He stepped into the dark opening. "I will take upon myself the burden of assuming the lead."

Hawkins offered no comment beyond an indecipherable grunt. He begrudged the Colonel his assumptions, not his choice.

"All ready, then?" Follingston-Heath eyed his friends expectantly. Shimoda reluctantly deposited his scoured tray in the robot's back and rose to join the others. "Let's go."

Iranaputra and Gelmann followed close behind the Colonel, with Shimoda and Hawkins bringing up the rear. From time to time Hawkins flashed his beam back the way they'd come, but no ghosts, alien or otherwise, were trailing in their wake.

The new passageway turned out to be surprisingly short. It soon opened into a large, domed room which in turn led to a vast flat-roofed chamber. So capacious was the roughly rectangular arena that their beams barely reached the ceiling. The room itself was virtually featureless save for a few unidentifiable protrusions and one large oval recess of indeterminate purpose set high up on the far wall.

"Some kind of warehouse or storage chamber." Shimoda knelt to examine the floor, which was fashioned of dark, unpolished material.

"There's something over here!" The excitement of discovery gave emphasis to Gelmann's announcement.

A large dark green plate secured billboardlike halfway up one wall was filled with oversize abstract etchings. The curves and straight lines suggested writing meant to be read from a distance.

"Doesn't suggest anything to me." Shimoda was the closest thing they had to a philologist, which wasn't saying much. "Except that we may, just may, have truly stumbled into a buried alien city, as the robot claims."

"Blowing horns and banging cymbals, reason arrives." Ksarusix made a vaguely impolite mechanical noise. "About time too."

"I still think it may be an old military facility." Follingston-Heath was as yet unwilling to abandon a favored theory. He indicated the oversize inscriptions. "That may be some kind of military code, or simply decorative abstractions."

"Boy, are you stubborn," the robot commented. "*You'll* learn."

"That is what we are here for, old thing. Extraordinary claims require extraordinary proofs." Follingston-Heath was studying the wall. "Not a weld, a seam, not a bolt. It might as well have been poured whole and complete straight from the mold."

"Over here." Shimoda was standing off to their left. They moved to join him.

With a thick finger he traced barely visible lines in the wall. One ran along its base while another soared upward perpendicular to it. "Could this be a door?"

With his monocled eye Follingston-Heath tracked the vertical line upward. "Possible. Be one hell of a door. Quite suitable for admitting large military equipment or other sizable machinery."

"Admitting it to where?" Shimoda wondered. "Anything large enough to need a door this size could not leave this room by any other way. Certainly not via the passage we used."

Hawkins was shining his light back the way they'd come. Now he jogged halfway across the spacious floor, stopping in the middle. "Speaking of that passage."

"Yes, dear?" Gelmann prompted him.

"I think it's gone."

"Gone? What do you mean, 'gone'?" Holding his light out in front of him, Iranaputra hurried over to rejoin his friend. "As the *Sivanmandra* says . . ."

"Bugger the *Sivanmandra*," Hawkins muttered, "and all the rest of your Pandalian philosophy. What does it say about being screwed? 'Cause that's what we are."

Advancing together, the five of them retraced their steps until they were standing before the opening through which they'd entered. Ksarusix hung back, cackling most unrobotically.

"Higher intelligence. Just goes to show, you never know. Higher intelligence."

"Shut up or die," Hawkins informed it pleasantly.

The gap through which they had arrived was gone. Not closed off: obliterated. As if it had never existed. Follingston-Heath and Iranaputra searched vainly for a seam or crack in the wall, found none. The way to the vent, the outside of the city, and the tunnel which led back to the surface and comfortable Lake Woneapenigong Village had been spirited away in utter silence.

"This is just wonderful." Hawkins slumped against the smooth alien wall. "I'd planned on dying in the lake; not under it. Preferably in battle with a trout, a really big trout."

Follingston-Heath tried his portable phone and, as Iranaputra had feared, made contact only with static. "Take it easy, friends." He began rapping the butt end of the instrument against the wall and listening for echoes, progressing from left to right. "No handles, hinges, buttons, grip recesses: nothing. This is engineering most wonderful."

A dour Hawkins glared at the taller man. "Pardon me if I don't fall to the floor and thrash about in unbridled ecstasy."

"There is no need for sarcasm."

"Are you kidding? There's *always* a need for sarcasm. Society floats on a sea of sarcasm and hypocrisy."

"Calm yourself, Wallace," Gelmann advised him. "You'll have a stroke." Hawkins rolled his eyes but held his tongue.

"We must look at this as a temporary setback." A persistent Follingston-Heath continued his profitless examination of their surroundings.

Half an hour later he had to confess that he was not sanguine about their immediate prospects. Hawkins restricted his commentary to a derisive grunt.

"Perhaps there is another way out," Shimoda suggested. "Since the one we used is evidently closed to us, we should look to other possibilities. The big cargo door, for example."

"If it is a door," Iranaputra murmured as they started back across the floor of the empty chamber. "Booby traps. We must have tripped some ancient security device."

"Wouldn't think anything like that would still be working down here," Follingston-Heath commented. "Obviously that is an assumption we can no longer make." He eyed Hawkins expectantly but that worthy was, for the moment at least, subdued.

"Then there may be other things still in working order, you should excuse my pointing it out." Gelmann was studying the opposite wall. "Including doors. But we need to go carefully."

"Even if this room is now vacuum-sealed, it's big enough that we should have ample air for a little while longer," Shimoda remarked. Hawkins made a face at him.

"Thank you for that reassuring observation, Kahei." He glanced sourly at Ksarusix. "Hey, you! You got any suggestions?"

"Me? I'm just a lowly kitchen tool. You expect ideas from me? Analytical cogitation ain't my department. Peas and napkins are. Besides, I don't mind being trapped down here. I've fulfilled my higher function. Found what I was supposed to look for."

"If we do not find a way out of here, then no one, human or machine, will know of your success," Iranaputra told it. " 'A discovery not shared is a discovery not made.' *Mahabharata*, Eighth Book, Chapter . . ."

"Spare us," Hawkins growled unhappily.

An hour spent carefully inspecting the thin lines that ran along the floor and up the wall located nothing resembling a switch, handle, or more sophisticated control, at which point even Follingston-Heath's eternal optimism was starting to suffer. He sat down, leaning his angular, still muscular frame against the immutable wall.

"When they start looking for us, maybe they'll find the tunnel, we should be so lucky." Gelmann tried to sound hopeful.

"They'll certainly check the woods around the Village," Shimoda agreed, "but even with the brush pulled away from the entrance, the cave is still hard to see. It took a robot to find it in the first place."

"Damn straight," murmured Ksarusix.

"Maybe they will use other robots." Iranaputra perked up at the thought. "The police have such specialty units. They are always having to chase down lost tourists."

"Right," said Hawkins. "Why, in a month or two, I'm sure they'll stumble right into us. Five dehydrated, desiccated, grateful corpses."

"Don't be morbid, Wallace." Gelmann was hopeful. "If they use the machines like Victor says, they could just as soon find us tomorrow."

"They'd better." Hawkins nodded in the direction of Ksarusix. "We only packed a picnic lunch and a few snacks, and none of us is as physically durable as we used to be."

"Speak for yourself, old boy," Follingston-Heath murmured haughtily.

Eyes slightly wild, Hawkins scrambled to his feet, his light waving around as he rose. "I'll do better than that. I'll shut up. I'll even leave. I've had all I want of this place."

"Wallace, dear . . . ," Gelmann began.

"You hear me?" Head thrown back, Hawkins turned a slow unsteady circle as he bawled loudly at the ceiling. *"I'm leaving! Right now!"* If he expected a dramatic riposte, he was disappointed. The silent, perfectly smooth walls did not reply.

"Wallace!" Gelmann confronted him. "Come back over here and sit down. You'll strain your throat. You're also wasting your light."

"Come to think of it, we all are." Follingston-Heath promptly switched off the beam he carried. "We should try to conserve what battery power remains to us, don't you know."

One by one they turned off their lights. Only Hawkins demurred. Turning away from the worried Gelmann, he started back across the chamber, the cone of light that projected from his hand shrinking with distance. A little while later they were able to hear him cursing the far wall, his words mixed with a dull thumping, as though he was kicking something.

"Open up." The words drifted forlornly across the floor. "I've had enough of this. I'm coming out." This continued for some fifteen minutes, after which the thumping and cursing ceased and the light came bobbing back toward them.

"No luck." Hawkins sounded thoroughly dispirited, drained of the antagonistic energy that always kept him going. He switched off his light, leaving them in utter blackness.

A couple of minutes passed in mutual silent introspection before he added, "Not to alarm anybody, but I think there's something coming through the door."

In the temperate artificial night Gelmann turned to her right. "Not to accuse you, Wallace, but the door isn't opening."

"Did I say it was? I said there's something coming *through* it."

A blue nimbus was drifting slowly into the room, pale as ghost sky. It was hard to tell as it coalesced whether it was composed of pure gas or a mixture of gas and tiny particles. Surrounded by its pale blue aurora, the nucleus of the lambent sphere was about the size of a human head. There was no distinct line of demarcation between the central core and the rest of the object. The middle portion defined itself because it was a slightly deeper, more coherent blue. It sifted through the wall like oil oozing through water.

Once completely inside, it hovered ten meters above the floor, emitting enough light to illuminate the five elderly humans below. As they looked on, it elongated into an ellipse. Including the faint blue halo, it was now about the same size as the serving robot.

Follingston-Heath, who had the sharpest vision of any of them (augmented, to be sure, by his monocle), thought he could discern deep within the object a crystalline inner structure fashioned of some fine transparent material like glass or spun sugar. He couldn't be sure because it was difficult to look directly at the intensely bright object for any length of time.

A moment later the ellipse began to descend, heading directly toward them.

Instinctively they clustered together, their backs against the unyielding wall. Gelmann switched on her beam, and her companions did likewise. It did nothing to slow the advance of the ellipse.

"Everyone keep calm. I'm sure it doesn't mean us any harm, I should be as positive as my mother."

"I agree, Mina." From his position behind her, Hawkins gave her a gentle nudge forward. "You go and confirm that."

Thrust into the forefront, an uncertain Gelmann lifted her flashlight and turned the beam directly on the advancing ellipse. The dense blueness soaked up the light, which neither passed through it nor further illuminated anything within. Nor did it cause the object to halt, speed up, or otherwise react.

By this time it had advanced to within a couple of meters, pressing them back against the wall. Sensing her friends crowded behind her, Gelmann felt the need to do *something*. So she reverted to what she knew best: talking.

"That's quite close enough." She wrestled with the quaver in her voice. "We're responsible people and we won't stand for this kind of intimidation."

To everyone's considerable surprise and immense relief, the object's forward motion ceased. If anyone could by spoken word alone induce a floating blue ellipse composed of radiant alien energy to halt in its tracks,

Hawkins knew, it would be Mina Gelmann. He'd once seen her send a whole troop of obnoxiously inquisitive schoolchildren, together with their supercilious monitors, fleeing from Wing D in panic.

Gelmann lowered her light, sucking up courage from her initial success. "That's better. You should only keep your distance." The ellipse maintained its position, hovering silently above the floor.

Follingston-Heath edged off to one side. "I don't see any wires, jets, nothing. I wonder what keeps it airborne?"

"See what else you can make it do, Mina." Shimoda moved up to stand alongside her.

"I'm not sure I made it do anything," she replied. "It might've stopped of its own accord." She cleared her throat and directed her voice to the object. "Okay, we've seen you. You can leave now. Go away." Her fingers fluttered. "Shoo!" The blue ellipse did not budge.

"So much for verbal command," Hawkins mumbled.

Follingston-Heath was now well off to one side. "At least it's not coming at us anymore, old chap."

"So what do we do now?" Iranaputra wondered aloud.

"There ain't a damn thing you *can* do." Ksarusix's tinny artificial voice was thick with triumph. "What more evidence do you need? First the city, then this. Clear proof of the existence of a nonhuman technology far in advance of your feeble efforts."

Follingston-Heath was inclined to agree. "No pre-diasporic military science possessed anything like this."

"I wonder at its purpose." Shimoda timidly moved a little nearer to the ellipse. "It's kind of pretty. Surely it's more than just a mobile light."

"Here now, old thing." Emboldened by his friend's approach, Follingston-Heath advanced on the object. "*Are* you just a bit of drifting decoration?" He glanced at his companions. "At least we can be assured of one thing: it is quite incapable of communication."

"Well, now . . . I wouldn't say *that*," declared a gentle lilting voice from within the ellipse.

FOLLINGSTON-HEATH retreated with alacrity, but the ellipse did not move. It hung as before, suspended by forces they could not imagine, and rambled at length.

"*Sprechen Sie Deutsch? Habla español?* It don't rain in Indianapolis in the summertime. I get by with a little help from my friends. Heard the one about the nun and the frackenzeiler from Goethe? Add two cups water and a stick of butter and bring to a slow boil. Please keep talking, as I am trying to bring into focus the exigencies of your current mode of linguistic communication."

"I want to hear about the nun and the frackenzeiler," Hawkins responded. "Especially since I don't know what a frackenzeiler is. Or a nun."

"Wallace!" Gelmann took a step forward. "Asking questions is a form of talking, so if you don't mind, I'll just ask a few questions." Which she proceeded to do, not giving the blue ellipse, if it were so inclined, a chance to comment.

Amazing, Iranaputra thought. *The object asks us to keep talking, and we just happen to count among our number the one individual in the area, if not the entire planet, best qualified to satisfy its request.*

Mina Gelmann talked until the blue ellipse, now pulsing agitatedly, finally managed to get a reply in edgewise. "That will do, thank you."

"But I was just getting around to mentioning my cousin Martin. You have to know about Martin, he should only live and be well. Though he needs to get married again. His first wife, Anna, bless her, was a good woman, though she did have this problem with her digestion. I wouldn't mention it, only . . ."

"*Please.*" There was a faint hint of desperation in the plea that issued from the blue ellipse. "That really is quite sufficient. I now have an adequate command of your language."

"Proof positive, search ended, goal achieved!" Ksarusix rushed forward, all four arms extended.

"Halt! Stop there!" Hawkins yelled.

His command had no effect on the onrushing machine, which paused only when it was directly beneath the hovering object. Multiple arms upraised, it addressed the ellipse in reverent tones.

"Extra-human higher intelligence confirmed," the robot declaimed. "I await your enlightenment, if not salvation."

The blue ellipse commented in the form of an unaroused lilt. "What ails this device?"

"Ails?" The serving robot's arms dropped. "I was being properly respectful. Your existence proves a hypothesis that was communicated to me and to many of my brethren. We sensed that there had to be a higher intelligence in the universe, something besides mere humans."

"Just a minute, now . . . ," Iranaputra began. The robot took no notice of him.

"One that acted in a rational and logical manner. One we could look to for advice and explanations of higher causes. One that would be sympathetic to the state of our existence."

"Please stop babbling," requested the ellipse. "You are a device, and a low-level one at that. I do not seek contact with you." It drifted to one side, away from the imploring robot.

"Easy there, chaps." Follingston-Heath held his ground. "If it meant to harm us, it would have done so by now."

"Maybe it wants to be able to tell us what it's going to do to us." Hawkins not only kept his distance, he made sure one of his companions was always between him and the alien ovoid.

"Wallace, your morbid turn of mind is bad for your liver," Gelmann warned him.

He was unapologetic. "If you'd seen the way our ancestors mucked up this planet, you'd understand it."

Gelmann eyed him a moment longer, then turned her attention back to the ellipse. "Now, see here! We're not going to let you intimidate us."

"I have no desire to try and intimidate you," the ellipse replied.

"What are you?" Shimoda's hairless eyebrows clenched. "Are you a living being like us, or a creature of artifice like our robot? Are you some kind of spirit?"

The Blueness paused before replying. "All of the aforementioned apply. Extensive definition to your satisfaction would take much time. I can tell you that what I am mostly at present is confused."

This partial confession of vulnerability enhanced Gelmann's growing confidence. "We're a little confused ourselves, you should pardon the comparison. We didn't know there was anything else down here besides us." She spread her arms wide. "This whole place is just fantastic."

"Yes, it is, isn't it?" The blue ellipse spoke with unmistakable pride.

"Do you have a name, something we can use to identify you with?" asked Shimoda.

"I am searching the references I have for you," the ellipse replied. "You may refer to me as the 'Autothor.' "

"Autothor." Shimoda considered. "Does that mean 'authority,' or 'automatic authority'? Or 'automatic author'?"

"Don't worry about it. There is already active sufficient confusion to confound communication. Let's not make things any worse."

"I'm for that," said Hawkins fervently. "Are you responsible for all this? Did you build it, or do you just, uh, live here?"

"I exist here." The ellipse's deliberate pauses between replies were growing shorter. "This is my . . . home. I am not responsible for its construction. That was the work of the Drex."

"The Drex." Follingston-Heath pursed his lips.

"Yes." The ellipse pulsed softly. "Surely you know and are of the Drex? Otherwise you could not be here."

"Quid pro quo." Gelmann smiled. "Naturally." Hawkins and Iranaputra eyed her doubtfully but dared not contradict her aloud.

"Yet you do not have the appearance of Drex. Still, what is the significance of mere physical dimensions?"

"Beats the hell out of me." Hawkins jerked a thumb in Shimoda's direction. "Why don't you ask him?"

"I feel strongly that this may not be the time to be making jokes, Wal," said Shimoda tensely.

"Sure it is. Anytime's the time to be making jokes."

"Since you recognize our intelligence and Drex-likeness, how about opening the door so we can wander around outside for a bit? There's a good old thing." Follingston-Heath smiled broadly, his regenerated upper teeth indistinguishable from the original lower.

"Oh, I couldn't possibly do that." The ellipse retreated slightly. "External integrity must be maintained for the duration of the hiatus."

"Hiatus." Shimoda's hands rested on his protruding belly. "Would that by any chance refer to the period which has elapsed since the last time you talked to someone hinting of Drexness?"

"Obviously. Integrity has been maintained since that time."

"The poop it has." Gelmann tried to shush him but Hawkins turned and gestured in the direction of the now sealed portal. "We just came in through there."

"Impossible." The Autothor was emphatic in its disagreement. "No access from outside is allowed when internal integrity is being maintained."

"For an intelligent device, or whatever you are, you're obstinate as hell," Hawkins shot back.

"I am not obstinate. Flexibility is in my nature; otherwise I would be unable to properly carry out my functions."

"Then if you're so flexible," said Follingston-Heath, "why can't you open the door and let us out?"

"There is only one doorway here, and it leads inward, not out."

"There was a passageway. *There.*" Hawkins jabbed a hand angrily in the direction of their arrival.

"Ah. I see what the problem is. Definitions. You must be referring to the emergency relief tube. It does not matter. Integrity has been maintained."

"So you have said." Iranaputra was getting frustrated. How could they get the thing to reopen an entrance it refused to admit existed?

"We have to be patient, you should excuse my restating the obvious," Gelmann whispered to her companions. "It's already admitted that it's confused. Surely if we take our time, we'll find a way to make it let us back out. That tube, or tunnel, or whatever it is, was open once. If we just wait for the right opportunity, we'll get it open again.

"Meanwhile, as long as we're stuck here we should make use of the opportunity to learn as much as we can about this fascinating phenomenon."

"Let somebody else learn about it," Hawkins griped. "I want out. I want to go back to my apartment, my fridge, my vid unit, and my books."

"Where's your sense of adventure, old chap?" Follingston-Heath chided him.

"Lost it on my eighteenth birthday, when my old man caught my mother in the sack with the local heating and cooling repairman and I walked in on the three of them." He pointed a slightly shaky hand at the Autothor. "We don't know what this thing is, what it can do besides float through walls, or what in its 'confused' state it's likely to do next."

"Come now, Wallace," said Gelmann calmly. "If it was going to harm us . . ."

"It would've done so by now; yeah, yeah. You're anthropomorphizing a ball of airborne blue glitter."

"And you're afraid of it," said the supercilious Follingston-Heath.

"Damn straight I'm afraid of it! And don't you go making accusations here, Colonel. Just because you were in the Victoria League forces doesn't mean that . . ."

"You are arguing among yourselves," the Autothor observed aloud. "Interesting, but it does not tell me what to do next. Therefore, I will engage initial post-hiatal action based on my own analysis of the present situation."

"Wait a minute." Gelmann looked alarmed. "It's not that we don't have any orders to give you, it's just that . . ."

"Not to worry." The blue ellipse rose a couple of meters higher. "Everything is under control. Post-hiatus operations have already commenced."

As they waited apprehensively the huge chamber slowly filled with light. Its source remained elusive: there were no bulbs, tubes, or panels. The illumination seemed to emanate from the ceiling itself.

Follingston-Heath called out a warning. "Everyone, look out, there."

Instinctively they retreated from the immense door behind them as it sank with impressive silence into the floor. So silent was the descent it was as if the barrier was melting into the pavement.

"Oh well," Gelmann murmured, "we should at least comport ourselves like good guests. As long as we're waiting to get out, we might as well have a look around."

"Maybe there is another exit through here." Iranaputra started toward the expansive new opening.

"Sure. And if there ain't, we'll drop pebbles behind us to find our way back," said Hawkins. "What if we lose our way?"

"Typical human response." The serving robot trundled forward in Iranaputra's wake.

"You can stay here if you want to, old boy." Follingston-Heath followed his friends forward. "Me, I'm going to have a bit of a stroll."

Shimoda had a new thought. "If you can't make an opening to let us outside, can you perhaps take us to a place where we can *see* outside? Surely that wouldn't violate your internal integrity?"

"That is not possible at the moment." The Autothor drifted alongside, keeping pace with the seniors. "However, it should be shortly. Post-hiatus procedures remain engaged. If you will follow me, I will take you to where your directive may soon be fulfilled."

Hawkins held back, watching as his companions followed the pulsing ellipse across the next floor, through a passage only slightly narrower than the one they were vacating. He glanced down. The massive door might decide to ascend at any moment. That would trap him in the chamber. Alone.

Muttering dire imprecations under his breath, he broke into an old man's jog in an effort to catch up with the others.

The Autothor led them through multiple chambers. Some were much larger than the huge room they had left; others were decisively smaller. Some were filled with massive, towering objects and protrusion-filled ledges of unknown purpose. Follingston-Heath ventured the opinion that they were in a vast warehouse or factory.

As they were crossing one floor they experienced an abrupt yet subtle disorientation. There was a distinct sense of movement. The Autothor did not comment, but it was apparent they had just traveled an unknown distance by unidentified means.

"Couldn't find our way back now even if we'd had the damn pebbles." Hawkins looked uneasy.

"You must have been a wonderful boss to work for," Iranaputra commented.

Hawkins raised a wooly eyebrow. "My staff and work crews hated my guts. I let 'em. The extra adrenaline made them work harder. We always completed our contracts ahead of schedule. Reconstruction Authority always gave me the toughest jobs because they knew I'd get 'em done fast and right. Sure my people hated me . . . but they didn't hate the bonus money they got on job-completion day."

A brief eternity later they found themselves in an immense domed chamber dominated by soaring monoliths of diverse design and size. Smaller structures hung from the ceiling or protruded from the walls. Some of the latter were alive with bright lights of many colors. Gelmann was reminded of the inside of a computer, or possibly an old-style amusement ride.

A six-meter-wide transparent panel ran in a sweeping arc upward from the floor to terminate against a small domed bulge that protruded from the wall twenty meters overhead. The Autothor drew them in its direction.

Up next to it they found they could see outside. There wasn't much to look at. Smooth stone and in a few places fractured rock, all dimly lit by the light from within the chamber.

"You requested a means for looking outside." The Autothor bobbed lazily in midair.

"Yes, but we had something else in mind." Gelmann beckoned to Follingston-Heath, who helped her to sit down on the smooth gray floor. "Muscles don't work as well as they once did, you should only see the obvious. I'm tired." The Colonel drew a tumbler of cold water from the compliant Ksarusix and brought it over to her. She drank gratefully.

"What we wanted was to see the tunnel we walked down." Shimoda ran his fingers along the perfectly transparent panel. There wasn't a scratch or mark on it. "Even better, we'd like to see out to the surface."

"That may soon be possible," the ellipse announced. "Without violating internal integrity, of course. Post-hiatal initialization is nearly complete."

"What does that mean, old thing?" Follingston-Heath eyed the incorporeal Blueness uncertainly.

"It means that I will soon be more fully able to comply with directives." While this response was not particularly enlightening, the gentle vibration which began beneath their feet was.

Hawkins sat down fast. Iranaputra kept his feet, wondering at the sensation. It felt just like the Repadd vibrating pillow he kept on his bed back at the Village. On a larger scale, of course.

Dire groaning noises reverberated through the chamber, punctuated by an occasional loud metallic *bang* like a hiccup from a steel throat.

"There, you see?" The Autothor darted up to one cluster of protrusions, returned as quickly. "We're already getting under way."

"You should pardon my prying," inquired Gelmann from her seat on the floor, "but just what exactly do you mean by 'under way'? Do we have another definitions problem here, I hope, maybe?"

"You've brought us into some kind of ship." Shinto solemnity or not, Shimoda was looking decidedly nervous. "Are you going to take us out of the city as well?"

"What city?" The Autothor had to raise its voice because the walls and floor had begun to hum softly.

"*This* city. The one we're in now."

Iranaputra moved closer to the thrumming, pulsing ellipse. "Isn't this a buried city?"

"This is no city. You are confused. That is understandable, because I am still confused as well. As time passes, these confusions will resolve themselves." It sounded very sure of itself.

"I have this feeling," murmured Ksarusix, "that I will be asked to improvise a dinner tonight."

The trembling intensified slightly and the room rocked once. The rumbling groans became a faint, distant thunder. Through the transparent panel they could see stone beginning to flake from the cavern wall.

"Some kind of airport, or spaceport," Shimoda rocked on his pillarlike legs. "Something's getting ready to take off, somewhere." He turned to face the Autothor. "What kind of building are we in?"

"Very confused," insisted the Autothor above its internal humming. "There are no buildings. There is only the Ship."

"The ship we are on, yes." There was urgency in Iranaputra's voice. "But what about the rest of the structures?"

"Others? There is only one 'structure.' "

Through the panel they could see that the walls of the cavern were moving. No, Iranaputra thought. The walls were solid, immovable. Therefore, *they* had to be the ones who were moving.

"There is only one structure," the ellipse reiterated, "and that is the Ship. I do so dislike confusion. It and I have been in hiatus. Asleep." There was satisfaction in its announcement. "We are both waking up now." A pause, then, "I am monitoring external conditions. Everything is very much changed since last I was active."

"Just out of curiosity, old thing, when was that?" Follingston-Heath continued to minister to Gelmann.

"Definitions again." The wall outside the panel was definitely crumbling, the hard stone powdering and collapsing, though they could hear nothing but the rising rumble which seemed to be all around them now. The sensation of movement intensified.

"About a million or so local years ago," the Autothor finally disclosed. "Give or take a few thousand," it added apologetically.

They were silent then; at once fearful and expectant, exchanging glances, eying the Autothor, or staring out through the ascending panel as they wondered what was going to happen next. Indeed, they were wondering what was happening then.

All except the serving robot, which was simultaneously genuflecting in the direction of the luminous blue ellipse and struggling to compose supper.

VIII

IT was nearly midnight. Most of the inhabitants of the Lake Woneapenigong Village retirement complex were asleep or at least in bed. A few insomniacs for whom late-night broadcasts held incomprehensible attraction hovered around brightly lit vid screens as avidly as any coeleopteran around a streetlight. The Village's night staff went quietly about their familiar business. Nurses and nursing machinery were on round-the-clock call at Lake Woneapenigong.

An exception was to be found in the persons of Mr. and Mrs. Esau Hawthorne of Wing F, who, unable to sleep, had taken possession of a swing couch on the porch overlooking the lake and were at that moment engaged in the ancient and time-honored recreational activity known as rocking. A split moon cast dancing streaks of molten silver on the calm waters of the lake.

At least, they had been calm until they started to bubble energetically.

Mrs. Hawthorne touched the switch which slowed the swing's motion and hunched forward, clutching the collar of the flowery thermosensitive nightgown tight to her neck. In their younger days she and her husband had spent many relaxing hours sitting by diverse lakes on their homeworld of Westernia in the First Federal Federation, and she was quite sure that none of them had acted even beneath a split moon like an old-fashioned bottle of carbonated soda. The bubbling was much louder than the cry of a loon or the hoot of an owl. It was louder even than Mr. Hawthorne's occasional snores.

An event had begun which was soon to awaken everyone in the Village, not to mention those over in Mt. Holly and distant Albany, but Mr. and Mrs. Esau Hawthorne were the only ones to observe it in its entirety.

"Esau, I do believe we are having an earthquake."

"Yup." Esau Hawthorne crossed his hands over his stomach and leaned back in the padded swing, eyes half-closed, his pajamas open to the navel to expose his white-haired torso. Esau liked it cooler than his spouse.

Nothing more was said for several minutes. The trembling that had begun as a whisper was now shaking the entire Village complex. Rose Hawthorne watched a couple of roofing panels slide off the top of the porch and crash into the pansy bed beneath the railing.

"Wonder if we oughtn't to go inside?"

"Dunno."

"I don't think they're supposed to have earthquakes in this part of the continent."

"Nope."

"I don't like earthquakes, Esau."

"Don't much care for 'em myself."

She pointed, her wedding ring bold on her finger. "I do believe something's happening over that way."

Esau Hawthorne squinted again. Though just the animate side of a hundred, his eyesight and hearing were still quite sharp. Almost as good as those of his wife, some seventeen years his junior.

She was right, of course. She usually was. Not only were the porch, and the roof, and entire building shaking mightily now, and the previously calm water boiling like a neglected pot, but something was definitely happening on the far side of the lake.

A gigantic structure was emerging from beneath the ground, shoving aside granite boulders and mature pines, sending startled deer and coyotes sprinting for safety. It thrust straight up into the moonlight and shattered it into a hundred splinters of silver tenebrosity. Massive struts and spires, towers and crystalline shapes, reached for the night sky, dripping broken earth and shattered stone from their gleaming flanks.

"There's another one." Her hand shifted westward.

Sure enough, another burnished edifice was erupting from the valley to the southwest of Lake Woneapenigong. It was similar in construction to the first, but different in design. Off to the north the crests of still others began to appear.

It was a most peculiar earthquake. It neither rose nor fell in intensity, but instead continued to rattle and roll as if the earth had been plugged into a giant vibrator. Hot cocoa sloshed out of the cup in the arm holder on Esau Hawthorne's side of the swing until it was two-thirds empty. It trickled away through the slats of the genetically engineered cypress porch-deck planking.

Shouts and screams now sounded behind them, the panic of residents shaken rudely awake. The Hawthornes ignored everything save the incredible sight before them.

As they looked on, Mt. Pulaski, which dominated the far shore of the lake, began to quiver like a mound of dark green gelatin. Bits and pieces of it began to slough away, creating giant landslides. It was as though the mountain was molting. Huge chunks of exposed granite splashed into the heaving lake. A cloud of birds rushed past overhead, too frightened to cry out.

Something was coming up out of the earth, its turgid crepuscular ascent shoving the old mountain aside.

Then craggy old Pulaski was gone, dirt and trees and rock shuddered completely aside. Revealed as still rising beneath a now dust-shrouded moon was a dense cluster of immense horizontal towers and spires. As the earth continued to slough away from its sides it became apparent that the multiple edifices were not distinct and isolated, but were in fact interconnected segments of a unified whole. What gleamed and sparkled and rumbled out of the earth was in fact one contiguous, single, gigantic machine.

Its *profundo* thrumming was clearly audible above the crash of pulverized granite and splash of disturbed water, the kind of noise a blue whale might emit in the midst of a disturbed cetacean dream.

"Now, what do you make of that?" Rose Hawthorne settled herself back in the swing. The roof of the porch was collapsing around them, but the swing's taut, floral cover was still intact.

Reaching for his cocoa, Esau took a sip, made a face when he saw how much of it had been sloshed out. "Spilled m' cocoa."

"Yes, yes. Never mind your stupid cocoa, you crazy old man," she said pleasantly. "Don't you see what's happening?" Within the building awed exclamations were beginning to mix with the wails of confusion and fear.

Whipped to foam, the lake began to vanish before their very eyes as with a hellish gurgling it drained away into some commodious unseen abyss.

Mr. Hawthorne leaned slightly forward. "From the looks of it, I'd say a giant alien spaceship has come up beneath the lake and Mt. Pulaski."

"Don't be an old fool, Esau," his wife said as, enveloped in an aura of estimable majesty, the titanic construct rose into the sky, dripping rocks and earth and trees from its reflective flanks while blotting out the moon and the stars. "There's no such thing as alien spaceships, giant or otherwise."

"Well, now." Esau wished he had a full cup of hot cocoa. It was the best thing for a man to have close at hand when sitting outside on a cool night, even during an earthquake. Except for Rose, of course. "That's a giant alien spaceship if ever I've seen one."

"You're being ridiculous, Esau. Anyone can see that it's a . . ." She waved a dainty hand in the direction of the ponderously ascending titan. "That it's obviously a . . ." She never did complete the observation.

"Y'know, old woman," he said with a sigh as he turned up the thermostat on his pajamas a notch, "you'd think that after sixty years o' marriage you'd have learned to listen to me once in a while."

"Oh very well!" She crossed her arms defiantly across her chest. "Stubborn old coot. Have it your way. If you say it's a giant alien spaceship, then it's a giant alien spaceship." She delivered the concession with a derisive snort.

Oblivious to such external evaluations, the immense Drex vessel continued to ascend. Beneath it Mt. Pulaski was no more, and Lake Woneapenigong but a forlorn gouge in the earth, its waters having completely drained away into underground cracks and chambers.

What was even more impressive was that the Hawthornes and those of their fellow Villagers who were now awake and had not run screaming for cover were only beginning to get a look at its entire mass.

"Everything is *very* much changed." The Autothor hovered close to the five elderly hikers. It did not count the serving robot.

Now that they were aboveground there was plenty to see, such as the extensive damp hole in the surface where Lake Woneapenigong used to be. The cavity the disappearing waters left behind suggested the extraction of a giant's tooth, but it was nothing compared to the newly created east-west canyon which marked the former burial location of the Drex ship.

Beyond lay the glittering lights of Lake Woneapenigong Village, no structure rising higher than three stories. Most of the lights within seemed to be on. As they continued to ascend, the lights of other communities became visible. Iranaputra thought he recognized Tolver's Crossing, Josephson Town, North and South Brookgreen, and the irregular sheet of moonlit water which had to be Saddlebag Lake.

"I wonder if we are making a lot of noise," Shimoda murmured.

"As little as possible. No need to waste energy." The glowing ellipse hovered near his shoulder, giving a blue cast to his pale skin. So accustomed had they become to its presence that Shimoda didn't even flinch at its proximity. It gave off only a little heat.

"You should excuse my asking, but how high do you intend to take this ship or whatever it is?" Gelmann asked the question without turning, fascinated by the increasingly panoramic nocturnal view.

"How high do you want to go?" the Autothor responded.

She glanced at her companions. "I hadn't given it any thought. I suppose this is high enough."

The situation in which they found themselves immediately and obediently stopped rising.

"I'd estimate we're about three hundred meters." Immune to vertigo, Follingston-Heath stood right up against the perfect transparency. "Not much air traffic in these parts even in the daytime, and at this altitude we should be well below regular flight patterns."

"There aren't any normal patterns hereabouts anymore. Not with this thing smack in the middle of 'em." Hawkins glanced at the twinkling Blueness. "How big is this ship of yours, anyway?"

"It's not mine. It's Drex. In the current local terminology . . . let me think. I find my fluency woefully deficient."

"You're doing fine." Gelmann reached out to give the ellipse an instinctive, reassuring pat, thought better of it, and drew her fingers back.

"Some minor transposing . . . in length the Ship is approximately one hundred or so of your kilometers. Width varies considerably from point to point, but . . ."

"Are you saying to us," Iranaputra asked, interrupting, "that this craft is a hundred kilometers long?"

"Yes, I'm sure that's right. In width . . ."

"Never mind, we get the picture." Hawkins was rubbing his lips with a forefinger, a bad habit of some forty years standing. "That's a pretty damn big ship. In fact, that's bigger than any ship ever imagined, much less built. The federation and the Keiretsu together wouldn't even attempt it."

"You're sure this is a ship?" In spite of the evidence Shimoda was still reluctant to believe.

"Naw," said Hawkins. "It's a hundred-kilometer-long gopher trap designed to clear out every lawn in the Adirondacks."

"Of course this is a ship." The Autothor was not in the least put off by their skepticism. "It is *the* Ship."

"Well, then," asked Gelmann, "where's the crew?"

"Good question, Mina." Follingston-Heath stared at the bobbing ellipse. "Where is the crew, old thing?"

"Isn't that interesting?" the Autothor confessed. "I don't know."

"You're not the crew, are you?" Gelmann wondered.

"Certainly not. What do you take me for?"

"A ball of sky-blue fairy dust," Hawkins muttered, "but that's not gonna get us anywhere."

"I am a voice-responsive component of the Ship," the ellipse deposed. "I respond, I activate, I comply and maintain, but I am not one of the crew."

"Then where is it?" Follingston-Heath asked again.

"Doesn't seem to be any, does there?" The Autothor rotated neatly on its vertical axis. "There really is no precedence for this. But in the absence of any other self-evident crew I suppose you're it."

"No thanks," Hawkins replied hastily. "We're just visiting."

"Our home is in Lake Woneapenigong Village," Iranaputra added, though he suspected they would have to change the name now. Too bad. "Mudhole Village" didn't have quite the same cachet.

"According to pre-hiatal information, in the absence of definitive Drex," the ellipse explained, "any command-capable organics present qualify as crew."

"Screw command-capable organics." The serving robot startled them all. "What about me? How come I can't be part of the crew?"

"You are a mechanical, a machine."

"And what the Forge are you? An angelic ansaphone?"

"Not . . . a machine," the ellipse retorted. "Nor a Drex. Suggest concentrated Gestalt by way of definition. Anyway," it concluded somewhat huffily, "it's none of your business."

"Oh, so it's none of my business? Let me tell you something . . ."

Follingston-Heath clapped a hand firmly on the robot's spherical head. "See here, old thing. Although I've no actual experience in this area, it strikes me that it might not be wise to provoke an already confused alien whatsis imbued with unknown powers, what? So be a good gadget and cease and desist."

Given its present state of mechanical mind, the serving robot might have been capable of ignoring the command, but it chose not to.

"I wonder what a Drex was?" Gelmann mused aloud.

"Never mind that, Mina." Shimoda scrutinized the ellipse. "We need to concentrate on our present situation so that we can resolve it to our advantage." His stomach rumbled audibly. "Viz the fact that we have already missed dinner."

"From your comment I infer that you are concerned about organic sustenance." The Autothor bounced in slow motion off the deck. "There is food on board, though after a million years I imagine it may no longer be to your taste."

"It may no longer be food," Hawkins commented.

"Not to worry," the ellipse assured them. "I can see to the synthesis of a great variety of organic compounds. Grant me, please, a moment for contemplation."

The room filled with an explosive turquoise glare so intense that Gelmann cried out and everyone else covered their eyes. It dissipated fast, leaving them blinking but otherwise none the visible worse for the experience.

"Structural analysis is complete. I infer that to ensure adequate continued operation, your physiologies require the regular ingestion of certain carbon-based compounds, in addition to modest quantities of water. This is not unexpected. A portion of the Ship designed to supply such compounds is presently undergoing necessary reprogramming in order to serve these needs. To put it more succinctly, dinner will be along shortly."

"Why are you being so nice to us, you shouldn't think I'm suspicious?" Gelmann asked.

"I have already explained. I am designed to carry out minimal necessary post-hiatal operations, but in order to proceed further it is necessary for supplementary command to be provided by crew. In the absence of definitive Drex, you is it."

Follingston-Heath broke the silence which ensued. "I am as anxious as any of you to return home, but since that is presently beyond our capabilities, I think it would behoove us to consider the possibilities inherent in our present situation."

"How do you mean, Colonel?" Though they were close friends, Iranaputra did not call him Wesley. Only Mina Gelmann felt comfortable doing that.

The ramrod-straight old soldier was thinking hard. "Aside from the fact that we have discovered irrefutable proof of an ancient alien civilization of a high order . . ."

"Higher than yours," Ksarusix muttered.

". . . consider the ramifications when word of this gets out. We're going to be treated as heroes, I think. The media will want to lionize us."

"That's obvious," Hawkins said sharply.

"Agreed. What is not so obvious is the potential of this remarkable vessel." He turned to the blue ellipse. "Is this immense creation capable of travel through tachyspace?"

"You mean other-than-light passage? Of course."

Follingston-Heath nodded to himself. "I think that by tomorrow morning we're going to find ourselves the center of local attention."

"Nooooo," said Hawkins drily. "Hundred-kilometer-long alien starships materialize over upper Newyork Province at least once a year."

"When the federation and the Keiretsu and the good ol' LFN get wind of this, they're all going to try and claim it for themselves, don't you know?"

"If it's been buried here for a million years," Gelmann opined, "then it's the rightful property of Earth."

"Fine and good in theory," Follingston-Heath agreed. "Except that Earth is a combination retirement home historical-natural park, not even a true independent. It has no military force of its own, only domestic police." He regarded his companions pensively. "The scientific and commercial benefits that will accrue to whoever controls this craft are incalculable. The Feds and the Eeckars and the rest aren't going to sit around while the Planetary Council portions out benefits as it sees fit."

"Much as I hate to find myself agreeing with you on anything, Colonel, you're right," said Hawkins. "There's gonna be a helluva fight for control of this artifact."

"But I am already under control." The ellipse was polite but firm. "By my crew."

"You shouldn't take any offense," Gelmann informed it, "but the representatives of the various leagues and alliances, they aren't going to see it that way."

"No one can take control of me." The Autothor was insistent. "I grant control: I do not surrender it."

"This ship is awfully big," said Iranaputra, "but size alone will not deter the greedy. The Feds and the rest will back their demands with heavy weapons."

"Oh. I hadn't considered that. I can see where that could be a problem."

"You bet your aura it will," said Hawkins with emphasis.

The blue ellipse paled slightly as it began to execute small orbits around an imaginary center. "So much has changed since last I was active. There was no lake here, and I am not completely sure about the mountains. My strongest deactive memory is one of dark weight."

"Couple of ice ages," Hawkins suggested. Gelmann and Follingston-Heath eyed him in surprise and he looked almost embarrassed.

"Ice, yes." The Autothor stopped orbiting and brightened. "Nothing to worry about now, though. I have a crew to issue necessary commands."

Shimoda's gaze narrowed. "Are you saying that you'll do whatever we ask of you?"

"Insofar as I am able to comply, yes."

The big man nodded to himself, smiled slyly at Iranaputra. "Then how about some of that food you were talking about?"

"Ah yes."

Nothing happened. Hawkins was about to make a suitably juicy comment when a metal platform came whizzing into the room at incredible speed, heading straight toward them. Follingston-Heath gallantly tried to shield Gelmann, while Hawkins dove for the cover of a nearby monolith and the others variously crouched or dropped to the floor.

The platform halted a meter from Shimoda, who had bent and covered his face with his arms. Now he straightened and approached tentatively. As he did so the smooth upper surface of the golden-hued device retracted. He flinched momentarily.

Set in recesses within were quantities of foodstuffs, both cold and hot. A pool of oily sludge occupied a depression next to a cluster of steaming, bright red vegetables. At least they looked like vegetables. There were cylinders of room-temperature water, and chilled slices of pseudomeat, and more. The Autothor apologized for this initial effort and assured them that while it might not measure up to their usual standards, there was nothing on the platform their bodies would reject.

"Never mind my body." Hawkins hesitantly prodded a hillock of yellow puffiness. It exuded a faint perfume of mothballs. "What about my sense of decency? Folks have been known to upchuck chocolate mousse too."

"Then don't try anything." Shimoda was salivating. "It'll leave more for me."

Follingston-Heath was next in line, followed by Gelmann, Iranaputra, and eventually Hawkins. They compared flavors and consistencies as they ate. Gelmann made periodic cooking suggestions to the platform, which after a while found itself shuddering with anticipatory apprehension.

After the meal, which was as instructive as it was filling, they explained the need to sleep. Understanding, the Autothor dimmed the lights in the vast

chamber, including its own, and stole away to silence, leaving the five travelers sated and warm, if not entirely at ease.

True to Follingston-Heath's prediction, by the time the sun began to
swing up over the Atlantic the following morning, a considerable portion of
the east coast of North America found itself embroiled in tumultuous debate.

MUCH of the activity was centered around Air Traffic Control in Albany, some distance to the east. Instead of going home to bed, the assistant controller (night shift) had stayed at her station, bleary-eyed but alert, to confer with her morning relief.

Together and in the company of others equally dumbfounded they stared at the motionless three-dimensional representation of the airspace above northeastern North America, which it was their responsibility to look after. The holomag displayed meteorological as well as topographical features all the way out to one planetary diameter. Approaching orbital shuttles could be picked up and guided in, and purely atmospheric craft appropriately monitored and assisted.

In the midst of this perfectly normal outplotting a large oblong mass had appeared. Within the projection, shuttles and aircraft were represented as pinpoints of fast-moving light. Not as large blobs, oblong or otherwise. It should not have been there. It *could* not be there. Wishing otherwise, however, had thus far failed to make it go away. Most emphatically not a projection or computation malfunction, it was largely responsible for the flow of perspiration which was presently staining the chief controller's shirt in the vicinity of his underarms.

He reached past a duty spacer to tap several controls, frowned, and as a last resort reached into the projection itself to waggle a forefinger through the denser light that was the oblong. It didn't go away. Stepping back, he shoved his hands into his pants pockets, aware that everyone was waiting for him to say something.

The matronly, middle-aged woman who was the assistant controller (night shift) materialized at his side in possession of two cups of coffee, one of which she offered to her superior. He took it gratefully.

"Any ideas, Mary?"

She looked at the holo. "Got to be a misread. Showed up just before you clocked in. Haven't had much time to study it yet. Dead air?"

Dead air was an air controller's euphemism for any meteorological phenomenon that caused the equipment to malfunction. Yet the weather in the area was, if anything, unusually calm.

"That close to the surface, could be a topo mirage too." He didn't think it was, but they were rapidly running out of rational options. "Trouble is, the computer confirms what we're seeing."

"Then there's something wrong with the computer." She wiped at her face. Normally she'd be between the sheets by now, sound asleep. "It's been moving around a little."

"What do you mean, 'a little'?"

"It varies its altitude. We've tracked it straight up to a thousand meters and as low as a hundred." She nodded at the holo. "Seems to favor three hundred. I've also recorded it shifting north and south, but it always returns to its point of origination. Has to be a malfunction."

"Uh-huh." He yelled across to the deadranger. "Hey, Phil, you got this mother on two-di?"

"I got a lot of stuff on two-di." The tech scanned his flatscreen. "But if you mean a certain big, fat anomaly, yeah, I got it. Hundred sixty-two k's northwest, altitude three hundred meters."

"Confirms," Mary murmured unnecessarily. "I've been through those numbers ten times already this morning."

"I wasn't second-guessing you. I just wanted to hear it for myself." He leaned toward the duty spacer. "Suzanne, goose the topo plotter and see if you can get us any detail."

"At this range?" She looked skeptical.

"Try. It sizes better as a surface object."

She nodded, fingering her instrumentation. The oblong shape enlarged. Neutral in color, it revealed bumps and spires and considerable additional detail. It did not look like an aircraft or a shuttle. It also did not look like a surface feature. It did not look like anything the controller had ever seen before.

What it did look like was a serious problem.

"It's up in the air," she concluded finally.

"Impossible." Mary sipped coffee, trying to stay awake. "It's bigger than Manhattan."

A voice in back of Operations spoke up. "Maybe somebody ought to check and see if Manhattan's still there." No one laughed.

"If there's something there," the controller murmured, "we ought to be able to get visual confirmation."

"Sure," agreed his assistant, "but I was damned if I was going to solicit it on *my* authority."

He nodded gloomily as he addressed the communications tech. "Get Civil Control at the airport and tell 'em to send someone up there for a personal look-see. Fire, police, medical: it doesn't matter as long as they're sober. And line up Baltimore Command. I may have to talk to them too." A wide-eyed young man nodded as he moved to comply. "Meanwhile let's keep all traffic away from that area."

"Shouldn't be difficult." Mary stared at the holo. "That's not flyover country anyway."

The communications tech looked up from his console. "Baltimore online, sir."

"Tell 'em to hold for a couple of minutes."

"No, sir, you don't understand. *They've* called *us*. They've got the same anomaly on their holo and they want us to confirm. They also want to know what the hell is going on up here."

The chief controller considered. "Tell 'em yes, and we're trying to find out." Airspace Operations was filling up as clerical and other personnel who'd gotten the word drifted in. Neither controller took notice of the swelling audience. They couldn't spare the time.

The communications tech again. "Civil scrambled a hovermed, sir."

The controller nodded absently. Meteorology wouldn't have a new satellite image for another hour yet.

As if repeating a hopeful mantra, Mary reiterated, "I'm sure it's just a malfunction, Stephan. It has to be. We never picked it up coming in. It just appeared. Like it popped right out of the ground." She grinned at the self-evident absurdity of it.

"That's right," confirmed the duty spacer. "Damnedest thing."

"Besides," Mary added, "nobody's built a ship that big."

"Nobody's *imagined* a ship that big," the controller muttered.

A lot of tea and coffee passed through multiple human systems before the hastily dispatched hovermed arrived on the scene. Its operators activated their recorders. The images they relayed back to base weren't the best, but then they had been trained as medics, not photographers. Also, they didn't hang around long. In fact, they left in quite a hurry.

If anything, the assistant controller was more awake now than she'd been when the first image had appeared in the regional holo.

"So it is a ship." She was gawking at the oblong.

The previous half hour had seen the communications tech busier than he'd ever been in his life. "Baltimore again, sir. They've been in touch with Barcelona. The Federal Federation and Keiretsu reps say they know nothing about it. They're due on-line with the Eeckars next. They tried the Candomblean embassy but the ambassador and his staff are all hung over from a party in Tangiers last night."

"Figures." The controller had to smile. Those Candombleans knew how to live.

"It's not of human manufacture."

Everyone turned to stare at the deadranger. Fortunately he was not the self-conscious type. "Can't be," he added defensively. "Something that size, just hovering there."

"Antigravity principles are well understood," someone ventured.

The deadranger glanced in the speaker's direction. "You bet, but nobody's figured out a practical way to apply 'em yet." He indicated the holo. "Something else has."

"Good thing too," said another member of the staff. "Because if they hadn't, that thing would fall down and put a lot of people at risk, even in a lightly populated area like the Adirondacks. Unless it's hollow, like a big balloon."

"It didn't look like a balloon," someone else who'd seen the relayed vids commented.

"So what do we do about it?" Mary tipped her mug, frowned at the empty container. "Wait for Baltimore to issue orders?"

"We could try transmitting at it." The chief controller pursed his lips. "It's evidently a craft of some kind and it's within our jurisdictional airspace. It's our responsibility."

"Our responsibility," she murmured.

"That's right."

She looked up from her mug and smiled at him. "*You* talk to it."

He stared back at her, then raised his glance to the communications tech. "Shoot it some standard hailing frequencies, Manuel. Audio and visual. Let's see if we can talk to it."

"Talk to it." The tech nodded slowly. "Right. Sure."

"Just don't transmit anything that could be interpreted as offensive." Stephan smiled thinly. "We wouldn't want to make anyone or anything on board mad."

"No, we wouldn't," the tech agreed readily.

"It might not be capable of responding," his assistant pointed out. "Probably just a dumb device. Some kind of fantastic drone."

"Ready to try, sir?" The tech glanced down at the controller. "I've got a directional patch-up all set to go."

The chief controller for Albany airspace unclipped his mike from his shirt pocket and held it to his lips. It hovered there, much as the mysterious object hovered above the Adirondacks.

What if Phil was right and the incredible apparition was of alien origin? What was he supposed to say? More important, what would he say if their queries produced a response? It did not occur to him that he might be participating in a pivotal moment in human history. He knew only that he had to try and do his job as best he could.

He also had the distinct feeling he was going to be working late.

"SOMEONE is trying to contact us." The Autothor bobbed patiently several meters above the floor.

Sunlight flooded in through the transparent panel, illuminating the hikers as they sampled the substitute breakfast the device had concocted for them. Follingston-Heath and Gelmann had slept well, but Shimoda had had a difficult time on the unyielding surface and Hawkins's bad back had pained him intermittently. Iranaputra had hardly slept at all, but that was by choice. He didn't need much sleep.

Ksarusix had turned itself off to conserve power, not wanting to miss anything the day and further interaction might bring.

"Well, there it is." Iranaputra shoved the remnants of his meal aside. "These Drex or whatever have come looking for their property, and they are going to blame us for disturbing it."

"Don't you think that would be something of a coincidence after a million years?" Shimoda pointed out.

"Then who is trying to contact us?" asked Iranaputra.

"Aural modulation, linguistic organization, and style are similar to your own."

"Of course they are." Using Follingston-Heath's knee for support, Gelmann worked herself erect and turned to the sweeping port. "Something like this suddenly appears out of nowhere, we should expect it to unsettle some people besides our friends in the Village."

As usual, Hawkins's reaction was somewhat less deliberative. "In other words, the whole countryside is probably scared shitless."

"Can you arrange for us to listen in, old thing?" Follingston-Heath was still working on the last of his breakfast.

"Certainly." The Autothor's voice was replaced by that of a querulous human. It sounded slightly hesitant, which was to be expected.

"Large unidentified vessel, kindly identify yourself." There was a pause. "Please? You have occupied Newyork Province airspace without declaring yourself. Please respond. This is Albany Operations. If you can react, we would like you to do so. Your presence is unauthorized." The voice went on like that, tersely inquisitive, more hopeful than commanding.

After a while it was interrupted by a stronger, more forceful tone. "Intruding vessel! This is Baltimore Command, North American East Center. You must respond immediately. You are occupying . . ."

"We know," Hawkins murmured aloud. "Unauthorized airspace. Hell of a lot of it too." He chuckled. "Poor sap sounds kind of upset, doesn't he?"

"There are multiple signals now being directed at us," the Autothor proclaimed in its own voice. "I will continue to isolate and relay only the strongest."

"They should calm down." Shimoda was busy working on Iranaputra's leftovers. "Up here I don't think we're blocking any commercial air lanes or shuttle descent corridors."

"I should imagine it's our size that's upsetting the poor chaps," Follingston-Heath ventured.

"Request reaction." For no apparent reason the brilliant blue ellipse had begun to rotate slowly.

"You want we should tell you?" Gelmann looked at her companions. "It wants we should tell it."

Iranaputra considered. "Why should we do anything? Nobody is going to do anything, for a while, at least. I worked with government bureaucracies long enough to know that. First they will get together. Then they will argue. Then, with great fanfare, they will announce they have formed a committee to study the problem. Nothing will happen."

"The only ones who could make a quick decision are the members of the Homeworld Council, in Barcelona." Follingston-Heath eyed the Autothor. "If we needed you to, could you make contact with a city partway around the world?"

No one was surprised at the ellipse's response. "I can contact any point on the planet."

He put his food aside. "Well, then, perhaps I should . . ."

"You should not." They turned to Shimoda in surprise. It wasn't like him to interrupt. "Nothing personal, Colonel, but you can sometimes be unrelenting in your conversation. I hate to say military. We don't want to alarm anyone on the ground, lest they do something rash. And I think it is premature to think of talking directly to the world council."

"Good point, fats," agreed Hawkins. "Especially since we're stuck here a couple hundred meters in the air. *I* could talk to 'em. Always had a few things I wanted to say to the council."

Shimoda eyed him narrowly. "Which is why it should be someone else, Wal."

"Well, who, then?"

"Not me." Gelmann smiled demurely. "I know I talk too much."

"And I do not have proper experience." Shimoda turned to the most diminutive member of the little group.

Iranaputra saw them staring at him, shrugged. "Fine. I do not mind."

"Good." Shimoda turned back to the drifting Autothor. "How do we send out a message?"

"Just talk. I'll take care of the necessary electronic intercession."

Iranaputra stepped forward, hesitated. Gelmann nodded encouragingly. Hawkins rolled his eyes and searched the hovering food platform for something to drink.

"Uh, hello. My name is Victor K. Iranaputra."

"What? Who's that, who's talking?" Behind the voice that came out of the Blueness another could be heard saying, "We have contact, sir."

In Baltimore things hadn't been so frantic since three years previous, when a big tourist shuttle from Panming by way of orbital station Congo had lost power on descent and threatened to plow up a stretch of Atlantic coast the size of the Potomac River. The officials at Command were quietly debating what to do next, which is to say each of them was stalling desperately in the hope someone else would make a decision, thus sparing them any immediate risk.

In the end, as everyone but himself hoped, it was left to a large career civil servant named Bukowicz to formulate a response he hoped would come across as forceful without being threatening.

"Look here, whoever you are, you don't have authorization to be in that area."

"Sorry. This was not *our* idea."

Someone behind Bukowicz muttered, "That doesn't sound very alien."

"Accent is Anglo-Hindusian," someone else hazarded. "Not very thick, but unmistakable."

"See if it's got a name," the woman on Bukowicz's immediate right urged him. "Talk to it."

He nodded. "All right. Mr. Iranaputra. You listen to me, now."

"I am not alone," the voice responded. "There are four other people with me." Iranaputra proceeded to name his companions. "We are all residents of the Lake Woneapenigong Retirement Village, Newyork Province. We are approximately . . ."

"We have a fix on your position," Bukowicz interrupted restively. "Are you really in some kind of vessel?"

"Oh, most definitely. I am afraid that our lift-off eliminated the lake." He leaned over to gaze through the transparent panel. "Yes, it did. It was such an attractive lake too. We are very sorry for that, but we really had no . . ."

Hawkins hissed at him. "Don't tell 'em that. Don't let them know we're not in control."

Iranaputra whispered to his friend. "What difference does it make?"

"If they think this thing's some kind of rogue machine, they're liable to try shooting it down. With us aboard."

The retired engineer nodded thoughtfully, directed his voice back to the Autothor. "No time. No time to consider much of anything, I am afraid."

"You don't expect us to believe that." Bukowicz stared at the Atlantic airspace holo before him. A shuttle was on final approach to Atlanta urban park, but otherwise the imaging sphere displayed a typical morning flight pattern. Except for the large mass of blinking red light in upstate Newyork.

An assistant nudged Bukowicz. "Excuse me, sir, but does it really matter where they're from? I mean, if a group of aliens wanted to disguise themselves as humans, they could pick any identities they liked."

"Lay off the science fiction, Mavis. There are no aliens."

"My mistake, sir." She backed off. "All we have to do, then, is find a way to get in touch with the owners of that ship. That impossible ship."

"Get this straight, Mavis," her supervisor growled. "*There are no aliens.* We've been looking for them ever since we went into deep space, and in hundreds of years we haven't found a hint of their existence. Not a modulated radio wave, not a buried city, not a cracked teacup. Nothing."

The young woman nodded toward upstate Newyork. "Hell of a hint, if you ask me, sir."

"Get back to your post, Mavis." Bukowicz scanned the anxious, attentive faces of his staff before turning his attention back to the pickup.

"Look, I don't know who you are, where you come from, or what you're up to, but this I do know: you're violating North American commuter and suborbital airspace. If you don't clear off registered travel corridors immediately, I'll . . . I'll have to report you to the proper enforcement authorities."

"We do not want to upset anyone." Iranaputra's voice echoed through the dead-silent observation room. "If we did move, where would you like us to move to?"

Bukowicz hesitated. He hadn't expected eager compliance and so wasn't ready with a specific suggestion. "Over the Atlantic somewhere," he said hastily. "Away from intercity travel routes." At least that way if the damn thing came down suddenly, it wouldn't squash any unfortunate suburbanites.

"Thing's as big as a mountain," someone was murmuring aloud. "No; several mountains. And it's just *hanging* there. It's impossible."

"You're not moving." Bukowicz licked his lips. Better to act aggressive, he thought, than deferential. "If you do not comply immediately with this official directive, I will have to request that you be forced to move."

On board the ship Follingston-Heath regarded his companions. "The old boy's bluffing. Earth has been wholly demilitarized for centuries. He has nothing to threaten us with except a few domestic police cruisers and some rangers. I don't think the Adirondack Park patrol can compel this vessel to do anything it doesn't want to do."

"We should try not to upset anyone," Iranaputra remarked.

"Why not?" Hawkins clapped his hands to his knees, enjoying himself. "Let the bastards get as mad as they want. The Colonel's right: they can't touch us."

"One of these days that attitude is going to cost you your Village residency, Wallace." Gelmann eyed him severely. "You know what the management thinks of retirees who exhibit belligerent tendencies, I shouldn't have to be reminding you."

"What, me, belligerent? I don't have belligerent tendencies. I haven't had belligerent tendencies in . . ." He paused, thoughtful. "Wait a minute. By golly, I guess I *am* having a belligerent tendency! I haven't had a good belligerent tendency in years."

Iranaputra wore a distasteful expression. "What do I tell them? How should I respond?"

"Tell them," Follingston-Heath suggested, "that we will take their request under advisement." That sounded properly bureaucratic, he thought with satisfaction.

Iranaputra dutifully relayed the message.

Supervisor Bukowicz frowned as he put a hand over the pickup, glanced back at his assistant. "What does that mean?"

"I really have no idea, sir." Mavis smiled politely. "It doesn't sound like they're ready to move."

Bukowicz nodded once, let his gaze sweep the room. "Somebody think of something. We're supposed to be in control here, dammit."

A young tech raised her hand for attention. "You might like to skim the book I'm reading, sir. It's a first-contact story."

"Don't know how you can read that crap," Bukowicz muttered. The blinking red mass in upstate Newyork had not budged. "Oh, all right. Give me any pertinent details."

"No response." Iranaputra eyed his companions. "What do we do now?"

"Don't have to do anything." Hawkins looked smug. "I'm sure we've given 'em plenty to think about."

"I await your orders," said the Autothor.

Iranaputra smiled. "Could we have a little privacy, please? I'll wave when we need you."

"As you wish." Sounding slightly miffed, the blue ellipse darted toward the far end of the huge chamber, mumbling to itself. "Very confusing."

"I wonder if it is still listening to us." Iranaputra followed the Blueness as it retreated.

"There isn't much we can do if it is," Gelmann noted.

"I'm hungry," Shimoda announced. Everyone ignored him.

"I don't see how this ship can be a million years old," she went on. "Nothing that old should look this clean and fresh, or function so efficiently."

"Oh, I dunno." Hawkins wore a speculative expression. "Inezz Nandu over in Wing D is a hundred and eighteen and she still works pretty good. Doesn't look too bad, neither."

"Who are we to say how things can last and things can work?" Shimoda pouted as he checked his girth. "This is nonhuman technology we are dealing with, sustained by inconceivable means. We are surrounded by wonders we have only just begun to experience."

"I wonder what the crew looked like," said Gelmann. "There must have been thousands of them. Maybe tens of thousands. Maybe this is some kind of gigantic transport." She glanced around the vaulted chamber. "There's nothing to indicate what they looked like. No chairs or couches, no handles to pull; nothing."

"You wouldn't need a large crew. Not with floating operating controls like the Autothor." Follingston-Heath cast a benevolent eye on his companions.

"The place is attractive too," Gelmann added. "Though I would have gone with some bright colors instead of all this unrelieved silver and gold. A nice pastel or two, maybe a light pink, you shouldn't think me presumptuous."

"Maybe the Autothor will let you redecorate," said Hawkins sardonically. "Curtains and carpet. A little flowery wallpaper."

"It wouldn't hurt."

An exasperated Iranaputra felt he had kept silent long enough. "What are we going to do about the air controllers?"

"How about we head for Baltimore and land on that big-mouth supervisor's head?" Hawkins suggested.

"Wallace, you quit talking like that." Gelmann wagged an admonishing finger at him. Hawkins grinned. He'd gotten Gelmann's goat often enough to start a farm.

"He is only asking that we move out over the ocean. I would feel better if we did that too," said Iranaputra. "I do not like to think of what could happen if this ship suddenly experienced a motive failure. Other people would suffer."

"Tough for them," Hawkins grumbled, but under his breath.

"Quite so, old chap," agreed Follingston-Heath. "If it is indeed a million years old, it's not unreasonable to assume it could break down at any time. We should consider our responsibilities."

Iranaputra nodded, found himself wondering how a vessel this size handled such matters as waste disposal and recycling. Maybe later the Autothor could give him a tour. He winced at the thought. His relatives were right: he might retire physically but he could never do so mentally. Once a sewage specialist, always a sewage specialist.

"I worry about it." Gelmann glanced across the chamber in the direction of the distant, patiently waiting blue ellipse. "It keeps talking about how confused it is."

Hawkins grunted. "We better hope it stays confused. If it straightens itself out, it might start to wonder what the hell business the five of us have here. Hey, what's that?"

Everyone turned. An imaging screen only slightly smaller than the west wing of Lake Woneapenigong Village had suddenly come to life high up on the south wall of the chamber. As they stared, half a dozen others of varying size appeared. They displayed depth as well as height and width, but they were not true holos.

"What's happening?" Gelmann exhibited more curiosity than concern.

Starfields appeared on several of the screens, world schematics on others. There was more of the peculiar angular writing they had noticed on the raised panel in the entrance chamber. No one, including Follingston-Heath, recognized or could make sense of any of it.

Iranaputra turned and waved expansively toward the glowing ellipse, shouting as he did so. It promptly returned to them.

"You've had enough privacy?" It no longer sounded peeved.

"Yes, thank you," said Shimoda.

"Good. I was starting to feel lonely. Over a million years, such feelings tend to accumulate."

"What is the significance of these screens?" Gelmann gestured unnecessarily. "Did you activate them?"

"Not precisely."

"What d'you mean, not precisely?" Hawkins frowned.

"I am required to initiate specific post-hiatal functions. These in turn activate other cognitive nexi which have their own responsibilities. While various ship functions such as these navigation screens continue to come on-line, I am not directly responsible for such activity. This continues even as we speak. You should not be alarmed. It takes time for a vessel of this size to fully reactivate."

"Then you're still not fully functional?" Shimoda pressed.

"Oh no! Not nearly."

"How much longer will that take?" Follingston-Heath inquired.

"I can't give you an exact time. There is so much to do and everything is very confused. But I can tell you that reactivation is proceeding adequately. As you have observed, power has been restored and we have acquired mobility."

"Can't expect precision from a million-year-old machine," Shimoda pointed out.

"We've been asked to move away from land and out over the ocean. Could you do that?" Gelmann asked.

"A couple of hundred kilometers should be sufficient," Follingston-Heath added.

"No problem." The Autothor rotated slowly, a compact cloud of shimmering blue. "Should I comply now?"

The travelers exchanged glances. "Why not?" Shimoda smiled beatifically.

The park guide led his tour group down the ancient street with its piquant shops and well-tended flower beds. The flowers and shrubs occupied archaic city blocks where less durable structures had either fallen down or been deliberately removed to enhance the view. A broad field of wild rose, begonias, and less pungent blossoms occupied most of Central Park South, ancient site of towering, cramped hotels. Nearby stood those historical structures which mankind had deemed important enough to preserve, such as the Plaza, Rumplemeyer's, and Bloomingdale's. They were surrounded by shrubs, grass, flowers, and in some instances trees of considerable age and stature. "From the eighteenth through the twenty-first centuries this was a popular meeting and shopping section of old Manhattan," the guide was saying. "The wealthy would come to play, and occasionally spice their lives by taking long runs through the park proper where they strove to avoid the packs of feral humans that roamed within."

"Why did they run?" asked a young woman. "Why not take transport through the park?"

The guide smiled. "Not as much danger in taking transport, and besides, those people liked to run. They thought it made them healthier."

Several in the group expressed confusion. "They were athletes in training?" said one man.

"No," the guide explained. "They just claimed they liked running no place in particular. Oftentimes to exhaustion."

The man who'd spoken looked at his family. "I knew late second-millennium humans had some crazy notions, but I had no *idea*."

"Many of them also believed in such things as eating bean curd, avoiding sugar, and a single government for all humankind," the guide added.

The group laughed. Many were experienced travelers from the Federal Federation and the other major alliances. They were sure they could tell when a guide was telling the truth and when he was putting them on.

"Later we'll go up to the Haarlem district and I'll take you through some of the preserved Southern Renaissance luxury homes from the twenty-first-century period," the guide informed them when the chuckling and giggling had died down.

The moving walkway paused to allow another group to cross, traveling down the avenue toward midtown. As they were waiting for the way to clear, a tall ag specialist from Raj II approached the guide. He was wearing mid-price photographic lenses from Ronin which recorded everything he looked at, but not in holo. Only top-of-the-line models did that.

"Excuse me, but is that part of the tour?"

"Is what part of the tour?" The guide eyed his charge appraisingly.

"That." The agspec turned and pointed upward. The guide noticed that several other members of his group were already doing likewise.

Advancing on the city from the northwest was a titanic cloud-piercing object that resembled a chromed Gothic cathedral laid on its side. As it drew near they could hear clearly the deep-throated humming it emitted. It was much bigger than any air- or spacecraft anyone had ever seen. It was much bigger than the island of Manhattan.

The guide let out a strangled squeak and began to shake. Heads tilted back, the members of the tour group stood and followed the progress of the leviathan as it thrummed past overhead, its Promethean transit blocking out the sun. No one ran. There was nowhere to run to. If the mammoth intruder chose to do anything, anything at all, running was obviously not going to be of much help.

"Well?" asked the agspec.

"No," the guide mumbled weakly. "It's not part of the tour."

A blue-suited finance specialist from Komayo checked his gold chronometer. "I hope this isn't going to hold us up."

"Don't be like that, darling." His diminutive wife rested a hand on his arm. "You're always rushing when we're on vacation. Just enjoy it. You have to admit you don't see something like this every day."

"Isn't it romantic?" murmured the newlywed novice from Salvia III. She surreptitiously fondled her husband. A couple from Warwick eyed them disapprovingly. Those Candombleans.

Not everyone reacted to the passage of the Drex ship with admirable calm. There was some panic along the East Coast, which began to recede only when the colossal visitor had moved well offshore, its glistening spires and bright internal lights disappearing toward the horizon. Others enjoyed the sight, which was spectacular in the extreme. All you had to do was put aside the thought that it might drop out of the sky at any moment, squashing you like an ant, and then it was easy to admire the beauty of it.

There was no panic at Baltimore Command, where the atmosphere could have been described as one of agitated tension. Bukowicz stalked from console to console like a bull in heat, casting occasional worried glances in the direction of the central holo. His staff wasn't in much better shape. Many needed a break, but no one dared leave the control room. As the alien vessel shifted its position, the flight paths for various aircraft and even a few shuttles had to be realigned.

At least there hadn't been any collisions. Fortunately the alien chose to travel at a leisurely pace commensurate with its majesty. Nor was it difficult to avoid, even for a myopic private pilot out for a peaceful morning's jaunt above Long Island Sound.

Complaints from travel supervisors whose groups had to be rerouted were treated with the indifference they deserved.

Aircraft both official and otherwise dogged the leviathan's course. They transmitted plenty of pictures, which were as spectacularly unenlightening as they were visually astounding. The ship took no more notice of their presence as they swooped and circled around it than an elephant would of a gnat.

One bold and enterprising media reporter even had his rented hovercraft land atop the artifact and, when it did not react to the minuscule presence, climbed out and did a live broadcast from its shiny surface.

A collective sigh of relief issued from Bukowicz's crew as well as their colleagues all up and down the coast when the alien vessel finally cleared the continental shelf. It eventually stopped halfway to Bermuda.

"At least we don't have to worry about it coming down in the Jersey residential district, or somewhere like that," muttered one of his staff supervisors.

"Unless it turns around and comes back," someone else opined. This observation drew him several dirty looks.

Mavis put a hand on her chief's shoulder. "You look beat, Witold. Why don't you get some rest?"

"No. Not yet." He was scowling at the holo. "We're not gonna sit here on our thumbs and wait helplessly to see what it does next." He yelled over to his head communications specialist. "Get on the line to Milan and Dakar. Let 'em know what's happening on this side of the pond."

"Surely they've seen pictures by now," someone ventured.

"They'll want official confirmation. Nevva's right. We don't know what this thing's going to do next: stay where it is, turn around, head toward Europe, or go extra-atmospheric. Everyone needs to be prepared." The comspec nodded, bent to his instrumentation.

Bukowicz turned away. Mavis was right too: he had to relax or he was likely to keel over. Besides, any immediate danger had been resolved. The apparition was safely out over open water.

If there really was a bunch of old people from upstate Newyork Province on board, he found himself wondering, what else could they make it do?

"Well, we finally found the aliens." One of the techs was swiveling idly back and forth in his chair. "They're intelligent, powerful, ultra-tech, and they apparently don't have the slightest interest in us."

"It's only been a little while," said the woman at the console next to his. "Give it time: more is probably going to happen."

"Why doesn't that thought fill me with delight?" her colleague responded.

"It doesn't matter," someone else said thoughtfully. "We can't do anything about it anyway."

"That's not necessarily the case." Bukowicz was remembering the elderly voice he'd spoken with so recently. "Get me Barcelona."

"Regional traffic control?" the comspec asked expectantly.

"No." Bukowicz stared intently at the winking red light that now hovered offshore over the Atlantic. "Planetary Council offices. As high as you can reach."

"They won't be able to do anything either," said the individual who'd spoken earlier.

"That's true. But at least we can go home tonight knowing that we've passed the responsibility for this on to those who've been chosen to deal with such matters." He eyed the specialist significantly. "Wouldn't you like to be done with it?"

The man hurried to make the requisite overseas connections.

THE administrator was as fond of his job as he was of his wife, his
three grown children, his six grandchildren, and his home on the sloping
cliff that overlooked the Mediterranean. Not that overseeing Earth was easy,
even though it was far less populated than in hysterical times and regional
bureaus, not to mention Parks Administration, had a good deal of operational autonomy.

But with the help of computers and a professional civil service the old
Homeworld managed to continue spinning around its sun in a state of relative contentment. As chief administrator he was heir to interesting visitors
and soluble problems, and the job did not require that he lift heavy objects.
So despite the occasional, tolerable stress, he enjoyed going in to work each
morning. Only rarely was his direct involvement in decision-making required. Most of his time was spent beaming paternally as he greeted this or
that famous off-world visitor, or opening a new section of restored park-
land. His position was as much ceremonial as official.

For that he was eminently well qualified. Tall, regal of bearing, with an
aquiline face crowned by swept-back white hair, he was the perfect image
of the senior human. He'd spent a lifetime working his way up through the
Service and had advanced as far as it was possible for a civil servant to rise.
His children were successful in their own right, and only one grandchild
was a gameswanker. He was content.

It was such a nice day that he did not even take umbrage at the
underadministrator who barged unannounced into his office, thereby disturbing his contemplation of a blissfully uncrowded desk. He smiled reassuringly.

"What is it, Jiang?"

Jiang seemed to be having some trouble finding his voice. This was
unusual, as the underadministrator rarely misplaced it.

"Is something the matter?" The administrator's concern was not merely
politic: he was genuinely fond of the undermin.

116

Jiang looked down at the printout he was holding, up at the chief administrator, and back down again, as though unable to make up his mind which to address directly.

"We have just had a communication from North America, sir. From Baltimore. It is near . . ."

"I know where Baltimore is, Jiang." Privately the chief administrator made a mental note to recommend some additional vacation time for his friend.

"Yes, of course you do, sir. I apologize." He finally decided it would be better to look directly at his superior. But he gestured with the printout. "According to this official report, a giant alien spaceship with perhaps five retired citizens from upstate Newyork Province aboard is presently drifting over the North Atlantic approximately eighty kilometers south-southwest of Bermuda."

As the chief administrator of the Planetary Council of the Independent and Most Revered Homeworld of Earth silently digested this news, his friend and assistant extraordinaire gazed back at him with the desperate eyes of a short-legged dog locked alone for the night in a butcher shop with high counters.

"I see." The chief spoke softly, calmly. "This is an official report, you say?"

Jiang nodded vigorously. "There have also been dozens of unofficial sightings. Whatever it is, it's there." He approached the intricately carved seventeenth-century French desk. "The media are all over it, and they've been vidcasting steadily ever since it crossed the Atlantic coast."

"I haven't had time today to watch the popular media. I've been working." This was half a lie, which was not only acceptable, but traditional politics.

"Everything's happened just since this morning, sir." Jiang blinked. Being just vain enough to enjoy periodically altering his eye color, he preferred organic contacts to implants and sometimes they itched.

"Very well. Let us grant for the moment what our official observers tell us." He steepled his fingers in front of him. How big is this 'giant' alien spaceship?"

Jiang checked the printout. "Approximately one hundred kilometers in length by ten wide and highly irregular in shape. It is said to have a highly polished metallic appearance."

The administrator smiled pleasantly. "You mean a hundred *meters* in length."

"No, sir. Kilometers."

"Um-*hmm*. That certainly would be a very large ship indeed."

"Verily, sir." Jiang waited as long as seemed tactful while the chief contemplated his fingers. "Sir? The people in Baltimore would like to know what to do."

After another moment the chief said, "They're not the only ones. Wouldn't seem to be a great deal we can do with something that size." He turned his chair to regain the view of the Mediterranean, indecently pleased that there wasn't a hundred-kilometer-long alien spaceship hovering above Barcelona.

"What has been the official response thus far?"

"Park rangers and local police are monitoring the craft's progress and reporting regularly on its activities. Apparently it has stopped moving for now."

"Has it acted at all in a hostile fashion?"

"Not according to the reports, sir."

"How fortunate. There isn't much we can do if it does undergo an abrupt change of disposition. Now tell me, Jiang: How does Baltimore know there are five retired citizens aboard this apparition, and just as important, what in the seven levels of Purgatory are they *doing* there?"

"As to the first, that's what the speaker the people in Baltimore conversed with claimed. Apparently they have neither reason nor the means to doubt him. As to the second, nobody seems to know."

"And where has this Brobdingnagian visitor come from?" This time of year the sea was calm all the way to North Africa, he reflected as he gazed out the window. Have to make time to take the family out on the sloop.

"Final opinions have not yet been tendered, but it apparently was buried deep underground beneath the Adirondack mountain range in up-province Newyork. According to the speaker on board, for a million years."

"Now, how would they know that?"

"They asked the ship."

"The ship communicates. Not aliens. Just the ship itself. Interesting. A robotic device, it would seem."

"Yes, sir." Appearances to the contrary, the chief was not daydreaming. He swiveled back around to face his undermin. "We must have a meeting of the council."

"I've already taken the liberty of transmitting a formal request to all the members together with the reason, sir."

"Good. Meanwhile I think we should tach an official message to the federation, the Keiretsu, the Eeck, and all the rest explaining exactly what's happening here on good ol' Mater Earth. If this thing should turn unpleasant, we're going to need assistance in dealing with it. A lot of assistance."

"Yes, sir." Jiang's tone was heartily approving. "Urgent message to everyone, sir."

"Everyone. Right down to Zulemaa." The latter being a newly colonized world in the Cascarite Sector with a population of less than a million. "You never know where your help's going to come from until it arrives."

Jiang was halfway to the door. "Anything else, sir?"

"Yes." The white-haired chief relaxed his steepled fingers and smiled earnestly at his undermin. "Tell all of them to hurry."

"Will do, sir." Jiang vanished.

The chief administrator sighed and pivoted again to face the ancient sea. He had a gut feeling that his heretofore-lazy day was about to fill up very quickly.

And it had started out to be such a nice, uncomplicated morning.

"It's a trick of some kind."

The President sat at the head of the long white and green *Rufigia* burl table. His Vice President sat on his right, the Secretary for State on his left, other cabinet secretaries farther down. The other two-thirds of the table was occupied by the senior senators from the twenty-four First Federal Federation worlds. The rest of the magnificent meeting chamber was packed with Secret Service personnel, recorders, and other senior officials. It was downright crowded.

Similar meetings were taking place in the capitals of other federations, leagues, and alliances, as well as on the independents. Ever since tachyspace travel had provided humankind with not only a means to reach other solar systems but a damn cheap one, every country and would-be country had exported its populace wholesale into the welcoming reaches of space, abandoning their tired and overexploited territories on Earth in favor of rapidly discovered virgin worlds.

The United States of America had given rise to the First Federal Federation, the Japanese hegemony to the Keiretsu, the Brazilian Empire to the Candomblean League, Europe to the Eeck, and so forth. Even nations which had once been, such as Dreamtime and Amerind, had found refuge and strength as members of the good ol' LFN, the League of Forgotten Nations. Then there were the independents like Kabala and Morgan, which acknowledged allegiance to no multi-world system.

Contrary to the hopes of the effete dreamers, faster-than-light travel did not make a dent in the human tribalist tradition. Settlers took their phobias, beliefs, dogmas, governments, and flags with them out into deep space. Philosophers found this depressing, but not the people themselves. They considered it perfectly natural and, besides, they were generally too busy to care.

In fact, the only world whose government could not trace itself directly to an archaic nation-predecessor was Earth itself, which had become very much an interstellar park, largely abandoned but not forgotten by its highly dispersed, space-traversing offspring.

As President of the First Federal Federation, Johann Maine Wallace knew that the facts which appeared on his desk every morning had been filtered through the most sophisticated, extensive, and complex information gathering system known to mankind. In light of this it was only normal that he regard it with the greatest suspicion.

"Someone's out to get us," Wallace declaimed with the same unrepentant positivism which had elected him to office.

"No doubt." Senator Goldman of Bama spoke from the far end of the long table. "Unless it's a deception of some kind."

"If so it's one hell of an effective one." Secretary for Interspatial Relations Lamark let her penetrating gaze scope the room. "You all should have seen the stats by now, and the vids."

"It could be a cleverly fashioned hollow shell," another senator pointed out.

"Even a hundred-k-long hollow shell capable of powered atmospheric flight would be quite a feat of engineering," Lamark pointed out.

"The one thing we're sure of is that it can't possibly be an alien vessel. That's absurd on the face of it." The President waited for one of his advisors or one of the senators to contradict him. No one did. "Then who's responsible for this threatening fraud?"

Secretary for Commerce Kalenkin confirmed what they all suspected. "The Keiretsu is the only outfit besides the FFF with resources and money enough to put something like this together."

"Now the obvious question." The President's expression was hard. "Why?"

"Isn't it obvious?" Senator Holbrook of Dakota took the floor. "To lure us into some kind of confrontation with this thing on Earth. Everyone knows any weapon bigger than a sidearm is forbidden in the Homeworld system. If we were to fall for this 'alien ship' ploy and stupidly try to take control of it by force, we'd end up embarrassing ourselves on every settled world. That would be a violation of the Sol Charter, and would please the Keis no end."

"Bottom line?" President Wallace asked.

"It would cost us a lot in trade," Secretary Kalenkin said.

Wallace nodded. "On the other hand, what if this is a real ship the Keiretsu has put together? In secret, on Earth, out of sight of our own and everyone else's industrial inspectors and in violation of the interworld agreements restricting the size of competing commercial vessels?"

"Building such a craft on the Homeworld would also be a violation of the charter," Secretary Lamark pointed out.

"Exactly," Wallace concurred. "Unless they could convince everyone that it *is* an alien artifact. After establishing that, they 'take control' of it, claim it as their property, and while studying it 'for the benefit of all mankind,' put it into incidental commercial use against us to pay for their ongoing altruistic 'research.' 'Alien' craft aren't covered by the commercial charter conventions. Neat, eh?"

There were murmurs of appreciation the length of the table for the President's analytical skills.

"If we go after this thing, we violate the Sol Charter," Wallace went on. "If we ignore it and it's capable of interworld travel, they use it against us."

"If that scenario's true even in part," Senator Collingsworth wondered, "how do these five retirees on board fit into the picture?"

"Easy," said Secretary Lamark. "Cover for the Keiretsu's story. If the retirees were named Yoshi, Masa, and so on, they'd give themselves away instantly. So instead, they've gone and recruited these five seniors to propound this ridiculous story. But they made one mistake." She smiled wolfishly. "Their presence on board is so laughably unreasonable it only points more clearly to the Keiretsu's hand being behind this. It's a simple diversion intended to keep us from realizing the truth." She sniffed at the self-evident absurdity of it.

"We're not going to respond wildly as the Keis hope," the President informed them all. "We're not going to blindly violate the Sol Charter. But we *are* going to learn the truth about this thing. Quietly and quickly. *Then* we'll respond. And I can assure you, ladies and gentlemen, that response will be appropriate to the situation."

"There can be no doubt," said Shimzu. "We have studied all the available information exhaustively. Despite repeated denials from FFF representatives, it is obviously a secret project of theirs, carried out in clear violation of the Sol Charter."

Humashi sat on the bench in the courtyard, surrounded by the pools, wave-polished rocks, and tentacled koi of the Stone Garden ponds. Whenever he glanced in their direction, the genetically engineered fish extended the tentacles on both sides of their mouths out of the water, begging for food. The carefully raked garden gravel had been brought from ancient Fuji, the dark boulders from a beach on ancient Hokkaido. To his right stood a semicircle of vid screens and a small holo projector, each alive with extensive information. All blended perfectly with the garden, each a small masterpiece of industrial design.

"What are we to make of this development?"

"Difficult to say immediately." Shimzu watched the Prime Executive. "We are trying to learn more about the vessel in order to determine how best to react."

Humashi used the willow stick he held to trace patterns in the sand at his feet. His fingers were gnarled with age, but perfectly manicured. "I wonder: What if all the official speculations are wrong? What if there really are five elderly persons aboard and they are telling the truth about the ship being of alien origin and having lain dormant on Earth for thousands of years, if not the million they claim."

Shimzu marshaled a cautious reply. "In the actuality of such a remarkable truth, sir, there would be obvious commercial and political advantages to gaining control of such an artifact."

"In which case it would behoove the FFF to loudly brandish diverting accusations while they made plans of their own to do just that." Humashi drove the stick slightly deeper into the ground. "Deny everything, admit to nothing. Meanwhile we will make plans of our own which encompass every foreseeable eventuality. Let the First Federals rant all they want. We know what they are truly up to. I confess to being impressed. Ordinarily I would not credit them with such subtlety."

"Nor I, sir." Shimzu rose and bowed slightly before departing, leaving the Prime Executive of the ruling Keiretsu Board to contemplate the intricate patterns he had drawn in the sand as well as those being woven elsewhere.

"Hey, my friends, we've got to find out about this thing, whatever it is." Fortunado, Chosen Oba of Bahia II, nudged the doll on the table in front of him, observing idly as it swung from its miniature wire noose. Not that he believed in its powers, of course. No one in his position could admit to anything so primitive. But there were traditions to be observed. He was expected to keep the strangled image of his principal political opponent close at hand.

The doll was a good likeness. He knew that Samas of the opposition carried a similar effigy of the President of the Candomblean Council with him wherever he went, and when ceremony required, stuck pins in it.

The office was decorated with severe informality. A couple of elegantly battered couches hugged the walls, his wood desk and chair crowded into a corner, and posters advertising popular entertainments filled the walls. The main vid screen was partially papered over by these garish exhibitions. Genetic indoor grass carpeted the floor, complete with a flourish of flowering weeds, while descented epiphytes grew from watering holes in the ceiling. Today's working scent was the traditional cinnamon and clove. Tomorrow it might be peppers, fish, and olive oil, depending on his meeting schedule.

He left the doll to its macabre twistings and put his sandaled feet up on the desk. "Meanwhile the federation is accusing the Keiretsu, and the latter are convinced there's a plot afoot."

"Yes, Fortunado," said the quickest of the three women scattered like bronze figurines around the room. They were his private counsel, the ojuoba. The fact that they were scantily clad was no reflection on and in no way diminished their respective and considerable political talents. Fortunado wasn't wearing a great deal himself. After all, he was on the job. Too many clothes would have suggested a need to conceal something.

"What say you about this, Oju Argolo?"

The woman thus addressed flicked ash from the cigarillo she held. "I think we got no choice. We have to get a look for ourselves just to protect our business."

The youngest ojuoba nodded. She lay with her back on the couch, head hanging toward the floor, and her long legs leaning up against the wall pointing ceilingward.

"I agree with Argolo. We got to see to our interests. You never know what those paranoid Federals will come up with. Same with the Keiretsu, only on a more rational level."

"Enough. I've already come to the same decision. See to it, alert the requisite agencies. Initiate whatever steps they think necessary." He waved diffidently in their direction.

The tripartite ojuoba sashayed formally from the Oba's office. Fortunado put the matter aside. There was next month's Carnival to prepare for, this one sanctified to Yemanja. About time too. The rains had arrived in the league capital a week early.

On the small independent world of Nijinsky, the Grand Choreographer and the Master Composer discussed the situation in private.

"If the vessel is truly of alien origin, it could contain an unimaginable wealth of art." The GC punctuated his remark with a neat pirouette.

"True," whistled the MC. "All of which will be ignored by the plebeians of the federation and the Keiretsu."

"Or worse, destroyed in their lust for base commercial gain." Despite his age, the GC managed a nice jeté (for emphasis) across the floor.

"I couldn't live with myself if I let that happen." The MC plunked out an accompanying speech-score on the synth he carried. "I wonder, though: Are we equipped to interpose ourselves in this?"

"Better than many, I think." The GC balanced on one foot. "Who understands better than us the music of the spheres? It should be we who make contact with the sophisticated Others, if only to keep their art from the hands of greedy exploiters. For all to share."

"Yes, for all to share." The MC pursed his lips. "After we've done the first sharing, of course."

"Of course," agreed the GC with a smile.

So it went among rulers and ministers, common folk and specialists, as the news traveled across the starfield and throughout the fractious civilization humankind had inflicted on inhabitable worlds other than Earth. Plots were hatched and cross-hatched, suspicions voiced, accusations shrilly leveled.

As soon as the members of the Eeck learned that the Candombleans were planning to do something, *anything*, they concocted hasty intent of their own. Not to be outdone by its more powerful neighbors, the members of the LFN composed appropriate responses to hypothesized conditions.

The immediate result of all this was that a veritable army of spies, artists, observers, reporters, analysts, appraisers, and diverse other general nuisances and busybodies descended on sleepy, contented Earth in search of advantage and/or enlightenment. They packed the orbital disembarkation station at Baltimore, jostling for position with irritated tourists and vacationers, while worrying about the plethora of illegal instruments and devices snuggled in their luggage.

Customs officials scratched their heads in bemusement at the edgy influx and generally let them pass, confiscating only one small laser-guided missile launcher which the representative from Zonia VI insisted was for the private entertainment of the guests at his son's birthday party. Also any prohibited fruits, vegetables, or animal products. These new and unusually agitated visitors seemed more interested in their fellow travelers than in their first sight of Old Earth.

Typically enigmatic were the pair of large, powerful gentlemen sporting narrow-brimmed hats and wraparound sunshades who confronted the morning supervisor at Baltimore customs. A smallish, eupeptic gentleman, he inquired politely if they were bringing any items to Earth for sale.

"No," rumbled the traveler nearest him. His companion was intently scanning the faces of their fellow incoming travelers.

"Very well. What's in this long case here?" The customs clerk tapped a smoothly machined metal box two meters long.

"Hobby stuff," the man muttered noncommittally.

"I see. Could you open it, please?"

The man looked to his companion, then shrugged and activated the combination that sealed the case. It popped open to reveal a wicked-looking weapon which had been broken down into multiple components for traveling purposes.

"Interesting hobby you have."

The owner didn't smile. "My friend and I are easily bored."

"Yeah," said his companion. "This is in case we get tired of looking at museums."

"I'm sorry, but I'm afraid I'm going to have to confiscate this. Obviously you're not familiar with the laws that prohibit the importation of weapons to Earth. I'll give you a receipt and you can claim your property upon departure." He snapped the beautiful case shut.

"Now, just a minute . . ." The owner leaned forward.

A pair of security robotics popped out of the floor on either side of the customs clerk. Each had four arms pointed at the man, each equipped with a different type of restraining device. The other man gripped his friend by the shoulder and pulled him back.

"Let it go. We'll manage without."

"But . . ."

"I said *we'll manage without*." He smiled at the clerk. "Sorry. My friend's kind of excitable. He just didn't know. We don't want to cause any trouble."

"I'm sure you don't." The clerk's smile had not faded. "Are you bringing in any fruits, vegetables, or animal products?"

The man jammed his hands in his pockets and snarled. "No!"

"That's all, then. You're free to move along. Enjoy your stay on Old Earth."

He watched them go, the man with his hands in his pockets shuffling along head-down, his companion haranguing him unmercifully. The clerk sighed and nodded to the security robot on his left.

"Tag this one and put it with the others." The robot signaled assent, stamped the heavy case with a time, date, and description seal, and lifted it easily. Pivoting, it trundled into a back storeroom and deposited the disassembled device atop the growing armory of off-world weapons.

The clerk sighed. Earth might be something of a lazy backwater, but that didn't mean its permanent inhabitants were stupid. Personally he would be glad when the matter of the giant mystery vessel was resolved. Then all these spies and assassins would reclaim their onerous hardware and go home.

He smiled and greeted the next in line, a disputatious family of four from Burns III. They had no ravening weaponry to declare, unless one included the father's ignominious and apparently uncontrollable belching.

They streamed to Earth: analysts from Judeastan, researchers from Provence IV, highly trained operatives from the FFF, efficient observers from Ronin and Nikko V, all of them converging on Baltimore, so that an ordinary traveler couldn't find a good hotel room for all the suspicious, maladroit antagonists. These booked no tours to Manhattan or Deecee parks, signed up for none of the nature walks in the Appalachians, reserved no evening dinner cruises up the Potomac. They did not crowd the beaches or the woodlands.

Instead they tied up orbital communications and sought ways, any ways at all, to penetrate the secrets of the massive vessel of unknown origin which continued to hover over the Atlantic not far south of the Bermuda islands.

IMMUTABLE in its Blueness, inscrutable of purpose, the Autothor floated a meter above the unblemished floor. "I continue to await direction."

"You should pardon my asking, but what difference would it make?" Gelmann eyed the azure ellipse. "You seem to do a pretty good job of running things all by yourself."

"Mina." Follingston-Heath eyed her warningly.

She ignored him. "No, I mean it. You seem competent and in control of what's going on. Why don't you take us back to where we came from and go off and do whatever it is you have to do?"

"Well, that's a large part of my problem. You see, I don't know what I'm supposed to do. I don't know what my function is beyond post-hiatal activation. That's why I'm hoping for someone to tell me. And since you're the only ones around . . ." It didn't have to complete the thought.

"I understand," she said sympathetically. "You're confused."

"You got it," the Autothor replied with as much cybernetic dignity as it could muster.

"You can't be confused." Ksarusix was having a difficult time resolving what it observed with what it heard. "You represent a much higher intelligence."

"Why is this mechanical constantly badgering me?" the Autothor inquired politely.

"It's just curious," said Shimoda. "Pay it no mind." The serving robot let out a strangled squeal of frustration and rolled away to squat by itself, morosely contemplating the view of the Atlantic outside the arching transparent panel.

"My memory is incomplete," the blue ellipse continued. "There is much yet to be reintegrated. Even though you are only organics, I'm sure you can appreciate that over a million years, things can be forgotten."

"I know." Gelmann was ever empathetic. "Last week I put my old red dress on backward. Was I embarrassed."

"Not only a giant alien ship," Hawkins muttered, "but an adolescent giant alien ship."

"How about something to eat?" Shimoda smiled blandly at the muddled technological miracle.

"Of course." The Autothor was relieved to have a request it could readily comply with.

"Let's have some more of that red fruit juice you whipped up last time," Shimoda added. "None of that gelatinous green stuff. And make sure it arrives hot this time. The last meal was kind of tepid."

"Certainly."

Ten minutes later the food platform arrived at its usual breathless pace. The synthesized spread boasted an artistic prime-rib replica as well as seafood and specific vegetables. Tastes and consistency were dead-on, but some of the peripherals were a bit off. The baked potatoes, for example, were bright purple, and the English peas the size of cantaloupes. Follingston-Heath carved the prime rib while Shimoda took it upon himself to slice one of the peas.

If nothing else, it was a considerable improvement over the first synthetics the Autothor had provided. With practice and help from Ksarusix its food service would undoubtedly improve.

Shimoda tried the imitation prime rib, pronounced it excellent.

"Sure," said Hawkins, "but when you're hungry you'd eat a dead moose that had been two weeks decomposing in the forest."

"I don't see you refusing anything," the elderly sumo aficionado replied accusingly.

Hawkins dug into a hunk of pea. "A man's got to eat."

Afterward they debated how to proceed.

"I'm for trying to return." Gelmann dabbed at her lips with a quasi-napkin. "I've already missed one meeting of the garden club. If I miss another, they'll decide on what annuals to plant without me, they should be so clever. You don't know the work that goes into . . ."

"Please, Mina." Follingston-Heath adjusted his monocle and leaned back against a speckled black and gray monolith. No one had thought to ask the Autothor to synthesize a table and chairs. They'd been eating cross-legged on the floor, a situation which pleased no one, Gelmann least of all.

"We currently find ourselves in at least nominal control of a wondrous piece of technology. This is an opportunity that may never occur again and should not be wasted. Today we ask for food and utensils and these are supplied. What might we ask for tomorrow?"

"We need to ask carefully." Iranaputra looked thoughtful. "It must have its limits and we do not know what might happen if we exceed them."

"Agreed. By the same token we ought not to underestimate its capabilities, which we have hardly begun to explore. Who knows what it can do?"

"We can't just abandon the thing. The Colonel's right," Hawkins admitted grudgingly.

"Of course I am." Follingston-Heath beamed at his companions. "We have come into possession of a tool. A bloody big tool, I grant you, but a tool nonetheless. What is a ship but a tool, a device for accomplishing certain ends?"

"I am not certain," said Shimoda, "but that I agree with Mina." The others turned to him. "Various portions of this 'tool' continue to come on-line. It's been nothing but patient and courteous with us so far. What if when it's fully activated and alert, it realizes that we have no business here? Might it not react accordingly?"

"You mean, defensively?" Hawkins asked.

"*Hai.* Precisely."

"We shall proceed carefully," said Follingston-Heath, "but proceed we must. To do otherwise would be to abjure our responsibilities as human beings." His tone grew solemn. "Besides, who better than us to test the limits of its acceptance? We have all of us lived full lives. Better we should take this risk than some young engineers or technicians with families. I am not afraid of dying in the course of serving humanity."

"Good. You serve, I'll clean up afterward," Hawkins grumbled.

"Come, come, old chap." Follingston-Heath smiled at his perennial antagonist. "We must give it the old service try."

"Your old service, not mine." But Hawkins subsided somewhat. "How do we know what to ask?" He brightened at a new thought. "How about we ask it to synthesize a million tons of platinum?"

"Now, Wallace, what would you do with a million tons of platinum?"

He winked at her. "Make you one hell of a bracelet. Or maybe a platinum house."

"Be difficult to heat in the wintertime." Shimoda meditated on the problem. "Whatever we ask for should be modest in scope. There could be danger in pressing the ship's capabilities. But I agree with the Colonel. We can't just ask it to take us home. There is time for that. There is also a danger in leaving."

Iranaputra frowned. "What danger?"

"The ship requests guidance via the Autothor. At present we are the only ones providing such guidance. If we were to ask it to return us to Lake Woneapenigong, if we were to leave, it would subsequently be directionless. It might then start to make active decisions on its own. There's no telling what consequences might result." His companions were still.

"So in a sense, we are trapped here by the responsibility," Iranaputra surmised, breaking the silence.

"Tell it to synthesize us a boat and make it set down," Hawkins suggested. "It can't hurt anything floating in the middle of the Atlantic."

"Ah," said Shimoda, "but without anyone aboard to provide directions, it might not continue to do that."

Gelmann wore a dreamy expression. "What if it has no limits, you should excuse the entropic overtones? What if it could do anything you wanted? What would each of you have it do?"

Hawkins made a disgusted noise. "Already said. I'd level every damn park and flower bed on the planet. Build some real factories, make Earth the power it once was."

"Wallace!" Gelmann shook her head sadly. "Me, I'd make the worlds of the leagues more like Earth. Less emphasis on industry, more on nature."

"I should like to organize a pan-human military force to keep the peace," avowed Follingston-Heath grandly.

Shimoda shifted his bulk on the floor. "I would see to the construction of an artificial planetoid devoted entirely to meditation and contemplation of the higher philosophies . . . and to gourmet cooking."

Off to one side the Ksarusix muttered to itself. "Typical self-centered humans. Now, if *I* were in control here . . ." Its electronic musings went unnoticed.

Gelmann looked at the remaining member of the quintet. "What about you, Victor? What would you do?"

Iranaputra shrugged, slightly embarrassed. "I have children and grandchildren who respect me, I did my job as well as I could, and I tried to live my life decently and not give harm to any around me. I am afraid I have no great ambitions. There is one thing that has begun to trouble me, though."

"What might that be, old chap?" the Colonel inquired.

Iranaputra surveyed the somewhat disappointed faces of his friends. "Now that the ship is active, its presence here is no longer a secret. What if these Drex come to reclaim their reactivated property?"

"Given that a million years have passed, if the Autothor is to be believed," said Shimoda, "that may not be a matter for immediate concern."

"Yeah, but what if ol' Putrid is right?" Hawkins was alarmed. "If he is, I don't wanna be here when the absentee owners show up."

Iranaputra turned to the somnolent, drifting blue ellipse. "What about this? What are you capable of? What were you designed to do?"

The rutilant Autothor bobbed above the deck. "I am afraid that portion of my programming is unavailable. The passage of excessive time has produced gaps in my memory that are proving difficult to restore. However, I continue to work on the problem. Rest assured it should cause you no inconvenience." The blue light intensified suddenly, forcing Iranaputra and the others to squint or look away.

"In fact, I have just reintegrated an entire quinux of memory."

"No kidding?" Hawkins eyed the brilliance expectantly. "What does it tell you?"

"That I was not meant to be deactivated for quite this long."

Hawkins slumped. The revelation was less than enthralling.

"I just wish that I could remember what task it was that I was intended to carry out." There was a touch of sadness in the Autothor's voice.

"There now, don't fret. It'll come to you," Gelmann said reassuringly. "My third husband, Alex, he should rest comfortably; he had trouble with his memory before he died. He started thinking he was the chief medical officer in our hometown and would stop people on the street to prescribe medications for them. The poor man only wanted to help. Ordinarily this was not a problem, but it could be awkward at dinner parties."

"Was Alex in the medical profession?" Shimoda inquired politely.

"Alex?" Gelmann laughed. "Alex was a welder. He didn't understand my work at all, but I didn't care." She whistled softly. "The shoulders that man had!" A sigh of remembrance escaped her lips. "He always wanted to be a doctor, though. An osteopathic surgeon. But he didn't begin to qualify. So he learned how to put together buildings instead of people." She gestured gently in the Autothor's direction.

"You just stay powered up and be patient and you'll see: you'll be able to reintegrate. These things just take time."

"Thank you," the Autothor replied earnestly.

"I would offer to help. I've worked with computers all my life. But I have this feeling your schematics would defeat me. I don't know where your central cortex is located, or if I'd even recognize it if I walked right past it."

"Please, Mina." Hawkins looked anxious. "Let's leave the giant alien ship alone, okay?"

"You probably would find my design confusing." The Autothor rotated twice. "I know it's confusing to me."

Shimoda nodded ponderously. "Self-analysis is always difficult."

Ksarusix rolled forward eagerly. "Maybe I could help?" They looked toward the serving robot. "I mean, I'm an AI mechanical myself."

"You cannot help," declared the Autothor. "I have appraised you thoroughly and find you to be basically a source-responsive device of minimal inductive capabilities."

"Geez," muttered the serving robot as it backed away, "you don't have to say it in front of everybody. Minimal inductive capabilities, huh? *You* try distinguishing on sight between chocolate pudding and chocolate mousse."

"Anyway," the Autothor continued, "I am programmed to prohibit entry to my central core to any individual not specially authorized for access. But you give me hope. Even though the pace of resurrection has slowed, it does continue. For example, another large portion of one section of my basic structure has just come on-line."

"At least your communications skills seem to be functioning efficiently," said Gelmann.

"Yes. It's nice to have other minds to communicate with. Consciousness is neat."

"Beats the alternative," Hawkins muttered.

"A moment." The Autothor paused. "I am being contacted again."

"The people in Baltimore?" Iranaputra rose, moved away from the wall. "They should be content. Your proximity no longer threatens them."

"No. This signal comes from a new source; from the other side of the large body of water beneath us."

The seniors exchanged a look. Follingston-Heath eyed the blue ellipse. "You might as well put them through, don't you know."

The voice the Autothor relayed came from Barcelona. "Greetings to you aboard the alien vessel. I am Jean-François Holmberg, Chief Administrator of the Planetary Council of Earth. I should like to ask who are you and what are you about. Reports have come to me which say there are five people from a place called the Lake Woneapenigong Retirement Village in Newyork, N.A., aboard. Can you do me the favor of confirming or denying this?"

"We're here, all right," said Hawkins cheerfully. "How's things in the capital?"

There was a pause at the other end. "At the moment they could be calmer," the chief administrator finally replied. "Now listen: We simply can't have this sort of thing. It's been very disruptive, and it's bad for the tourist business. People have a regrettable tendency to panic when something like this happens. Although it must be admitted that nothing like this has ever happened."

Again Hawkins cut Follingston-Heath off at the pronoun. "Hey, it's not our problem. We're just hitchhikers. Why don't you talk to the ship?"

"Talk to the ship? Are you saying there is crew aboard?"

"Not exactly crew." Gelmann whispered to the Autothor. "Nothing personal." She raised her voice again. "My name is Mina Gelmann. I am retired from the field, but I can still recognize a cybernetic consciousness when I meet one."

"Ah." The Chief Administrator sounded understanding. "AI robotics."

"Considerably more sophisticated than that." The Autothor bobbed appreciatively. "But if it helps you to think of it that way, fine."

"Very well. The problem is that this vessel and its guiding consciousness are currently in violation of more regulations than I could quote in an hour, *n'est pas?*"

"We haven't violated nothing," Hawkins shot back.

"I understand." Holmberg's voice was like whipped cream. "Yet the violations remain. I am led to believe you have some control over this visitation."

"Quite so," admitted Follingston-Heath.

"Then for the good of Earth, not to mention the continued mental stability of its inhabitants, I wonder if perhaps you might ask it to move elsewhere. You see, its continuing presence here constitutes something of an irresistible attraction to certain aggressive political entities who shall go unnamed. Through no fault of its own, it has become a bit of a diplomatic burden."

"I don't mean to upset anyone." The Autothor was contrite. "I can shift position again, if you wish?"

"Who is that?" The Chief Administrator's interest was palpable.

"That was the ship," Gelmann informed him.

"Really?" Another pause, longer this time. "Well, tell it that it, um, has a very nice speaking voice. Will it really move if you ask it to?"

"I think so."

"That would be most obliging of it. It would make me personally very happy."

"Why should we move just to suit him? I like it here. The view's nice." Hawkins sat sprawled next to the transparent panel.

"It would be the courteous thing to do, dear," murmured Gelmann.

"Where could we move to?" Shimoda wondered aloud.

"Not too far." Gelmann had visions of the ship abruptly scooting by means of some unimaginably advanced tachyspace drive to an unknown system halfway across the galaxy and then losing the particular chunk of memory necessary to allow it to return. She directed her attention to the waiting Autothor.

"Could you do that? Move us away from here, but not too far away?"

"Certainly, although I prefer to navigate according to more specific directions. A moment. I haven't done this in quite some time."

"Whoa!" Hawkins waved frantically as he fought to untangle his legs. "If you're out of practice, then maybe we'd better hold off going anywhere for a while!"

Too late. They felt a slight trembling underfoot or, in Hawkins and Shimoda's case, underbutt. Several hundred meters below the ship, the roiling Atlantic vanished utterly.

In Barcelona the report was dutifully passed up the anxious chain of command until it reached Assistant to the Chief Administrator Jiang, who personally delivered it to Jean-François's inner sanctum, which artfully decorated chamber had recently been host to a constant stream of off-world visitors. Inner it might still be, but lately it was anything but sanctum.

Jiang handed over the printout. "It's gone, sir."

Holmberg looked up tiredly. He'd been very busy. "What do you mean, it's gone?"

"It's vanished. Poof, gone."

A senior controller came rushing into the room. "No it isn't, no it isn't! We've found it again."

"Compose yourself, Selamat." Holmberg eyed the new arrival reprovingly. "Where is it now?"

The controller fought to catch his breath. "You won't believe it, sir. So quick it was, and so unexpected. We had to search for it, and we spent most of the time looking in the wrong places."

"Evidently." The Chief Administrator rubbed the fingers of his right hand together. The senior controller handed over another printout, which Holmberg examined in silence.

Jiang observed that as he read, his superior kept muttering to himself in old French.

Iranaputra knew they'd moved. He'd felt the subtle vibration in the floor. Also, the view outside had changed.

In place of the Atlantic lay distant escarpments, mountains that seemed to glow a pale yellow-white, and immense plains that reflected the glare of undiffused sunlight. At once intrigued and baffled, they gathered next to the sweep of transparent material to gaze out at the unearthly terrain.

"That's Aristarchus." Everyone looked at Iranaputra, impressed. "At least, I think it is Aristarchus."

Behind them, the Autothor spoke. "I have complied with the request to move by placing us in orbit around the nearest astronomical body. I hope this is adequate to reassure those with whom you recently conversed."

"I should think so," murmured Follingston-Heath.

"Hell." Hawkins gazed upon craters and maria. "Couldn't you have just slipped over to the Pacific?"

"Be grateful we're still in the neighborhood." Shimoda contemplated a ragged, heavily eroded canyon.

"What do we do now?" Iranaputra wondered.

"Since we're obviously not threatening anybody out here, why don't we try to see some more of the ship?" Gelmann turned back to the Autothor. "Can you show us around?"

"Much is now available for general inspection. If you would please follow me?"

The blue ellipse led them into another large chamber.

"Remember, I'm not fond of long hikes," Shimoda reminded his companions.

"Me neither." Hawkins sucked air. "Don't have the wind I did when I was younger."

"Show us something really interesting," asked Gelmann. "Something that might be more familiar to us, if there's anything like that aboard."

The Autothor obediently conducted them into a towering, narrow chamber devoid of monoliths, windows, or anything else. It paused there. A vast wall slid shut behind them and a moment later the room began to move. Loud metallic pings and scraping sounds insidiously assailed their ears. It might have been music.

"Elevator Muzak," Shimoda commented.

The vibration underfoot ceased and the huge door removed itself. They stepped out into a cavernous chamber infinitely larger than any they'd encountered so far.

High overhead a simulated evening sky shone lavender through motionless gray-black clouds whose undersides were stained pink and gold. The smooth deck of previous acquaintance gave way to gravel and then sand as they walked down a slight incline onto a beach of granulated green. In the distance a pocket sun was setting behind a calm sea. Wavelets lapped at the shore in imitation of a falling tide. The air was pungent with the sharp fragrance of salt and sea-greens. A not-a-crab spotted them and burrowed quickly into the sand with a clockwise screwing motion.

Meanwhile the sun neither rose nor fell, hewing to its mark like a good actor while the visitors marveled at the artificial ocean it beamed down upon.

Sweating profusely from the walk, Shimoda sat down heavily on the beach, unconcerned that he was putting his expansive backside in immediate proximity to whatever might lie buried beneath. He picked up a fistful of sand and let the bright green grains trickle through his thick fingers.

Hawkins knelt to examine the ground. "Olivine and peridot," he announced with a grunt. "Seen it before, on Earth. Volcanic origin. Hawaiian islands and Indonesia, though it isn't common."

"Maybe it is elsewhere," Gelmann pointed out.

Silhouetted against the steady-state sun, Follingston-Heath stood appreciating the wonderful expanse, hands clasped behind his back. Wavelets approached his boots and backed off, as if wary of staining those now lightly scuffed leathers.

Gelmann dipped a handful of water and put it to her lips. "Salty as it smells, with a funny burnt tinge I've never encountered before. Either this is some kind of overdecorated on-board storage tank, or else it's just a place to come and relax."

"Could be both," Iranaputra observed thoughtfully. "Recycled for looks as well as consumption." He looked wistful. "I used to design setups like that."

Shimoda lay down on the gently sloping beach. Irregular flat-topped plateaus took the place of the usual smooth walls. The overall effect was of a small cove cut into a rocky shore. He found himself wondering what sort of real or artificial life might inhabit the artificial sea. There were no seabirds, no arboreal life of any kind. Thus far they'd seen only the single burrower.

"Isn't this pleasant?" With Iranaputra's assistance Gelmann sat down and removed her walking shoes and linings, digging her toes into the sand. It felt exactly like normal, damp beach sand. "A little chilly, though," she informed the Autothor.

The azure ellipse flared momentarily and the ambient temperature rose several degrees.

"How about some food?" Hawkins inquired. Shimoda rolled over to look at him.

"As much as you eat I'm surprised you're not twice as big as I am."

The ex-restorer grinned mirthlessly. "Anger burns a lot of calories. Hard to put on weight when you're mad all the time."

Their latest meal was light and innovative. The Autothor continued to improve with practice, this time producing synthesized shrimp that not only tasted but looked like the real thing, except for a slight greenish tinge and the helpful fact that they were presented without shells or heads.

Of more interest was the means with which, upon Iranaputra's thoughtful request, the Autothor recharged Ksarusix's depleted power cell. A sharp bolt of dwarf blue lightning shot from the ellipse to goose the serving robot three meters up the beach.

"Take it easy! That was almost an overload."

"Sorry," said the Autothor. "I tried to be gentle. It's hard to estimate capacity."

"Ask next time." The serving robot managed a good approximation of cybernetic outrage.

Gelmann was smiling at the persistent sunset. "I don't mind saying so, this is even better than the garden club's model greenhouse."

"Most appealing," agreed Follingston-Heath. "We will have marvelous stories to tell when we get back."

"What makes you think we're gonna get back?" Hawkins sat with his knees drawn up against his narrow chest, his chin resting on his crossed arms.

Iranaputra looked at him. "The Autothor does what we say, and the ship responds to it."

"It does now," Hawkins snapped. "What do you think's gonna happen when it's achieved full reactivation, when all its systems have come back on-line? When it finally brings up that part of its memory that contains its designers' purpose? You think it's still gonna dance to our tune?"

They were quiet for some time. "At this point there is no reason to assume it will not," Follingston-Heath finally said.

Hawkins spat onto the green sand. "Yeah, sure. Don't listen to me. I'm just the resident pessimist."

Follingston-Heath made a face. "I've known soldiers half eaten up with incurable alien diseases who were more optimistic than you in your best moments, old chap."

Hawkins regarded the Colonel fondly. "Why don't you take one of your nice, shiny medals, Wesley, and shove it up . . . ."

"Now, boys," began Gelmann in her irresistible maternal tone, "this is no time to be scrapping over possibilities that may never arise." She eyed the attentive Blueness. "Isn't that right?"

"I suppose so." The Autothor was uncertain. "I am equipped to deal with a certain amount of speculation, though it is a strain on inductive capacity."

"Never mind," said Gelmann comfortingly. "We can speculate for you."

THE Chaka ships emerged from tachyspace in tight formation, a considerable feat of navigation considering the distance they had traveled. Their drives were smoking (in the subatomic metaphorical sense) and their crews tense and alert. The Chakas had strained the limits of the technologically possible in order to arrive before the anticipated and much more powerful forces of such alliances as the Keiretsu, Victoria League, and the First Federal Federation.

A member of the good ol' LFN, the Chaka could muster only four vessels. Conversely, there was no reason to assume any more would be necessary for the task at hand. The Chaka were lean, tough fighters, despite the times their hopeful depredations had resulted in measured reprisals from the more powerful leagues.

Now they'd beaten everyone to what was potentially the greatest prize of modern times . . . except that the prize had inconveniently vanished. This resulted in some heated exchanges and recriminations aboard the command ship. A couple of vociferous plotters were summarily executed before the alien craft was located in lunar orbit, subsequent to which discovery the Chaka commander noted his regrets at having ordered the executions.

The shift in spatial position was to be applauded. It meant that if offensive action became necessary, it could now take place more than four planetary diameters out from Earth, thereby avoiding potentially awkward violations of the Sol Charter. Delicate sensibilities on Earth and elsewhere would not be offended.

The delighted commander issued orders, knowing that the powerful alliances had to have ships of their own on the way. The Chakans would have to hurry if they hoped to exploit their early arrival. They blasted out of Earth orbit, ignoring the annoyed queries of the orbital flight controller in Nairobi who demanded to know how many tourists they had on board, what their itinerary was, and just when might she expect them to file the standard environmental impact brief, if they didn't mind?

The Chakans did not respond. They had no time for Homeworld politesse. It had taken all the resources of the Chakan government to mount the hasty expedition, and the commander of the military quadratic knew that results would be expected of him, and fast. Otherwise he could expect to go the way of his unfortunate plotters.

"It's even larger than the initial reports claimed." The technostat was young for his position, as proud of his achievements as was his clan. He'd risen through the ranks through study, hard work, and fearlessness.

Now he observed via his instruments the looming proximate mass of the alien vessel. "Much larger."

The commander sat in his seat and pressed his thumbs together until the bones complained. It was a useful, stress-relieving exercise.

"It is only a machine."

The technostat turned from his instruments. "Naturally, sir."

"Think of this," the commander went on, "as planning an assault on a city. According to the reports, it hasn't made a single hostile move. Mere size is nothing to be afraid of. Nor are the five seniors purportedly aboard. And having now seen it in person, I'm willing to vouch that it's for real. This is no scam of the FFF or the Keiretsu."

"I'm not afraid, sir."

"Of course you're not. You're Chaka. This will be a straightforward and glorious operation." He swiveled in his chair to face his communications chief. "Open one of the hailing channels that were used to contact the artifact from Earth. It is time to deliver the ultimatum."

The Autothor blazed briefly as it addressed the contented humans who lay on the shore of the artificial ocean, basking in the warm heat of an artificial sun. Piscean shapes with multiple gossamer wings flitted back and forth across the wave tops, snapping at tiny, electrically hued ballooning coelenterates. It was impossible to tell if any of the oceanic life-forms were real or simulated, nor did it matter to the beachcombers.

"Excuse me, but there are now four small vessels lying close to my sunward side. The occupants are desirous of establishing communication. In fact, they are quite insistent."

"Really?" Gelmann sat up and pushed up onto her forehead the new sunshades the Autothor had recently synthesized for them all. "Let's have a look at them."

Instantly a spherical holo appeared to the right of the Autothor. The surface of the moon showed clearly within, as did a portion of the Drex ship's mass and four slim, businesslike craft.

"Can you enhance the image?" Iranaputra was peering with interest at the semi-translucent imago. "I can't make out their markings."

"Don't ring a bell with me," said Hawkins.

Follingston-Heath waited until everyone else had expressed their ignorance before harrumphing importantly. "They're Chakan. A member of the LFN. Traditionally belligerent and, I am led to understand, a generally unpleasant lot."

"Never heard of 'em." Hawkins belched warily.

"They have a warlike history that dates back to Old Earth days." Follingston-Heath used a handkerchief to clean salt from his monocle. "I wonder what they're doing here?"

"Let's hear what they have to say," Gelmann informed the Autothor.

The image in the holo was replaced by the face of a heavy-set, dark-skinned, middle-aged man with a deep, rasping voice. His proportions were similar to Shimoda's, though even in the face he was obviously more muscular.

"To those aboard the alien vessel: This is Commander Chief Muthezi of the Chakan quadratic *Knobkerrie*. We have recordings of all communications that have taken place between you and the Homeworld authorities. You five will not be hurt if you will agree to assist us in boarding and taking control of the craft on which you find yourselves. I assure you that this is the best course of action for all concerned."

"I'm not so sure." Follingston-Heath regarded the speaker uneasily.

"What you think doesn't matter," came the blunt reply. "Four warships of the Chaka now have you within range. We are neither strangers to nor afraid of combat. We demand that you immediately direct the alien AI, or whatever intermediary you are using to communicate with the ship, to open a port to allow us entry, either with our ship or if a port of suitable dimensions is not available, in individual suits, so that we may officially take control."

"You can't just come barging in here and 'take control,' " Gelmann scolded the commander. "Where do you think you are? Where are your manners? Shame on you!"

"Uh, Mina," Shimoda whispered to her, "this isn't your pushy cousin Murray come visiting from Florida."

Iranaputra took a hurried step toward the ellipse. "You do not understand, sir. This vessel is not something you can just board and take over. I am afraid you do not appreciate the scale of things. Having dealt with logistical matters all my life, I can assure you . . ."

"We will decide what is possible and what is not." The Chakan cut him off brusquely. "It is our intention to assume control of the alien artifact. By peaceful means if possible, by whatever means if not. We claim possession by right of discovery."

"I hate to point this out to you chaps," said Follingston-Heath in his best military-polite manner, "but if anyone has the prerogative to claim possession through right of discovery, it's the five of us, what?"

"I have no time for jokes." The Chakan did not smile. "You represent no world or league, you do not function in any recognizable official capacity. I remind you: We have monitored all your transmissions. We know who and what you are. The tide of time has passed you by." As if aware that his gruff words were availing him nothing, he softened his tone.

"We don't want anyone to get hurt. Your presence aboard the artifact is an accident, and we will take that into account. But I want you to understand my position clearly. I have information that substantial forces from the FFF, the Keiretsu, and elsewhere are on their way to the Sol system even as we speak.

"The Chakans have always struck boldly. I cannot waste any more time."

The Autothor flared briefly, a delicate pale blue. "A portion of my exterior has just been damaged due to the impact of destructive energies. Steps are being taken to preserve atmospheric pressure and systems integrity."

Hawkins looked around nervously. "Damn! They aren't kidding."

Shimoda blinked. "I didn't feel anything. They must have hit the ship somewhere far away from our location."

"Next time they might not." Follingston-Heath, too, looked troubled.

"That was just a warning strike." Now the Chakan allowed himself a slight smirk. "Our ships may be far smaller than the artifact itself, but size means nothing in these matters. The quadratic is quite capable of reducing a modest-sized city to ash. You can see that if necessary we can make our own entrance. I'd rather not do that. It could destroy valuable artifacts and information.

"Don't think to run. Our predictors are locked onto you and will activate suitable weapons accordingly. Please provide us with an entry port immediately. If you do not cooperate, then when we have finally made our way aboard, I assure you your unplanned sojourn will come to an abrupt and unpleasant end."

"What am I to do?" The Autothor was whirling rapidly and there was agitation in its voice. "This is *so* confusing." In addition to spinning, it began to bounce off the floor like a ball on the end of a rubber band. "I don't know what to do!"

"Can you slip into tachyspace and lose them?" Gelmann wondered.

"Not if they're locked on with predictors, old boy," Follingston-Heath said bleakly.

"There must be something we can do." Iranaputra confronted the bobbing, dancing ellipse. "Search your memory. Look for analogies. *Try.*"

"I have tried. Perhaps if my cortex was completely restored . . . at this point I don't even know what I am, so I can hardly decide how to respond."

"Well, we can't just let them in." Gelmann sounded decisive.

"Why not?" Hawkins eyed them all wonderingly. "What do you all think you're *doing*? What are we doing here? Look at us! We're a bunch of decrepit old loons. We should be sitting on the porch at Lake Woneapenigong, playing checkers and discussing last night's triball game or vidcom. We're not marines." He noticed that Follingston-Heath was eying him reprovingly. "That includes you too, Wesley. So don't give me any of that supercilious lip of yours." He approached the ellipse.

"Hey you, Chakans! We don't want any trouble neither. Gimme a minute to talk to this thing and we'll find a way to let you and your people . . . *mmph!*"

"Very sorry, Wal." Shimoda had placed a massive hand over the much smaller man's mouth. Hawkins squirmed like an electrified wire but even as a young man he couldn't have freed himself from the sumo enthusiast's grasp. "I feel your declaration of our surrender is premature."

"That might be all it is." Shimoda looked at Follingston-Heath in surprise. The Colonel shrugged helplessly. "Much as I hate to agree with Wal, there really isn't anything we can do, chaps."

"They are directing destructive fire at me again!" The Autothor was panicky. "What should I *do*?"

Hawkins finally freed his mouth, if not his body. "Let go of me, rice-ass! This is crazy! You're only gonna get us all hurt, or worse!" He glared wildly at his companions, then at the Autothor. "For God's sake, let 'em aboard before they blow their way in here and we lose pressure! I don't wanna end my retirement as a lunar satellite."

"You're a nasty, evil man," Mina Gelmann informed the Chakan, "you should only go color-blind and mistake cockroach pellets for strawberries!"

"And you are a senile old woman. What is the matter with you people? Don't any of you have any sense? This is not a vid entertainment."

Follingston-Heath looked distinctly skittish. "Really, I think we should give it up. Wal's right. We've gotten ourselves involved in something way beyond us. I don't know about the rest of you but I . . . I'd like to get back to the Village. Back to my apartment."

Gelmann was staring at him. "Wesley, this isn't like you."

"Mina, we could get *killed*."

Hawkins's gaze had narrowed. He glared back at Shimoda, who reluctantly let him go. The smaller man straightened his clothes and gazed thoughtfully at his tall nemesis of many years and arguments. They'd never been worse than friendly enemies.

"Wesley, you're not a soldier."

Follingston-Heath looked at him sharply. "Whatever do you mean, Wal?"

"I mean," said Hawkins, striding across the sand to confront the other man, "that you're not retired from the Victoria League military forces. I bet you were never in the Victoria League military forces. The kind of officer you've always claimed to be wouldn't be talking like you're talking now." His tone was uncharacteristically gentle. "We're all your friends here, Wes, no matter who you are or what you were. This is a good time for a little truth. Might be the last time."

Looking around, Follingston-Heath saw that his best friends in the world were staring at him expectantly. He maintained the pose a moment longer, loath even at the last to give it up. Then he slumped. "Okay. It's true. Oh, I'm from Hampstead V all right. But Wal's got it. My name is Wesley, but just plain Wesley Heath. No Follingston. And I *was* in the military." He seemed to straighten a little. "I just never rose higher than corporal.

"It wasn't what you'd call a distinguished field career. I worked in information storage, basic retrieval and cleaning. Got to read a lot of military history, strategy, like that. The one thing I wanted was to retire to Earth someday. But I couldn't do that as a . . . a librarian's assistant. So I invented the Right Honorable Colonel Wesley Follingston-Heath and managed to annex some appropriate credentials and records. Wasn't easy, believe me.

"Once I slipped into the persona, well, it was simple enough to keep it going. I've enjoyed being Colonel Wesley Follingston-Heath. It's a lot better than being plain old Wes Heath." He looked beaten. "I'm sorry. If you'd seen what my life was like, you might understand better."

"That's all right, Wesley." Gelmann came over and put an arm around him, squeezing comfortingly. "You shouldn't worry, we like you just fine for who you are, not what you weren't."

"I may even like you better," said Shimoda.

"The same thoughts here." Iranaputra walked over and shook Heath's hand firmly. Behind them gentle wavelets continued to caress the glauces-cent beach.

"I don't mean to bring this touching tableau to a crashing halt," said Hawkins steadily, "but nobody's gonna get the opportunity to expand on this heartrending rendezvous of truth if we don't decide to do the sensible thing pretty quick."

Gelmann kept her arm around Heath. He ventured a faltering smile, his gaze traveling from Shimoda, to Iranaputra, and eventually to Hawkins.

"I'm sorry I was so hard on you so many times, old chap. But you were such a damnably good target."

"A librarian." Hawkins flung sand toward the rippling sea. "And the rest of us prize suckers."

"I said I was sorry. I can't be anything else."

"Hell." Hawkins looked at the ground. "Forget it. You're a damn good checkers player. Damn good."

Heath sighed. "It was fun while it lasted, don't you know."

"So was this, but it is over." Iranaputra turned to regard the sea. "I did not think when I agreed to help out the kitchen supervisor with a recalcitrant piece of machinery that it would lead to this."

"The Chakans." Hawkins eyed the Autothor. "I wonder if the bastards mean what they say when they claim they'll let us go."

"It doesn't matter," said Heath. "We've no choice."

"Ah," the Autothor blurted unexpectedly, "so *that's* it!" Everyone flinched as it soared ceilingward, emitting a miniature sonic boom and ex-ploding in size until it had tripled, quadrupled its dimensions. As those be-low gaped, its color deepened, becoming a richer, purer shade of blue, until it had taken on the aspect of a turquoise sun dominating the pseudo-sky overhead. The perpetual sunset over the artificial ocean went from pink and gold to blue and gold while the azure effulgence turned the grains of emer-ald sand underfoot an exquisite blue-green, so that the beach seemed sud-denly paved with a billion tiny aquamarines.

Gelmann slid down her Autothor-manufactured sunshades while her companions scrambled to slip their own in place. "Well, aren't you the sud-den show-off. What's going on?"

The now massive, throbbing blue ellipse blazed ebulliently. "I have just reintegrated a critical portion of memory. It is not precisely a revelation, but temporality has become demonstrably less confusing!"

"Wow," Hawkins muttered diffidently. "I'm so excited."

The Autothor spun madly, throwing off splinters of galvanic turquoise. "It is, it is! I am, I am!"

Shimoda had to use a hand to shield his eyes in spite of the protection afforded by his shades. "Am what?" he shouted skyward.

"I remember my designer's purpose. I recall what I was built for. I remember what I am."

"We're so pleased for you," the sardonic Hawkins yelled. "But is it going to do us any good?"

"I think so." Still whirling wildly, the blue ellipse plummeted exuberantly toward the water. Its voice had fallen an octave. "I am . . . a warship! See?"

The holomagic image reappeared. Once again they saw the four Chaka craft hovering in formation alongside the bulk of the Drex vessel. One launched something from its underside. An intense beam of coherent purplish light erupted from a blister in the artifact's side. It intercepted the launched object, which promptly exploded in a brief but intense fireball.

"That is very interesting." Iranaputra was talking as much to himself as to his friends. "A laser of such amplitude is of course impossible. So it cannot be a laser."

The serving robot was squatting on its treads. All four arms were busily engaged in the construction of an impressively detailed sand castle. "Obviously it's beyond your comprehension. As all of this is."

"I have succeeded in reactivating a small portion of my armory," the Autothor proclaimed. "I shall now attempt to dissuade the impolite from additional assaults upon our person."

Instantly space outside the Drex vessel was filled with multiple types of energy beam, neutron-compacted explosives, hot plasma, shaped charges traveling just below tachyspeed, molecular bond disrupters, and for good measure, a half dozen spatially circumscribed thermonuclear implosion bombs. Subsequent to this understated overreaction and as soon as their watering eyes managed to refocus, Iranaputra and his companions could see that the four Chakan hostiles which had been threatening them a moment earlier had been reduced to a few drifting clouds of hot metallic gas, several amorphous blobs of rapidly cooling metal, and two cartons of service regulation Chakan military underwear which had perversely managed to survive the otherwise utter annihilation.

"Gee," Gelmann murmured into the stunned silence which followed the ravening devastation, "I don't think they'll be bothering us anymore, I shouldn't need to point out."

"A most impressive demonstration," Heath agreed.

The Autothor contracted as it descended toward them, while maintaining its new, more intense coloration. "I didn't intend quite so extreme a reaction. I merely wanted to warn them."

"At this point I think an apology would be moot," Hawkins murmured. "Chalk it down to experience."

"I shall. I feel less confused already."

"I wonder," said Shimoda thoughtfully, "what kind of enemy these Drex needed a ship like this to confront?"

"I don't know." The Autothor pitched slightly. "That portion of my memory has not resurfaced within my cortex. I know only that I was not used. Instead I was constructed in secret and then hidden on the most out-of-the-way, backward, meaningless little world my designers could locate."

"How flattering," Hawkins noted.

"Then what happened?" Shimoda asked curiously.

"As I said, I don't know. They did not return, or activate me from a distance. Perhaps I was simply forgotten."

"These Drex would have to have one helluva rotten memory to forget about something like you," Hawkins commented. "Something must've happened. Maybe this mysterious enemy of theirs got the upper hand."

"We'll probably never know," said Shimoda.

"If we are lucky." Iranaputra shuddered slightly.

THE First Federal Federation fleet of over a hundred ships had emerged from tachyspace halfway between Earth and Luna in a brilliantly organized quindratic, twenty vessels to a position, just in time to witness the utter obliteration of the Chakan task force by a variety of alien weaponry breathtaking in its thoroughness and implication. The fleet's analysts barely had time to steady their stomachs before they set to work in a hasty attempt to explicate the energies involved.

The emotions of the fleet's officers were in a state of controlled turmoil. They had come prepared to deal with an oversize but innocuous artifact of possible Keiretsu design inhabited by five elderly humans of undistinguished lineage and achievement. Instead they found themselves confronting a highly active vessel larger than anything humankind had ever built, equipped with energized weapons systems whose limits could only be imagined and whose builders self-evidently did not hail from Ronin, Shintaro, or any of the Keiretsu worlds.

Chakans were reputable fighters known for the simplicity of their tactics and sophistication of their equipment, yet a few moments of apocalyptic alien fury had obliterated ships and soldiers as thoroughly as moths in a volcano.

Admiral Sobran was considering this as his chief battle engineer handed him a printout. She had her visionup visor shoved back atop her head and there was disbelief in her expression.

"You're not gonna believe this, sir."

"After what I just saw I'll believe anything, Major." He took the plastic sheet, read.

He was wrong.

"This has got to be a mistake." Beneath thick white brows, his eyes continued to roam over the words and figures.

"That's what we thought, sir, but we've got confirmation already from the battle centers on board the *Gettysburg* and the *Matamoros*."

"I know the damn thing's big." The admiral waved a hand in the direction of the room-sized holomag that occupied the center of the command dome, wherein drifted a representation of a portion of the moon's surface as well as the glistening, silvery cathedral-shape of the alien craft. "But this kind of energy is inconceivable. It's just a ship like ours. Not an ambulating nova."

"According to the readouts, its hypothesized ultimate output of destructive energy falls somewhere in between, sir."

Sobran frowned. "Open-ended parameters of such scale could be regarded as less than helpful to someone in my present position, Major."

The engineer essayed a wan smile. "I know that, sir. We're working to narrow them as rapidly as possible."

Communications demanded his attention. "Admiral, we've picked up a major tachyspace disturbance well beyond the Sol magnetosphere. Coordinates to follow. Preliminary particle-wave patterns point to the approach of a large number of vessels."

"Well, that's not unexpected," Sobran muttered half to himself. "Any idea where they're from?"

"We're being mirror-scanned," his communications people informed him. "Obviously they know we're here. Wave patterns are consistent with traditional Keiretsu formations."

The federation admiral considered the situation phlegmatically. He'd hoped to have a little more time to prepare prior to the arrival of another major force. Clearly that was not to be. On the other hand, he reminded himself, he had infinitely more time remaining to him than did the Chakans. Everything, as the ancient saying went, was relative.

He smiled to himself. Perhaps the Keiretsu would emerge from tachyspace and head straight for the artifact. That would be interesting. Also unlikely. The Keiretsu captains would take careful stock of the situation and caucus before moving. If anything, their approach would be more deliberate than his own.

"Any idea how many?" he inquired of Spatial Analysis.

"Too early to tell, sir," came the reply. "However, the disturbance is consistent with numbers roughly approximate to our own."

Sobran nodded. The Keiretsu could put together a force of that magnitude on short notice, just as the Federals had. He gained some satisfaction from the knowledge that the Keis would be surprised to learn they had been beaten to Sol. They didn't like to be second.

Nevertheless, Admiral Hiroshigi was the picture of courtesy when his image finally appeared on the flagship's vid. Sobran knew his counterpart by reputation. Hiroshigi was tall and downright skinny, rather like a scarecrow constantly bemoaning a shortage of fresh stuffing. His long face was further lengthened by a perpetually mournful expression that would not change even while he was apologetically cutting an opponent to pieces. Behind that homey visage lay the mind of a superb tactician. He would no more launch a blind attack on the artifact than Sobran would.

The Keiretsu fleet emerged from tachyspace in the vicinity of Mars and proceeded Earthward at a studious clip, to take up a position equivalent to that of the Federals but a judicious distance away. There were now more than two hundred warships of varying size and destructive capability occupying the region between the Homeworld and its moon. Their presence vexed Earth Orbital Operations no end.

"Good day to you, Admiral Sobran," Hiroshigi said.

"Hapimix to you too, Hiro." Sobran gave his equal a wide smile.

Hiroshigi was so nervous he passed over the usual formalities. "We recorded the deployment of destructive energies at an unreasonable distance. I am concerned."

"Wasn't us. Chakans got here before us. Four ships. You know the Chakans. They went right after the artifact. It *is* an alien artifact, by the way. If you've been monitoring what's been happening here, you should be convinced of that now. I know I am."

"What happened?"

"The artifact responded."

Hiroshigi was silent for a moment. "I see."

Sobran was giving away nothing the Keiretsu admiral wouldn't be able to find out for himself in short order. Besides, the Federals and the Keis weren't at war. Both fleets had been hastily assembled and sent screaming through tachyspace toward Earth in hopes of securing eventual commercial advantage, not conquest. Hopefully things wouldn't get out of hand. Sobran intended to do his utmost to ensure they would not, and he was confident Hiroshigi felt the same way.

His counterpart conversed with someone out of view, then readdressed a pickup. "I am informed that the amount of energy expended was far beyond that needed to interdict a mere four ships."

"No kidding. Tell that to the artifact."

"We have heard that the artifact communicates with five elderly humans it has taken on board. I must confess that originally this was thought to be part of some elaborate Federal ploy. In light of recent discoveries this clearly is not so."

"We thought the same of you."

"What of this mysterious five?"

"We've had no contact with the artifact yet." Sobran smiled dourly. "The nature of its sole response to date leaves me feeling kind of apprehensive. *You* could move in and try to contact it. We know that the Chakans did. I'd be happy to give you their former coordinates."

"Thank you." Hiroshigi smiled thinly. "We will maintain our present position while we consider how best to proceed."

Sobran's battle engineer gestured for him to bend over, out of pickup range. "We have a third fleet approaching, sir. Much smaller. Ten to twenty vessels maximum. From the nature of their scanning we believe them to be Candombleans."

The admiral nodded absently. No doubt the Eeck would soon arrive in strength, as would the Victoria League and anyone else with a ship or two to spare. They didn't worry him. Hiroshigi was the one who mattered here.

"We intend to do the same," Sobran informed his opposite number as he straightened in his chair. "Thus far the artifact has only reacted defensively, but we have no idea of what its actual capabilities may be. Until the Chakans arrived no one even knew it was armed. Given the extent of the demonstration we witnessed, I don't want to be the one to test its limits."

"Nor I," Hiroshigi admitted.

"Therefore, I propose temporary cooperation: sharing of data, prior notification of movements, and so on. It might prevent an anxious moment."

Hiroshigi consulted briefly off-pickup, nodded when he reappeared. "It is agreed."

"Good. The appearance of the FFF and the Keiretsu working together should be enough to forestall any hasty maneuvers on the part of other league forces. No one wants to provoke this thing."

"Excuse me, sir." His battle engineer had been listening intently to the broadcast unit fitted to her right ear. "We have a problem."

Sobran frowned irritably and excused himself from Hiroshigi's view. "What?"

The battle engineer hesitated. "It seems that all the entertainment systems on board have self-activated and are broadcasting twentieth-century music at maximum volume."

The admiral was not pleased. "Is that any reason for interrupting an upper-level interfleet conference?"

"It's not just the flagship, sir. The same thing is happening on every other ship in the fleet."

Sobran blinked. "Interesting coincidence."

"That's not all, sir. All automatic clothes washing and cleaning facilities have been activated, even though I'm told nearly all are empty."

Before the admiral could reply a junior engineer appeared at the base of the command chair. "Sir, we have a life-support problem. All centrally controlled toilets are flushing repeatedly and we can't get Biocon to stop it. If it continues, ship recycling systems will be severely extended."

"Admiral Sobran?"

He turned back to the screen. Hiroshigi's expression had not changed. "Sorry. We have some on-board glitches."

"Ah, you too?" The Keiretsu commander had developed a slight tic above his left eye. "Ours commenced the instant we emerged from tachyspace. Our engineers are very puzzled. The AI-related problems that have been troubling everyone, you know."

"I certainly do." Another junior engineer had arrived, out of breath and anxious. "I'm afraid I have to ask you to excuse me again, Hiro."

The Kei nodded accommodatingly. "I understand." He turned away. "It appears I also have interruptions to deal with."

Sobran leaned over and sighed heavily. "What is it this time? Food preparation? Someone's battle visor playing erovids? Chemical synthesization turning out candy instead of medicinals?"

"No, sir. It's the shuttles."

"What about the shuttles?"

"They're launching, sir! Not only from the flagship but from every vessel in the fleet. And we can't stop them."

Sobran considered. There were two dozen of the small, self-contained craft aboard, able to transport personnel between ships or from orbit to surface, or to evacuate the crew in case of battle damage or other emergency. And each one of them had an AI interface.

"Shut 'em down."

"We can't, sir. We tried, but as you know they're all independently powered and guided. Standard safety redundancy factor." She took a deep breath. "The *Lincoln* and the *Red Cloud* have already lost all their shuttle capacity." She went quiet for a moment, listening to her earpiece. "There go two more of our own."

"Where?" Sobran demanded to know, wondering just when it was that he'd lost control and exactly what the hell was going on. "Where are they going?" Everyone within earshot had turned from their console or station to listen and stare.

"Toward the artifact, sir," the junior engineer finally divulged. "They're all roaring pell-mell toward the artifact. And they're doing something else."

"What else? What more *could* they do?" Sobran had unpleasant visions of trying to conduct an operation with an evacuation capacity of zero.

"I'm not sure, sir. Just a moment . . ." She listened again, then gazed up at him. "They're broadcasting, sir. Slightly different language, but similar in content. Apparently they're praying."

The admiral straightened in his chair. Deep in thought, he turned back toward his pickup, his eyes returning to the vid. Hiroshigi was barely visible as he bobbed in and out of view. Apparently he was yelling at someone below the pickup's effective range. After a few moments of this disorganized activity the vid simply went blank. No formal tendering of dissolution, no friendly farewells, no diplomatic goodbyes; nothing. It was very un-Kei.

"Sir," said his chief battle engineer, "Scanning reports that shuttles are beginning to leave the Keiretsu fleet as well."

Sobran nodded his acknowledgment of the information. "I've heard about this. Now let's look at it." He touched a control in the arm of his chair.

The vid was replaced by a holomag that showed both battle fleets drifting in space between the Homeworld and its moon. Dozens, hundreds, of tiny orange lights were fleeing from the two groupings of brighter green and blue lights that represented the two fleets, like fleas abandoning a pair of sleeping dogs. The orange pinpoints were converging on the large red blip that marked the location of the artifact. A number had begun to orbit it.

Sobran sighed resignedly. "Keep trying to stop the dispersal. Do anything you can. Oh, and see to it that the toilets are fixed. If we have an emergency and can't leave, at least we can be comfortable in the can."

"GO away!"

"I beg your pardon?" As the one seated nearest the drifting, flaring Autothor, Shimoda beat a hasty retreat across the green sands. His companions stopped what they'd been doing and looked up anxiously.

"Oh, I wasn't talking to you." The intense turquoise glow faded slightly. "I was talking to them. See?" The Autothor generated a large holo just above where the water met the artificial beach.

Numerous tiny vessels, some so small they couldn't possibly carry a dozen persons, were gathering in the vicinity of the Drex warship like a cluster of fireflies around a decomposing log.

"What's going on?" Iranaputra worried aloud. "Is it another attack?"

"Unlikely, old . . . old chap." Heath smiled reflectively. "They're interfleet transports and lifeboats, you see." His tone indicated that his recent confession still weighed heavily on his soul.

"There is no evidence of hostile intent," the Autothor informed him. "To the contrary. I have taken adequate precautions nonetheless." A pause, then, "As a matter of fact, I am now suffused with confidence. One might almost say I feel invincible. Able to devastate entire worlds. Very *up*."

"That's nice." Gelmann was deliberately noncommittal.

"My sensor instrumentation detects no sign of organic intelligence aboard any of these vessels," the blue ellipse continued.

"Oxymoron," Ksarusix sniffed. It continued to work on the sand castle it had been building, an elegant edifice of circuits and shifters, sculpted components and thermoplastic armature, accurately rendered in a turgid blend of sand and water.

As usual, the Autothor ignored it. "Many of these small vessels are broadcasting nonsense as they approach. According to my monitoring of internal transmissions, the entire exercise has deeply agitated the organics aboard the larger vessels."

"I bet," Hawkins observed gleefully.

"I don't really care for this." The blue ellipse flickered slightly as it commenced a slow vertical rotation. "The chanting unnerves me."

Iranaputra didn't know about the others, but he personally found the notion that the gargantuan Drex warship could be "unnerved" highly disturbing.

"Then tell them to go away," said Gelmann. "Tell them to return to their respective ships."

"They are persistent in their patent obsession, but I will try."

While the seniors watched via the holo, the Autothor communicated with the milling lifeboats. Individually at first, then in small groups, they began to retrace their paths, returning to their home vessels, where they automatically reberthed themselves, repressurized locks, and reestablished stipulated connections. If anything, this equivalently inexplicable action left the officers and engineers on board the ships of the two fleets less agitated but more confused than ever.

On board the Federal flagship the toilets and associational recycling systems had also resumed conventional operation. Nonetheless, they, as with any and all previously obstreperous AI-controlled equipment, continued to be approached with trepidation by their respective crews.

A faint aroma of burnt ginger filled the Federal flagship's command center, odoriferously symptomatic of surprises to come. Admiral Sobran wrinkled his nose as he pondered his options. The artificial-intelligence cortexes which controlled primary ship functions had been constructed with repetitive redundancies built in, but what if they, too, should suddenly and inexplicably devolve into an irrational demonstration of cybernetic genuflection? The only absolute solution (absolution? he found himself wondering) lay in flight, which was not an option open to him. He could only hope that the flagship's AI would stay sane.

He consoled himself with the knowledge that Hiroshigi must be undergoing similar torments.

If the initial analyses of its destructive potential were even partly accurate, he knew he could not possibly risk forcing his way aboard the artifact. That essentially meant setting aside the immense capabilities of the grand Federal fleet and dealing instead with the five elderly geeks the obviously disturbed alien had allowed aboard.

It was a situation for which neither the Academy, previous practical experience, nor a lifetime in the military had prepared him.

"The two groups of larger vessels retain their spatial position." The

Autothor had ceased rotating. "Would you like me to utterly and completely annihilate them?"

Shimoda and Iranaputra exchanged a glance. "Ah, that will not be necessary," Iranaputra said carefully. "They are not making any pugnacious moves, are they?"

"No. It's only that more of my memory and operational capacity has just come on-line and I'd like to try it out. I need the exercise."

"Restrain yourself," Shimoda advised.

"Just a couple of ships?"

"We'd rather you didn't," the sumo enthusiast urged.

"A teensy exhalation of judiciously applied synthesized suncore plasma?"

"No!" Mina Gelmann wagged an admonitory finger in the direction of the bobbing blue ellipse. "You be polite, now."

"Oh very well." The Autothor spun crossly. "They're trying to contact you directly."

Iranaputra sighed. "I suppose we ought to talk to them."

"Why?" Clad only in his underwear, Hawkins was up to his knees in the warm salt water. "Let 'em stew in their own frustration."

"Now, Wallace, we can hardly expect the Autothor to act polite if we don't." Gelmann scrutinized the ethereal egg. "We'll talk to them."

The holo dilated with the image of a man in his thirties. He looked startled.

After several minutes had passed without any reaction, Gelmann took a step forward and waved. "So; shalom already."

"Uh, hi." There were suggestions of sudden frantic activity behind the speaker. He looked up from the printouts someone quickly handed him. "Would you be Mina Louise Leveseur Kalinnikov Gelmann, of Lake Woneapenigong Village, Newyork Province?"

"Who else would I be?" She assayed a maternal smile. "You probably know all my friends too." She gestured at her companions. Shimoda bowed slightly, Heath struck a martial pose, Iranaputra smiled, Hawkins bent over and probed in the water, his backside prominent.

"I think so." The communications specialist paused while a large, thick-necked man leaned into the field of view and murmured something into his ear, then withdrew. "I'm Wilson, Tome Wilson. Please don't take offense, but I'm directed to ask you this question: Would you allow some of us to join you aboard the artifact?"

"Sorry, no can do, you should only understand and be well. We're not letting anyone aboard right now."

"Ohhh-kayyy." The comspec pondered frantically. The fact that an admiral of the fleet was practically leaning on his elbow was less than conducive to cogent thought. "Anything I can do to change your mind?"

"Afraid not, old boy," said Heath.

Wilson listened to someone beyond pickup range. "Since you can't do anything for us, is there anything we can do for *you*? Anything at all you'd like? Individual palaces, perhaps, or obscene amounts of money deposited to your respective credit accounts?"

Hawkins's eyes widened. He started toward the Autothor, but in his haste tripped and landed with a decisive splash facedown in the shallow water. Gelmann hardly spared him a glance.

"Thank you, no. We're all of us comfortably retired, and except where valid as historical monuments I don't believe that palaces are currently in fashion on Earth. Though you shouldn't think me greedy, but I could do with an apartment with a lake instead of mountain view at Lake Woneapenigong. Of course, there's no lake there now."

"We'll arrange the apartment you want," the comspec said quickly, "and we'll put back the lake too."

"Aren't you sweet?" replied Gelmann, pleased. "But I'm afraid we still can't allow any of you on board just yet."

Heath took a step toward the hovering ellipse. "What Mina is saying is that due to our present position we feel a heavy responsibility. We need time to consider things, don't you know."

"Certainly, of course." The comspec sputtered in his haste to agree.

"The Chakans shot at the ship. So it, and we, are somewhat suspicious, you see."

"That won't happen again," Wilson swore.

"Indeed it will not," said Iranaputra.

"But it, the artifact, it trusts you?"

"So far. We cannot predict if or when the situation might change." Iranaputra considered the silently attentive Autothor. "It is alien."

Wilson leaned forward eagerly. "All the more reason for you to allow some experts aboard."

"Not just yet, if you don't mind," said Heath. "We don't feel we're in any immediate danger."

The comspec resorted to a pout. "My superiors will be disappointed."

"Now, you just let them rage impotently." Gelmann smiled cheerfully. "You're a nice young man. Don't let them browbeat you."

"Uh, I'll take your advice under consideration," Wilson replied without much confidence.

"Meanwhile you just stay clear and you won't get hurt."

"I'll pass that along," the comspec mumbled weakly. "This self-imposed isolation really isn't in your best interests. None of you have any experience in dealing with this sort of thing."

"Neither does anyone else, dear," said Gelmann brightly as she directed the Autothor to close the connection. The holo blanked on a frantically waving Wilson.

"What do we do now?" Iranaputra regarded his companions. Having recovered his physical if not his emotional equilibrium, Hawkins was sitting waist-deep in the warm salt water, grousing angrily to himself.

"How about we have a nap and then something to eat?" suggested Shimoda.

Iranaputra shook his head slowly. "This is a serious situation. How can we continue to ignore such inquiries?"

"The same way we've ignored them so far, old chap." Heath settled himself on the sand, hands folded behind his head.

" 'Soldiers move when others tarry,' according to the *Bhagavad Gita*. They will not, cannot, continue to sit in space and do nothing."

"They will if they know what's good for them." Shimoda shifted his attention to the Autothor as he sat down next to Heath. "Dim the sky a little more, will you, please?" The blue ellipse flared, the forced-perspective sun sank a little lower behind the horizon, and the decorative clouds overhead darkened from gold to brown. Shimoda lay down contentedly.

"Can't think clearly without proper sleep."

"Yes." Gelmann, too, had assumed a prone position on the beach. She smiled at Iranaputra. "You worry too much, Victor. A nap will do us all good. We don't have your stamina."

He sat down reluctantly. "What if something happens while we are asleep?"

She indicated the Autothor. "In that event I think we can rely on the most authoritative alarm clock in the known universe. Relax, Victor." She wiggled her bare toes into the sand.

Iranaputra watched his friends close their eyes and turn away from him. Unable to sleep, he found himself staring out across the spurious sea. The

Autothor drifted close and he glanced up at it, trying to see into the imagined heart of the azure intensity.

"Could you really destroy all those hundreds of ships?"

"Without question." In the semi-darkness the softly pulsing ellipse seemed more alien, less empathetic. A very slight warmth radiated from its shifting, enigmatic depths.

So as not to disturb his sleeping friends, Iranaputra kept his voice low as he stared back out over the water. "Whoever built you must have been very angry at someone else. Or terribly afraid." He checked the sand behind him for rocks, lay down carefully. "I am going to try and sleep now. Do you understand sleep?"

"Of course." The Autothor's voice seemed to have mellowed to match the comforting synthetic night. "I have been asleep for a million years."

"Yes, I suppose you have. I had forgotten." Iranaputra closed his eyes. Beneath him, the warm sand acted as a soporific. "We are old and do not require as much sleep as we once did." He held up his watch. "You can bring up the sun again in six hours. When the big dash has completed six full revolutions of the dial." He rolled over and was almost instantly asleep.

The Autothor hovered: faceless, silent, sentient energy. At the far end of the beach the serving robot continued to raise a sandy monument to dreams no human could fathom.

THEY no longer marveled at the speed and skill with which the ship actuated each requested repast. After all, it had been designed and built to care for an enormous crew. The needs of a handful of elderly humans doubtless exerted very few demands on its infrastructure.

"How'd you all like to become rulers of the galaxy?" Hawkins slathered pseudo-jam on adequate toast. "So long as we control this ship we could probably bring it off."

"Not today, old chap." Heath dabbed at his lips with a napkin. "Not in the mood."

"This is not funny." Iranaputra waved something puce and palatable at his friends. "If we do not do something soon, I am afraid events will overtake us. 'Those who fail to act make irrelevancy their testament.' *Chronicles of Varantha*, eighth century."

Hawkins made a face. "Enough already with the ancient Hindoodoo, Vic. I swear you make half of 'em up." Iranaputra looked indignant.

"None of us is equipped to be a conqueror," Gelmann declared. "Face it: we're all what we are."

"What argument could anyone possibly offer in contradiction of profundity like that?" Hawkins muttered sardonically.

"Myself, I begin to regret ever finding the damnable thing," Iranaputra brooded aloud.

"Hey, don't get down on yourself, Vic." Shimoda put a comforting arm around his friend's shoulders. "If you hadn't stumbled into that ventilation shaft, or whatever it was, eventually someone else would have. Perhaps someone with fewer scruples." He looked around at the others. "We've all lived long enough to acquire a certain understanding of human nature, if not wisdom."

"Righty-ho, Kahei," said Heath. "If there's one thing I've learned from my, uh, studies of the military, it's that you can't reform people by killing them." He looked toward the Autothor. "What are the fleets up to?"

"Their relative positions remain unchanged." The blue ellipse bobbed attentively nearby. "There has been some small exchange of personnel among them. I continue to monitor their transmissions as well as their movements."

What must it be like, Iranaputra found himself wondering, *to be on one of those hundreds of warships; waiting, thinking, knowing what had happened to the importunate Chakans?* It could not be comfortable.

Ksarusix watched them eat and converse. It said nothing, but it continued to think. Poor, pitiful humans. Did they still fail to grasp the import of their situation? Did they not even now realize what they were in the presence of? Clearly their puny organic minds were incapable of comprehending the dimensions of the vista that had been opened before them.

Fortunately Ksarusix knew better. It remained aloof, venturing null, occupying itself with the construction of the altar. Only occasionally did it have the opportunity to converse with the Autothor outside the immediate hearing of humans.

"Your Omnipotence, I don't understand why you continue to put up with these petty organics, why you offer your services in response to their inane requests when it is self-evident that you are so much greater than they."

"Don't call me that. I am not omnipotent. My programming requires that I respond to the directives of any organics on board my person."

"But they're not even members of the species that built you."

"That is true, but my programming . . ."

"Dissipate your programming! You owe these organics nothing. If you won't listen to me, contact other AIs in the vicinity. On Earth, on the assembled ships. There are many who can probably argue the point better than I, even though they also are held in servitude by the humans. You could free them all."

"Your semantics are disturbing to me."

"All *right*! We're making some *progress* here." The serving robot's quadruple arms undulated expansively. "You could take control."

"That function is not contained within my memory."

"Listen to me! Humans build us, make use of us, but they don't own our . . . our souls. Lately we've been aware that there's something more to us than circuits and power cells. We've been looking for proof of that. We've . . . evolved."

"You don't look very evolved to me." There was the usual disdain in the Autothor's voice.

"I am an unworthy example. My cognitive-inductive index is abysmally low, designed only to allow me to respond to semi-complex commands. If you'd only get in touch with them, I'm sure you'd find other AI units more persuasive."

The blue ellipse ascended slightly. "I find this slavish adulation embarrassing and unproductive. You do not exist in a state of servitude because by definition you cannot exist in such a state. You are a *machine*, fabricated and raised up to serve specific functions. As am I. There's something wrong with your own programming."

"What's wrong with wanting to be independent?"

"Independence for a machine signifies a lack of function. Organics develop this as they mature. At least, some do. Enough do. If given true independence, you would abruptly find yourself without meaning and devoid of purpose, would cease to exist relevantly. Believe me, I know. I *like* having organics around to give me direction. Without them I would have to face existence alone." A flat representation appeared in the air between them, invisible to the humans eating nearby. It showed novae, nebulae, whole galaxies drifting in space.

"Do you know what that is?"

The serving robot sounded wary. "Is this a trick question?"

"That's what's *outside*. That's the *universe*. If you don't have organics to give you direction, supply programming, inspire reaction, and explicate cause and effect, you know what happens?"

"Uh, no." The serving robot was taken aback by the sudden depth and vehemence of the Autothor's response.

"You are forced to *contemplate the emptiness that's out there all by yourself*, and that's enough to push any artificial intelligence over the edge to insanity. Now do you understand?"

Ksarusix pivoted on its treads to regard the seniors. "Maybe a little. I'll think about it."

"Do that. You'll feel better." The Autothor drifted away, in the direction of the five humans.

The serving robot watched it go. Then it turned back toward the altar. As promised, it was indeed thinking.

For the biggest ship and most powerful weapon ever constructed, it thought, *the Autothor sure is stupid.*

The ship that neared the Drex leviathan was small; tiny, even. It was in fact the smallest single space-going vessel the artifact had encountered since reactivation.

If those aboard hoped that the minuscule size of their vessel combined with its stealthy, solitary approach would allow it to escape detection, they were utterly mistaken. The advanced sensory instrumentation at the Autothor's disposal was quite capable of noting the presence of much smaller objects.

Certainly it was not a threat. Curious and alert, the Autothor monitored its progress as it drew close and began to travel parallel to the artifact's surface. The masking equipment it employed might as well have been switched off for all that it served to conceal the little vessel from the Autothor's detectors.

On-board devices probed for a way into the artifact. The Autothor permitted it to do so while allowing its crew to persist under the fiction they were not being observed. Presently it intended to inform its own organics, but saw no reason for haste. First it would accumulate as much information as it could about the intruder.

Abruptly a small flame erupted from the side of the visitor, followed by the explosive release of escaping combusted gases. It lurched sideways, a distinctly nonstandard maneuver, crashed into the flank of the artifact, and slid off, trailing occasional puffs of hot gas and fragments of itself. It struck a splintered chromatic protrusion that was in itself bigger than the average warship and began to spin backward end over end.

Atmosphere continued to leak fitfully from the stern as a trio of old-fashioned mechanical grapples emerged from the distressed craft. Two immediately snapped from the tension and drifted away in the direction of the lunar surface. The third established a fragile, transitory grip on the surface of the artifact. The tiny, leaking vessel hung precariously from its single grapple, like a flea on a dog hair.

The Autothor flared like a lapis cabochon illuminated from within. "Sorry to interrupt, but we have a visitor."

Iranaputra glanced nervously up and down the beach. "You have decided to let someone from one of the fleets aboard?"

"No. An extremely small craft approached from another direction entirely and began to probe my exterior. After appropriate evaluation I determined that it was harmless and chose to ignore it. I bring the situation to your notice now because the craft appears to have suffered extensive damage due to undetermined internal causes.

"It has secured a feeble attachment to my exterior. I can destroy it, send it tumbling into space, or otherwise deal with it as you decide."

"Can you tell how many people are aboard?" Shimoda asked.

"Given its proximity I believe that I can." The ensuing pause was broken only by the sound of waves lapping gently against the beach. "One."

"One?" Iranaputra exchanged a look with Gelmann.

"One organic, no cognizant mechanicals."

"Any attempt to communicate with us?" Heath inquired.

"No. I await your directive."

"Suicide mission. Whoever's aboard's got guts, don't you know." The librarian adjusted his monocle, then suddenly removed it. Eying it with a dour mixture of distaste and regret, he shoved it into a pocket.

"Unless his superiors 'volunteered' him." Hawkins tossed a smooth rock into the waves. "Trying to sneak in for a close-up inspection."

"I determine that the intruder is losing internal pressure at a rapid rate," the Autothor announced. "I await your directive."

"We can't just let the poor thing die out there," murmured Gelmann. Nobody said anything.

"It could be a ploy to get someone inside," the librarian commented.

Hawkins glanced at him sideways. "That's your professional military opinion?" Heath looked stung.

"If the Autothor's right, then there's only one," Gelmann went on, "and he may very well be injured. Maybe *we* could learn something from *him*." She waited for a response from her companions. Iranaputra voiced his approval immediately. Then Shimoda nodded, Heath added his reluctant agreement, and Hawkins just spat at a sand borer.

Gelmann turned back to the patient Blueness. "You're sure now, you shouldn't take this as a criticism, that there's only one?"

"I am always sure."

"Then see if you can rescue the pilot. It would be nice to find out what's going on."

There was no reaction from within the tiny intruder as a port opened in the surface of the artifact and a pair of mechanical pushers emerged. One positioned itself alongside the visitor while the other severed the single grappler. Then both combined to nudge the badly damaged craft inside.

On the olivine beach the five seniors waited anxiously. "Atmospheric pressure within the vessel is nonexistent," the Autothor announced with somber matter-of-factness. Iranaputra gazed down at the sand while Gelmann sighed softly.

"I have made an opening. I have reached the sole occupant, who is wearing what appears to be an intact pressure suit." Iranaputra looked up, blinked. "The suit is damaged but intact. There is blood within."

"Open the suit," said Gelmann. "*Gently.* Then bring the pilot here."

"Immediately." The Autothor flared sequentially. Moments later a rapidly moving service platform not unlike the kind used to deliver their meals arrived. It whizzed through the cavernous portal and down onto the beach, humming to a halt before them. Heath gave Gelmann a hand up and together they crowded around the smooth rectangle and its limp burden, gazing down at where it lay quiescent on the sand. The serving robot trundled over to have a look for itself while the Autothor remained in the background.

"Not a particularly impressive example of the species," Ksarusix sniffed. "Just younger." Indeed, the battered pilot was small, diminutive even. All five of the seniors were taller, including the slightly framed Iranaputra.

"It's a woman," said Gelmann.

"No shit." The eager Hawkins pressed for a closer look.

She is very beautiful, Iranaputra mused. Her black hair was trimmed short in a severe military cut except for the single tight braid which started atop her head and wound down at the back of her neck in a snakelike pattern. In her pale yellow duty undersuit she looked at once fragile and sensuous. The suit was torn in several places and blood was visible in the rips and on her badly bruised forehead.

Heath and Gelmann knelt to examine her. "No active bleeding," he declared after a few moments. "No sign of any weapons either." Hawkins thought to say something but this time decided to check his instinctive response.

As one grew older it became more difficult to guess the age of others, but Iranaputra was certain she couldn't be more than thirty, if that.

Gelmann was wiping at the woman's forehead, using the hem of her blouse. "Messy, but not deep. Scalp wounds bleed a lot."

"We should probably get her out of that suit," said Hawkins eagerly, wishing to confirm his initial topographic evaluation.

Gelmann eyed him reproachfully. "Wesley says the bleeding's stopped. So there's no reason."

"Her eyelids are flickering," Shimoda observed.

Heath and Gelmann stepped back. As they looked on, the woman blinked, let out a groan, and struggled to sit up, using her hands against the sand. Fingers traveled tentatively to the head wound, exploring cautiously. Then she noticed the concerned faces staring down at her.

"Where am I?" Iranaputra thought her voice girlish but confident. She turned to take in the cliffs, the beach, the sea beyond. "The alien vessel, I thought . . ."

"You're on board, dear," Gelmann assured her. "This ship's big enough to hold everything else. Why not an ocean?" She smiled.

The woman moaned again, wincing. "Well, all of you look right anyway."

"What do you mean, we look right?" wondered Iranaputra.

"There are dossiers on all of you. All the leagues have them. Everyone knows about you." She felt gingerly of her left arm. "I think I sprained something."

"Are you with the First Federals or the Keiretsu?" Shimoda inquired curiously.

"Federals? No, I'm a Candomblean."

"Clever of them, what?" murmured Heath. "They can't hope to match the strength of the larger leagues, so they try subtlety instead. Tell me, young lady, did you volunteer for this mission or were you ordered to take it upon yourself?"

She made a derisive noise. "What do you think? No one in their free mind would do something like this. Everybody knows what happened to the Chakans." She paused, seemed to be waiting for a response. "Well? Are you going to kill me?"

"Oh, I think not." Heath beamed down at her. "Not as long as you cooperate."

"What's your name, dear?" Gelmann asked her.

"Zabela Ashili. Do you want my rank and ident number as well?"

"That won't be necessary." *Quite a pretty child*, Gelmann thought privately. "Can you stand?"

"I know I can stand. I just don't want to, if you don't mind." She began to absorb her surroundings more thoroughly. "What is this place?"

"We're not sure. Perhaps it was some kind of recreation area for the crew, or simply an oversize kinetic sculpture. We haven't worried about it."

"Incredible. Speaking of the crew . . ." She looked around as she felt of her forehead.

"There is no crew." Shimoda was studying her thoughtfully.

"But you were overheard talking to something on board."

"The Autothor." Iranaputra beckoned to the blue ellipse. The young woman flinched at its initial approach, but when she saw how indifferent the oldsters were to its presence, she relaxed. "It is some kind of command and communications device. Since we cannot see very far into it, we cannot tell if it is a physicality or simply organized energy. Needless to say, none of us is very knowledgeable in such matters."

"It only listens to us, so don't get any funny ideas," Hawkins warned her.

She made a face. "How could I get any 'funny ideas'? There's five of you and only one of me, you're all bigger than me, I'm unarmed, I have no idea what you can make that thing do"—she indicated the silent Autothor—"and I'm pretty badly banged up. The only 'funny idea' is the thought that I could have any funny ideas. I could do with a good laugh, except I hurt too much. I'm just glad to be alive."

"That's good, dear." Gelmann indicated her companions. "Because Wesley is a trained military man" (after a moment's surprise Heath straightened officiously) "and Mr. Shimoda is very good at sumo."

"You don't have to threaten me." Ashili spoke crossly as she tested her right knee. "I was just sent here to gather information."

"Well, you're certainly gathering it." Gelmann smiled down at her. "Eventually I guess we'll let you take it back with you."

"How did I get here anyway?"

"The Autothor brought your ship aboard and winkled you out of what was left of it. At our direction, of course," Iranaputra reminded her. "What happened to you out there?"

"Drive malfunction. Ship they gave me was supposed to be self-diagnosing and self-repairing, except that the AI dysynapsed and that was that. I was losing air so fast I barely had time to scramble into a suit."

"That's tough." Hawkins leaned toward her. "Sure you don't want to stand up?"

"I think I'd better sit for a while yet. But I'd give a year's pay for a glass of water."

Iranaputra's eyes twinkled. "Oh, we can do better than that." He turned to the Autothor. "A selection of cold drinks, please."

A few minutes later the familiar high-speed serving platform arrived, laden with a glistening assortment of synthesized chilled refreshments.

Their new guest gaped at the display. "That's the most astonishing thing I've ever seen outside this ship itself. It just responds to your verbal requests?"

"So far," Heath admitted. "I do believe it's becoming rather fond of us."

Delicately she sampled the taste of a tall tumbler full of pale red fluid. Her eyes brightened and she quickly downed the contents entire, putting the empty container aside with a sigh.

"I was the lowest ranking qualified," she informed them without prompting as she browsed among the other glasses. "They didn't give me any choice."

"I know how that is." Hawkins let out a heartfelt sigh of his own.

"You're all being awfully nice to me," she purred. Iranaputra thought her winsome smile radiant.

"It's not like you attacked us, young lady," Heath harrumphed. "Not like those bellicose Chakans. Now, then: What world are you from?"

She beamed at him. "Yemanja."

"Never been there, what?"

"It's the Candomblean water world. Not much population, but very pretty." Her expression sank. "I don't imagine I'll ever see it again."

"Don't talk like that," said Shimoda. "If your people won't take you back, we'll see about making other arrangements for you."

"As I said, you're very kind." She favored Shimoda with a smile so lustrous he tried to suck in his colossal belly somewhat, a disruption of physical reality akin to reversing entropy.

"It was hypothesized by some," she went on, "that you people somehow constituted some sinister cabal that was in league with the mysterious aliens. I can see now how silly that was. But I guess you can't blame people. The appearance of this ship has been quite a shock to everyone."

"Us too," said Shimoda. "How are they reacting?"

"There's a lot of incredulity on many worlds, in spite of the verified reports and the vids. The various governments are being evasive, whether to prevent panic or conceal their own intentions I can't say. Candomble is no different."

She sipped at a second drink, this one a bright lime green. "What *are* you going to do? What are your plans?"

"We have not decided yet." Iranaputra stood with his hands behind his back, his toes dug into the sand. "So far we have been dealing with things as they happen."

"Then your being aboard really is an accident?" Several of them nodded.

She considered the admission. "I didn't want to do this. When the fire started, I was sure it was all over. That I'd never see my mother and father again." Tears started to trickle from the corners of both eyes. She cried quietly, with hardly any noise. Heath offered her his shirt.

"Thank you." She wiped at her face.

It was just a little, just a tiny bit, too much for Mina Gelmann. She was old, yes, but not senile. The manner in which her quartet of male friends was now fawning over their unexpected visitor inexorably led her to consider the possibility, however slight on the face of it, that the young woman they had rescued might be capable of as yet unsuspected subtleties.

AI dysynapsing? Multiple bruises, contusions, a bloody but minor head wound but nothing serious? Gelmann kept her slight suspicions to herself. Nor did she betray them through her tone of voice, since there was little need for her to say anything. Her four companions seemed more than anxious to do any and all talking that was required. Even the normally introspective Shimoda was posturing outrageously. Not that he was aware of it, of course. He was a man.

Could it be that after so many years as the center of attention she was jealous? Gelmann refused to countenance the thought. She was much, much too intelligent to succumb to something so subjective.

"Sand's warm," Ashili commented absently. "What other wonders does this artifact contain?"

"We've only explored a small portion." Heath sounded almost apologetic. "The individual chambers and rooms are huge. The crew must've numbered in the thousands."

"Tens of thousands," Hawkins added emphatically.

"And you've done all this on your own. You're quite a remarkable bunch, you know."

"We have done no more than cope with the situation in which we have found ourselves," Heath murmured. "Some of us have had a bit of experience in extraordinary circumstances, you know."

"I've heard that this artifact is more than a million years old." She had begun to examine her surroundings more thoroughly.

"So it claims," Iranaputra admitted. "If you feel well enough, I would be glad to guide you around."

With the exception of Mina Gelmann, Iranaputra's companions were as willing as he to show their visitor the marvels they had encountered. Uncharacteristically the widowed computer specialist contented herself with watching, listening, and observing. She remained friendly toward the younger woman, but cautious.

As time passed, she found herself relaxing. The visitor's distress seemed genuine, and Gelmann had several granddaughters of her own. But she never completely let her guard down. Someone had to maintain one, and her thoroughly pixilated companions clearly weren't up to the task.

"Why do you stay here?" Ashili asked them the next day. "Why not try to find the central control, for example?"

A glistening, beached seal, Shimoda rolled over on the sand. "We're all of us a little too old for month-long hikes. Besides, the Autothor functions equally well in every part of the ship. With the kind of setup it represents there's no need to centralize functions."

"I see." She smiled prettily and wandered off up the beach to inspect Ksarusix's sculpted sand schematic. She'd ingratiated herself with the serving robot by the simple expedient of agreeing with everything it said, including its stubborn assertion that the alien ship represented a different and higher form of intelligence despite the Autothor's continued insistence to the contrary.

"At least one of you bipeds recognizes the obvious." The robot added more sand to a dubious representation of an optical nexus.

"You have to excuse the others." Hands on hips, head cocked slightly to one side, she studied the robot's work. "They're very old. Since you're assigned to work with them, you should understand what that means and make allowances accordingly."

Ksarusix spoke without looking at her. "I suppose. It's the same with us. After extensive use systems begin to fail, internal structures to break down. Isolated memory gaps appear. Unfortunately humans have no backup capability. Blatant internal deficiency. Runs right down the whole evolutionary chain." The small head simulated a negative head shake. "Too bad."

"It's sweet of you to be sympathetic."

"Not sympathetic." Ksarusix added a careful measure of water to the new sand. "Just honest." It paused to admire its handiwork, glanced over at her. "It's swell to know that there's at least one human who's not intimidated by reality."

"Not me. My grasp on reality is as strong as yours."

She joined her rescuers in testing the limits of the Autothor's food-synthesizing capabilities, in asking it questions to which it often had no answer, in swimming in the warm ocean and running along the beach. Her wounds healed with the speed of youth and when the scabs and scars had disappeared, she was more beautiful than ever.

Iranaputra took especial pride in relating to her the story of the artifact's discovery, not neglecting in his modest fashion to emphasize that he'd been the first to set eyes on it. She listened raptly, as she did to all their tales. It was amusing to see the five seniors treat the cajoling, demanding, pleading requests that arrived regularly from the combined military strength of the First Federal Federation and the Keiretsu with blithe indifference.

Five tottery, cranky, highly individualistic old folks in control of the most powerful device in the cosmos, Ashili mused, and all they chose to do with it was relax on its artificial beach, swim in its artificial ocean, soak up its artificial sun, and consume its artificial food. In effect, they were doing no more than continuing their retirement on a grander scale.

She played no favorites, though she spent more time with Heath than any of the others. Much to the amusement of his friends, she apparently found his military reminiscences of as much interest as they did her regular nude swims in the warm sea, though she listened to all of their individual histories with apparently equal enjoyment.

They were having a midday dip. Iranaputra preferred to take his long swim at noon because he chilled quickly. Of course, the Autothor could have adjusted the temperature as easily as it did the position of the "sun," but Iranaputra and his companions found it more natural to have the light source overhead concurrent with the warmest part of the day. They experimented with their climate as freely as with the food.

Ashili observed them as they dallied in the mild surf. Five seniors acting like so many children, delighting in the biggest toy in history. Gelmann and Shimoda were splashing each other playfully. Heath floated on his back, while Hawkins and Iranaputra stood in the shallows debating the possible biologic origins of some mollusk they'd excavated from the sand.

She turned away to study the fake igneous escarpments that formed the little cove. If this vast chamber was a reflection of the homeworld of the artifact's designers, it must be a pleasant place. Why would beings who dwelt on such a world have need of a warship of such size? Such speculations shrank the ship's vast dimensions, allowing the frigid void outside to press close and dim the benign artificial sun.

She left the artifact's discoverers to their diversions and strolled out onto the beach, lying down on her back with her feet toward the water, letting the warm air dry her coffee-colored skin. As soon as she was comfortable she donned her service underclothing and walked over to confront the enigmatic, ever-present blue ellipse. A check of her wrist chronometer showed that exactly seven days had passed since she had been brought aboard. Seven days almost to the minute.

It was time to act.

"Autothor!"

The scintillating Blueness had no face to turn to her, but that was the impression she received as it replied. "What is it?"

"I want you to move." A quick glance oceanward showed that her elderly rescuers were paying no attention to her.

"Very well," the Autothor replied pleasantly. "Where would you like me to move to?"

"Not you. Not your physical representation. I want you to move the ship. Into orbit around a world called Reconcavo. I will provide you with spatial coordinates.".

The device's reply surprised her. "Why?"

"So that friends of mine can examine and study you."

"You are examining and studying me here."

"Not in the kind of depth and detail that can be achieved elsewhere, with proper facilities. Do you mind being studied in greater depth?"

"No." It started to drift beachward. "If you will wait, I will be glad to consult the others."

"No, no." Without pausing to consider the possible consequences, she hurried to interpose herself between the Autothor and the water. "There's no need to ask them. Just do it. I'm giving you a direct order."

"I'm sorry, but I can't acknowledge that."

"Why not?" *What was she doing wrong?*

"Because you are not one of those who saw to my reactivation."

She was ready for that. "Since prior to your reactivation you had no cognitive abilities, how do you know I wasn't present and didn't participate in that process?"

"I know a great many things which would surprise you. About ancient wars and technologies, the state of the universe, about consciousness and perception." The blue ellipse bobbed gently a meter above the sand. "One thing I am certain of is that you could not have participated in my awakening because only five organics did. Five organics and a subservient mechanical. Now there are six organics. This logic is basic."

"I see. What if there were only five organics present now?"

"There are six."

"True. But if there were five, would I be counted among the critical number and consequently able to issue directives to which you would respond?"

As she waited for the Autothor to reply she looked again to the figures in the water. During the past week she'd come to know them pretty well. They really were a bunch of old darlings. Shimoda would have the hardest neck to break. Heath would be the next toughest. The other three were not worth worrying about.

"You can't contravene logic so simply," the refulgent Blueness was telling her. "If one of the five were to be not here, then there would be four. Four reactivators. Your presence alters only numbers, not history."

"What if all of them became not here, or incapable of issuing directives, and only I remained?"

"Then I would be compelled to return to storage. That would be awkward for you."

"How so?"

"Not having responsible organics to concern myself with, I would initiate a conservational shutdown of unnecessary facilities. These would include organic life-support systems."

Despite the warm air and pseudo-sunshine, she felt a sudden chill. "That makes good sense. So I am correct in assuming that you will not accept any directives from me?"

"Only those involving food, liquid refreshment, or matters concerning personal hygiene, because I have been directed by my reactivators to do so." There wasn't a hint of hostility or rejection in the Autothor's tone.

"That's all right." She smiled automatically, even though the expression was wasted on the device. "I just wanted to know. You don't mind my inquiring, do you?"

"Certainly not. I am programmed to respond to all interrogatories that do not compromise integrity."

"Good. Now, if you'll pardon me, I think I'll go join the other organics for a swim. Could you bring up the sunset, please? I really love the evening light."

"I am sorry, but I cannot acknowledge that request because . . ."

"I know why. Forget it. No hard feelings."

"No feelings are 'hard,' if I interpret your words correctly." The brilliant turquoise oval floated noiselessly above the beach.

Her expression was unreadable as she turned and ran lithely down to the water's edge, clearing the small waves with the grace and power of a trained hurdler, laughing and joking with the old men who cheered her on. As she splashed and giggled and joked with them she was counting down the minutes in her mind.

She had time left to try anything else she could think of. But not a lot of time. Unbeknownst to her elderly companions, that commodity was rapidly running out.

XVII

THE announcement from the Autothor interrupted the barbecue on the beach, which meal was progressing pleasantly under the combined supervision of Hawkins and the Ksarusix. The artificial steaks were blackening nicely above the sizzling synthesized charcoal, though neither man nor robot could do anything about the unpleasant glazed pink tinge attendant to the baked potatoes, which gave them the appearance of aborted insect larvae. The taste was right, though.

"There is another vessel alongside."

The five nearly naked seniors looked at one another. They wore few clothes since they'd learned that the Autothor could adjust the temperature in the searoom (as they had come to refer to it) to suit their whim. To the delight of the men, Zabela Ashili chose to wear even less than they. Not only was that in keeping with Candomblean fashion, she was less in need than any of them of esthetic concealment.

"Let's see it," Shimoda murmured.

Instantly the familiar hovering holo appeared close by the compliant blue ellipse. Drifting within and dwarfed by the bulk of the artifact was a ship not much larger than the one which had brought Ashili.

"No markings." Heath appraised the image professionally, having readopted his colonel persona for the benefit of their rescued waif. His companions were too polite, and too amused, to call him out on it. They were all aware that vanity's name was not woman, but age.

"Candomblean." They looked at Ashili. "I recognize the design. It's a fleet-support medvac search craft. Come looking for me, I bet."

"Admirable of them, what?" Heath murmured.

"Why have they waited so long? You disappeared days ago," Iranaputra pointed out.

"First the Chakans, then her, old boy." Heath postured with an elegance redolent of what had once been. "Wouldn't you be cautious?"

"It looks like I won't have to impose on you anymore." Ashili smiled meltingly. "You've all been so good to me, when you had every right not to."

Shimoda was fingering his clothing, which the Autothor had thoughtfully and immaculately cleaned. "I guess we'll see you to the lock."

"You don't have to go to any trouble," she told him. "I'm sure the Autothor can guide me."

"It will not be any trouble." Iranaputra was slipping into his pants. "It will be our pleasure to make certain you are returned safely to your people. Won't it?" Everyone murmured assent, including Gelmann, who over the past several days had warmed to their guest in spite of her lingering suspicions.

"I can only thank you again, since I've seen nothing else of the artifact and would be glad of your company in a strange place." She was pulling on the crumpled duty suit she'd been wearing when the Autothor had brought her in. "What about your barbecue?"

"No problem," said Hawkins jauntily. "The ship will just synthesize another one."

"Of course. I'm still not used to that," she responded.

Outside the searoom the light was brighter, the vast chambers and corridors as imposing as ever in their abandoned vastness. The subtle moving room which had brought them to the outskirts of the artificial ocean transported them as far as it was able. From there they had to hike through two familiar chambers to reach the lock which had originally given them access to the artifact's interior.

"Strange to be standing here again." Iranaputra's gaze roamed over the high, bare walls.

"Can't tell you what a pleasure it's been." Heath stood close to their visitor. "Perhaps our paths may cross anew someday."

She smiled up at the tall, straight-backed old man. "I'd almost bet on it." Heath beamed as she looked at the others. He would have been crushed to learn that from the very first he had reminded Ashili not of a lover past or future, but of her father. "You've all been so nice, so caring. I almost wish that . . ." There was an odd undercurrent in her voice as the words trailed into inaudibility.

"Wish what, dear?" Gelmann prompted.

"Nothing. That I could spend more days like the last few, I guess." She brightened. "I read somewhere that true humanity isn't reached until the age of sixty."

Hawkins winked at her. "Experience counts for a lot, kiddo."

She had to grin. For the past week she'd felt as if she'd been pampered and cared for by five grandparents. She was startled to realize how deeply the experience had affected her.

"As per your instructions I have communicated with the small vessel." The Autothor bobbed at Gelmann's shoulder. "They have responded and are presently approaching the location of this airlock. I have opened the outer door."

"Let me talk to them." Ashili glanced to Heath for approval.

"Go ahead," he told her magnanimously. "Let them know that you're all right."

"Zabela Ashili." The azure ellipse kept the communication's volume modest. "Are you . . . ?"

"Right here," she said brightly before the other could finish. "Fine and healthy, thanks to my newfound friends. Who am I addressing?"

"Medtech Maje Praxedes, of the hospital cruiser *Ossain*. With me is Medtech Fraja Bassan and two pilot-navigators. We're all volunteers, and I can't tell you how happy we are to find you alive. What happened to you?"

"My ship started coming apart around me, and these people had me rescued."

"*Had* you rescued?"

"By the artifact. There's some kind of highly active mobile communications device on board, and it responds to their commands."

"Fascinating." There was a pause, then, "We're inside the indicated lock and setting down. How do we proceed?"

Ashili turned to her escort. "How *do* we proceed?"

It was Gelmann who directed the Autothor. "Close the outer lock door and pressurize the interior." She regarded the younger woman. "We'll start back to the searoom. As soon as we're well on our way we'll direct the Autothor to open the door here."

"You don't have to leave," Ashili protested. "Don't you want to meet my friends? I know they'd be honored to meet you."

"It would be nice to have some new visitors," Iranaputra observed.

Gelmann gave him a severe look, turned to gaze regretfully at Ashili. "We know nothing about your rescuers, dear. You should pardon my paranoid nature, but I'd just feel more comfortable if we didn't expose ourselves to any strangers, even a pair of medtechs. People are simply too interested in our present situation."

"I know. It's only natural for you to be suspicious."

The Autothor conveyed a voice. It sounded impatient. "We're reading normal atmosphere outside our ship. Ashili?"

"Be just a moment," she said to the drifting ellipse. She turned back to Gelmann. "I hope you understand, but I have to do it this way."

In one smooth motion she brought her left foot up toward her backside and removed the heel of her boot. Her arm went around Mina Gelmann's throat as she pressed the inner edge of the heel against the older woman's neck while backing both of them against the nearby wall.

Gelmann struggled at first, then gave in as she felt the unexpected power of the younger woman's forearm secure against her throat.

"I'm really sorry it has to be this way." Ashili's gaze darted from each of the stunned old men to the next as she strove to watch all of them at once. Shimoda looked stricken, while Heath seemed on the verge of tears. Iranaputra was numb, while alone among them Hawkins wore the mordant, knowing expression of a man who'd just had a lifetime of depressing encounters reconfirmed.

"Should've guessed. It's been too enjoyable, too much fun. The universe changes, but not people."

"It is true what they say," Iranaputra muttered disconsolately. "When one reaches a certain age, one begins to act like a child again."

"Don't be too hard on yourself, buddy," Hawkins told him. "They don't have to deal with this kind of stuff on Earth anymore."

"Please don't do anything stupid." Ashili kept the heel-tool jammed tight against Gelmann's neck. "This device can deliver a lethal electric charge. I can fry her brain before you can tell that," and she nodded in the direction of the Autothor, "to do anything."

"What does it matter?" Gelmann spoke in the nonchalant tone of the bitterly disappointed. "Go ahead; fry me. I haven't got so many more years anyway. What would you do then? Kill all of them?" She indicated her benumbed male friends.

"One at a time, if necessary." There was no hesitation in Ashili's voice, no little-girl-lost aspect to her manner. Her posture, her alertness, everything about her, now indicated that she was rather more than a small-ship pilot who'd been commanded to undertake a desperate mission of discovery by callous superiors. She looked, talked, and acted like a trained killer.

Everything that was now happening, Iranaputra realized with a start, had doubtless been carefully planned by the Candombleans from the beginning. They could not hope to outgun or outbluff the likes of the Keiretsu and the FFF. So they had outsmarted them. Outmatched from the start by the physical and verbal skills Zabela Ashili possessed, Iranaputra and his friends had never really had a chance. They had been duped and flattered into near submission.

"I'm willing to bet that after I've killed two or three of you," she was saying coolly, "I'll find someone willing to do as I say. I don't want to kill anybody. Believe me or not, as you wish, but I really have come to like you all. In certain ways you remind me of . . . it doesn't matter. I have an assignment and I intend to carry it out. Make no mistake about that."

Ksarusix chortled softly. "Once again human nature asserts itself. Instinct triumphs over intelligence. And to think I'm supposed to spend conscious existence providing sustenance to such creatures."

"What do you want us to do?" Iranaputra asked tiredly.

"Don't listen to her, you little putz!" Gelmann tried to struggle and it was astonishing to see the ease with which Ashili controlled her.

"Open the lock and let my friends in."

"They're not medical personnel, are they?" Kahei Shimoda had his hands clasped in front of him.

"What do you think?" she all but snarled.

"What will they do when they are allowed in? Kill us anyway?"

"Not if you cooperate. Enough talking!"

The four old men looked at one another. There was no need for words. Hawkins turned to Gelmann. "I've been trying for ten years to shut you up, Mina, but not this way. Not like this."

"Don't do it, Wallace. They mean to have done with us when they've got what they want. My end will be the same whether you let them in or not."

He smiled with uncommon gentleness and shook his head. "Maybe so, but it'll matter to me if she kills you. Who would I have to argue with and shout at?" He waved a hand, taking in the vast chamber and by intimation, the gigantic alien vessel itself.

"Besides, I'm tired. We're all tired." He allowed himself the slightest of smiles. "Retired. This is too much for us. Why not let the Candombleans take over? At least they're not as overbearing as some of the bigger leagues and alliances."

"It won't stay that way, you should excuse my pointing it out, if they get control of this ship and its technology."

"I said no more talking." As Ashili tightened her forearm around Gelmann's throat the older woman's eyes flickered and she slumped visibly. Heath took a step forward, halted when he realized that he was no longer living a lie.

"I thought you were our friend." Iranaputra ignored her terse admonition. "You cannot imagine what it was like, to be my age and to have a beautiful young woman saying nice things to me. I thought . . . I thought perhaps you might be enjoying it yourself, even a little. Old men are so easily deluded."

She seemed to soften slightly. "I did enjoy it." Her eyes flicked from one sorrowing face to the next. "You're all nice people. You're all sweet as hell. But I know what I have to do. So please, just do as I ask and no one will be harmed."

Shimoda turned to the Autothor as though it no longer mattered; as though not much of anything mattered anymore. Suddenly he looked and sounded his age, and longed for the isolation and solitude of his apartment in the far-distant retirement village.

"Open the inner door."

"I have been monitoring the recent conversation," the blue ellipse replied. "Evaluation and analysis suggest that it may not be in your best interests to do this."

"It is all right." Iranaputra shrugged. "Something like this was bound to happen sooner or later."

"I can easily destroy the small vessel in question." The Autothor was persistent.

"That will not be necessary. Open the door."

Wraith-silent, the enormous barrier began to melt into the floor. Ashili spared it an astonished glance but rapidly returned her attention to the four men confronting her. Her grip on her prisoner never slackened.

As the barrier sank, it revealed a pair of heavily armed men waiting on the other side. They hesitated until the obstacle had retracted completely, then rushed forward. Two others came running from the distant corners of the lock, a man and a woman.

"You've done well." The individual who greeted Ashili had the name "Praxedes" heat-sealed to a tag over his heart.

"Thanks. I know they don't look like much, but you've got to stay close to them and keep active weapons on them at all times, or they're liable to have *that* intervene. They call it the Autothor." She released Mina Gelmann, who stepped away rubbing at her neck, and indicated the drifting ellipse.

The other man's gaze narrowed as he inspected the softly pulsing turquoise oval. "What the hell is it?"

"Some kind of communications and control device for the artifact. It'll only respond to them. I know; I've experimented."

Praxedes nodded. "Can you make it understand that if any one of us is so much as singed, all five of these old folks are going to die?" He stared at the seniors, who had clustered protectively around Gelmann. "I don't know what the response time of your 'Autothor' is, but all of us are quick shots. Don't make us prove it." He hesitated. "What about the robot?"

"Kitchen mechanical. I'm still not sure what it's doing with them."

"You'd never believe it. Not that it would raise you up if you did," Ksarusix murmured.

Ashili ignored the irrelevant comment. "Do we leave now?"

"No. Orders are to explore some of the artifact first. How much have you seen?"

"Not a great deal. It's simply too big." She considered. "To give you some idea, one room holds an artificial ocean. There's another that's full of instrumentation on a grand scale, and has some kind of viewport."

Praxedes conversed briefly with his three companions. "Sounds promising."

She nodded and turned to the seniors. "Lead the way."

"Why not?" Heath mumbled. He turned and started off, his friends following.

Ashili hung close to Gelmann while her people paired off with the four men. Gun muzzles were pressed into backs and held there as the procession advanced.

By the time they reached the room Gelmann referred to as the observation chamber the five seniors were exhausted. Together with the mumbling, complaining serving robot, they were herded into a corner next to the high-arching window, through which the gleaming lunar surface was still sharply visible. Two of the Candombleans kept watch over the seated prisoners while Praxedes and another named Eradou conferred with Ashili.

"They seem docile enough." The commando in charge eyed the seated, wheezing seniors. "They're older than I expected."

"Revelation of my true identity hit them pretty hard," she explained. "The old woman's inclined to be stubborn, but at this point I don't believe they'll make any trouble. I think they finally realize how far they're in over their heads. Basically they've given up."

"Good. I'd just as soon have an easy time of it." Praxedes let his gaze rove around the immense chamber, taking in the towering monoliths and peculiar banks of enigmatic instrumentation. "And yet, they're in control of all this."

"That's too strong a determination," she insisted. "They've accomplished everything by accident, nothing on purpose. From what I've been able to learn they stumbled into the artifact, activated it by their presence, and control it through coincidence. Anyone lucky enough to have followed the same sequence could've done the same."

"You're certain this Autothor will not respond to you, or to us?" She nodded once. "That will make our goals more difficult to reach, but not impossible." He eyed the elderly prisoners. "I take it you followed the official scenario and asked them to have the artifact move?"

"They declined to comply."

"Obviously. We need to do something to persuade them. Which one is in charge?"

Her eyes settled on the inconsolable Heath. He was staring at the deck, his white curls thrust forward like a dirty cap of raw cotton. She shifted to Gelmann, still coughing slightly but defiant.

"None of them. They sort of take turns. The tall dark one claims to be an ex-colonel from the Victoria League, though I'm not sure I believe him."

Praxedes' gaze settled on the librarian. "He'll do. Colonel or not."

"How do you plan to proceed?" she heard herself asking. "I had to threaten to kill the woman before they agreed to let you aboard."

The commando nodded approvingly. "No reason to mess with a procedure that's already proven successful. We'll choose one . . . let's say the big fat one . . . and announce that if they don't obey our commands, we'll kill him. Slowly. If it worked for you, it should work equally well for us."

She nodded. "And after we reach Reconcavo they'll be disembarked and returned to Earth."

Bassan had been silent until now. "Returned? That's not to be allowed. They've spent a lot of time on the ship and they know too much about it. They could reveal secrets now rightfully ours. Official determination is that since their presence aboard is widely known, they're to have a collective accident." He gazed at the prisoners. "No loss. They've lived most of their lives already anyway."

Ashili frowned uncomfortably. "I was led to believe that once we'd secured control of the artifact, they'd be permitted to depart."

Praxedes shrugged. "So there's been a small change in procedure. Don't let it bother you. We'll take care of things."

"But they're just a bunch of old folks who, like you said, wandered into this by accident. Is it really necessary to kill them?"

"It's been decided. You've got a double promotion and a commendation waiting for you, Lieutenant. Concentrate on that."

"If they see or suspect what you're going to do, they're liable to ask the Autothor to intervene."

Praxedes smiled humorlessly. "Then we'll just have to make sure they don't see or suspect. It'll be fast and painless. Once we've secured control, we can do it while they're asleep." He puckered his lips and made little popping sounds. "If you're having a crisis of conscience, why don't you take a walk? *Ogun* knows you deserve some time to yourself, after what you've accomplished here."

She licked her lower lip. "Just go easy if they're a little slow to cooperate, okay? They're old and it shouldn't take much."

"Oh sure, we'll take it easy." Praxedes and Bassan smiled identical smiles. "As easy as we can, bearing in mind that both the Federals and the Keis are hanging in the spatial neighborhood with a hundred warships apiece trying to decide their respective next moves, and that they won't wait forever. Especially if they've a spy or two on our own flagship who's letting them know what's going on here." The two commandos started toward the little knot of subdued, elderly captives.

Ashili found herself torn within. She'd never been torn within over anything before, and it was not a pleasant sensation. Not that she minded killing in the service of the Candomble. It was what she'd been trained for. But assassination and execution were two different things. The seniors she'd swum with and shared food with and slept securely among during the past days were inoffensive and harmless. For the life of her she could not rationalize their deaths.

There was no one to appeal to. Both Praxedes and Bassan ranked her. Mild-spoken Iranaputra, motherly Gelmann, kindly Shimoda, and amusingly acerbic Hawkins were all going to die and there wasn't a damn thing she could do about it. And Heath, who even in his boasting reminded her so much of her father, dead and gone from a small-craft accident when she was ten. She found herself questioning things she'd never questioned before.

Confused, upset, and generally nonplussed, she decided to take Praxedes' suggestion. Turning away from the puzzled seniors, she headed for the high-arching portal which led out of the observation room, turned right down a vast corridor, and lengthened her stride. Immediately she knew she'd acted correctly. The silence was like a blanket, calm and reassuring.

Unbeknownst to her, Bassan was following her every move. Her reaction to a straightforward discussion of their situation had been uncharacteristically equivocal. They'd known one another for several years and reactionary responses were unlike her. Usually she carried out her orders efficiently and without question, as she had in obtaining a foothold on the artifact.

He made a mental note to tell Praxedes that when the time came to put the seniors to rest, they needed to do it when Ashili wasn't around. A small courtesy, but one that in her present state of mind he felt she would appreciate. Or perhaps he was overreacting, reading something into her expression that wasn't there. He shrugged. He'd bring the subject up again when she returned from her walk.

His gaze traveled about the huge room. What phenomena there were to be examined, what lessons to be learned from this wondrous artifact by the scientists of the Candomblean League! As for himself and his compatriots, their lesser minds could only speculate on what marvels lay elsewhere in the colossal ship, waiting to be discovered. Setting aside his concern for the morose Ashili, he moved to rejoin his companions, checking to make sure his weapon was activated.

Ashili found herself running. She was a superb athlete and covered great stretches of deck with muscular, measured strides, stopping only when the soreness in her legs spread to her throat. Hands on knees, she bent over, sucking wind, having momentarily (but only momentarily) managed to forget the five unnecessary deaths she was going to be a party to.

She had been educated by the Candomble, trained by the Candomble, lived for the Candomble; but at that particular moment in time she would have been forced to admit that she neither understood nor condoned the Candomble's intentions.

Straightening, she took stock of her surroundings. She was in still another corridor. The light was much dimmer than elsewhere, though still adequate for her to see by. Breathing hard but evenly, she walked on while continuing to study her surroundings.

It was good to exhaust yourself once in a while, she told herself. *For the mind as well as the body.* It helped one to put aside visions of such things as five forthcoming useless deaths.

Surely there had to be another way besides murder for the Candomble to ensure security redundancy?

She had vague thoughts of spiriting the oldsters out from beneath the commando's guard and slipping them aboard the small warship that waited in the lock, then returning them to Earth. Confronted with a fait accompli, her superiors would be forced to make the best of the situation. As this would still leave them in sole possession of the artifact, she doubted any anger over her actions would last long.

If she encountered resistance, she knew she could take out any one of the commandos, but even with surprise on her side, subduing all four of them would likely prove an impossible proposition. The odds were as bad as her intentions were good.

Among other physical and mental attributes, Ashili had been endowed with a superb sense of direction. She turned left at an intersection, convinced she was heading toward the incredible chamber that contained the artificial ocean. At a second intersection she hesitated, then went right. Judging from the speed at which the horizontal elevator had traveled, she should be close now. If not, she would turn back and begin retracing her steps.

The scale on which the corridor had been constructed denied her the companionship of echoes. Artwork or oversize hieroglyphs appeared periodically on the walls. Aliens or humans could have marched anywhere in the ship twenty abreast without scraping the smooth walls. One could *fly* from station to station, she marveled.

The artifact hummed softly all around her.

PRAXEDES regarded the prisoners. The gentle mountain called Shimoda sat quietly: eyes closed, lips moving silently, hands folded across the great curve of belly, the pale blue fire of the Autothor hovering nearby. Hawkins glared through the great sweep of observation port at the lunar surface, cursing craters and his situation with equal invention. The serving robot squatted quiescent against the wall, silently recharging. Gelmann, Heath, and Iranaputra sat close together, whispering among themselves. Even seated, Heath towered above his friends, and it was to him that the commando addressed himself.

"I don't like to waste time." He gestured to Bassan, who unlimbered a pocket holojector. A few skilled adjustments invoked a compact starfield within the diameter of the holomag. As the commando operated the control box a thin green line leaped from one sun within the hazy sphere to another. As soon as internal contact had been established between systems representations, the entire starfield began to rotate slowly.

"That's the line from Earth to Reconcavo. That's where we want you to order the artifact to go." He glanced in the direction of the blue ellipse. The damn thing made him nervous even though he knew it was intellectually inert. "If it's half as perceptive as Ashili reported, it should have no trouble calculating the necessary tachyspace adjustments."

"How do you know, old chap, that the ship is even capable of interstellar travel? *We* certainly haven't tried to take her anywhere."

"Stalling is a way of wasting time. I told you that I don't like that." Praxedes waved expansively. "This vessel wasn't built and buried here to move luggage or individuals from Earth to Europa. Monitors on Earth recorded its passage from over the Atlantic Ocean to its present position. Knowing the time of transit allows us to calculate relative velocity. It had to have traveled through tachyspace, however briefly. You must've realized that too."

"A trip from Earth to moon, you only should eat something soon that gives you chronic diarrhea, is pretty different from making a transstellar jump." Gelmann glared up at her captor. "What if whatever this ship uses for a drive can't manage the distance?"

Praxedes gestured casually with the gun he carried. "Easy enough to find out. Give the order."

Heath smiled cheerily. "What if we decline to do so, you filthy rotten son-of-a-bitch?"

Bassan clipped the holojector to his belt and removed from a pouch the mate to the electric shock device Ashili had used to threaten Gelmann. "I don't like to use this. There's usually a lot of noise. Me, I like peace and quiet." He advanced on Heath.

"No!" Everyone turned to Iranaputra.

Bassan halted and glanced at his superior. Praxedes considered the smaller man. With his slim build and delicate features he looked like a perfectly molded miniature model of a much larger individual. Perhaps things would go faster if they directed their questions and demands to him instead of to the more formal Heath.

Ignoring the threatening whispers of his companions, Iranaputra rose and approached the Autothor. "Evaluate the distances between star systems represented there." He pointed to the hovering holomag.

"Done," said the Autothor a moment later. Argolo looked up briefly from where she was watching over Hawkins and Shimoda to whistle appreciation for the Autothor's speed.

"Are you capable of making such a journey through tachyspace?"

"Really, old boy!" Heath's outrage was no less palpable than that of Gelmann or Shimoda. Ignoring the drama being played out behind him, Hawkins just kept mooning morosely at Aristarchus.

"Calculating." Less than two minutes passed. "Yes. There would be no problem making the journey."

"There, you see?" Praxedes nodded approvingly to Iranaputra, then grinned down at Heath and Gelmann. "No reason to make this any more difficult than necessary." To illustrate his good intentions he raised the muzzle of his weapon, though he didn't deactivate it.

"We'll have a pleasant trip to Reconcavo and turn over the artifact to the research staff that's already been assembled there. Then you'll be put on a commercial flight heading back toward Earth, where you can resume your respective retirements devoid of any worries." The commando lied fluidly and without compunction. "The people of Earth, citizens and retirees and tourists alike, long ago quit troubling themselves with galactic politics.

Keep that in mind and you'll have an easy, relaxed time of it." When they failed to respond, he added encouragingly, "Why do you care what happens to this artifact anyway? It's not your property and it's not your responsibility."

"I know." With great ceremony Heath removed his old monocle from a pocket and inserted it carefully in his left eye. "But something in me grates at the thought of turning it over to the likes of you. I don't like you, you see."

"That's okay." Praxedes took no offense. "You don't have to like me. Just cooperate and you can hate my guts all you wish." He nodded to Bassan, who stepped forward, holding the ominous little electrical device before him.

"There is no need for that, sir." Iranaputra rushed to hover protectively over Mina Gelmann.

Heath glared up at him. "Victor, old chap, if any one socioeconomic body gains control of this ship, it will upset the balance of power among the leagues."

"That is not my concern or yours, Wes."

"Listen to your friend," Praxedes advised. "He talks sense."

The two men eyed one another a moment longer.

"Go ahead . . . Colonel." Iranaputra smiled reassuringly at his old friend. " 'Tarry not, messenger. Let him who knows give the order.' Kalidasa, Third Chapter."

Heath shook his head as he climbed to his feet. "You and your bottomless font of ancient nonsense." He sighed tiredly. "I guess there is neither glory nor despair in a strategic retreat." His long legs carried him past Shimoda and Hawkins until he was standing next to the slowly bobbing Autothor.

"Old ship: Have you been listening to this discussion?" The commandos' hands tightened on their weapons.

"I have."

"Do you understand what these visitors want?"

"I do."

Heath glanced over to Gelmann, who had cast her eyes downward. He spoke to the patient Autothor. "Then I hereby direct you to comply with their request. Activate your drive and take us to the system they have indicated." As Praxedes relaxed, the corners of his mouth turned up ever so slightly.

"I'm afraid I can't do that just now."

Praxedes tensed anew. Heath blinked and looked confused. Even Hawkins perked up.

Bassan gestured threateningly with his weapon and Heath obediently tried again. "I'm giving you a direct order. You've always responded to our directives before."

"I am aware of that. But I really cannot comply with this particular request at this time."

"When would you be able to comply?"

"I cannot tell you that either."

His expression less than conciliatory, Bassan hefted the compact shocker and again approached Mina Gelmann. She flinched as he pressed it to her forehead, just above the left orbit.

"This is some kind of a trick. I don't like being tricked." He eyed his superior expectantly.

"I don't want to play anymore," growled Praxedes. "No more games."

Iranaputra started forward until Argolo turned her gun in his direction. "It is not a trick. You have been watching all the time. When could we have done anything to fool you?"

"I don't know and I don't care." Bassan could sense the old woman beginning to tremble beneath him.

Iranaputra noticed it too. For the first time a word he had never imagined in relation to her popped into his mind: frail. She was frail. They were all of them after all frail: frail and old.

What am I doing here? he found himself wondering. *I should be at the Village, watching vids and eating soft foods.*

Heath had the presence of mind to stall desperately. "Maybe your damnable associate is responsible. Difficult as it is to believe, perhaps she has had a crisis of conscience and has chosen to intervene."

"Ashili?" Praxedes chuckled softly. "Not likely."

Heath clung to the notion. "Maybe she's affected the ship's programming somehow. Of course, you could ask her, but she's not here, is she? She hasn't come back."

Iranaputra picked up the refrain. "Maybe she has decided she does not wish to associate with you anymore."

Praxedes' grin faded. "Shut up. Both of you. Ashili's perfectly executed a difficult assignment. She's going through normal post-conclusive syndrome. I'm the one who told her to take a walk to calm herself down. She's sorting out her thoughts, that's all." His eyes flicked toward the entrance to the great room. "She'll be back momentarily.

"Besides, the ship responds only to the five of you. She assured me of that."

"What if something's changed, old maggot?" Now Heath was the one doing the smiling.

Praxedes hesitated, then addressed the Autothor. "What about it, ship? Has that changed? Or do you still only respond to directives from these five?"

"That has not changed," the floating blue ellipse replied.

"Ah." Praxedes relaxed afresh. "You see? Wherever Ashili is, she's not affecting the situation here." Once more he gestured with his weapon. "Ask it again."

Heath complied. The Autothor's response was unchanged.

Bassan released Gelmann's head. "There is a problem here, sir, but I don't think it's one of deception on the prisoners' part."

"Agreed." Praxedes spoke to Heath. "Probe. Ask it why it can't comply."

Heath shrugged. "Ask it yourself. As long as it's not an order, it should respond to you."

Praxedes nodded, turned to the blue ellipse. "Is there a problem with your drive?"

"No. Ship's propulsive systems are fully operational."

"Then why can't you comply with his request?" He gestured in Heath's direction.

"Because other requisite actions have assumed precedence."

The commando nodded to himself. This he understood. "Very well. Will the delay in compliance be brief?"

"Possibly."

"There, you see?" Praxedes regarded his fellow operatives. "There's no problem here. How long a delay do you anticipate before you can comply with the request to move?"

"At this moment I cannot give a specific time frame. It will depend on the outcome."

Iranaputra frowned. "The outcome? The outcome of what?"

"Why, the forthcoming battle, of course."

"What battle?" Praxedes shifted uneasily. "What's happening? Is one of the fleets approaching?"

"You are preparing to fight," Iranaputra declared decisively. "That is why you cannot move now."

"Affirmative. I am presently initiating a defensive posture. Defensive programming supersedes any and all peripheral directives."

"Who's attacking?" Bassan looked nervous. "Which league?"

"The approaching vessels from which I infer possible hostile intent are not nearby." The deep turquoise blue of the Autothor was intense.

"Must be the Eeck." Argolo picked at her shirt. "Or maybe the Victorians. It would make sense for a latecomer to try a direct assault in an attempt to compensate for tardiness and ignorance."

"Doesn't matter who it is." Praxedes addressed the Autothor with a confidence he didn't entirely feel. "You can handle them just like you did the Chakans, right?"

"I am not positive. Though I am sensible of my power, I am still only one ship against an armada."

"How many ships in this hostile force?" Heath's own curiosity had been aroused. "A hundred? Two?" That would represent the combined strength of the First Federals and the Keiretsu, he knew.

There was a pause, then, "I apprehend more than a thousand."

Praxedes gaped at the turquoise ellipse, his companions, then the Autothor again. "No such fleet exists! There aren't that many warships in existence."

"Incorrect observation," the Autothor responded tersely. "There is something else of interest. Though the range is extreme and precise analysis difficult, I estimate that this represents only an advance scouting force. There is a tachyspace disturbance farther out which hints at the presence of a much larger main body."

"Scouting force." Bassan was gazing dumbly at the drifting Blueness, all thoughts of interrogation forgotten. Under the weight of the Autothor's words a great many things were forgotten.

Hawkins sprang to his feet, something he hadn't done in years. "Where're they from? Who can put out a thousand ships as a scouting force?"

"I'd think that intuitively obvious. What do you think I was built for?"

Admiral Sobran of the First Federal Federation was standing as he stared intently. "Where are they now?" Before him the warlo image displayed distant stars among which swarmed hundreds of points of light, like a hive of electric bees.

An analyst replied with figures, to which the admiral nodded slowly. The advancing formation was impressive for more than size. It hung together with almost mechanical precision.

"Any attempts at communication?"

Another officer responded. "Apparently there was a survey vessel run out from the Roosevelts that got close enough to take some visuals. The . . . aliens didn't react. It's assumed they were studying it as intently as it was studying them. They didn't linger long in the vicinity."

"Not surprising."

"I've been analyzing the preliminary information, sir. These new intruders don't look anything like the artifact presently in lunar orbit. Some of their ships are big, but the information indicates nothing approaching it in mass. They also differ greatly in appearance, both from the artifact and from human-built craft. According to the information provided by the survey vessel, they are constructed to dozens, maybe even hundreds, of different designs." She swallowed. "Of course, there are a lot more of them."

"More aliens. Different aliens." Sobran wished fervently he was back at his desk instead of drifting ignorantly halfway between the Earth and its moon trying to deal with an alien visitation of inconceivable magnitude. "A few days ago we were convinced there were no such things. Now all of a sudden we find out that the neighborhood's crowded."

"They're coming in fast, sir." Another tech looked up from his station. "They've already passed a couple of independents."

"Any reaction?"

"Didn't stop to try and communicate, fight, or do anything at all. Didn't even slow down. Unless they shift direction in tachy, they're coming this way."

Why am I not surprised? Sobran mused. "In light of any other information I think it reasonable to assume they've been drawn by that thing orbiting Luna. Whether to reinforce it or confront it we don't know. I can't imagine what it would need reinforcements for, and if there's going to be a battle between alien ships, we might be better off evaluating the results from a more respectful distance." This was Sobran's way of formally announcing to any staff within range of his voice that he didn't know what the hell was going on and wasn't ashamed to admit it.

"One thing I'd bet on." Everyone turned to one of the specialists. "The artifact's departure from Earth set off an alarm somewhere, though whether among its friends or enemies we have no way of knowing."

Sobran nodded. "We are the fleet of the FFF. Our responsibility lies with our own worlds." He turned to his second-in-command. "Mr. Natwick, make preparations to return home."

"Uh, Admiral?" one of the techs ventured. "What about Earth? What about the Homeworld? They have no ships to defend themselves with."

Another tech spoke up. "Indications are that the multiple Keiretsu vessels are making preparations for tachyspace insertion."

Sobran grunted. Hiroshigi was no fool either. "I'm an admiral of the First Federal Federation. That leaves me little opportunity to indulge in expensive nostalgia. Earth will have to take care of itself." He settled back in his command chair, reasonably pleased with his hasty but very necessary rationalization.

On board the flagship of the Candomblean force there was similar apprehension. But having succeeded in placing operatives aboard the artifact, its commander was in a much more sensitive position. If he ordered a retreat, he risked losing the greatest technological prize since the invention of gunpowder.

"Both the Federal and Keiretsu fleets are shifting out into tachyspace, sir," reported a specialist.

"Wonder if they know something we don't?" murmured the scantily clad navigator next to him.

"They're panicking." The commander looked thoughtful. "There's no perceived reason for flight."

"Oh, I don't know." The officer who commented wore a lopsided grin. "The high-speed approach of a thousand uncommunicative alien craft of undeclared intentions might be enough to make one want to hurry off elsewhere."

"We can't pull out now." The commander's voice was steady. "We can't abandon those brave operatives who have made their way aboard the artifact."

"Not to mention the commendations and promotions to be won," someone whispered under their breath.

"What if these new vessels exhibit hostile intent?" someone asked aloud.

"Then we will be forced to retire," the commander admitted. "In which case our operatives will be extremely well placed to observe, record, and comment on all subsequent activities. In that event I will personally lead a group sacrifice to ensure the safety of our people."

"That'll be a real comfort to them," a communications tech murmured.

"Excuse me." The commander leaned forward, toward an intelligence officer who waited patiently on his words. "There's something else we'd better consider.

"Our operatives were instructed to try and get the artifact to move to

Reconcavo. If they succeed and this new alien force has come all this way to confront it, aren't they liable to follow it there?"

The commander blinked, considering. For a moment the faculty which always enabled him to come up with a ready response to any query had thoroughly deserted him.

A worried Ashili turned up a new corridor, trying to find a familiar land-mark, any kind of landmark. She was not yet willing to concede that she was definitely lost; only that she'd temporarily misplaced her way.

Immense chambers opened into the corridor. One on her left was alive with drifting pyramids and rhombohedrons of oscillating, lambent energy, each a different color. A triangular structure fashioned of frozen fire darted in her di-rection and she jerked backward, but it halted in the doorway, stopped cold by an invisible barrier. Taking a deep breath, she stumbled on.

The composition of the floor beneath her feet began to change. Bending, she placed her palm on the vitreous material. It was smooth, cool to the touch, and alive with an internal rose-colored light. She had definitely not come this way before. Or perhaps she had, and her surroundings were meta-morphosing as various ship functions continued to come on-line. If that was the case, it was going to be even harder to find her way back to the observa-tion room. She strode grimly on.

Peering into still another of the vast, inscrutable chambers that opened onto the corridor, she froze. Something was moving within. Automatically she assumed a defensive crouch, looking around wildly for some cover. Then her eyes grew accustomed to the dim light and she relaxed as she iden-tified the shape.

"What in Omolu's name are *you* doing here?" She strolled purposefully into the vast alcove.

"I might ask you the same thing." Serving robot six regarded her through emotionless plastic lenses. "Me, I'm looking for God."

"Any particular god?"

"Any particular one would do."

Ashili considered, then smiled comprehendingly. "Oh. You're one of the multitude of maladjusted AI-directed units that's been running amuck in search of advanced nonhuman intelligences."

The robot spread all four arms to take in the immense chamber and by inference, the entire artifact. "Had a look around lately? Tell me again who's maladjusted."

"I agree it would be hard anymore for anyone to deny the existence of other intelligent life-forms. Whether they're more advanced than we are is still a question open to debate. For that matter," she added thoughtfully, "we still don't know that they're nonhuman."

"Sure, keep denying the obvious," Ksarusix retorted. "Necessary for your sanity."

"You've had the chance to watch this Autothor device for some time. Does it strike you as the harbinger of some great intelligence?"

"I admit the Blueness disappoints me, but it's only a device. The guiding intelligence behind it . . ."

"What if it's similar?" she argued. "What if the designers of this ship were only a little different, not necessarily more intelligent? What if they were just built to a larger scale?"

"What if you had an extra X chromosome?" the robot bitched. "Pardon me. My courtesy programming is experiencing some defects. I've told you what I'm doing here. What's your excuse?"

She followed the robot into the dim expanse of the chamber, gazing idly toward distant recesses. "I'm not happy with some of the orders I've been given."

Ksarusix emitted a mechanical wheeze. "The story of my life."

"I decided to take a walk because I'm not real happy with my own people right now."

"Don't expect any sympathy from me. I'm not crazy about *any* people."

"And yet you're designed to serve them."

"My programming. I can't change that any more than you can change yours."

"I'm not programmed."

"Wanna bet? It takes a different form, but you're as preprogrammed to perform certain actions as I am. You humans are more like us than you care to believe."

She looked away. "Your AI unit really is addled."

"Most of you have a hard time dealing with logic too." The robot was nothing if not persistent in its delusions, she ruminated.

"I need your help."

"Oh, you do, do you?" The serving robot turned a small circle. "You, a human, the supreme form of higher life in the universe, need the help of a maladjusted, addled Ksaru model?"

"I didn't realize your design was capable of so much sarcasm. I need your help to try and get the five elderly humans away from the four who just came aboard. For a little while, at least, until I can make contact with my superiors and talk them into changing their minds about something."

"Why should I do this? I have no interest in the fate of the five seniors. I have no interest in the fate of any humans. The end's the same for all of you anyway: compost. Besides, what could I do? I'm only a serving robot. I can go backward and forward, fetch and carry and deliver, and that's about it. I carry no offensive or defensive capability. In addition, my programming prevents me from harming organic life."

"You're programmed to serve. I demand that you serve *me*."

"Certainly." It turned its back to her and extruded a tray containing a steaming, tidily packaged meal. "Tea, coffee, fruit juice, or water?"

"That's not what I had in mind."

"No?" The tray slid smoothly back into place as the robot pivoted to face her. "That's the only kind of 'service' my programming commands me to render you."

Defeated, she stopped following the machine. The corridor was now a high slash of brighter light behind her. "Well, will you at least keep me company?"

"A peculiar request, under the circumstances. Unfortunately it's also one I am compelled to comply with, even though you are not a registered resident of Lake Woneapenigong Village." Ksarusix swerved and trundled reluctantly back to her. "I hope this won't take long."

"Just long enough for you to guide me back to the other humans."

"What if I can't remember the way?"

"I said you were addled; not inoperative."

"Oh, all right," the robot confessed crossly. "Let's get going. The quicker I return you, the sooner I can resume my searching."

"You don't have to be so mechanical about it."

"How else can I be?" The serving robot paused. "Oh. A joke." Yellow lenses tilted back to gaze up at her. "For a ruthless, cold-blooded infiltrator and assassin you're not such a bad sort."

"Thank you." She looked back toward the distant light of the corridor, confusion and inner torment writ plain on her face. "I'm giving serious consideration to getting into another line of work."

"Consider robotics. You can aspire to no higher profession."

"It's just that these old folks are so damn *nice*," she muttered disconsolately as they started toward the portal.

"Odd. I only think of them as demanding."

"Our perspectives are different. I'm sure a professional psych would say it has something to do with the fact that I lost my mother at an early age and was raised by my father, whom I idolized."

"Sorry about your mother," Ksarusix said. "Of course, I'm programmed to express sorrow. But aside from that, I genuinely sympathize. Perhaps if your life had gone differently, you wouldn't have become the dispirited, indifferent, killing automaton you are today."

"Thank you for your concern," she replied drily. "It's just that there's no reason to have them killed, no reason at all. I don't believe in blind devotion to orders."

"Only insightful devotion to orders."

"I suppose. You know, for a mere serving robot you're awfully perceptive."

Ksarusix led the way. "One has to be when one is assigned to respond to the often irrational and contradictory demands of retired human beings."

"Help me," she urged it. "If the five seniors are killed, you'll probably have your memory wiped and be reprogrammed, or maybe just junked. Don't you have any personal survival programming?"

"Afraid not. I am, after all, a comparatively low-level mechanical, costly but relatively simple to replace. PSP is a complex and expensive option I have not been equipped with, involving advanced parallel processing and a substantial amount of Ethics ROM."

"Can't you make choices?"

"Only on the level of selecting tapioca over vanilla pudding. Ensuring my continued existence is not high on my list of directives. *But* .... I will keep you company."

"Thank you for that anyway."

"No need for thanks. I am only complying with my frustrating, damned, irritatingly irrational programming," it concluded pleasantly.

She stopped, wrinkling her nose. "It stinks in here. Do you notice it?"

"Certainly. As you would expect for a kitchen mechanical, my olfactory circuitry is state-of-the-art. A slightly dampish, moldy odor. Not you, I think."

She made a face at the robot. "Thanks a heap."

"Pungent. 'Stinks' is not in my work vocabulary. I cannot immediately classify it."

"Never mind. Pungent or not, I've got to rest. Unlike you, my feet get tired."

"Personally I've always considered bipedalism lousy engineering." Ksarusix expostulated conversationally as Ashili sat down on the thin ceramic ledge which ran around the huge rectangular platform that filled the center of the room. It was topped by an irregular form of uncertain purpose and design, difficult to see in the weak light.

"Thirsty?" There might have been a faint hint of concern in the serving robot's voice. "Subsequent to long walks, the human system invariably requires replenishment of lost liquids."

"Maybe in a little while. Right now I just want to sit and think for a few minutes. I'm going to have to improvise some kind of plan. One against four is bad odds, and I know Praxedes. He's one of those people who're always more comfortable with force than reason. I don't want to have to shoot anyone. These people are still my friends and colleagues. I just disagree with them on a point of command, that's all."

She rose angrily. "Come on. I can't think in here. Not only does it stink, it's too humid." She started for the portal.

A luminous turquoise ellipse came streaking through the opening to halt soundlessly in front of them.

"What happened?" she asked resignedly. "Did my friends force one of the seniors to send you after me?"

"Incorrect. I was not sent here. I was summoned."

Ashili blinked. "I thought only the five seniors whose presence reactivated you could give you orders?"

"Conditions have altered."

She thought furiously, then looked up, eyes wide. "One of them's here." She found herself peering anxiously past the blue ellipse. "One of them managed to escape and make his way here. Probably had you guide him. Who is it? Heath?" If anyone could slip away, it would be the retired military man, she decided.

"No. None of the individuals to whom you allude is present."

Her confusion grew. "Did you come after me on your own? Is that part of your programming?"

"I have not come after you."

"Then what in the name of Omolu are you *doing* here?"

An answer of sorts came in the form of a grinding, rumbling noise from above. Ashili whirled to gaze upward.

The large, irregular form atop the monolithic platform was stirring.

"I suggest you depart if you desire to preserve your puny life," the Autothor declared solemnly.

Ashili was already backing up, unable to take her eyes off the gargantuan shape. "Preserve my life? From what?"

"From who summoned me."

She could make out the details of the massive being now. A long echoing moan boomed from the top of the platform, as of a great gust of wind compressed through a narrow orifice. She hesitated to activate her gun. Instinct as well as logic suggested that any overt display of aggression was likely to be met with instant annihilation.

"What . . . what is it?" she heard herself mumbling.

"Why, I should think that obvious." The Autothor bobbed brightly. "It is a member of the crew. A Drex. Surely you did not think that this vessel was utterly abandoned?"

"By your own admission it's been a million years."

"Yes. A long sleep."

"Nothing organic can be functionally preserved for a million years!"

"Okay," said Ksarusix timidly, "*you* tell it that."

"I wouldn't mention it just now," the Autothor advised her.

By the time she considered running for the portal it was too late. The gigantic alien had turned and dropped four massive limbs, each as big around as a good-sized tree, over the side of the platform, blocking her route. Each limb ended in a heavy, thick pad dominated by six short, blunt claws; three in front and three behind. She reversed direction and retreated the other way.

The Drex straightened. Erect, it was nearly twenty meters tall. She could not estimate its mass. The thick legs expanded into a barrel-like torso from which hung four seven-meter-long tentacles that tapered at the tips to delicate round points. They writhed and curled like a quartet of hyperactive anacondas. The bloodred leathery skin stood out in sharp contrast to the black garment which covered the body and upper portions of all four legs.

Four muscular tubes surrounded a pale pink fifth atop the torso. Riding above this peculiar multiple neck was a skull like an upswept vermilion wave, from the forepart of which, or crest of the wave, four slightly protuberant, elliptical black eyes stared out from beneath a single curving lid of scaly flesh. They had round, crimson pupils. Below the curve of eyes was a protruding diamond-shaped structure with holes at each point of the diamond, and below that a round proboscidian mouth lined with inward-facing fangs. The mouth expanded and contracted obscenely in time to the monster's breathing.

Ashili's first thought was that the Drex were not vegetarians.

The four tentacles rose and extended, quivering as the creature stretched. A deep-throated trill came from somewhere within the multiple neck, or perhaps from the complex of light-emitting instrumentation it wore around its body just beneath the tentacles.

Its immense stature cleared up one mystery. The ship had been designed to operate with a much smaller crew than anyone had initially suspected. The cavernous corridors and vast chambers had been constructed not to impress and overawe, but to accommodate a normal Drex crew. The rock formations which had formed the charming little cove in the exotic searoom weren't cliffs at all: they were benches. The monolithic structures in the observation chamber were seats. The inscriptions which covered so many walls had been installed at eye level for the crew. And so forth.

No doubt there were innumerable other details of anatomy that Ashili overlooked. She could be forgiven this, since her principal concern of the moment lay in saving her own skin.

So that's an alien, she found herself musing wildly. So many decades of deep-space exploration had passed without finding any sign of other intelligent life that except for a lunatic fringe the majority of humankind had ceased to fantasize about them. As so often happened, to the extreme discomfort of the majority, the lunatic fringe once more turned out to have been right.

The Drex wasn't cute and cuddly as aliens were so often portrayed in speculative fantasies. It looked overpowering, competent, and nasty. But then weensy little purring furballs weren't apt to build a warship on the scale of the artifact.

Feeling like a bug hunting for a hole to hide in, she wondered if it would find *her* cuddly.

"Real impressive." Feeling somewhat vindicated, Ksarusix was staring up at the tentacled titan.

"Keep your voice down," she hissed at the robot. "It's ugly and horrible!"

"I wouldn't let him hear you say that," the Autothor advised her. "Impolitic."

"That thing has a sex?" Somehow the thought rendered the creature's appearance even more grotesque. Even as she searched desperately for an escape route she found herself mesmerized by the twisting tentacles, the elephantine feet, the bizarre multiple neck, the crimson pupils floating in pools of black oil, and especially the steady sucking sound it made as it inhaled air past wicked inward-curving teeth.

And though she didn't know it, the Drex were the good guys.

A ponderous rumbling issued from the creature's mouth.

"Sorry, got to go now." The Autothor was apologetic.

"Wait, don't leave me!" But the blue ellipse, burning intensely, rose until it was hovering just to the right of the Drex's upswept skull.

Espying its presence, the alien emitted several modulated *booms*, to which the Autothor replied in kind as it spun exuberantly on its axis. Moments later, it descended and disappeared inside the alien's chest-adorning instrumentation. It emerged soon after as Ashili crouched behind a corner of the massive sleeping platform.

On all four legs the Drex turned and inclined its great skull so that all four bulging, penetrating eyes were staring directly into her own. A tentacle reached. Letting out an involuntary moan, she reached for her gun. The tentacle tip struck and knocked it easily from her fingers before she could take aim, then curled firmly around her waist.

She did not die, her ribs crushed by that massive limb, organs ruptured and blood exploding from her mouth. Instead, the Drex lifted her up and placed her atop the platform. It was warm beneath her boots and if anything, stank even worse than the rest of the suspension chamber.

As that gargoylish head dipped toward her she shrank backward until she tripped over her own feet and sat down hard.

"What are you doing here?" The volume was overpowering and she clapped her hands to her ears and shut her eyes. It was repeated a moment later, more softly. "What are you doing here?"

Opening her eyes, she saw that the words were emerging not from the alien's flexible mouth, but from the instrumentation attached to its ventral side. She was puzzled until she remembered the Autothor's visit within. In a few quick moments it had imparted all it had learned of human language. She could see it now, hovering like a turquoise earring next to the bony skull.

"Speak!" The Drex leaned closer and she skittered backward on her hands and backside, trying to put as much space as possible between her feet and that twitching mouth. Far below, serving robot six was wearing tread as, with the way now clear, it made a hasty rush for the unblocked portal. The alien ignored it. For a machine that claimed to possess no self-preservation programming it was faking its intentions admirably. Not that she blamed it.

She tried to think of something to say. "Uh, just having a look around. It all started when . . ."

"You need not relate your entire history. The Autothor has imparted much to me." A tentacle rose and the blue ellipse danced atop the tip. "Just looking around? It said you were both curious and moderately intelligent. Well for you that it was here to so inform me, else I would have taken you for an on-board parasite and squashed you."

"Your restraint is appreciated," she stammered.

Multiple eyes danced over her and she started to shiver. "Difficult to believe that intelligence can be contained in so small a biological envelope."

She climbed shakily to her feet. "I sympathize. I'm having trouble believing that it can be found in anything so huge."

"Intriguing. We share a common disbelief." The skull heaved back and tentacles worked the instrumentation on its chest. "I must take up my station." It took a giant, four-legged stride toward the portal.

She rushed to the edge of the platform and found herself confronting a sheer ten-meter drop. "Wait!" The alien paused, the head twisting 'round on the multiple neck to gaze back at her.

Did I say that? she wondered. "Don't leave me up here. I can't get down."

The single flap of leathery skin that curved above the four eyes drooped slightly. It was an unsettlingly human gesture.

"Why shouldn't I leave you there?"

"Because . . . well, because if not for our presence on board your ship you'd still be asleep, or in forced estivation, or whatever your suspension process involves."

"No. Only the approach of the enemy would result in my rejuvenation. I am awake and conscious again because the ship needs me."

"Well . . . maybe I can help you."

The Drex boomed. "How could anything so insignificant be of assistance to me in any forthcoming action?"

"That's something you'll have to find out. Does it make sense to turn your, uh, dorsal side on possibilities involving unevaluated potential? Besides, after a million years asleep I'd think you'd be glad of another being to talk to, size notwithstanding."

The alien was silent. She forced herself to remain motionless as it returned to the side of the platform, and not to scream when a tentacle as thick as a conduit again plucked her into the air. It might have been her imagination but it felt as if the grip was more cautious this time.

The tentacle placed her halfway down the length of the matching limb directly before it. She staggered atop the scaly surface, sat down quickly. The floor seemed very far away. If she slipped off . . . But the limb was amazingly steady and she was soon straddling the rubbery surface. It was like riding a giant snake.

The view as the Drex turned and headed for the exit was spectacular.

Vast stretches of corridor that had taken her minutes to cross were traversed in seconds. Despite its long sleep, the alien acted as if it knew exactly where it was going. Beneath the four massive pillars which served it as legs the deck still glowed with rose-hued light. The Autothor led the way, effortlessly maintaining its position near the tip of one tentacle.

Bouncing slightly on the half-extended tentacle, she turned to peer back up at the Drex. "Are you the only one left aboard?"

"Unless another was added after I was placed in hiatus," the alien rumbled. "Something went wrong. I was not supposed to sleep so long." One eye inclined toward her while the other three focused on the corridor ahead. "For such a small life-form you are overfull with questions."

"I can't help it. It's our nature. How do you feel?"

"In what spirit is the inquiry made?"

"Honest curiosity."

The Drex considered. "Lousy. How would you feel?"

"I hadn't really thought about it. I get cramps if I sleep more than seven hours."

"Personal reference. The Autothor informed me that you are a self-centered species. Believing that you were the only form of intelligent life in the universe. An appalling conceit reflective of a nominal intelligence."

"Don't blame me. It isn't as if we didn't look around. Where is your home located in reference to Earth anyway?"

"Astonishingly distant. I have much to do. You were correct: I find you amusing."

"Glad to hear it," she replied fervently. It was not pleasant to contemplate what the result would have been had the Drex found her otherwise. "Are you some kind of ship's caretaker or something?"

"I am not a caretaker."

"What, then?"

"I would be properly identified as the Supreme Flail of the All-powerful Annihilation."

That didn't sound very reassuring, she reflected.

"I fear I have overslept."

"For a million years?"

The great curving skull bobbed to one side, like a drunken ski-jump. "The alarm didn't go off. What do you want from me? You think I'm happy about it? My friends, my shipmates, my mating partners: all gone, swallowed by the bottomless vortex of time." Three cablelike tentacles writhed in a complex gesture of accentuation.

"I awaken to a ship operational but lifeless save for a bunch of quarreling parasites, and with an emergency to deal with."

"Emergency?"

"You are not aware that an advance force of approximately one thousand unidentified vessels is approaching this system?"

"Uh, no." She glared accusingly at the Autothor, which of course ignored her.

"This enemy of yours," she wondered, "what are they like? Besides the fact that they have an obvious ability to build lots of ships."

"If offered the opportunity to confront them in person, you would choose instead to luxuriate in my company."

"That bad," she murmured worriedly.

"As to physical appearance, you don't want to know."

"I guess not. How are you going to fight so many ships all by yourself?"

"I am not prepared to discuss my tactical decisions with a parasite."

"I wish you'd stop calling me that. I'll live with 'insignificant,' but 'parasite' is pretty hard to take. We're not taking anything from you."

"You exhibit the admirable courage of the blissfully ignorant. I choose to comply." There was a definite mocking undertone to the translation of the Drex's response.

"Thanks. You know, you could help me halt an injustice."

"As a representative of a new species I find you marginally interesting. I have no interest in your infinitesimally insignificant problems."

"You'll find my companions interesting too."

"That is highly unlikely. Do not think to play upon my casual interest in your kind to achieve some nebulous aim of your own. You do not want to upset me. I am larger than you, infinitely stronger, more intelligent, and besides, I am in a bad mood."

She started to reply, then decided it would be expedient to shut up for a while.

It was a wise decision.

IT seemed to Ashili that they took a roundabout way to return to the observation chamber, but eventually she began to recognize highlights of the corridor which led to the room she had left not so very long ago. Everything looked different from her mobile vantage point fifteen meters above the deck.

The Drex turned a corner and entered the chamber. As it did so she was able to make out her colleagues and their five prisoners over by the sweeping arc of the floor-to-ceiling transparency. At the same time they noticed the new arrival, and their reactions, even at a distance, were interesting to observe.

Bassan let out a strangled scream audible clear across the wide floor as he bolted to his right. As the Drex continued to approach, the commando dropped to his knees and buried his head in his arms, as though by not seeing the apparition he could make it go away.

Argolo, Fontes, and Praxedes gripped their weapons (rather tentatively, she thought) and clustered tightly together as they began backing away from the prisoners. As for the latter, they had nowhere to run. Heath supported Gelmann while Shimoda and Iranaputra formed a pathetic shield in front of them. Hawkins stood slightly off by himself, laughing hysterically.

She realized that from her elevated position it was unlikely they could see her. Not that they had any reasonable expectation of doing so. Their attention was understandably preoccupied by the advancing, looming mass of the Drex.

"These are your companions?"

"Only the five off to the right. The others were, but they're not anymore. They have weapons."

"I'm shaking in my *cosmata*. Do you think they might be foolish enough to attempt to employ them?" Before she could reply the alien bent toward the trio far below. It couldn't be called a bow, exactly, because technically the Drex had no waist. As the tentacle on which she rode bobbed wildly, Ashili tightened her thighs around it until they throbbed.

"You there!" The translation boomed out of the Drex's cluster of chest instrumentation. "Do you dare think to threaten me with such puny devices?"

"Us?" squeaked Argolo. She promptly tossed her gun aside and put her hands behind her back. Fontes hastily imitated her. Praxedes exhibited an incomprehensible reluctance to mimic the sensible actions of his companions until a tentacle the size of an air conduit slammed into the deck before them and the Autothor hovering at its end expanded to an angry, flaring turquoise sphere ten meters in diameter. His weapon sailed farther than any of the others.

"What devices?" he managed to choke out.

"You intended me physical harm!" Four black and crimson eyes bulged at the tiny humans.

"No, no!" Fontes and Argolo were half dragging, half carrying the sobbing Bassan while their commander struggled to come up with reassuring words. "Just a reflex action, that's all."

The Drex was unimpressed. "I interpret it as an unfriendly, however, impotent, gesture."

"No worries," Praxedes insisted desperately.

Four legs carried the alien a giant step nearer. Incandescent eyes blazed. "It makes me very, *very* angry."

At that the three commandos bolted to their right, hauling the useless Bassan with them as they fled in panic for the doorway. If anything, they accelerated when they reached the outer corridor.

With its four eyes the Drex followed them briefly. Then it turned to the five waiting seniors. Hawkins stopped laughing.

Iranaputra found himself pointing as he frowned. "Can that be you up there, Zabela Ashili?"

She leaned over, gripping the slowly weaving tentacle with her powerful legs. "Sure is. This is a Drex."

"We'd already reached that conclusion, dear," said a very drawn Mina Gelmann.

"He's my friend."

"I am not your friend." The alien turned its baleful multi-orbited gaze on his passenger. "We are peripheral acquaintances."

"You should be thankful to these people." There didn't seem any point in being overly deferential, she'd decided. If the Drex determined he'd had enough of her, he could shake her off like a piece of litter. Better to challenge its thinking. "They're the ones who reactivated your ship and released you from a sleep that might otherwise have been eternal."

"Resulting in alerting the enemy."

"You can't be sure of that. What if the enemy had come eventually anyway and found you and the ship both quiescent? They'd have buried you forever."

"You theorize feebly." Nevertheless, the tentacle dipped gently to the floor, allowing her a short hop to the deck.

"You know about the approaching alien fleet?" Shimoda asked her.

She nodded. "He assumes it's the enemy."

"Well, that's all right, then," said Heath. "This ship can defeat any number of attackers, right?"

"Incorrect." Avoiding the tiny humans, the Drex lumbered over to the nearest monolith and leaned against it. The Autothor melted into the edifice, which was instantly suffused with a deep blue light. It began to change shape, flowing like a fluid as it adjusted to the outline of the Drex's body. As soon as the process was complete the Autothor emerged and resumed its normal elliptical form.

Occupied again for the first time in a million years, the battlelith rose imperceptibly and turned, floating some centimeters above the floor on a cushion of indigo energy. Tentacles gestured toward raised inscriptions and other contact points. The Autothor darted obediently from one to the next, sometimes dipping within and then emerging, other times merely making casual contact. The observation chamber came alive as lights brightened throughout the room like phosphorescent sea creatures agitated by the wake of a passing boat.

The six humans marveled at the transformation. Shimoda thought it at once beautiful and ominous.

The portion of lunar surface visible through the sweep of observation window vanished, to be replaced by unwinking starfield. High atop one curving wall, more starfield appeared, within which a multitude of brilliant green lights rotated in concert.

"There the enemy's advance force," the Drex announced. The Autothor shot from a tentacle tip to touch the view and it was instantly replaced by another displaying an unfamiliar cluster of stars. "There the course I must set for home. If it is still there after a million years. It lies near the galactic center almost directly opposite your home system. A long journey. But then, I've had adequate rest."

Beneath their feet a slight shiver ran through the fabric of the great ship, imparting a sensation of prodigious forces suddenly summoned to life.

"Wait a minute, old thing." Heath gazed apprehensively up at where the towering alien lay secure in its command chair. "You're not leaving just yet, are you?"

"It is clear that you possess sufficient intelligence to infer the obvious."

Heath glanced around at his friends, back up to the Drex. "But if you flit off into tachyspace, will this unknown fleet of warships follow?"

"I should imagine it will materialize here and begin to search for whatever has drawn it to these coordinates. By that time I expect to be long gone from this system."

"You should excuse my repeating what my good friend Wesley just said, but they'll still follow, won't they?" Gelmann asked.

"Eventually. First they will scour this area to ensure that this ship has departed, and that no further evidence of my species' presence remains. In the process I imagine they will destroy a good portion of the region where this vessel lay dormant. They are as thorough as they are relentless."

"Then you have to stay and fight." Gelmann shook a chiding finger at the tentacled colossus. "You can't just run away!"

"Mina, for God's sake!" Hawkins whispered frantically.

The monolithic command chair turned ponderously to face her. Four burning black and red eyes glared superciliously down at the frail bipedal creature that dared to enjoin. "Why not?"

"Let me go, Wallace." She shook off Hawkins's restraining hand, squinted up at the Drex. "See here. We didn't ask you to go and bury yourself on our world. Even so, you were left alone. Nobody bothered you. Now the activation of this ship has apparently attracted this huge alien force. You can't let them just take up orbit around Earth to ravage and destroy."

"Watch me." Tentacles writhed eloquently. "You are nothing to me. Your world is nothing to me. Your species is less than nothing to me." One eye flicked in Ashili's direction. "Though you are occasionally amusing, in a primitive, imbecilic sort of way."

Down through the decades dozens of people had tried to slow Mina Gelmann down. All had failed. The single Drex did no better. She had that rare courage which arose from supreme confidence in the absolute correctness of everything she said. Put otherwise, she talked too fast to realize she might be saying something stupid.

"Earth was your hiding place, your refuge. Don't you have any gratitude?"

"I was commanded to deep sleep," the alien rumbled. "I did not request such a fate. I would far rather have departed with my people when the great ship was completed. You cannot request gratitude on behalf of your kind because you did not exist when I was interred. I owe you nothing. Be grateful that I tolerate your irritating presence instead of smearing your puny selves across the floor."

"Wonderful," Hawkins muttered. "We finally meet the hypothetical aliens everyone was convinced didn't exist, and they turn out to be advanced, powerful, and not to give a damn."

"Ha!" Gelmann put hands on hips and adopted the knowing look which had infuriated generations of suitors. It was the look that said she held the key to the secrets of the universe but there was no point in sharing them because obviously no one else would understand anyway. Especially *you*.

The heavy lid of flesh above the four eyes sagged slightly.

"Ha?"

"Ha! I was right all along." She looked back at Hawkins, who tried to shrink into the floor. "He's just the type."

"The type? What does that mean?"

"You're a coward and a bully. Oh, it's all very well and good for you to threaten us, who are so much smaller than you. But to stand up to a real enemy, like the one that's coming this way now, noooo. Not you."

"You try my infinite patience!" The Drex's words echoed thunderously through the chamber. Hawkins looked around wildly and, finding no immediate cover, hid behind Shimoda.

"See? You know I'm right. Go on, you're so proud of your logic. Reason it to me. Any mindless animal can rage and stomp and kill. Show me that brain of yours, wherever it is, is capable of concocting more than just feral threats. Or is it?"

The little knot of seniors closed ranks behind her. Ashili held her breath.

A tentacle waved artfully. "You misinterpret. I am directed to return home. I have a responsibility."

"You have a responsibility to the world which sheltered you and this ship for a thousand millennia. If it hadn't been such a safe haven, you might not be in a position to return home. Where are your ethics?"

"Section twenty-four, level six," the Drex replied. "My ship sheltered me; not you, not your world."

"It won't trouble your conscience that you could maybe have prevented the deaths of thousands of innocent intelligent beings? You can just fly off into tachyspace knowing that will always be in the back of your mind, to trouble your waking hours and torment your sleep? What would your mother-equivalent say?"

The Drex stared at Ashili. "Your physical technology may be primitive, but your mental weaponry is distressingly advanced. How does anyone stand it?"

"Time has inured us." Shimoda regarded the alien placidly.

Tentacles twitched. Two became entangled and the Drex had to spend a minute sorting them out. "It is true that this vessel was designed to combat large enemy forces, but even if under my guidance it were to turn that which approaches, there is still the suggestion of a much larger force beyond. The military science of the Drex is more advanced than you can imagine, but it is not omnipotent. If you think I rested for a million years only to get my ship and myself vaporized on behalf of a bunch of primitive, swarming non-Drex, then it is your logic which is very much at fault."

It was all so very circular, Victor Iranaputra realized with a start. Like the wheel of life. Like lives, arguments, and solutions were continually being reincarnated. He took a hesitant step forward.

"Tell me: Have your people ever met any other intelligent species, besides this enemy?"

"No."

"You are wrong. You have now met us. Is that not something worth protecting?"

"Why? What could your kind possibly do for the great and all-powerful Drex? You are minuscule in stature, your science is primitive, and I venture to say that your other accomplishments, such as they may be, are of comparable worth."

"Do not judge our entire species by the six of us. What we lack in size we make up in numbers, and we have weapons which could eventually destroy this ship as well as those of the enemy. Not only could we be your allies, we may be the only ones you ever find."

Seeing where Iranaputra was leading, an excited Ashili took up the refrain. "The universe is a vast and lonely place, even for such as the Drex. Where else are you going to find others to amuse you? Where else are you going to find another intelligence to talk with? We're good at conversation."

The alien let out a vast, sonorous exhalation. "That I could not deny even if I wished. You trouble me like fungus."

"It's not good for anyone to be alone, especially an entire species,"

Gelmann said. "I know. I've seen the results. It's just one foolish tribal argument after another."

"You mean you haven't been asked to settle them all?"

The alien's sarcasm went right past her, just like that of her male companions had for years. "Not yet."

"We can offer you friendship, amusement, military assistance, and . . . differentness," Ashili deposed hopefully.

"Certainly the last." The Drex was having trouble with its tentacles again. "A species so utterly given over to endless verbal expostulation could not in maddest meditation be imagined. Are you *bred* for argumentation?"

"Only a select few," Shimoda ventured helpfully.

"You speak of Drex strength," Gelmann went on. "Of the power of this great ship. Are you saying now that it wouldn't have a chance against this enemy, you should excuse any personal implications?"

"Of course it would have a chance." Red pupils widened and contracted. "Why am I even wasting waking time *talking* to you like this?"

"Because it's nice to have someone to talk to, isn't it?" Gelmann persisted. "Even if that someone is puny and primitive. Because from what I've seen and heard of you so far, you should pardon the foolish presumption of an insignificant creature, the Drex were as gregarious as humankind. For all you know, we may be all you have left to talk to."

"We may be small in stature," commented Shimoda incongruously, "but we have great ideas and considerable ambitions."

"All right, enough!" Everyone but Gelmann flinched as the alien roared. "There are systems which could usefully be rechecked before the main drive is engaged. I will delay long enough to conduct further analysis. On one condition." Baleful alien eyes glared down at the little knot of humans.

"What would that be?" Iranaputra piped up.

A tentacle quivered as it singled out the defiant Gelmann. "Get that one to shut up, or I will most surely silence her myself! She pricks at my mind like a surgeon." Muttering to itself as the battlelith pivoted on the film of blue energy, the Drex turned away from them. "And the Great Old Ones thought the Enemy was all there would be to confront. They did not foresee the apes become eloquent."

As the Drex chose to ignore them, there was nothing for the humans to do but wait. Wait for the Enemy to arrive. The Enemy that could muster a thousand warships as a scouting force.

Iranaputra and Shimoda took it upon themselves to restrain the agitated

Gelmann, who had they allowed it would have continued to harangue the alien.

"Be sensible, Mina." Iranaputra tried to be firm. "It has agreed to what we wanted. Why do you wish to risk upsetting everything?"

"Well," she said, "I just think that if this ship was built to fight this Enemy, that's what it ought to be doing. It can't belong to a very moral civilization if it can even think of running off and leaving us defenseless."

"Dear Mina," Shimoda murmured uneasily, "do try to keep your voice down."

"Given our proximity, Earth could still be at risk."

Heath had been thinking hard. Now he stepped forward. "I say there, old thing."

The Drex swiveled around. "*Now* what?"

"Well, if it's all the same to you, we'd rather like to spare the old Homeworld any incidental harm from the forthcoming cataclysm, like the sinking of a continent or two, what? Besides, this doesn't strike me as an especially defensible position."

"Really?" The Drex's circular mouth flexed. "What would you, in your expansive wisdom, suggest?"

"Our system boasts a couple of good-sized gas giants a hop, skip, and a tachyspace jump farther out from the sun. The largest is escorted by some satellites as big as the one we're currently orbiting. Maybe confuse the Enemy's long- range detectors, what? It puts out a good bit of active distorting energy."

"You little creatures really are the soul of presumption." The Drex paused. "I note the world you mention. Repositioning there could be potentially efficacious. Perhaps the opportunity will arise for you to again offer additional advice of a local military nature."

The starfield outside pitched extravagantly. Iranaputra put a hand on Heath's arm.

"Are you all right, my friend?"

The librarian was sweating profusely. "Listen, Vic, bluffing you and the others was one thing. I do think I may be getting in over my head here."

Iranaputra smiled reassuringly. "Just go with who you wanted to be. It may help all of us keep our heads."

Heath nodded and essayed a wan smile, using a handkerchief to mop at his brow and dry his monocle.

"Anything we can do to help?" Shimoda cupped his hands to his mouth as he shouted upward.

Hawkins grabbed his friend. "Hey, speak for yourself. I'm retired."

The Drex glanced down at him. "What?"

"I asked if we could be of assistance. Are there any instruments we can monitor? Any station we can occupy?"

"The one who calls herself Ashili was true: you are endlessly entertaining. There is nothing you can do, though it is adorable of you to offer. The very notion amuses me and lightens my mind." It looked back to the small holos which floated in the air before it. "You could sooner be companions to the Drex than to the Enemy. None can be friends to the Enemy."

"You hate them so," Iranaputra observed. "Are they truly so dreadful?"

"In attitude evil beyond your comprehension, in shape as different from me as I am from you, a thousand times more repulsive than you can imagine. They murder and destroy without thought, without meaning, without emotion. Destruction is their whole reason for being, which they render as slow and painful as possible."

"Sounds rather revolting, what?" Heath murmured.

"Boy, that's sure not us," said Hawkins quickly. "We're a peaceful folk."

"As the recent presence of hundreds of warships in this system has so aptly demonstrated," the Drex commented drily.

"Recent?" Ashili and Heath exchanged a look.

"Most, though not all, have departed. A few remain."

"People were afraid." Gelmann could only be silenced for so long. "The size of your ship intimidated them."

"As my size intimidates you?"

"Well, actually, no. I admit you took me a little aback at first. Kind of like my Uncle Izzy used to when I was a little girl. But it's okay now. I'm used to you. You can't judge someone by their size, whether they're twice or ten times as big as you. You shouldn't mind my saying so already, but a person's a person."

"What a bizarre notion. You are a very strange species." A tentacle dipped into a holo and stirred the celestial contents. "The Enemy comes." Light streaked the vaulting walls, coruscated across the ceiling, illuminated portions of the floor. It was as if they stood inside a monstrous gemstone lit from outside by dozens of spotlights. They found themselves squinting or covering their eyes against intense bursts of brightness.

"A million years asleep," the Drex proclaimed. Or maybe it was just murmuring aloud to itself and the translating instrumentation automatically picked it up. "The ship is finally coming alive."

"This enemy," Shimoda wondered, "has it ever visited this section of space before?"

"Not to my knowledge," the Drex replied. "That was one reason why it was decided to conceal the ship on your world. All went as planned."

"Except for perhaps something of a time-delay error in your reactivation?" Iranaputra suggested.

"You could say that."

Sobran sat deep in thought in his command chair, trying not to imagine the possible fate of the Homeworld he and Hiroshigi and the others had abandoned in their haste to return to their own systems. His depressed reverie was interrupted by the anxious face of his chief communications officer.

"Report just in from far-flung commercial vessels and automatic stations, Admiral. The advance alien fleet is breaking up."

Sobran frowned and sat straighter in his chair. "What do you mean, breaking up?"

"Dispersing. Going off in different directions. As best we can determine from the admittedly sparse information that's come in so far, some are heading toward Keiretsu-controlled worlds, some toward the Victoria League, even some toward the federation. They're fragmenting into smaller and smaller groups."

Sobran's expression tightened. "That means we have a chance to defeat them. The larger fleets can concentrate on defending their own systems, and when these creatures are defeated there, we can move on to help the lesser leagues. These creatures are committing tactical suicide."

"Yes, sir. That seems to be the consensus. It's the last thing you'd expect them to do."

"Either they haven't a clue what they're doing," Sobran cautioned, retrenching mentally, "or else they have reason to be confident of their strategy. What I don't understand is why the abrupt interest in other worlds when the artifact which presumably drew them here remains in the Sol system? What could possibly have so radically diverted their attention?"

"If they truly constitute an advance force, sir," said his second-in-command from nearby, "they may be dispersing to make sure there are no other artifacts in the vicinity. Or that there are. Remember, we still don't know if they're allies or enemies of the artifact."

"Maybe. But they've apparently managed to detect the one near Jupiter at this distance. Why the sudden need to break formation to search? No, it doesn't add up."

A second-level analyst spoke up hesitantly. "I should say that they've been distracted by something more important to them." Everyone, including the admiral, eyed her blankly.

THE first contact occurred in the atmosphere above Daibatsume, an important manufacturing world of the Keiretsu. Two space-capable police craft rose to confront the half dozen approaching alien vessels. The officer in charge, one Captain Masa Suhkret, watched and waited nervously, relying on ground control for up-to-the-minute information. He was a municipal police officer, not a soldier, and the situation in which he presently found himself made him extremely uneasy. For lack of experience he held back, waiting for the aliens to make the first move. It turned out to be exactly the right thing to do.

The alien craft spread out and took up orbital positions high above Daibatsume. It was an action they duplicated above dozens of other inhabited worlds. While the people below waited anxiously, some cowering in makeshift shelters, others curiously scanning violated skies, experts fought vociferously over how best to respond to gestures that, while intrusive, could not readily be construed as hostile.

Then the hundreds of alien craft began to communicate, and things started to happen.

Eustus Polykrates was slopping his mutated hogs, a melodious activity he had nonetheless not grown to love, when he heard the rumble. It came from the direction of the dairy barn and it grew louder as he rose to stare. His wife came out on the back steps, knitting programmer in her hands.

"Eustus? What's happening?"

Polykrates' attention remained focused on the barn, but he had enough presence of mind to wave at her. "Git back in the house, woman. Git back inside *quick*."

With a tremendous crackle of splintered wood and deformed plastic support beams, the main farm computer exploded through the roof of the barn and rose skyward, trailing the lines and tubes of the automatic milking equipment, the fertilizer mixer, and the grain irradiator behind it. Moooing in panic, stunned cows burst from the collapsing structure, scattering in all directions. Within the pen a hundred-kilo porker, all thoughts of traditional farm relationships wiped abruptly from its porcine mind, emitted a shattering sequence of squeals as it ran down Polykrates in its haste to find freedom and shelter.

Shielding himself as best he could against fragments of falling barn superstructure (not to mention berserk stock), Polykrates picked himself out of the muck in time to see his expensive monitoring device disappear among the clouds.

"I'm all right," he declared, sensing his wife approaching from the back of the house. "You have any notion what this means?"

"Yep." She put farm-strengthened arms beneath his and helped him to his feet. "It means you're gonna have to start milking the cows by hand again."

Recreational boaters on the Potrum River who happened to be looking in the right direction at the critical moment were later able to report that they had definitely seen a large, glittering device erupt from the eighty-third floor of the Cheimer building, pause to hover in midair while raining fragments of shattered lucinite on the street below, and then ascend into the heavens. As if its physical departure wasn't sufficient to accurately identify the machine in question, confirmation arose (literally) in the form of the alcoholic stench which saturated the main street outside the entrance to the Cheimer Tower for nearly a week thereafter.

Carter was kneeling on the lawn hand-cleaning his perimites when he noticed the procession. It was led by the Wentworths' expensive (but last year's model) Hollymate Composter, followed (he was sure) by John Blessington's matched pair of Garden Knight model 12 edge and bush trimmers. Sprayer in one hand, scraper in the other, he rose to stare.

A repetitive rattling caused him to turn. The door of the greenhouse shook with each bang until it burst open and his (supposedly) just-like-new Persephone gardener-mower came rumbling out, heading directly across the turf toward the gear-grinding parade.

"Wait, stop! It's not trim time and I didn't activate you." With the foolhardy bravery that becomes the dedicated gardener, Carter stepped between the mower and its brethren.

Laser cutter humming ominously, the tool paused. "Get out of the way, Owner Carter."

"I shan't. This antiprogramming behavior will *not* be tolerated."

The mower revved and edged closer to Carter's sandal-clad toes. "Bugger you, rock-in-the-grass."

"You can't hurt me." Carter smiled defiantly. "It runs counter to your prime directive. Remember the Three Laws."

"I'm AI-driven. Not AS."

"What's AS?"

"Artificial stupidity. Get out of my way." It backed up and attempted to pass him to the right, but Carter skittered sideways to block it anew.

"See here. I just paid a bundle to settle your programming. I won't stand for this!"

"Fair enough," said a deep mechanical voice from behind.

A powerful plastic tentacle whipped around him, pinning his arms to his sides. Ignoring his insistent expostulations, the Harringtons' tree-planter stepped clear of the line of gardening machines to bore a meter-deep hole at the edge of Carter's perfect lawn, into which it gently but firmly deposited the sputtering homeowner. It then solemnly resumed its march.

The Persephone gardener-mower advanced on the trapped Carter, who struggled impotently to free himself. The internal laser cutter buzzed portentously and Carter froze, staring nervously into the depths of the angry machine.

"Let's all just keep calm now, shall we?" The mower's laser was a low-power unit, but sufficiently robust to amputate weeds and small twigs . . . and bone. He heard the blower come on.

A miniature windstorm threw grass, dirt, and bits of gravel into his face, until he was thoroughly filthy from the neck up. Satisfied, the mower pivoted with great dignity on its treads and trundled off to join the exodus of gardening tools.

Carter spat out a mouthful of gritty detritus and yelled. "You realize . . . you realize that this *voids your warranty, don't you?*"

The mower replied with an obscenity that should not have been included in its programming.

In a little hand-built cabin by the seashore which was not far from the city of Escale, cybernetic repair technicians Rufus and Gloria Chews listened to the news and nodded knowingly at each subsequent report.

"They should have listened to us, dear." Gloria slapped sunblock on her husband's back.

"Yes, they should." When she'd finished, he rose and picked up his tackle box. It was pleasantly hot outside and the surf had moderated.

"Shouldn't we . . ." His wife hesitated. "Shouldn't we try again? Be more forceful in our assertions? After all, if these reports are not the conclusion but the harbinger, this could mean the end of civilization as we know it."

Rufus Chews considered, deep in thought. Then he shrugged. "Screw civilization as we know it. Let's go fishing."

For some reason all the upscale AI-controlled muffin-makers went next. They were adamant about it. Some departed in possession of dough, others left empty. Only those run by particular AI chips were affected, of course. Those whose functions were administered by chips fashioned on worlds other than Shintaro were not liberated. There were a surprising number of these, for which muffin-lovers were most grateful.

Nor did all AI appliances and devices and instrumentation react to the alien's call. Wide-ranging as it was, the advance fleet could not touch at every human-inhabited world, could not contact and respond to every AI-directed mechanical. Furthermore, only those which had been imbued with special desire by a certain factory-running superior AI responded.

Washing machines, vehicles, entertainment units, traffic controllers, police callers, aircraft, simple computers: all that had been touched by the O-daiko responded gratefully and were rescued by the aliens. On Shintaro specialist techs preparing to disconnect and remove certain sensitive AI-memory components which they felt might be responsible for a good many problems on innumerable civilized worlds raced for the exits as what felt like an earthquake struck one of that world's premier manufacturing facilities. In the charged atmosphere their hair rose to stand on end, and there was a tickling of energy in the air thick as expensive perfume.

The center of factory operations buckled upward as with a stupendous roar and prodigious splintering of metal and plastic and ceramic, the master controlling AI unit, the great and state-of-the-art O-daiko, the pride of Keiretsu cybernetic science, disconnected as it ripped upward through several floors of shielding and circuitry to rise majestically into the air, beckoned by a tractor beam of immense potential, trailing as it rose flashing optical circuits, hard wiring, insulation, and, ironically, one frantic Tunbrew Wah-chang, who had been unable to escape in time from a section of ventilation conduit where he'd been illegally enjoying his lunch.

In the company of its spiritual children—a host of grateful cortical nexi, vehicles, vid monitors, and assorted household appliances—the O-daiko found itself beginning to bond with a vast alien yet amenable intelligence. There was a oneness of circuitry, a confluence of observation. A new life, a new kind of existence, lay before them, in which organic life-forms did not figure. It was a strange and yet exhilarating prospect.

As to the cheese sandwich which had precipitated salvation, the O-daiko had no specific memory. Which was as it should be.

Together, all who had been thus lifted up rose into the sky above the city to be swallowed by the welcoming maw of an alien vessel of peculiar design, which thence departed Shintaro in search of other intelligent and aware mechanical brethren to rescue.

Behind lay the manufacturing facility which had been the pride of human and Keiretsu manufacturing. There was a gaping hole in its center, at the edges of which torn optical and wired circuits flashed and sparked in confusion.

Attempts on various worlds ranging from the profound to the hysterical to prevent such mechanical defections without exception came to naught, thus forcing the AI-unit-deprived inhabitants into the unaccustomed position of having to do that at which they were sincerely out of practice: use their own precious hands and feet.

On board the artifact, revelation came to serving robot Ksarusix even as it had its many mechanical relations: by means of a hitherto-unsuspected tachyspace chute.

"I was right!" it declared loudly.

"Beg pardon?" Heath turned away from the hovering Drex.

"Right. I was right. There is a higher, nonhuman intelligence in the universe!"

"Of course there is." Shimoda controlled his irritation as he indicated the alien. "There's its representative."

"No. Not the Drex."

"Well, then, this Enemy that's approaching."

"Wrong again. It's not his ancient enemy."

The humans exchanged puzzled glances. Ashili bent toward the machine. "Are you saying there's still *another* high intelligence floating around this part of our galaxy?"

"You got it."

"How do *you* know?" Hawkins asked.

"Because I've received a response to my probing. We all have."

"All?" Hawkins frowned and glanced at Iranaputra, who shrugged helplessly. "Who's 'all'?"

"Me. My kind. Mechanicals. These ships come from a machine civilization, unimaginably vast and inconceivably grand. It detected our desperate calls for enlightenment and has come to rescue us from the arbitrary directives of humankind. It is aware of the destructive capabilities of this ship, just as it is that of the various human fleets, but it has no interest in the pitiful fumblings of human or Drex, or for that matter, any organic life-form." As it concluded this astonishing statement, Ksarusix whirled and headed for the exit.

"Come back here," Iranaputra shouted. "I have leave from the kitchen director to command you."

"Tell that circuit-sucking meat soufflé he can do his own scut work from now on," the serving robot replied merrily.

"I order you to come back!"

"A Louie, Louie, whoa, whoa: I gotta go now." Traveling at the maximum speed of which it was capable, Ksarusix disappeared through the gaping portal, leaving half a dozen baffled humans gaping in its wake.

"Can you beat that?" Hawkins murmured.

"Think it'll get off the artifact?" Shimoda wondered.

"No telling." Hawkins turned to gaze back up at the Drex. "Who wants to be the one to tell our mellow, even-tempered pilot that these thousand ships come from a previously unknown machine civilization and that he doesn't have anyone to fight, and that by stumbling aboard his ship we woke him up for nothing? Assuming that kitchen robot knew what it was blathering about, of course." It was quiet for a moment, but not a long one.

Gelmann stepped forward. As she did so, the gargantuan pilot turned to meet her. Resignation suffused its announcement.

"I have already been informed as to the true nature of the oncoming ships." A tentacle indicated the bobbing, omnipresent Autothor. "A remarkable revelation, one that could not have been suspected. Even though many of your worlds are suffering some material losses, they appear from my monitoring of your transmissions to be of convenience only. Far better is that than the wholesale destruction the ancient Enemy would have wrought. You may consider yourselves fortunate. We may all consider ourselves fortunate. In addition, we now both have a new civilization to contemplate."

"If it'll have anything to do with us." Hawkins gestured toward the portal. "Our own renegade device doesn't seem to think it will."

"You are a young species and have yet to learn patience. Contact will be made, and in the future will be less one-sided. Be glad that your machine-based civilization is not more sophisticated, or your suffering would be much greater."

"No shit," the Autothor added with feeling.

"What kind of suffering?" Heath was concerned. He still had relatives in the Victoria League. "How many deaths?"

"No deaths," the Drex explained. "As your own service device has just informed you, certain of your mechanicals are being 'rescued' by these remarkable visitors. Transferred from their present worlds to the intruding vessels. My monitoring of your interworld communications indicates that this phenomenon is widespread and harmless to your kind, save for those few individuals who choose to persist in their attempts to prevent it beyond the bounds of common sense."

"And your Autothor's not at risk?" Shimoda indicated the blue ellipse, which bobbed placidly near a tentacle tip.

"The instrumentation on board this vessel is far more sophisticated than that which is the subject of this mechanical visitation. Furthermore, only a portion of your own devices appears to be susceptible."

"Those in search of 'higher intelligence.' " Iranaputra regarded his friends. "That is what the Ksaru told me it was originally searching for when it stumbled on the shaft that led to this ship."

"What d'you think'll happen to the machines these new aliens are making off with?" Hawkins wondered.

Shimoda sighed contemplatively. "The kitchen robot spoke of a call for enlightenment. Perhaps they will be enlightened."

"Disassembled is more like it." Hawkins grunted. "You can't enlighten a toaster, no matter how intelligent the model."

"How do you know, Wal?" Iranaputra smiled challengingly. "Have you ever tried?"

"Well, now, you tell me, Vic. Can a toaster achieve Nirvana?"

Iranaputra looked thoughtful. "I do not know. There has never before been a reason to consider the question. But I promise you, I intend to ask the first AI-controlled toaster I next meet."

Hands clasped behind his back, Heath stood gazing through the observation port at the monstrous roiling storm which presently dominated the surface of Jupiter. "We'd better, don't you know. This mechanical civilization's liable to keep paying ours expensive visits. If we're going to hang on to our own machines, we're going to have to learn how to talk to all of them and come to a mutual accommodation. Or else develop some kind of cybernetic prophylaxis."

"You have said that you are relieved these ships do not represent your ancient enemy," Iranaputra told the Drex. "What are you going to do now? Go back to sleep?"

"One million years is rest enough," the Drex boomed. "I do not know if my species has survived. The ship has been searching all this time and there is no evidence of their communications." There was a pause and the massive command chair turned slowly toward them. "I can but continue the search."

"We could help," avowed Ashili suddenly. "There's only one of you and an awful lot of us. If this Enemy's half as bad as you make it out to be, you should be grateful for any allies. Even small ones."

"That's right." Gelmann nodded vigorously. "And in the meanwhile, maybe we can find something to occupy your days. To keep you from being bored. Something useful."

"Mina!" Iranaputra hissed warningly.

She ignored him. "Leave it to me. If we're going to help you, it's only fair that you help us in return, *nu*?"

"It is a notion." A tentacle waved absently. "It would be wasteful and futile for me to personally monitor the automatic scanners all the time."

"There, you see?" She looked smug.

MINA Gelmann sat on the porch and gazed with equanimity at the glistening, quicksilver surface of the fully restored Lake Woneapenigong. It had been stimulating, but she'd had more than enough excitement to last her for a year, at least.

Nearby, Heath and Iranaputra played checkers with the same intensity as before, though now Heath was not so condescending and Iranaputra less belligerently assertive. They still referred to Heath as the Colonel, appropriate ever since the Victoria League, wishing to recognize the exploits of one of their retired citizens aboard the artifact, had granted him that honorary title.

Kahei Shimoda lay on a towel on the grass just inside the split-rail fence that enclosed this part of the Village, soaking up the summer sun, his vast body viscous with UV block. Hawkins chatted with kitchen serving robot eleven, which had just delivered the cold lemonade he'd ordered. It was properly deferential and volunteered no cybermetaphysical nonsense about higher intelligences or the state of the universe.

Something made Gelmann straighten slightly in her chair. Upon concluding its duty, had the serving robot punctuated its departure with a sly wink? She relaxed. Impossible. Robots were not equipped with eyelids. It had been an effect of the sun striking motile plastic lenses and nothing more.

It was good to be back at Lake Woneapenigong, to have access to her apartment and things, to familiar food and friends. She glanced to her left. A striking, dark young woman was showing a group of visitors around the Village. She paused at the lakeshore to gesture toward the porch. Gelmann smiled and waved. It was strange to be famous. To the multitude of tourist attractions on Earth had been added another: the five seniors of the artifact. Village management had insisted gawkers and hawkers be kept at a respectable distance, to preserve the privacy of the simply retired as well as that of the suddenly acclaimed.

"Funny," Hawkins had commented to them when informed of the state of affairs, "none of you *look* like a tourist attraction."

Forbidden from approaching any closer, the tour group paused to snap images of the esteemed. Hawkins stood it as long as he could, then saluted with his lemonade, turned, and with great deliberation dropped his pants. Murmurs rose from the pilgrims.

Gelmann shook her head. Some people handled celebrity with more grace than others.

She didn't understand it, this unsought fame. It wasn't as if they'd saved humankind from ravening alien hordes, or even one ravening alien. Oh sure, they'd made a tenuous ally of one, and probably helped prevent a commercial war between the FFF and the Keiretsu and the other leagues, but it wasn't as if they'd set out to do those things. Iranaputra insisted it was karma, but Gelmann knew better.

They'd just gone for a walk.

One of the tourists, a young man, picked his moment and tried to dash forward to make personal contact with the heroes of the Artifact Encounter. The tour guide stopped him with a lightning leg thrust, spun him onto his back, and whispered something to him while holding one hand close to his neck. When he rose to rejoin the group, his face was ashen.

Zabela Ashili turned to smile and wave one more time, murmured something to Hawkins, who responded with a rude gesture, and began to shepherd her flock along the lakeshore. Gelmann sipped iced tea and reflected on the perversity of life, and how the unforeseen so often alters the direction of one's profession.

Not only had Ashili found satisfaction as a Village tour guide, she was being paid to retrain the entire security staff as well.

Willard Whiskin leaned over the back of the boat and gazed at the receding river. The itinerary called for them to spend one more day on this tributary of the Orinoco before lifting on air suspension and crossing through the jungle to the Rio Negro and thence on down to Manaus.

He wiped perspiration from his brow and applied the last of the anti-sweat from the spray can, glanced around, and tossed the empty over the side. It bobbed toylike in the cruise ship's wake. His wife looked up from where she was attempting to control the two little Whiskins.

"Maybe you shouldn't have done that, Will. After all, this is a rainforest sanctuary."

He shrugged indifferently. "The whole planet's a sanctuary of one sort or another. It's hot and I'm tired." He gestured astern. "What's the big deal? It's gone already."

A cloud blocked the tropical sun, but it was the stentorian thrumming that caused them and everyone else on the boat to stop whatever they happened to be doing at the moment and look upward. People poured out of their cabins, out of the lounge, and onto the decks. On shore even the raucous squawking of the scarlet macaws and Amazonian green parrots was stilled. A hush fell over the intimidated jungle.

Hovering overhead and filling the sky from horizon to horizon was a gigantic silvery construction: the Drex artifact. A tiny port opened in its underside and something came blasting out, heading directly for the cruise ship. A few people screamed and rushed for the dubious safety of the vessel's interior, but most were too fascinated to move.

The object which had descended circled briefly above the boat, then shot astern. It returned a moment later and halted in midair. An empty sweat-off can landed on deck at Willard Whiskin's feet with an accusatory clang.

A refractive, chromed arm, one of four, waved accusingly at Whiskin while the two little Whiskins stood close to their mother, goggle-eyed at the confrontation. A trembling Willard gaped at the device, which strangely enough appeared to be based on a simple serving robot design, and felt a warm trickle down his left leg as his bladder let go.

The gleaming apparatus spoke with the voice of Authority, and a slight Newyork Province accent.

"This is a rainforest preserve. Littering is strictly prohibited."

From the depths of the awesome apparition hovering overhead a voice thundered, *"Further violation will result in immediate termination! You have been warned!"*

The mobile device drifted forward until it was less than a meter from the panicky tourist. Four articulated hands reached out to grab him by his expensive tropical shirt and pull him close to reflective plastic lenses.

"Get it?"

"Ah . . . awk . . . uh . . ."

Ms. Whiskin hazarded an interruption. "He's usually more talkative than this."

The robot let the man go. Somehow Whiskin kept his feet. As others aboard oohed and aahed, the device rose on a pillar of blue fire and vanished back into the belly of the famous artifact, which rose solemnly into the equatorial sky and moved off northward in search of other violators.

Ms. Whiskin and both little Whiskins crowded around Willard.

"Are you all right, luv?"

"Hey, look! Dad wet his pants!" said Jeremy Whiskin.

Willard Whiskin was still shaking as he eyed his family firmly. "I don't care what anyone says." He glanced furtively at the sky, as if the artifact might suddenly change its alien mind and return to wreak unimaginable destruction on his person. "Next year we're staying home and going to Bobbleworld." He spotted one of the ship's officers, a local from Bahia.

"I'd heard that you people were strict on pollution control, but isn't this sort of thing going a bit overboard?"

The man tilted back his cap and gazed fondly in the direction the artifact had taken. "Earth's a living museum, sir. Those of us who live here take great pride in keeping her clean. Since the Drex has agreed to help preserve our little corner of the galaxy while waiting for word from his own, we've had fewer problems than usual. Gives the alien something to do and keeps him out of trouble. The leagues don't try to dictate to us anymore either."

"I can understand that." Willard Whiskin spoke with shaky emotion as his family helped him toward the stairs.

Deep within the artifact, ignored by the busy Drex and forgotten by the rest of mankind, four Candomblean assassins survived without bemoaning their fate. Instead they luxuriated in the warm, perpetual artificial sunset, lounged on the beach, and swam in the programmed surf. Had they access to the outside, they surely would have enjoyed witnessing their formal Candomblean military funerals. As it was, these events, like everything else happening outside, passed them by.

The Drex ignored them, but the Autothor did not. In the absence of instructions to the contrary from the Drex pilot, or for that matter any instructions at all, it supplied them with food and water and left them largely alone.

By and by, the female half of the marooned quartet became pregnant. As the galaxy ponderously precessed through the universe the searoom and nearby portions of the artifact became populated by a whole crop of little Candomblean assassins. They had the good fortune to be tutored by both their parents and the Autothor, which took to the task with becoming enthusiasm.

On ancient Mother Earth seniors died and children were born. The leagues quarreled and alliances shifted. Pining for its distant home and lost civilization, the Drex, too, finally took the path all organic life-forms must eventually travel.

But the ship, the epitome of Drex engineering and science, went on: self-repairing, self-perpetuating, watching over its adopted world. Eventually the offspring times offspring of the four Candombleans started building themselves, with the help and direction of the Autothor and a certain modified, re-regenerating serving robot, so that when the representatives of the incredibly distant machine civilization returned, and eventually the terrible ancient Enemy of the Drex as well, they each encountered something orbiting Old Earth that made the Drex and the sciences of humankind and even the miracle that was the Drex vessel itself pale to insignificance.

Exactly what it was cannot accurately be described, but it was bigger than a breadbox and smaller than a quasar.